BRIAN AZZARELLO
writer

EDUARDO RISSO
art & colors

MOONSHINE

VOL. 2

JARED K. FLETCHER
letters & design

CRISTIAN ROSSI
color assistant

WILL DENNIS
editor

image

IMAGE COMICS, INC.

ROBERT KIRKMAN: CHIEF OPERATING OFFICER
ERIK LARSEN: CHIEF FINANCIAL OFFICER
TODD MCFARLANE: PRESIDENT
MARC SILVESTRI: CHIEF EXECUTIVE OFFICER
JIM VALENTINO: VICE PRESIDENT

ERIC STEPHENSON: PUBLISHER / CHIEF CREATIVE OFFICER
COREY HART: DIRECTOR OF SALES
JEFF BOISON: DIRECTOR OF PUBLISHING PLANNING & BOOK TRADE SALES
CHRIS ROSS: DIRECTOR OF DIGITAL SALES
JEFF STANG: DIRECTOR OF SPECIALTY SALES
KAT SALAZAR: DIRECTOR OF PR & MARKETING
DREW GILL: ART DIRECTOR
HEATHER DOORNINK: PRODUCTION DIRECTOR
NICOLE LAPALME: CONTROLLER

IMAGECOMICS.COM

Deanna Phelps: Production Artist for MOONSHINE.

MOONSHINE, VOLUME 2. First Printing. October 2018. Published by Image Comics, Inc. Office of publication: 2701 NW Vaughn St., Suite 780, Portland, OR 97210. Copyright © 2018 Brian Azzarello & Eduardo Risso. All rights reserved. Contains material originally published in single magazine form as MOONSHINE #7-12. "Moonshine," its logos, and the likenesses of all characters herein are trademarks of Brian Azzarello & Eduardo Risso, unless otherwise noted. "Image" and the Image Comics logos are registered trademarks of Image Comics, Inc. No part of this publication may be reproduced or transmitted, in any form or by any means (except for short excerpts for journalistic or review purposes), without the express written permission of Brian Azzarello & Eduardo Risso or Image Comics, Inc. All names, characters, events, and locales in this publication are entirely fictional. Any resemblance to actual persons (living or dead), events, or places, without satiric intent, is coincidental. Printed in the USA. For information regarding the CPSIA on this printed material call: 203-595-3636 and provide reference #RICH–815934. For international rights, contact: foreignlicensing@imagecomics.com.

ISBN: 978-1-5343-0827-5.

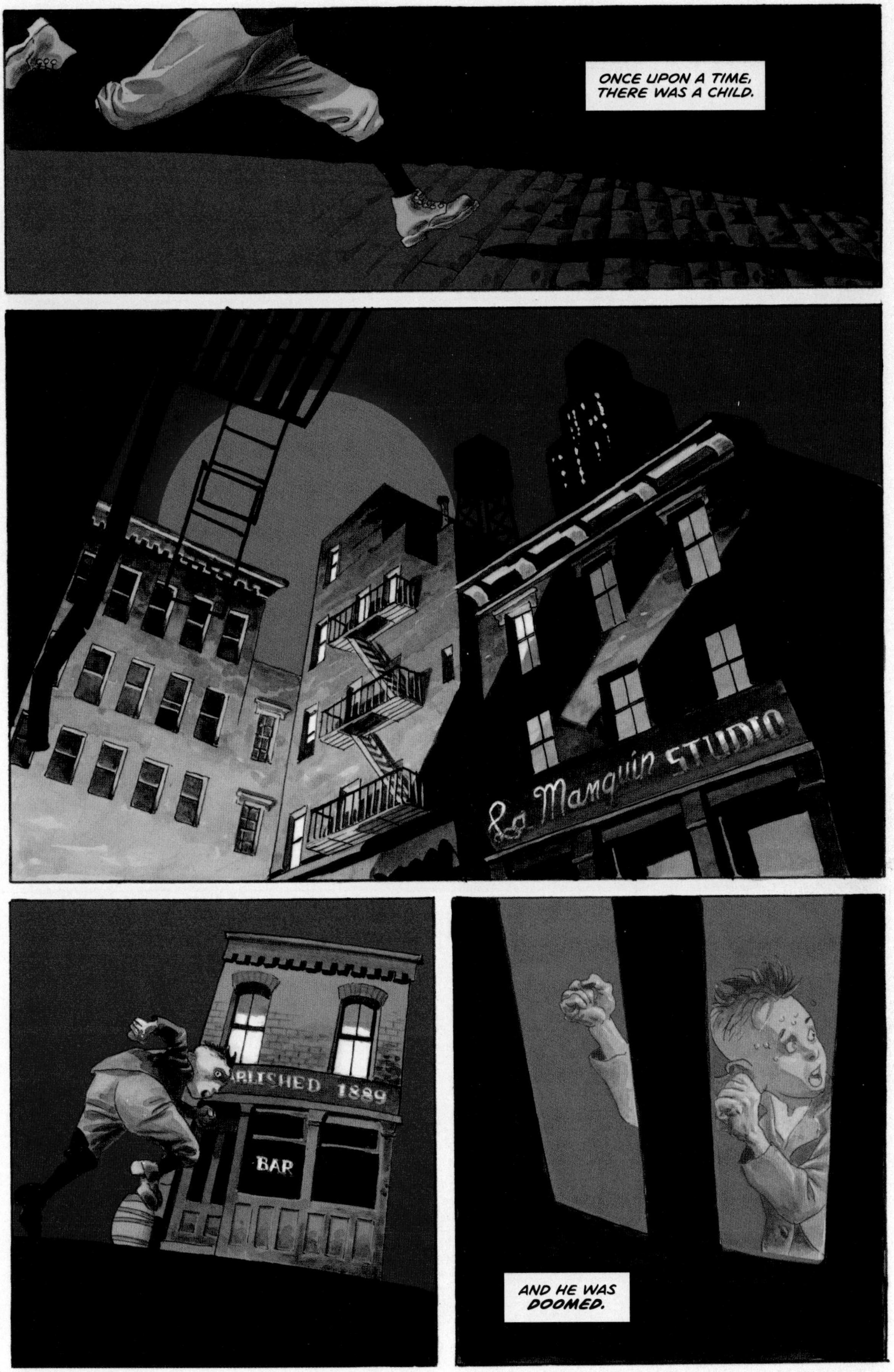
ONCE UPON A TIME, THERE WAS A CHILD.
La Manquin STUDIO
ABLISHED 1889
BAR
AND HE WAS DOOMED.

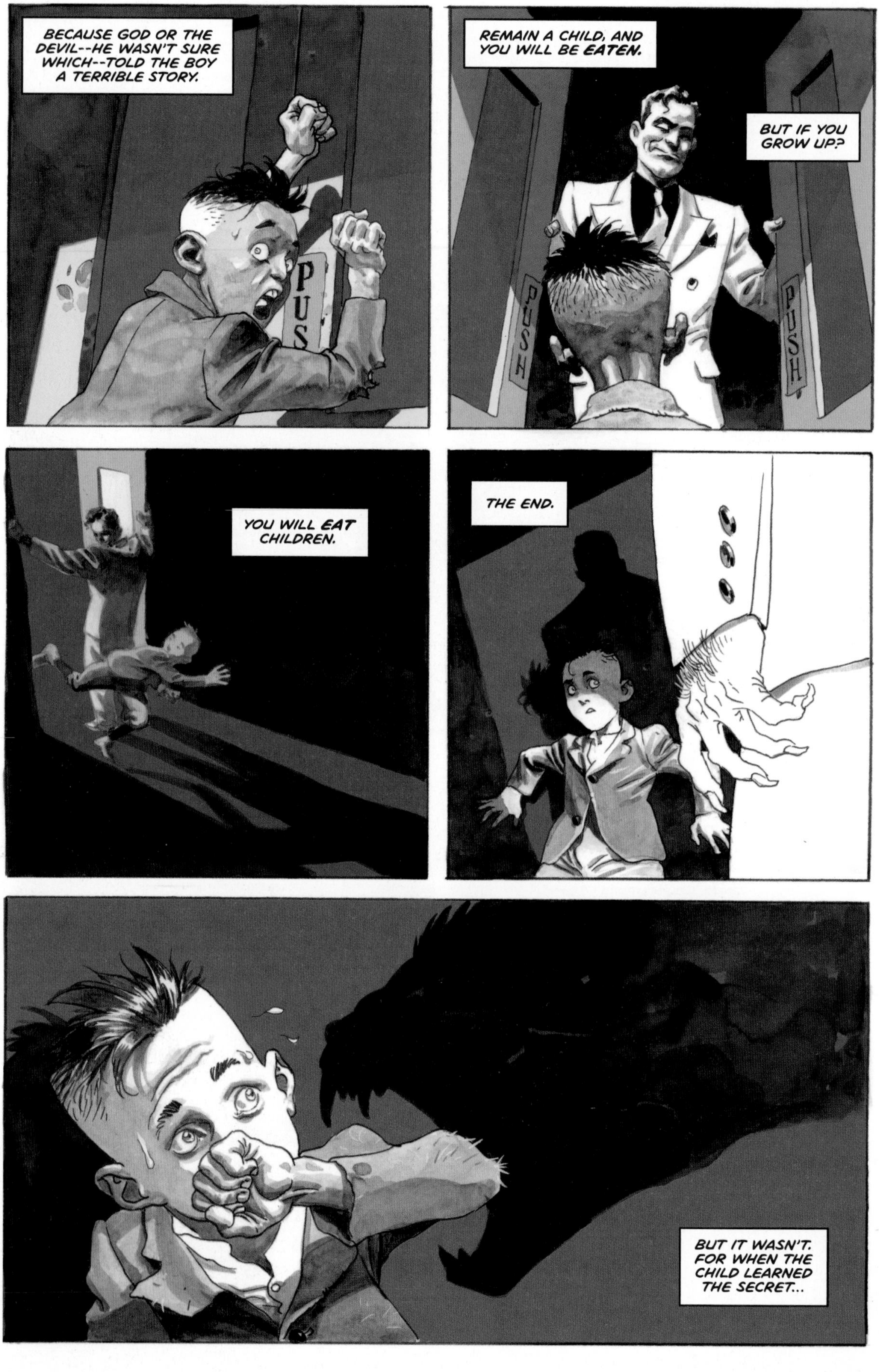
BECAUSE GOD OR THE DEVIL--HE WASN'T SURE WHICH--TOLD THE BOY A TERRIBLE STORY.
PUSH
REMAIN A CHILD, AND YOU WILL BE EATEN.
BUT IF YOU GROW UP?
PUSH
PUSH
YOU WILL EAT CHILDREN.
THE END.
BUT IT WASN'T. FOR WHEN THE CHILD LEARNED THE SECRET...

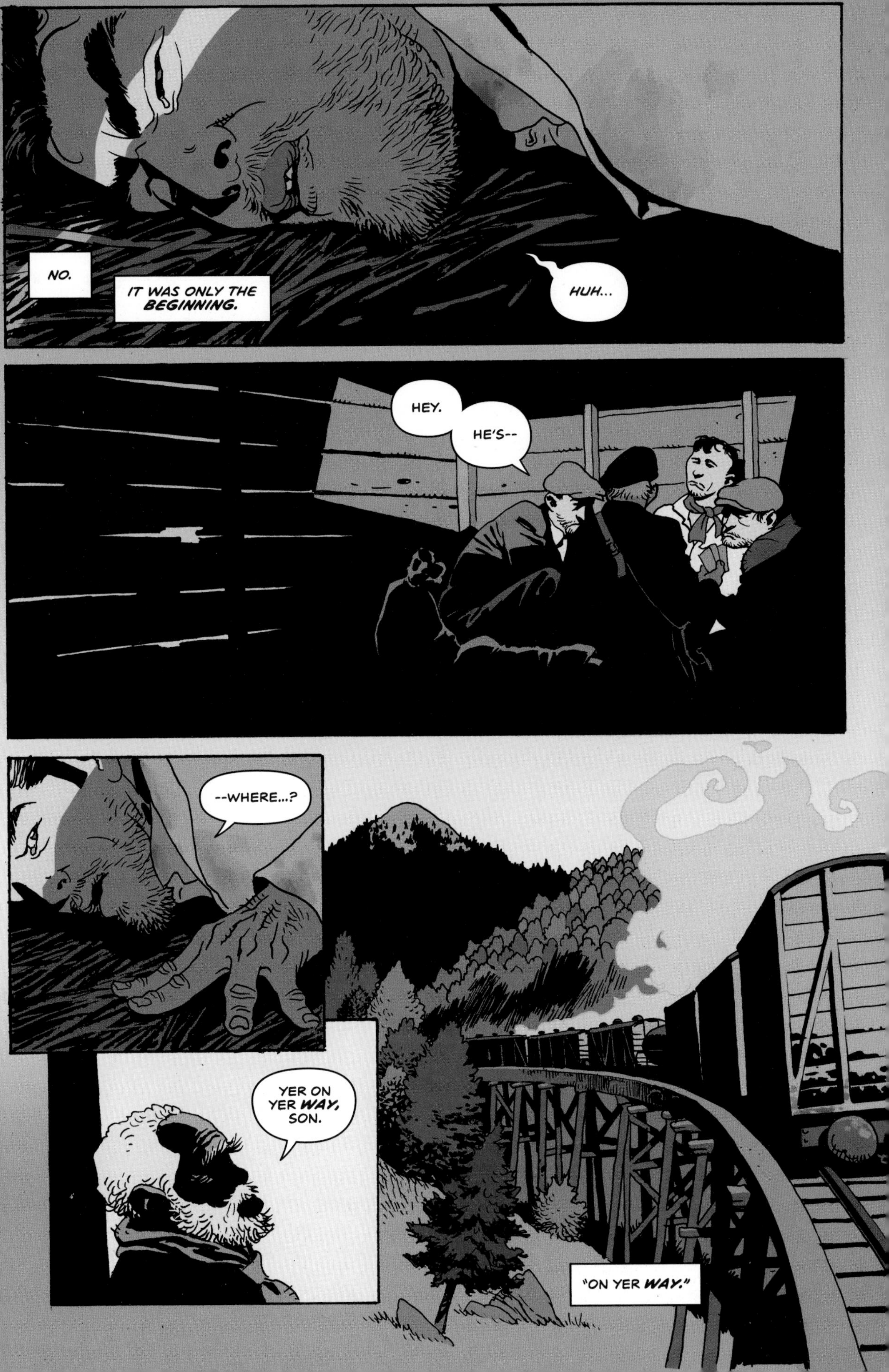
NO.
IT WAS ONLY THE BEGINNING.
HUH...
HEY.
HE'S--
--WHERE...?
YER ON YER WAY, SON.
"ON YER WAY."

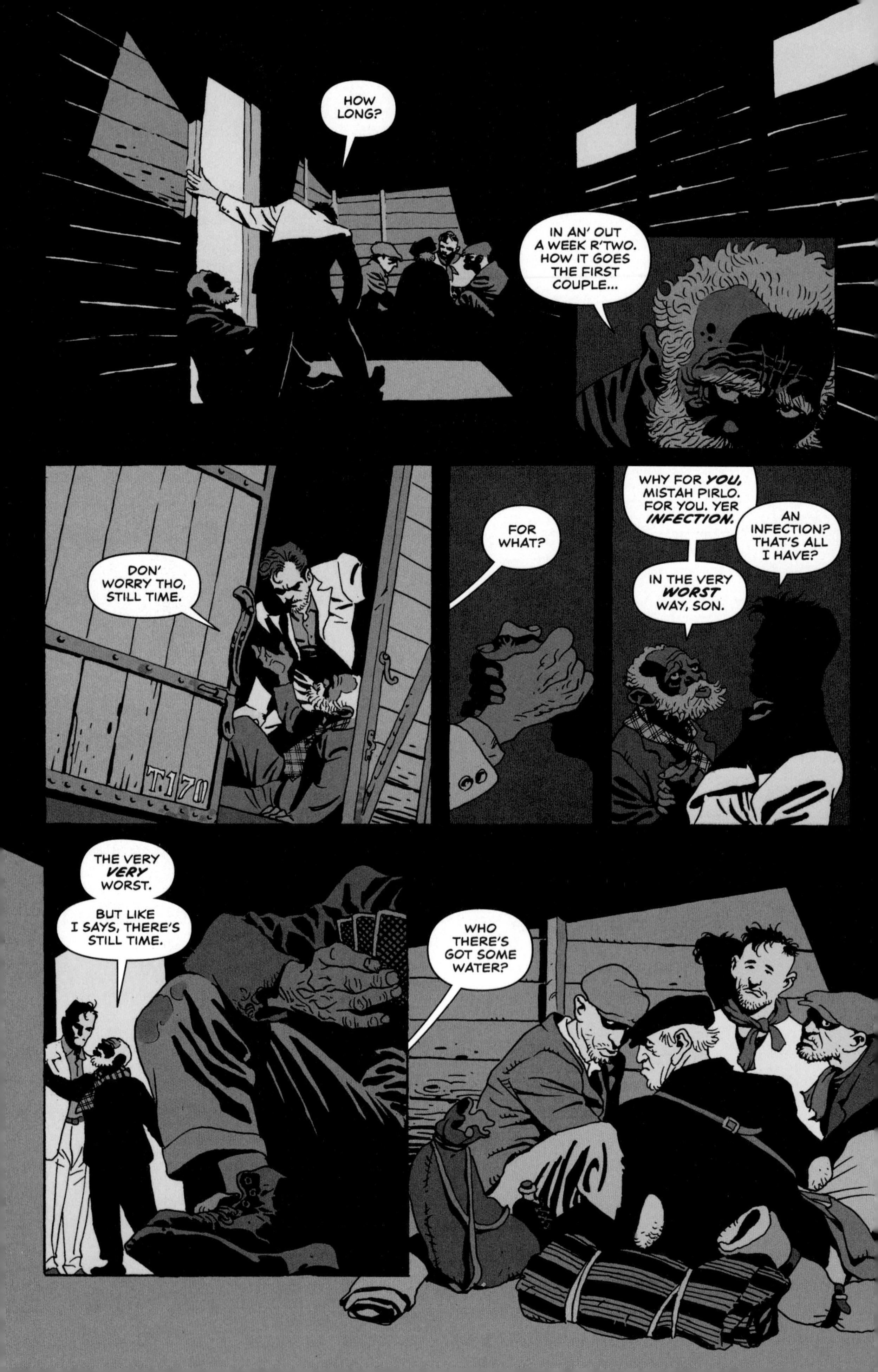
HOW LONG?
IN AN' OUT A WEEK R'TWO. HOW IT GOES THE FIRST COUPLE...
DON' WORRY THO, STILL TIME.
FOR WHAT?
WHY FOR *YOU,* MISTAH PIRLO. FOR YOU. YER ***INFECTION.***
AN INFECTION? THAT'S ALL I HAVE?
IN THE VERY ***WORST*** WAY, SON.
T.170
THE VERY ***VERY*** WORST.
BUT LIKE I SAYS, THERE'S STILL TIME.
WHO THERE'S GOT SOME WATER?

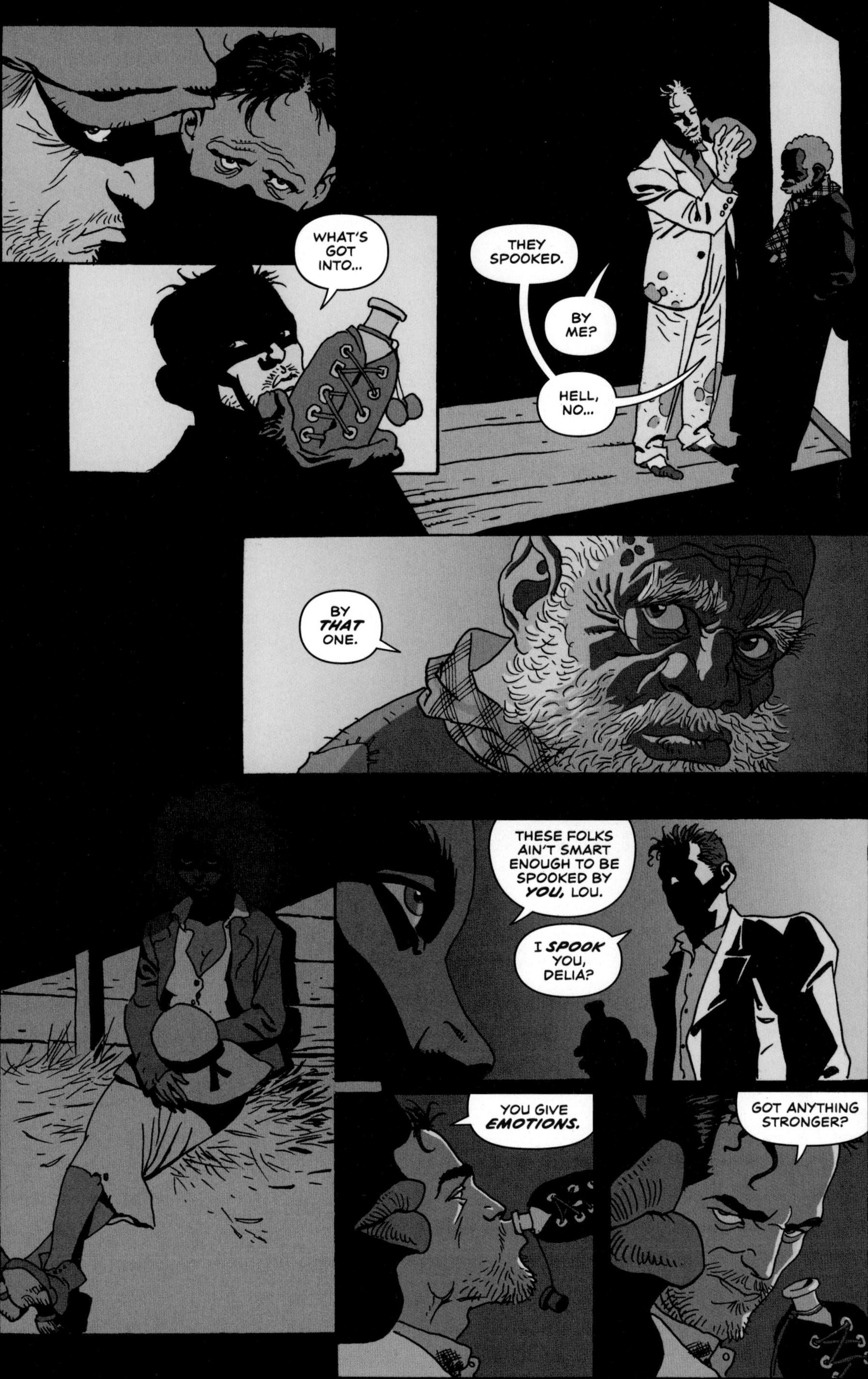
WHAT'S GOT INTO...
THEY SPOOKED.
BY ME?
HELL, NO...
BY *THAT* ONE.
THESE FOLKS AIN'T SMART ENOUGH TO BE SPOOKED BY *YOU,* LOU.
I *SPOOK* YOU, DELIA?
YOU GIVE *EMOTIONS.*
GOT ANYTHING STRONGER?

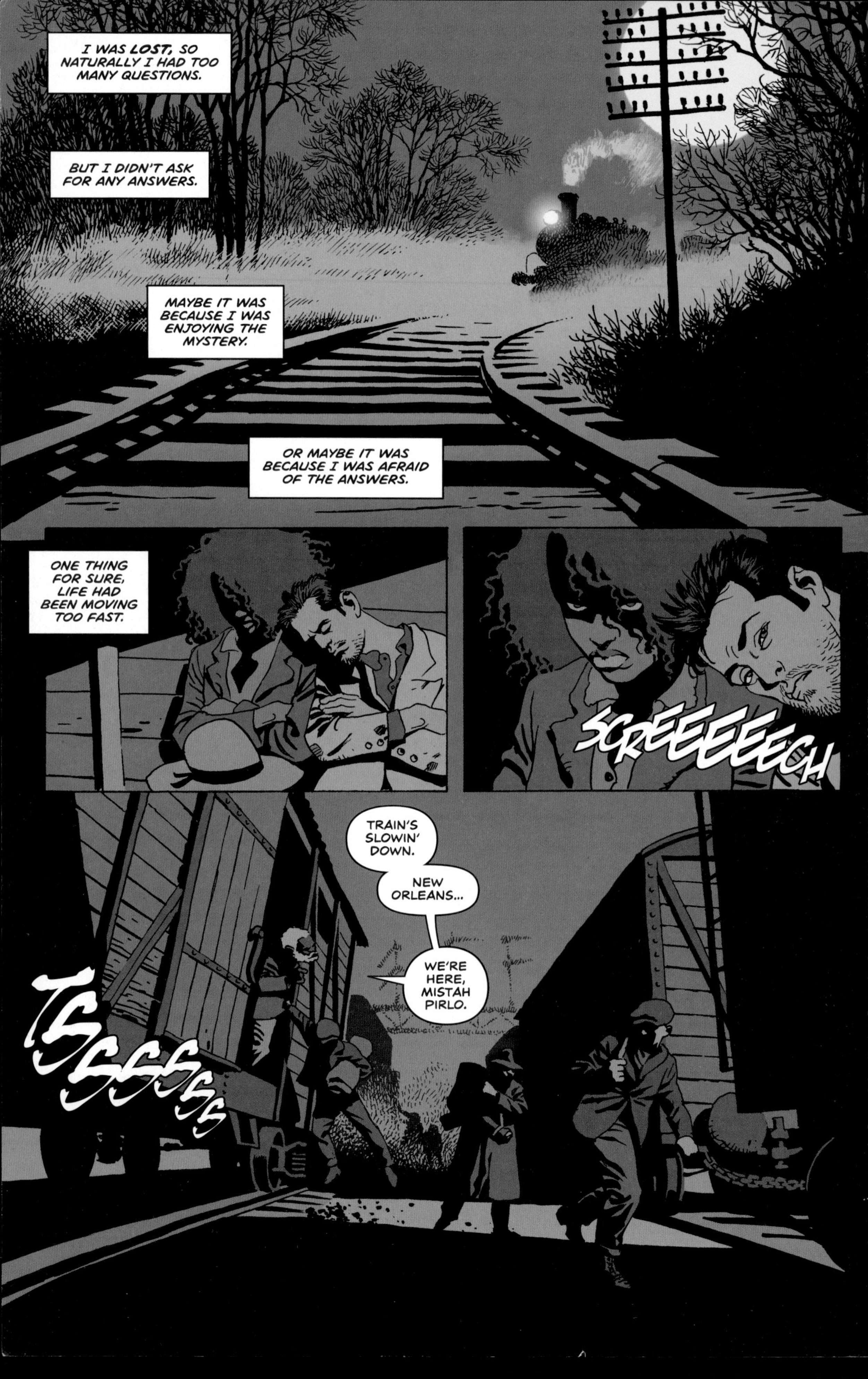
I WAS LOST, SO NATURALLY I HAD TOO MANY QUESTIONS.
BUT I DIDN'T ASK FOR ANY ANSWERS.
MAYBE IT WAS BECAUSE I WAS ENJOYING THE MYSTERY.
OR MAYBE IT WAS BECAUSE I WAS AFRAID OF THE ANSWERS.
ONE THING FOR SURE, LIFE HAD BEEN MOVING TOO FAST.
SCREEEEEECH
TRAIN'S SLOWIN' DOWN.
NEW ORLEANS...
WE'RE HERE, MISTAH PIRLO.
TSSSSSS

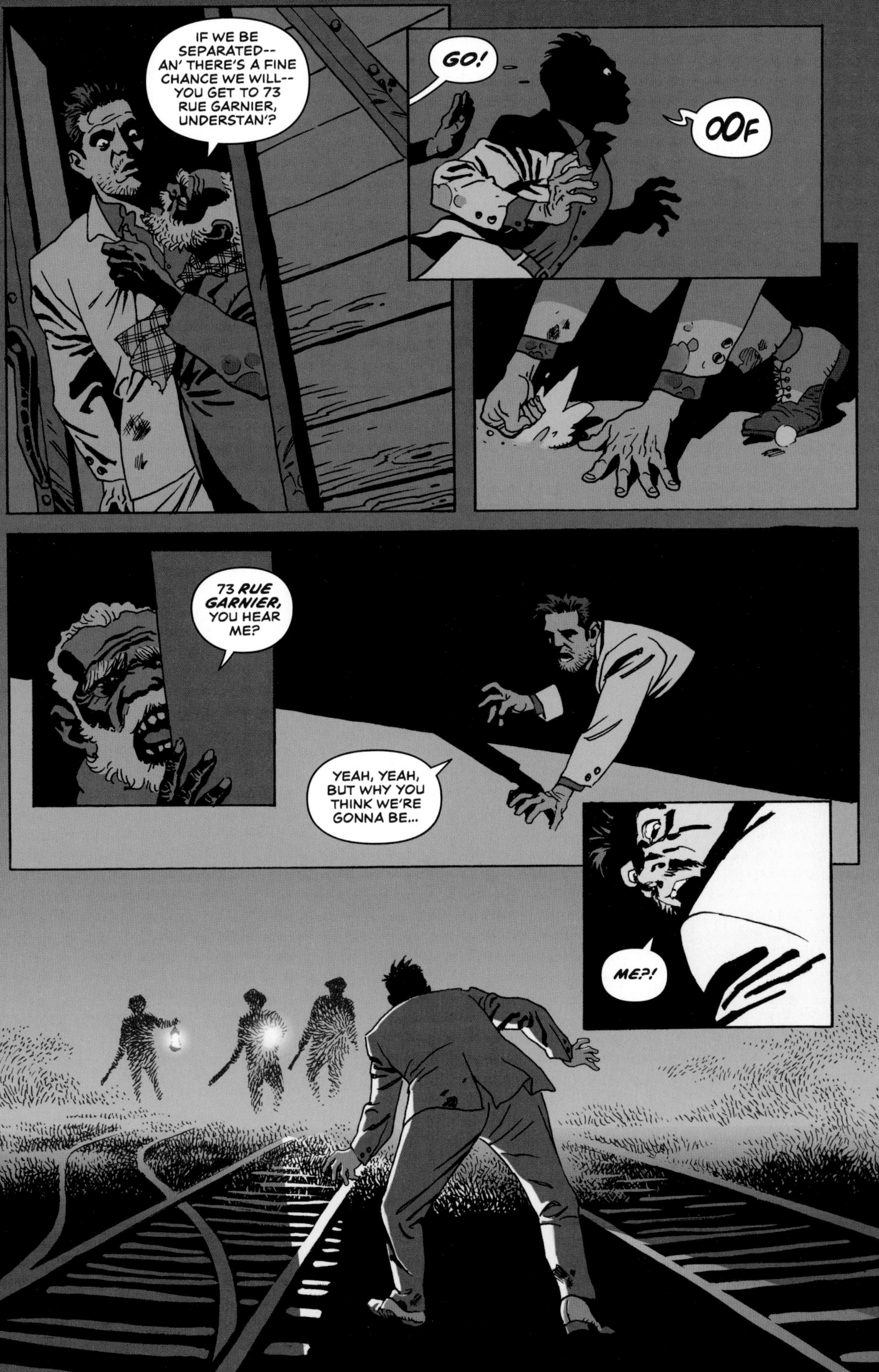
IF WE BE SEPARATED-- AN' THERE'S A FINE CHANCE WE WILL-- YOU GET TO 73 RUE GARNIER, UNDERSTAN'?
GO!
OOF
73 RUE GARNIER, YOU HEAR ME?
YEAH, YEAH, BUT WHY YOU THINK WE'RE GONNA BE...
ME?!

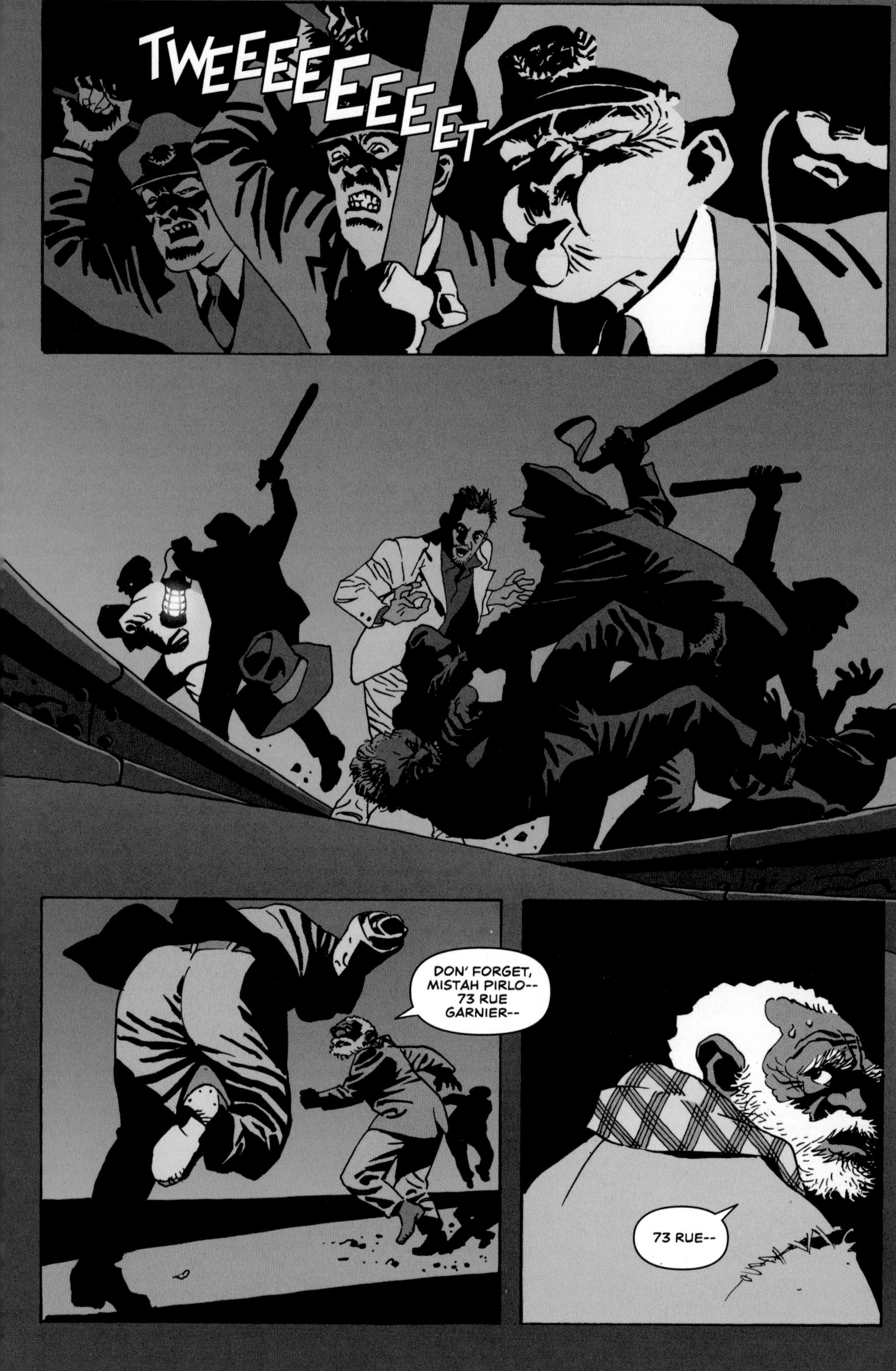
TWEEEEEEEEET
DON' FORGET, MISTAH PIRLO-- 73 RUE GARNIER--
73 RUE--

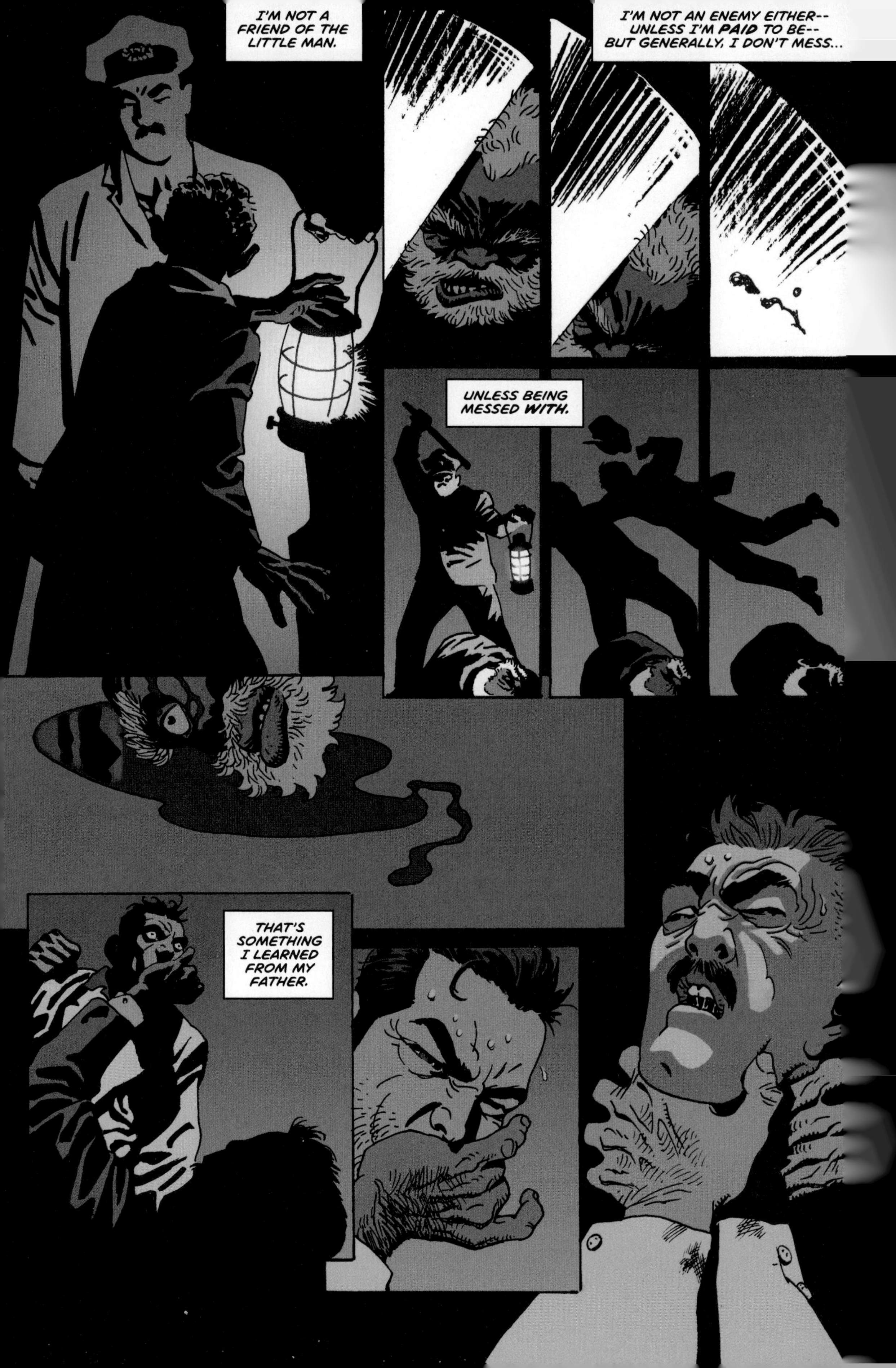
I'M NOT A FRIEND OF THE LITTLE MAN.
I'M NOT AN ENEMY EITHER-- UNLESS I'M PAID TO BE-- BUT GENERALLY, I DON'T MESS...
UNLESS BEING MESSED WITH.
THAT'S SOMETHING I LEARNED FROM MY FATHER.

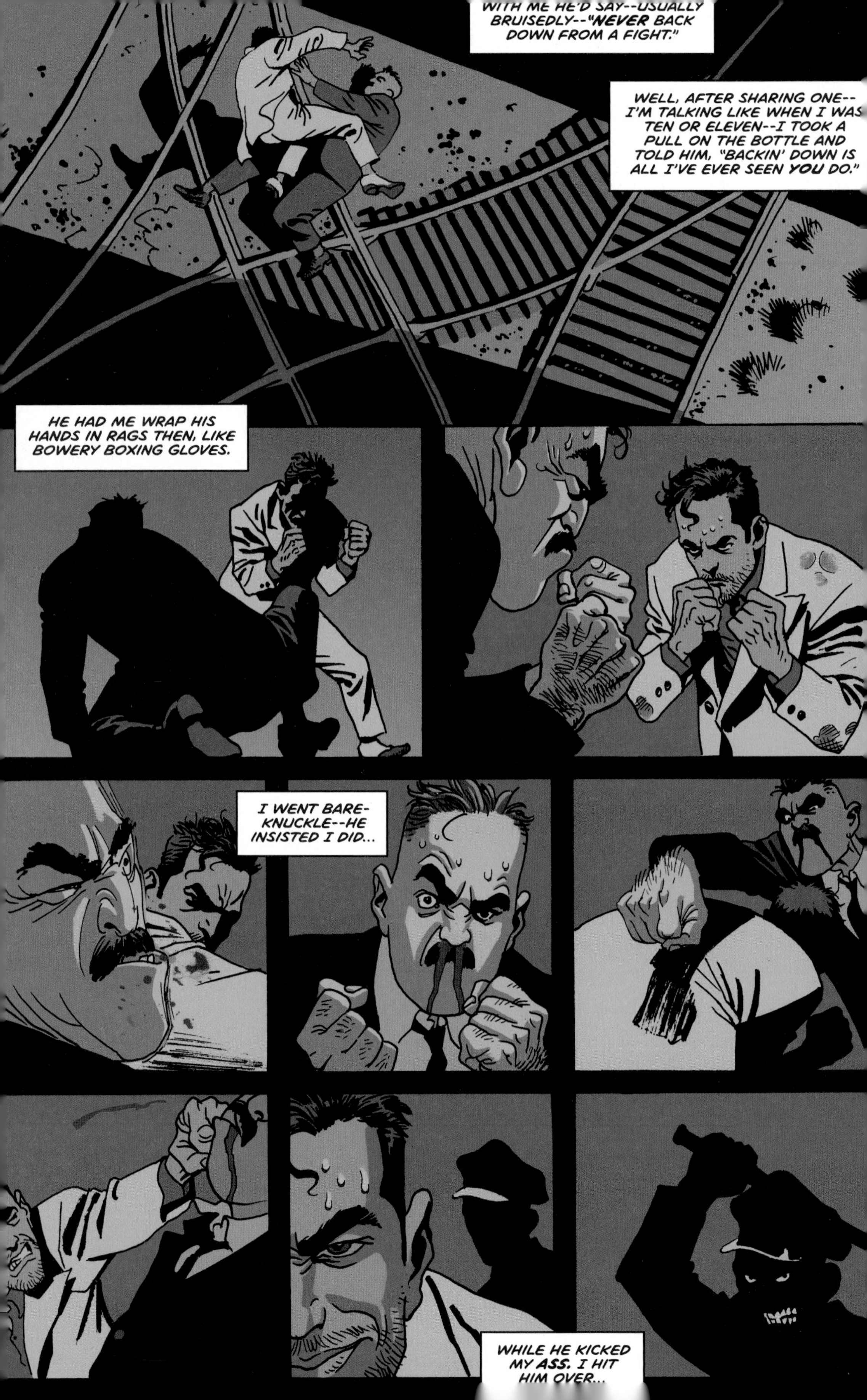
WITH ME HE'D SAY--USUALLY BRUISEDLY--"NEVER BACK DOWN FROM A FIGHT."
WELL, AFTER SHARING ONE--I'M TALKING LIKE WHEN I WAS TEN OR ELEVEN--I TOOK A PULL ON THE BOTTLE AND TOLD HIM, "BACKIN' DOWN IS ALL I'VE EVER SEEN YOU DO."
HE HAD ME WRAP HIS HANDS IN RAGS THEN, LIKE BOWERY BOXING GLOVES.
I WENT BARE-KNUCKLE--HE INSISTED I DID...
WHILE HE KICKED MY ASS, I HIT HIM OVER...

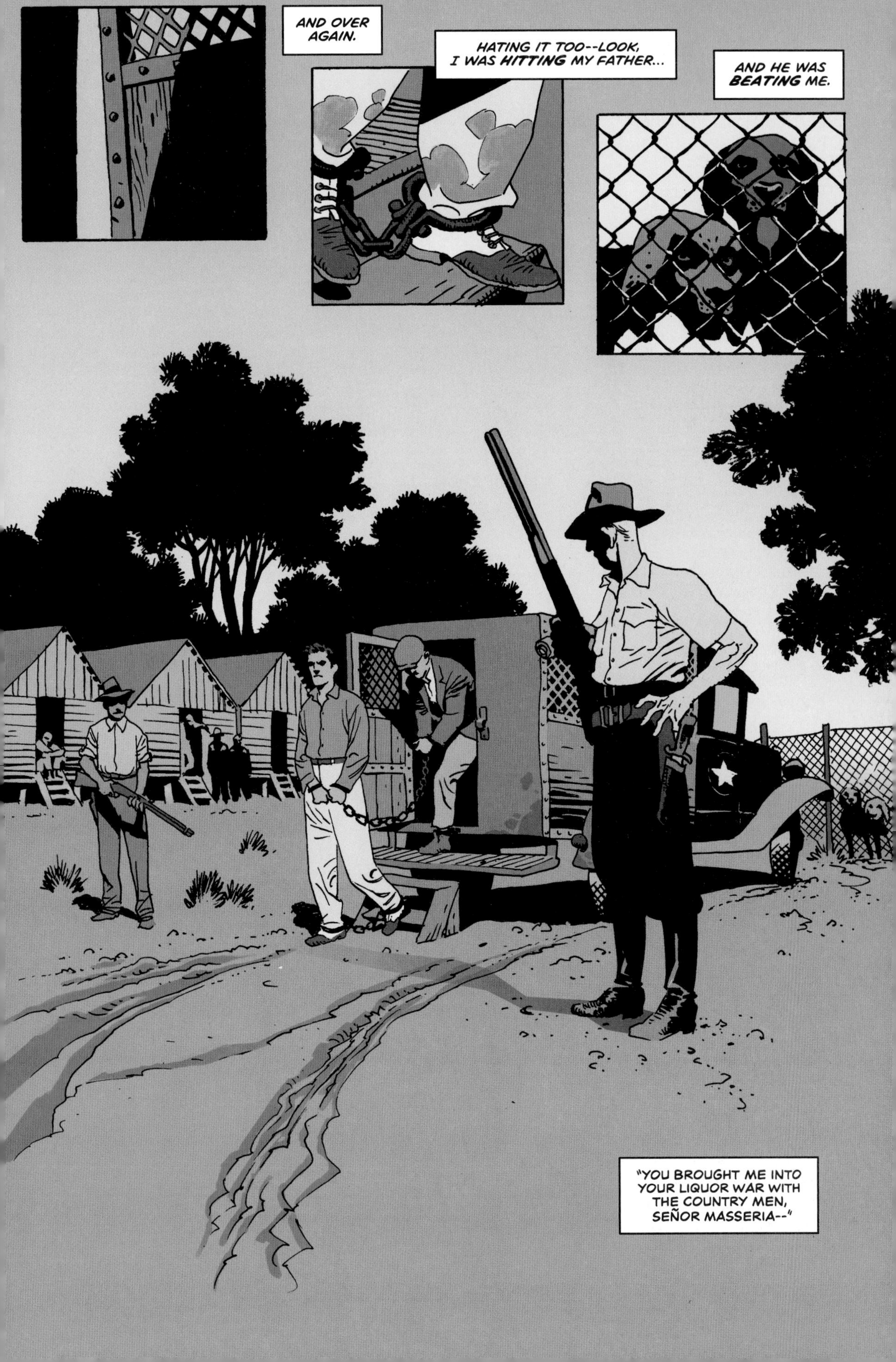
AND OVER AGAIN.
HATING IT TOO--LOOK, I WAS HITTING MY FATHER...
AND HE WAS BEATING ME.
"YOU BROUGHT ME INTO YOUR LIQUOR WAR WITH THE COUNTRY MEN, SEÑOR MASSERIA--"

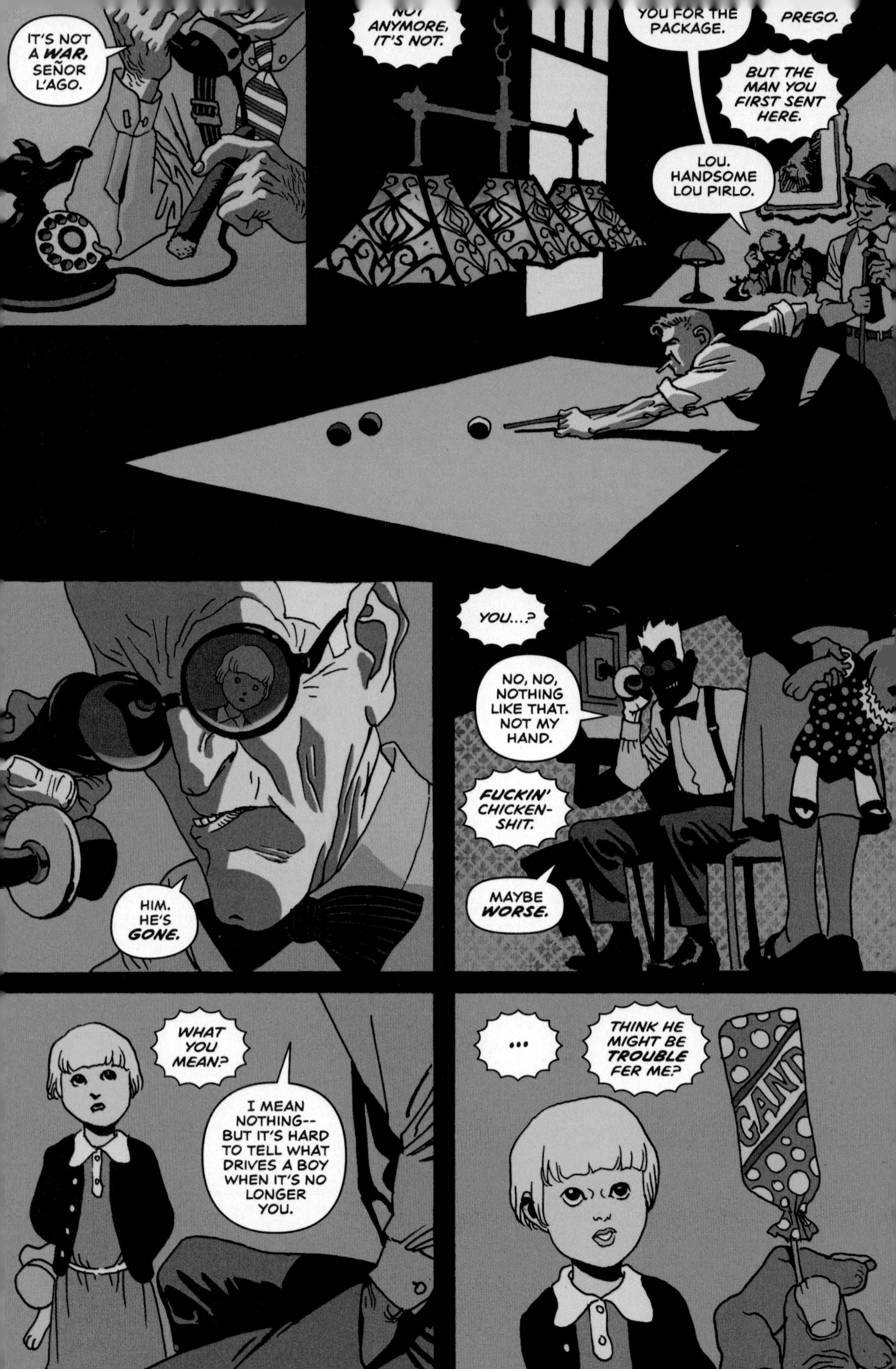
IT'S NOT A **WAR,** SEÑOR L'AGO.
ANYMORE, IT'S NOT.
YOU FOR THE PACKAGE.
PREGO.
BUT THE MAN YOU FIRST SENT HERE.
LOU. HANDSOME LOU PIRLO.
HIM. HE'S **GONE.**
YOU...?
NO, NO, NOTHING LIKE THAT. NOT MY HAND.
FUCKIN' CHICKEN-SHIT.
MAYBE **WORSE.**
WHAT YOU MEAN?
I MEAN NOTHING-- BUT IT'S HARD TO TELL WHAT DRIVES A BOY WHEN IT'S NO LONGER YOU.
...
THINK HE MIGHT BE **TROUBLE** FER ME?

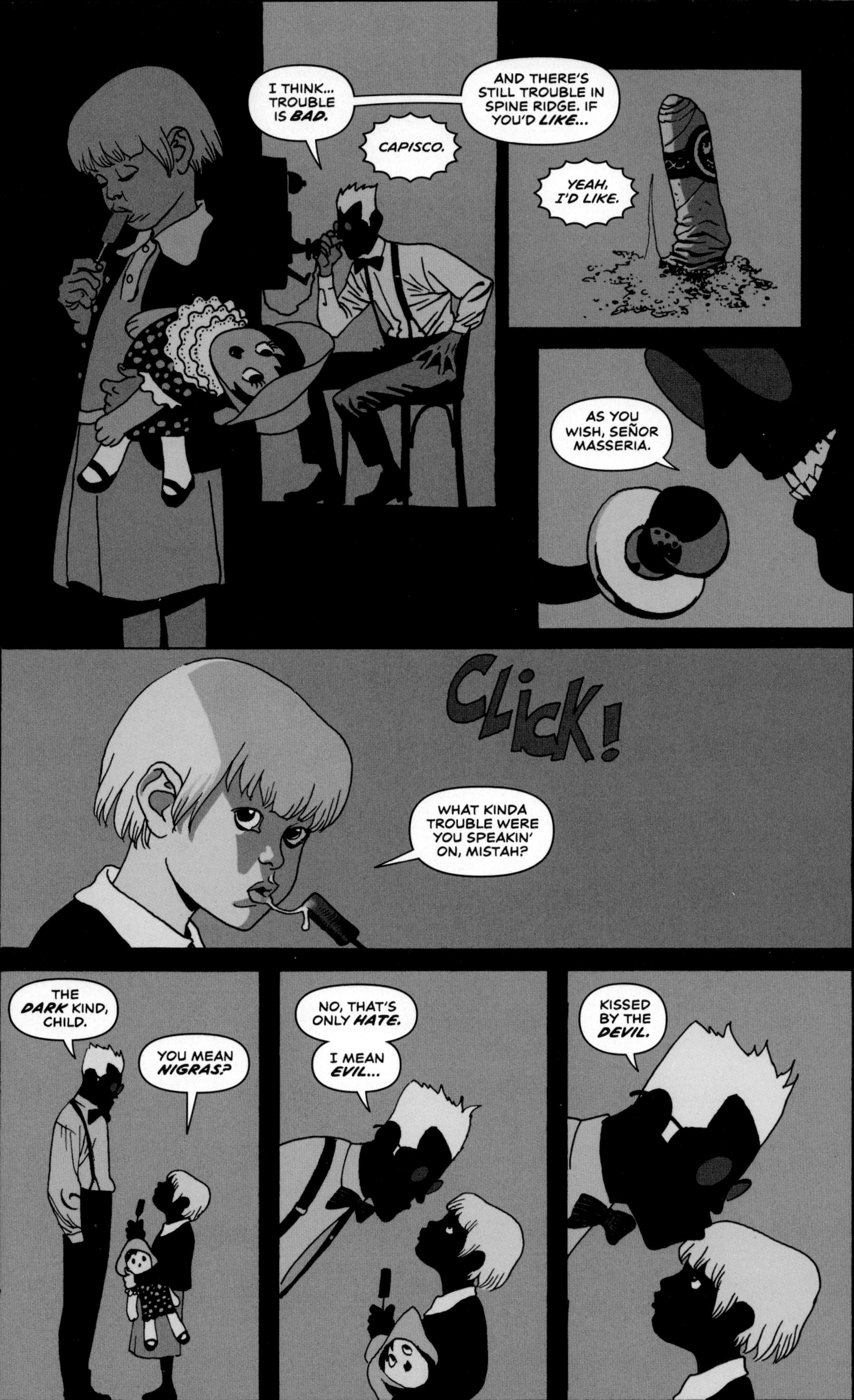

I THINK... TROUBLE IS **BAD.**
AND THERE'S STILL TROUBLE IN SPINE RIDGE. IF YOU'D **LIKE...**
CAPISCO.
YEAH, I'D LIKE.
AS YOU WISH, SEÑOR MASSERIA.
CLICK!
WHAT KINDA TROUBLE WERE YOU SPEAKIN' ON, MISTAH?
THE **DARK** KIND, CHILD.
YOU MEAN **NIGRAS?**
NO, THAT'S ONLY **HATE.**
I MEAN **EVIL...**
KISSED BY THE **DEVIL.**

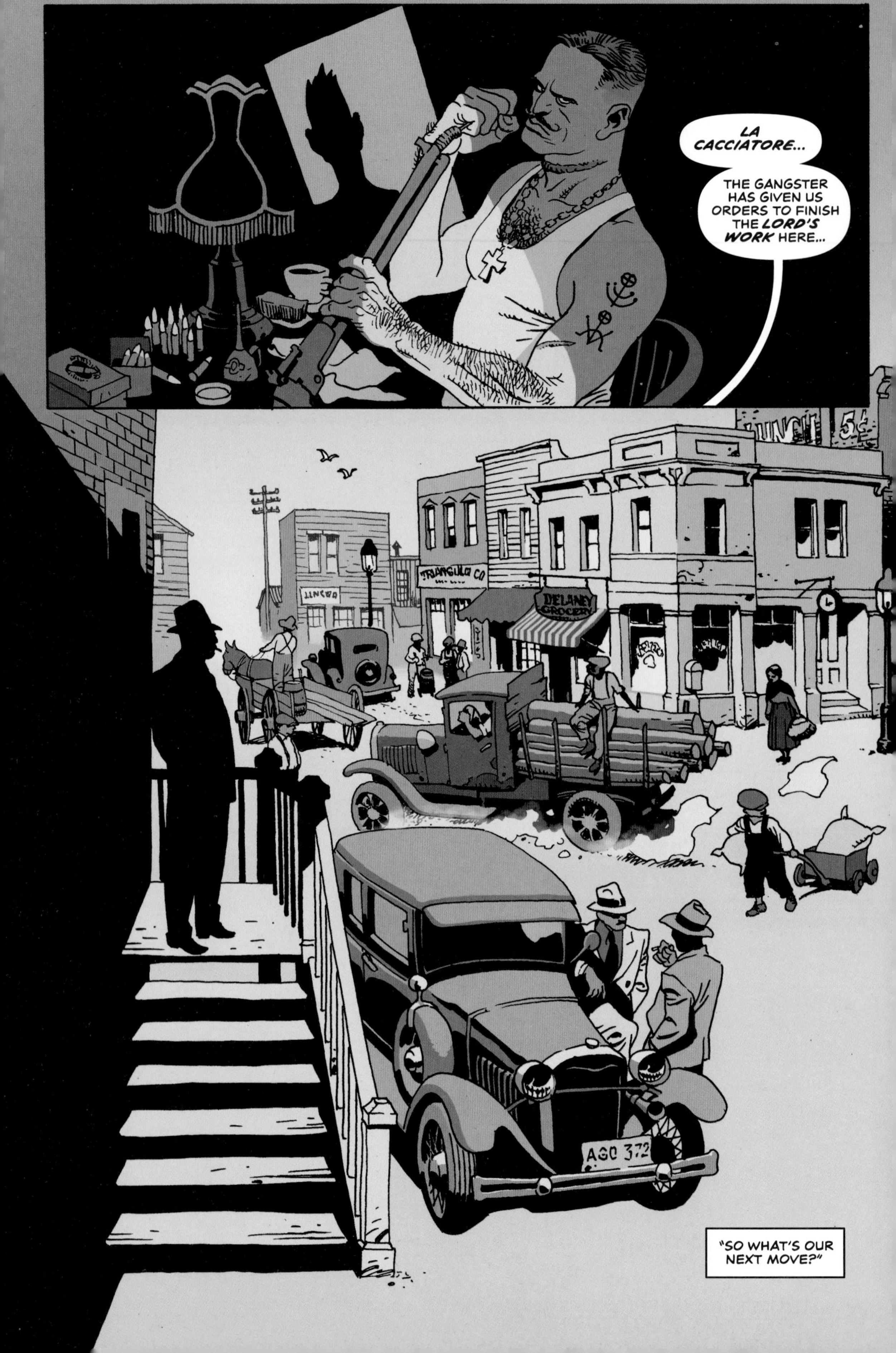

LA CACCIATORE...
THE GANGSTER HAS GIVEN US ORDERS TO FINISH THE LORD'S WORK HERE...
TRIANGULO CO
DELANEY GROCERY
AGO 372
"SO WHAT'S OUR NEXT MOVE?"

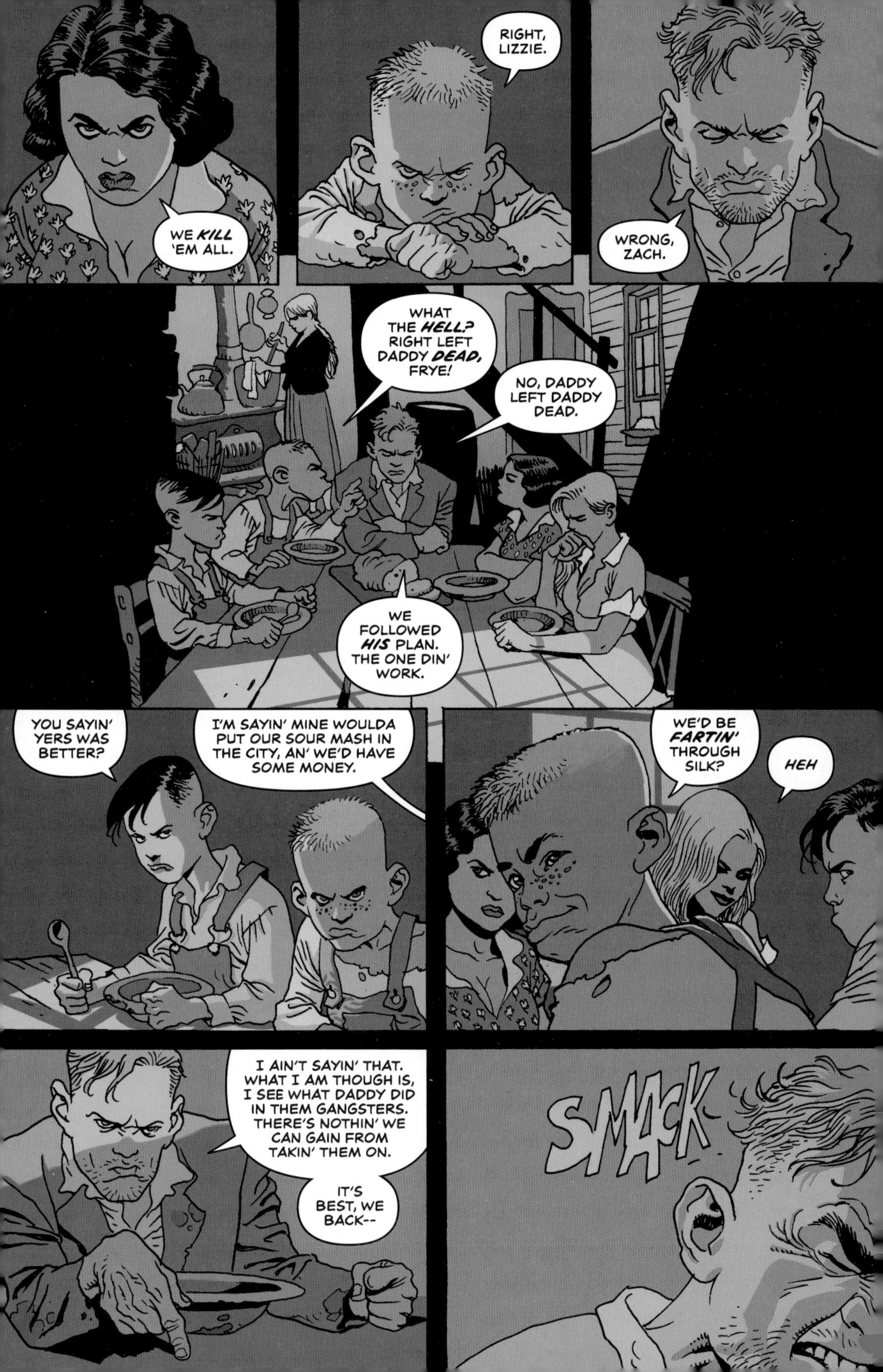
WE KILL 'EM ALL.
RIGHT, LIZZIE.
WRONG, ZACH.
WHAT THE HELL? RIGHT LEFT DADDY DEAD, FRYE!
NO, DADDY LEFT DADDY DEAD.
WE FOLLOWED HIS PLAN. THE ONE DIN' WORK.
YOU SAYIN' YERS WAS BETTER?
I'M SAYIN' MINE WOULDA PUT OUR SOUR MASH IN THE CITY, AN' WE'D HAVE SOME MONEY.
WE'D BE FARTIN' THROUGH SILK?
HEH
I AIN'T SAYIN' THAT. WHAT I AM THOUGH IS, I SEE WHAT DADDY DID IN THEM GANGSTERS. THERE'S NOTHIN' WE CAN GAIN FROM TAKIN' THEM ON.
IT'S BEST, WE BACK--
SMACK

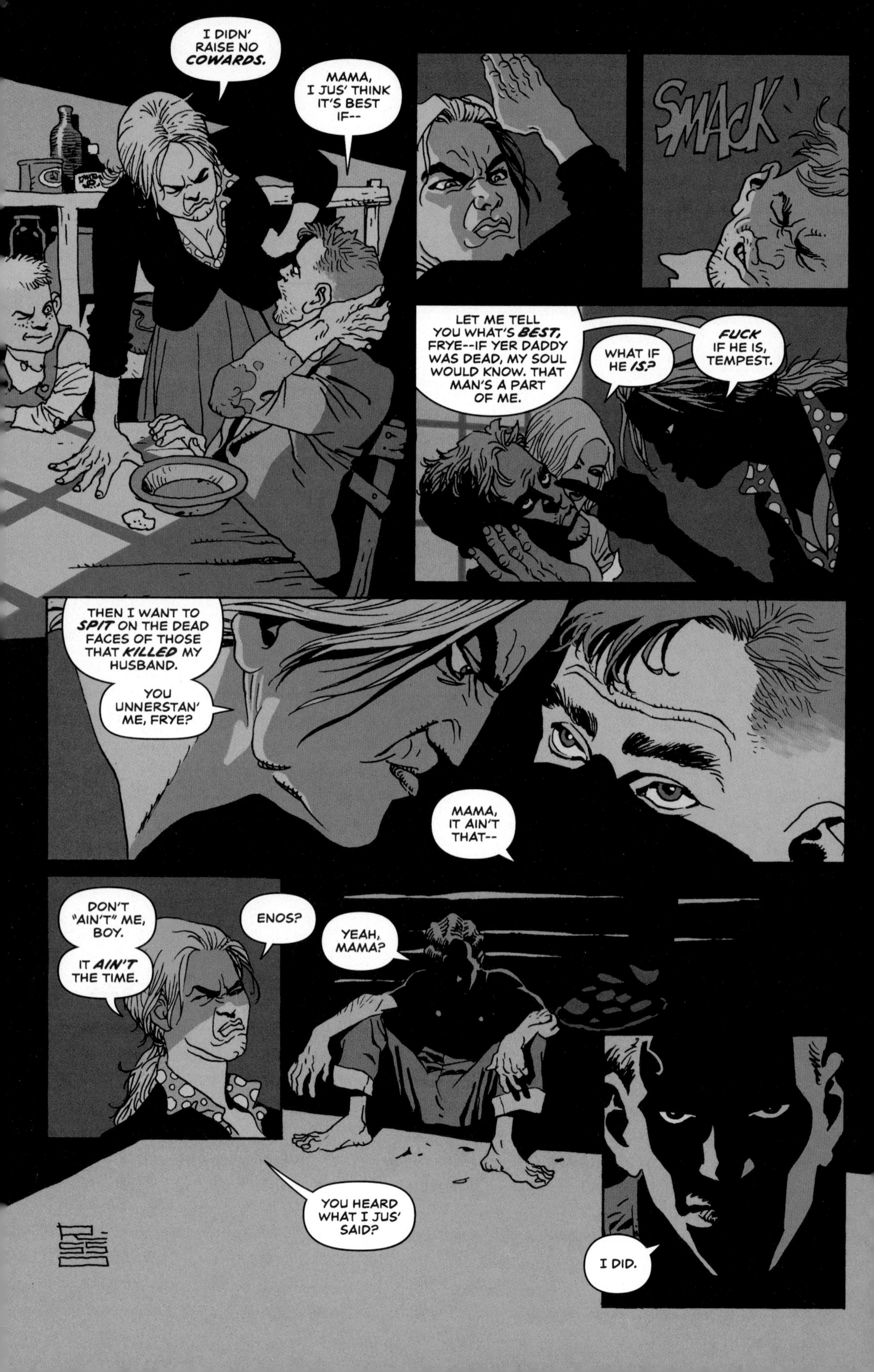
I DIDN' RAISE NO COWARDS.
MAMA, I JUS' THINK IT'S BEST IF--
SMACK
LET ME TELL YOU WHAT'S BEST, FRYE--IF YER DADDY WAS DEAD, MY SOUL WOULD KNOW. THAT MAN'S A PART OF ME.
WHAT IF HE IS?
FUCK IF HE IS, TEMPEST.
THEN I WANT TO SPIT ON THE DEAD FACES OF THOSE THAT KILLED MY HUSBAND.
YOU UNNERSTAN' ME, FRYE?
MAMA, IT AIN'T THAT--
DON'T "AIN'T" ME, BOY.
IT AIN'T THE TIME.
ENOS?
YEAH, MAMA?
YOU HEARD WHAT I JUS' SAID?
I DID.

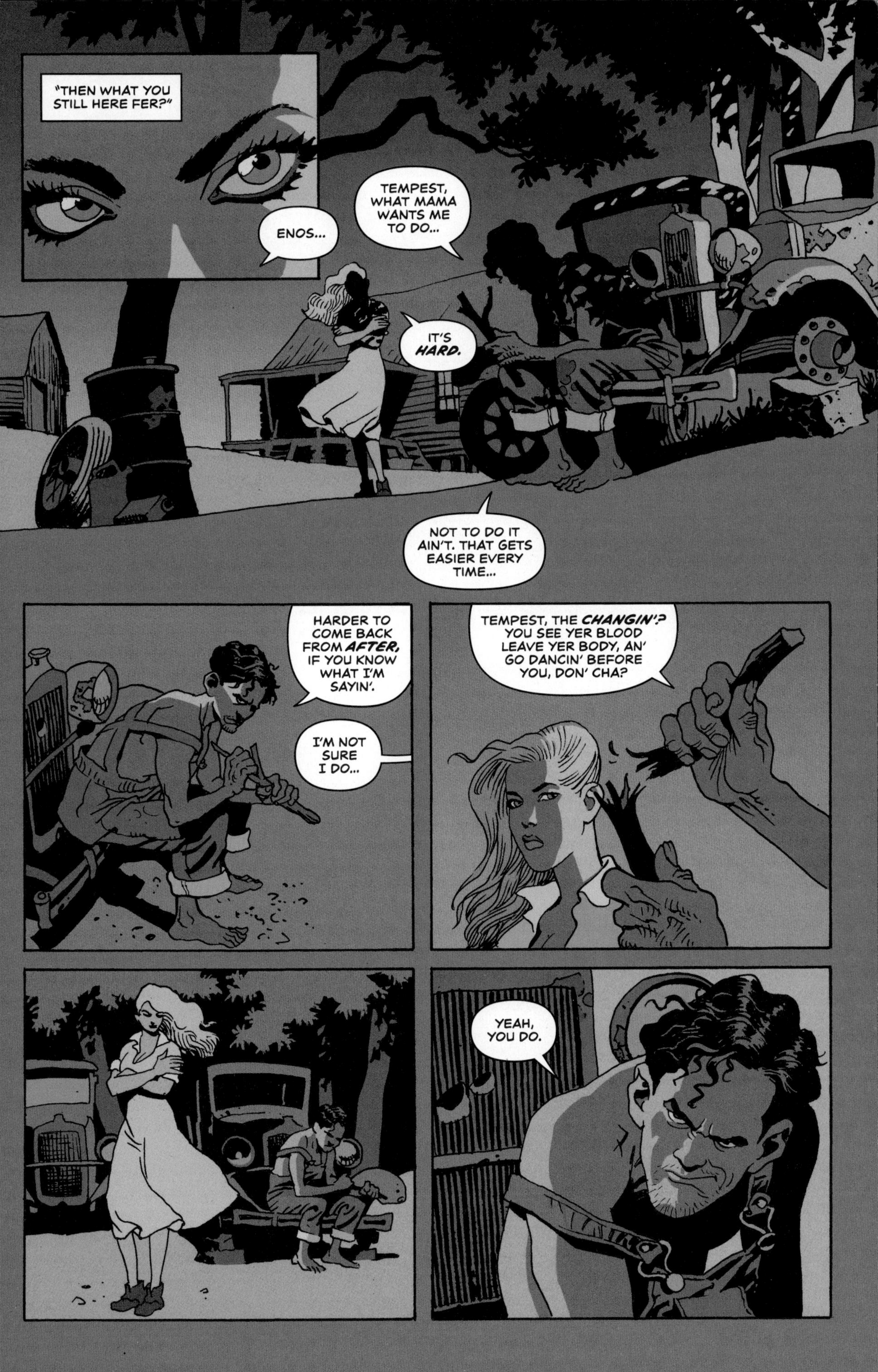

"THEN WHAT YOU STILL HERE FER?"
ENOS...
TEMPEST, WHAT MAMA WANTS ME TO DO...
IT'S *HARD.*
NOT TO DO IT AIN'T. THAT GETS EASIER EVERY TIME...
HARDER TO COME BACK FROM *AFTER,* IF YOU KNOW WHAT I'M SAYIN'.
I'M NOT SURE I DO...
TEMPEST, THE *CHANGIN'?* YOU SEE YER BLOOD LEAVE YER BODY, AN' GO DANCIN' BEFORE YOU, DON' CHA?
YEAH, YOU DO.

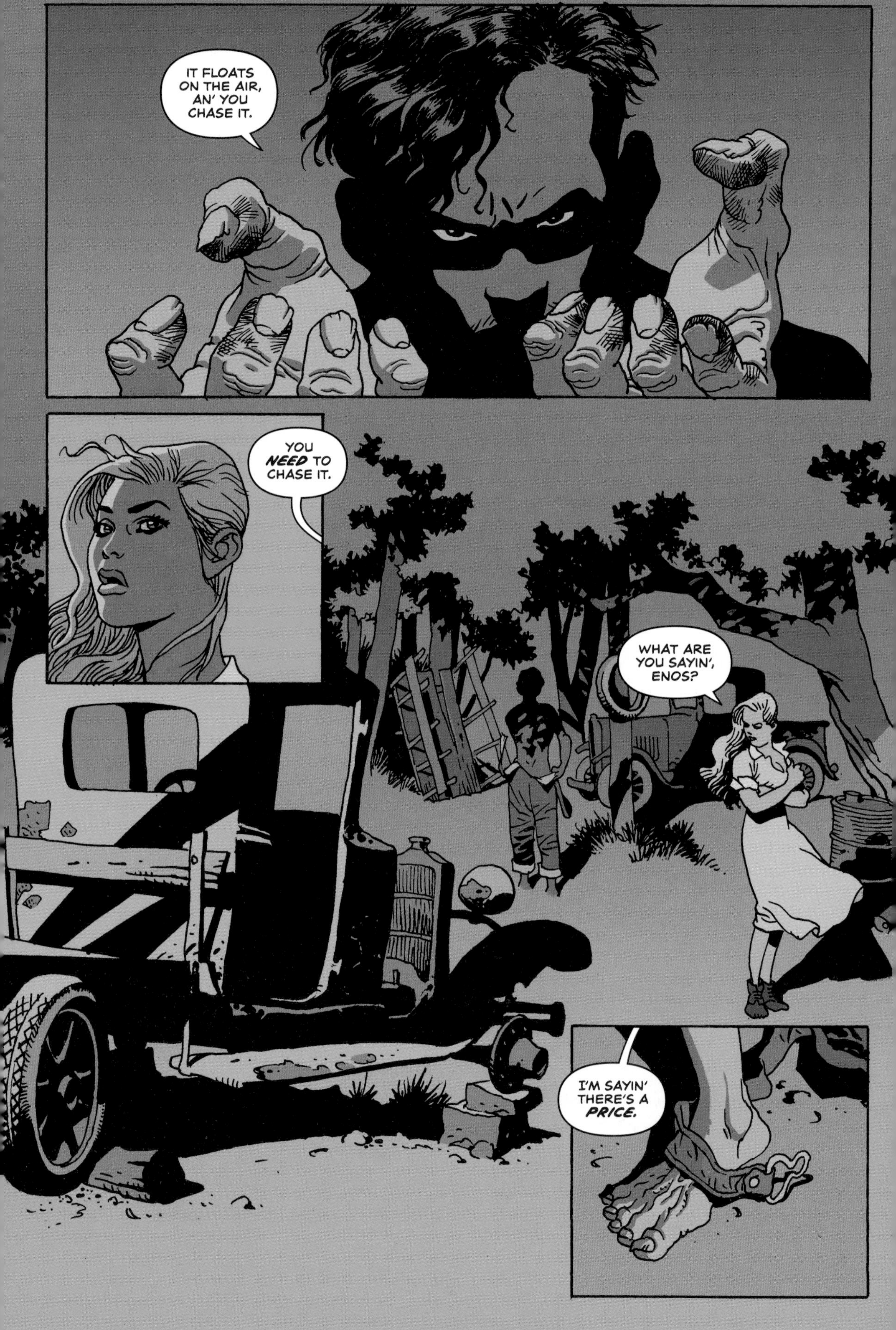
IT FLOATS ON THE AIR, AN' YOU CHASE IT.
YOU **NEED** TO CHASE IT.
WHAT ARE YOU SAYIN', ENOS?
I'M SAYIN' THERE'S A ***PRICE.***

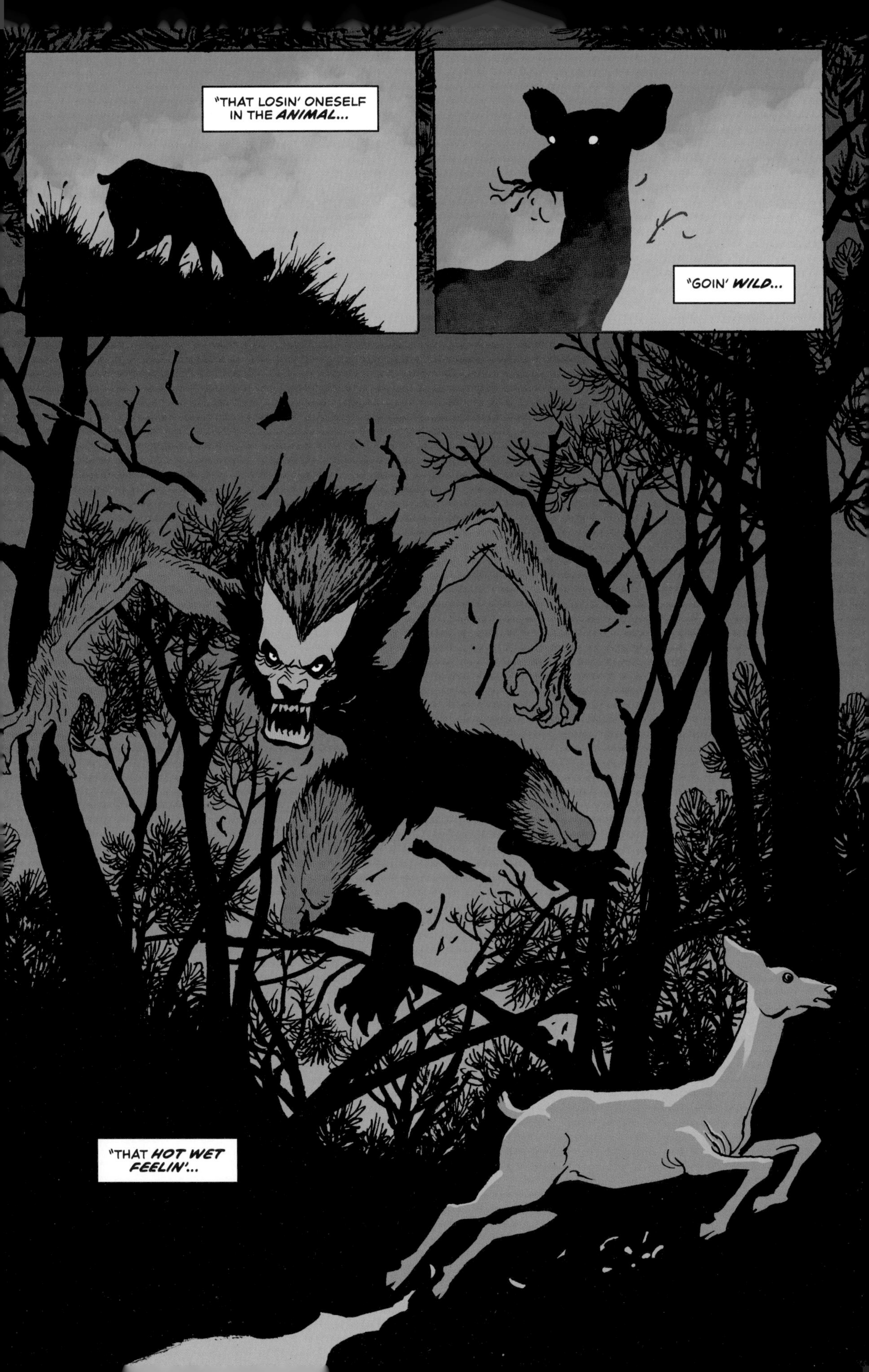
"THAT LOSIN' ONESELF IN THE ANIMAL...
"GOIN' WILD...
"THAT HOT WET FEELIN'...

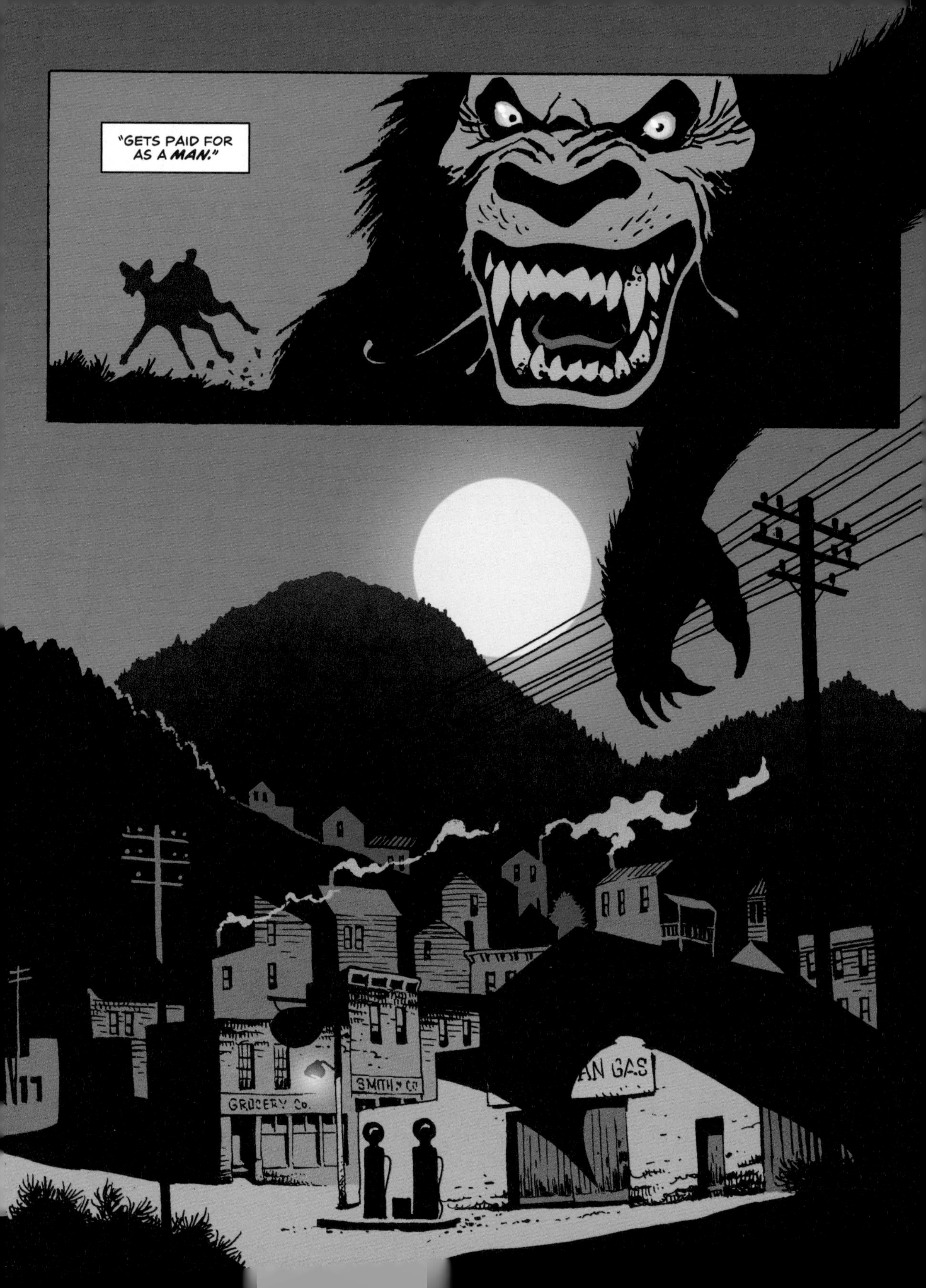
"GETS PAID FOR AS A *MAN.*"
AN GAS
SMITH & CO
GROCERY CO.

Chapter EIGHT

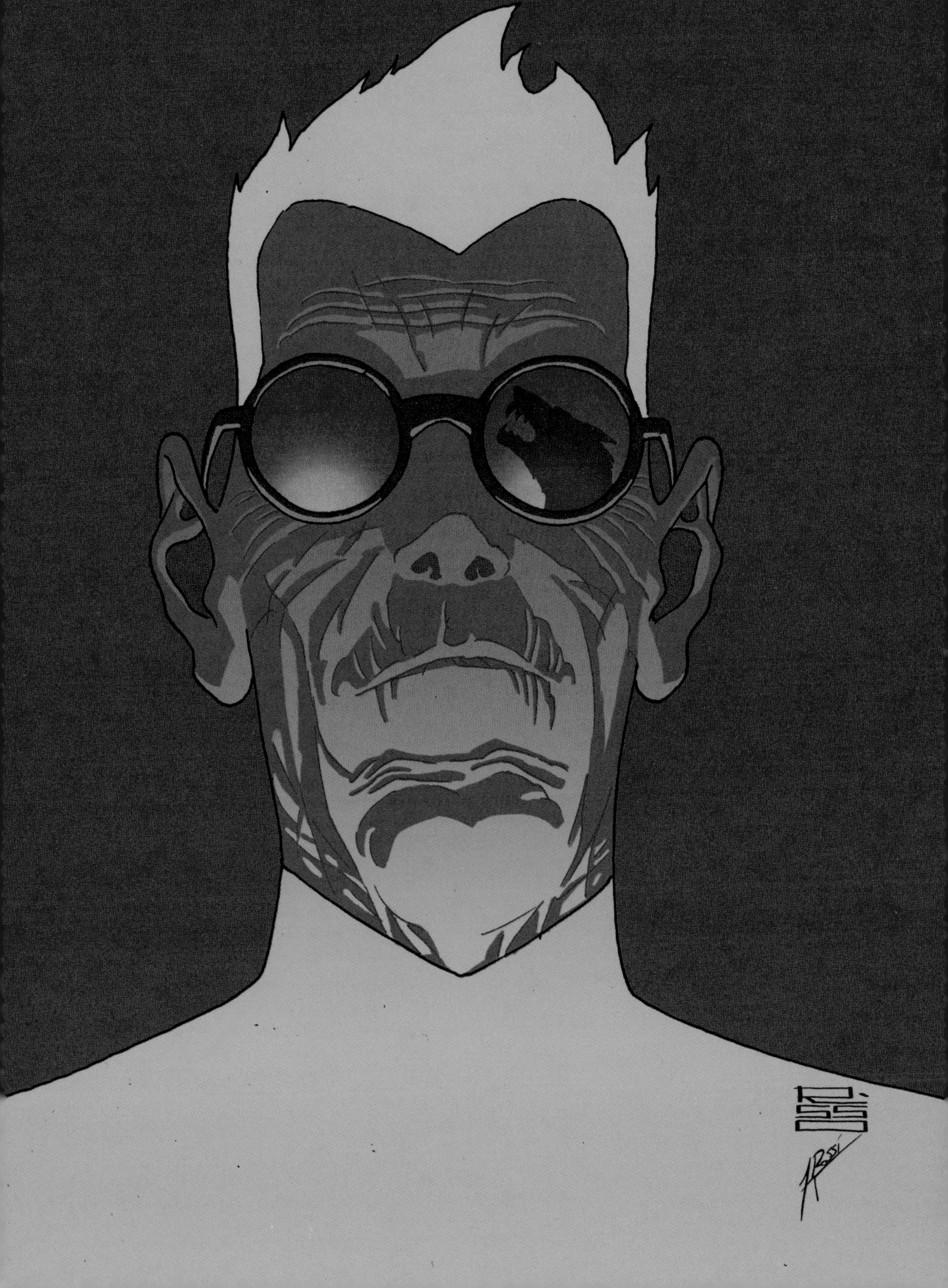

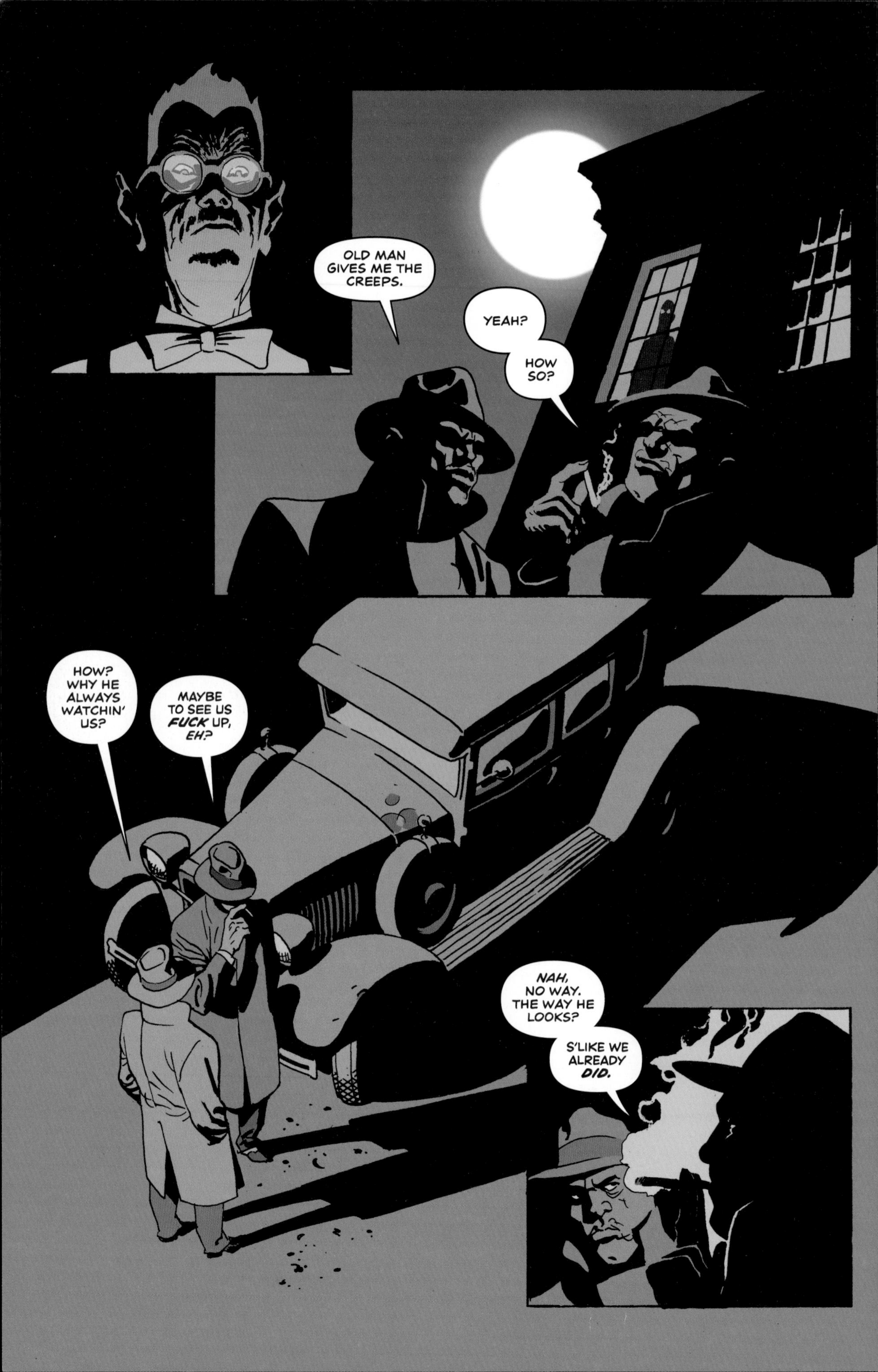
OLD MAN GIVES ME THE CREEPS.
YEAH?
HOW SO?
HOW? WHY HE ALWAYS WATCHIN' US?
MAYBE TO SEE US *FUCK* UP, *EH?*
NAH, NO WAY. THE WAY HE LOOKS?
S'LIKE WE ALREADY *DID.*

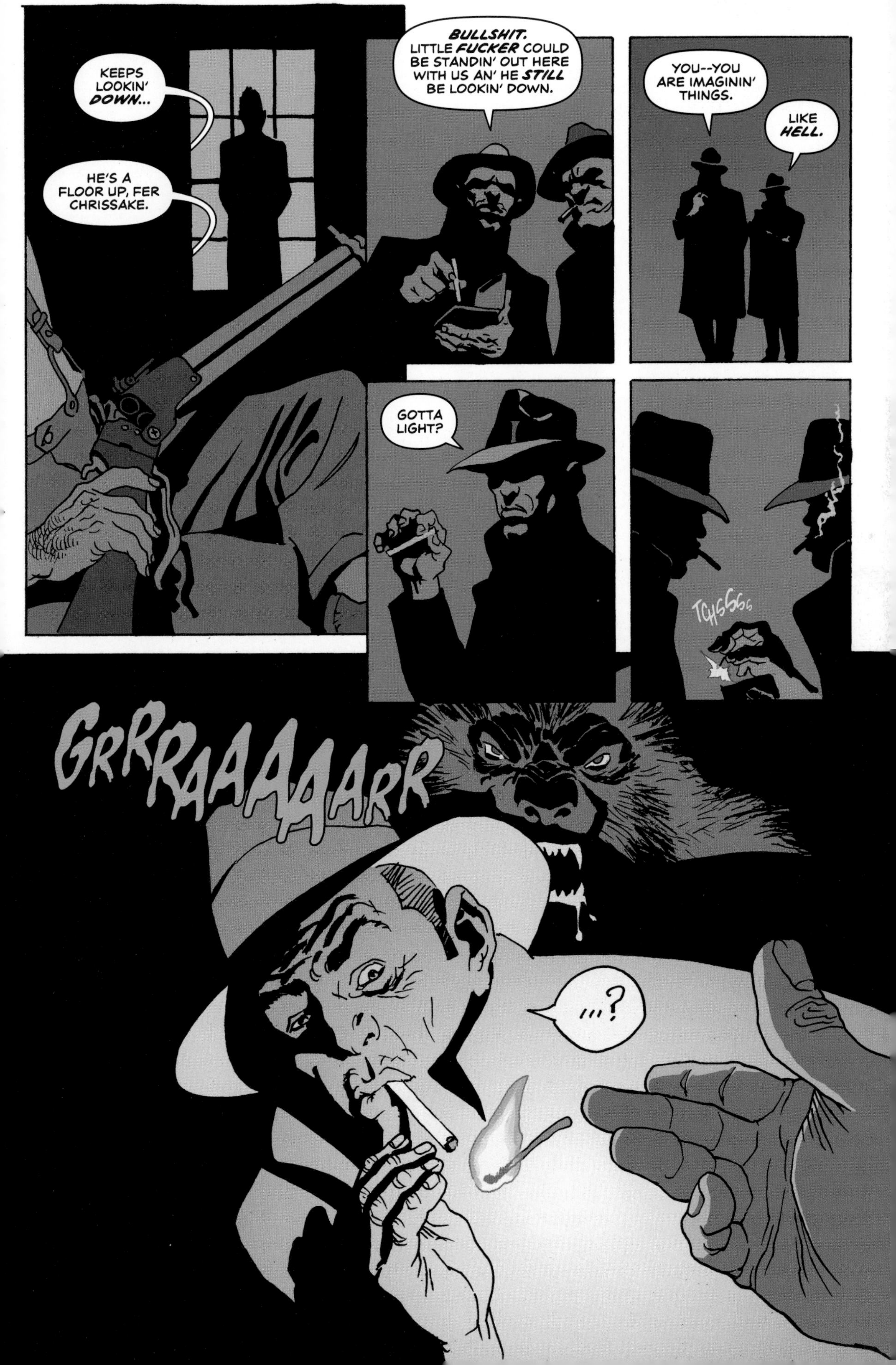
KEEPS LOOKIN' DOWN...
HE'S A FLOOR UP, FER CHRISSAKE.
BULLSHIT. LITTLE FUCKER COULD BE STANDIN' OUT HERE WITH US AN' HE STILL BE LOOKIN' DOWN.
YOU--YOU ARE IMAGININ' THINGS.
LIKE HELL.
GOTTA LIGHT?
TCHSSSS
GRRRAAAAAARR
...?

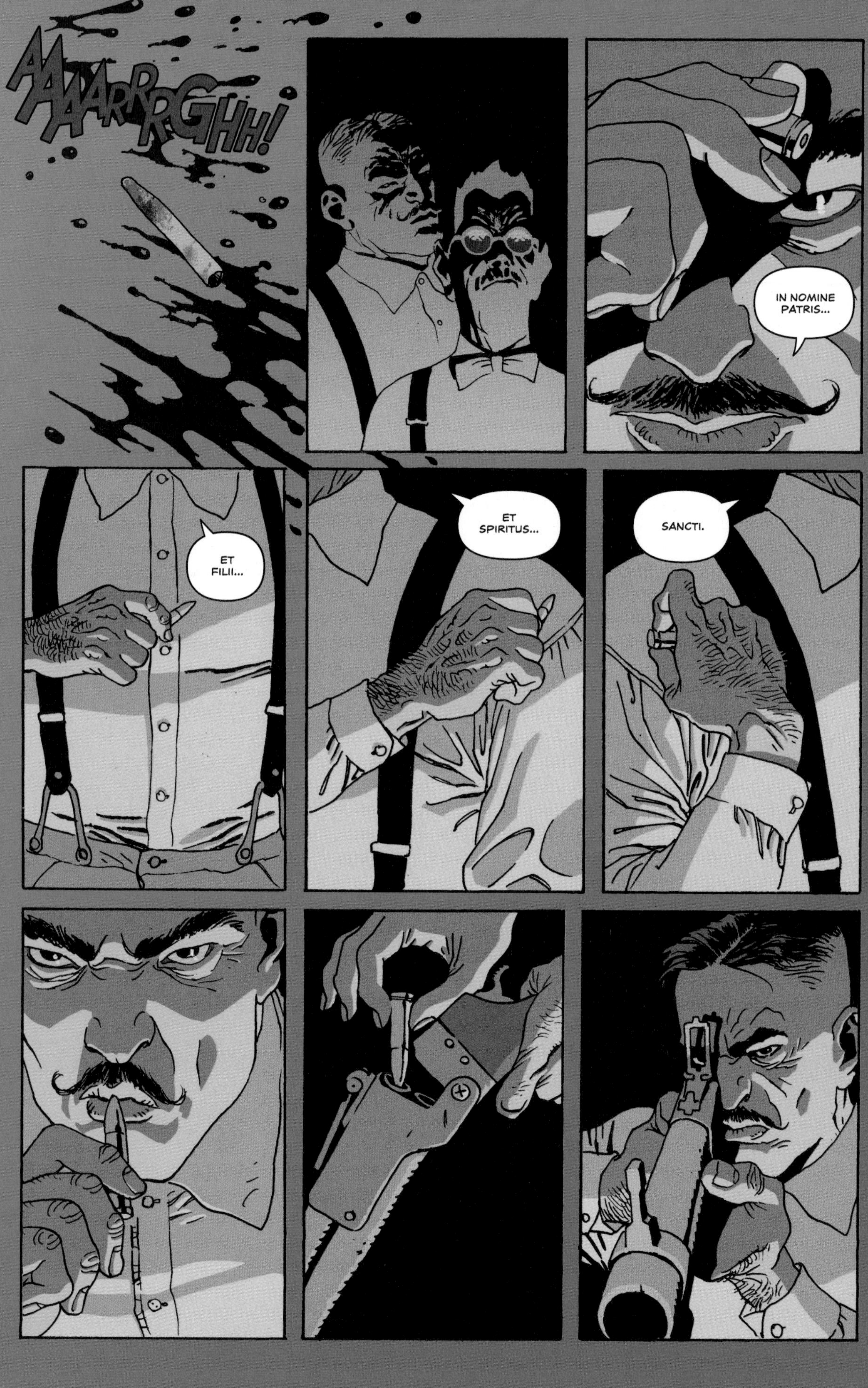
AAAARRRGHH!
IN NOMINE PATRIS...
ET FILII...
ET SPIRITUS...
SANCTI.

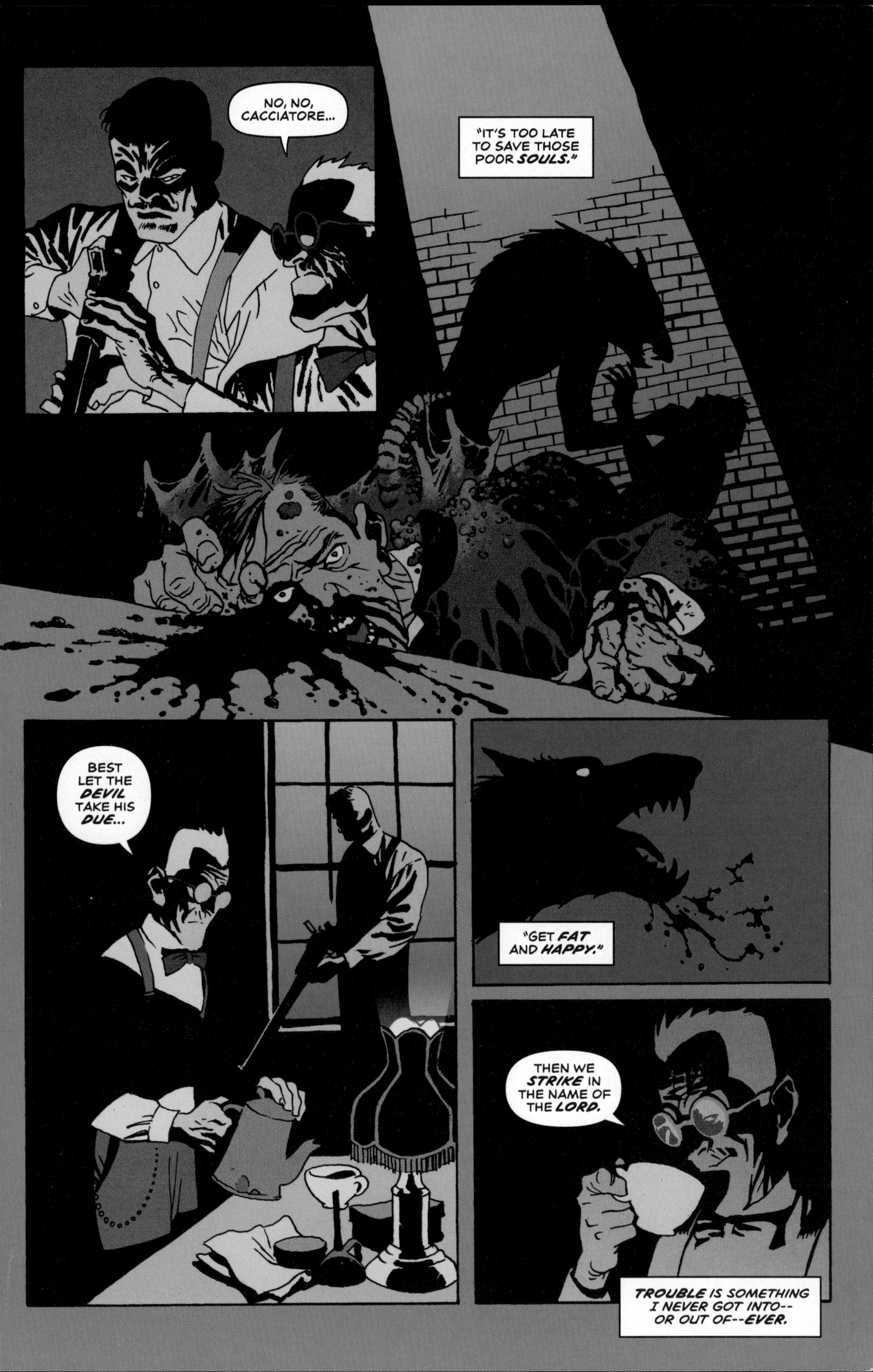
NO, NO, CACCIATORE...
"IT'S TOO LATE TO SAVE THOSE POOR SOULS."
BEST LET THE DEVIL TAKE HIS DUE...
"GET FAT AND HAPPY."
THEN WE STRIKE IN THE NAME OF THE LORD.
TROUBLE IS SOMETHING I NEVER GOT INTO-- OR OUT OF--EVER.

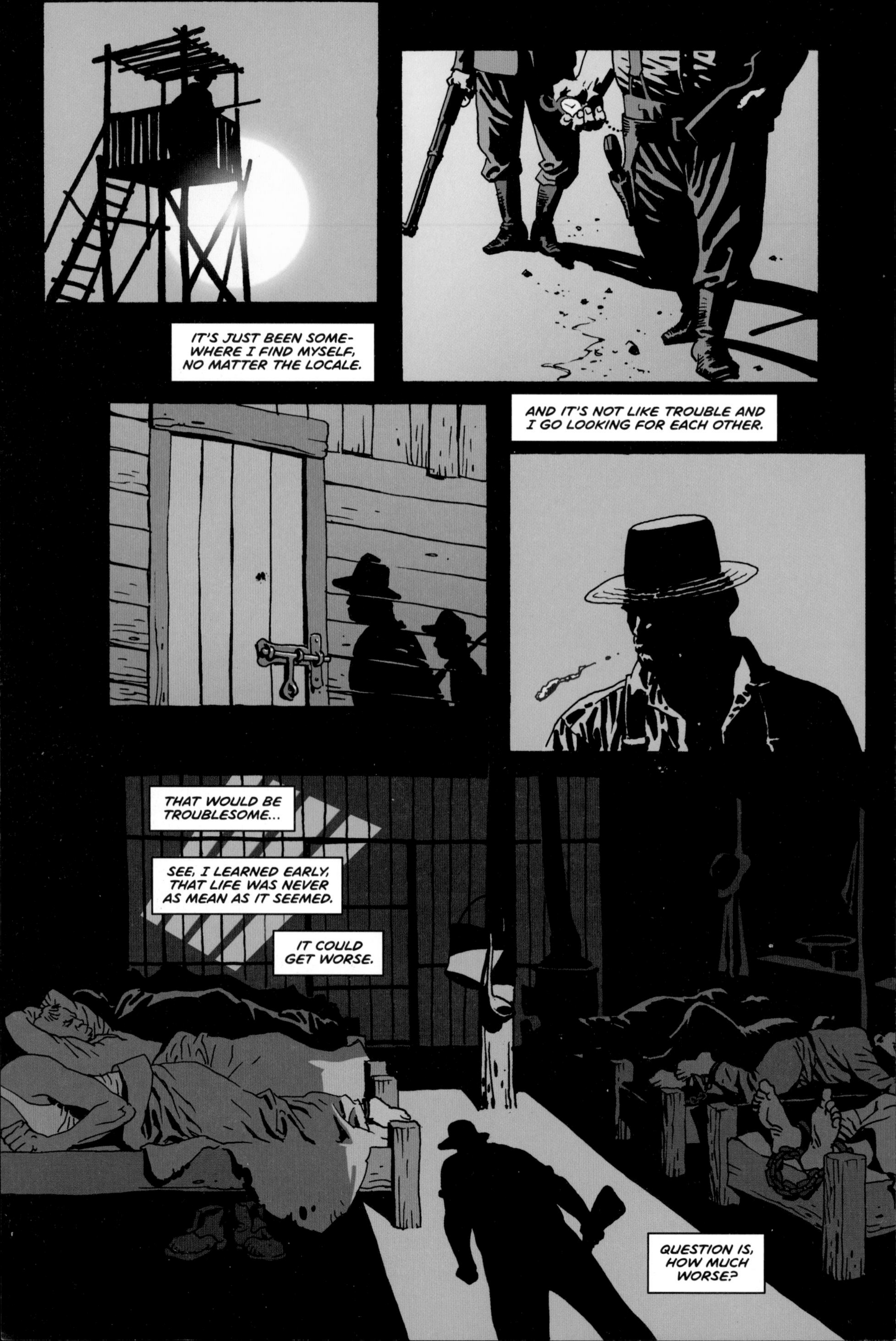
IT'S JUST BEEN SOME-WHERE I FIND MYSELF, NO MATTER THE LOCALE.
AND IT'S NOT LIKE TROUBLE AND I GO LOOKING FOR EACH OTHER.
THAT WOULD BE TROUBLESOME...
SEE, I LEARNED EARLY, THAT LIFE WAS NEVER AS MEAN AS IT SEEMED.
IT COULD GET WORSE.
QUESTION IS, HOW MUCH WORSE?

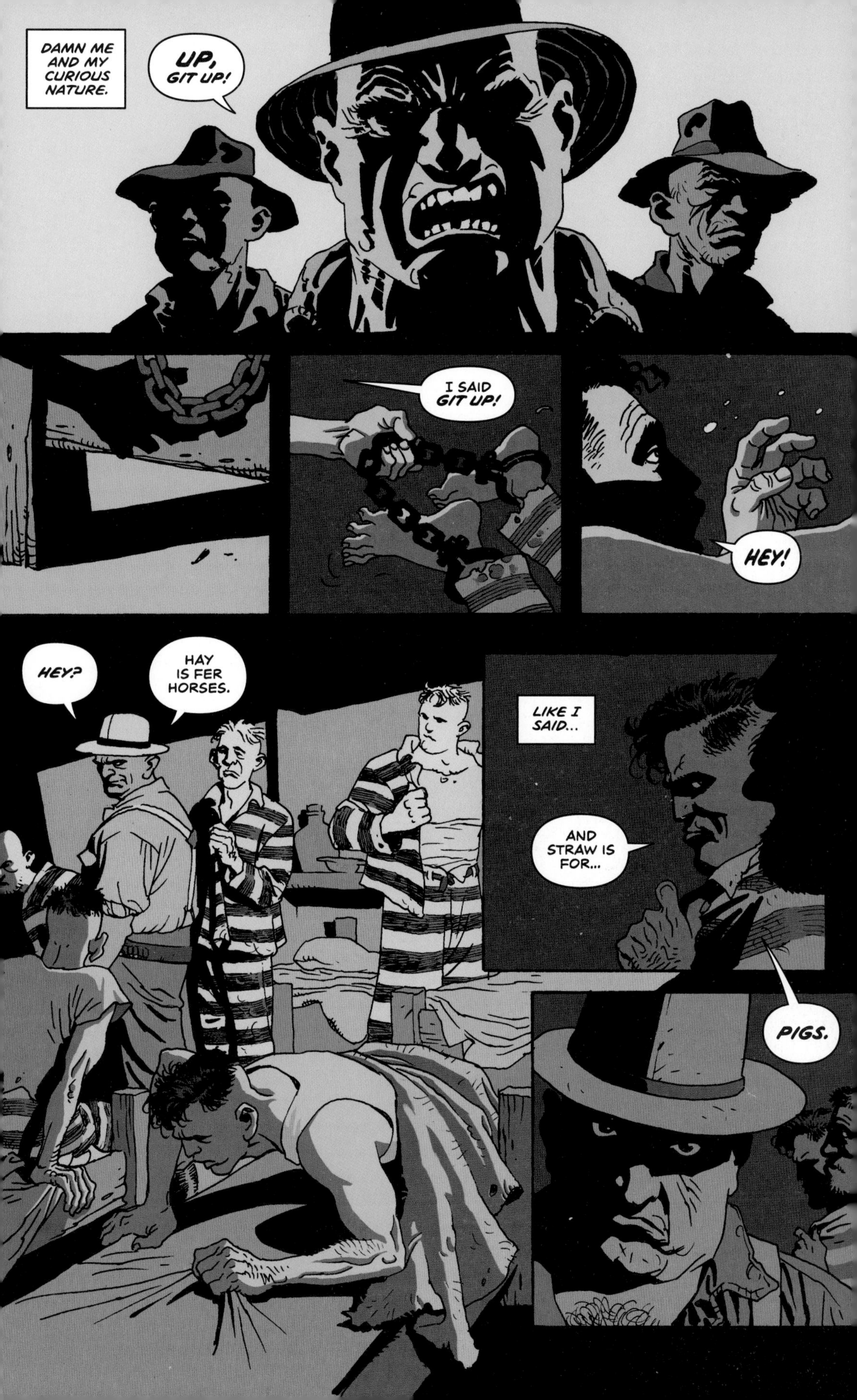
DAMN ME AND MY CURIOUS NATURE.
UP, GIT UP!
I SAID GIT UP!
HEY!
HEY?
HAY IS FER HORSES.
LIKE I SAID...
AND STRAW IS FOR...
PIGS.

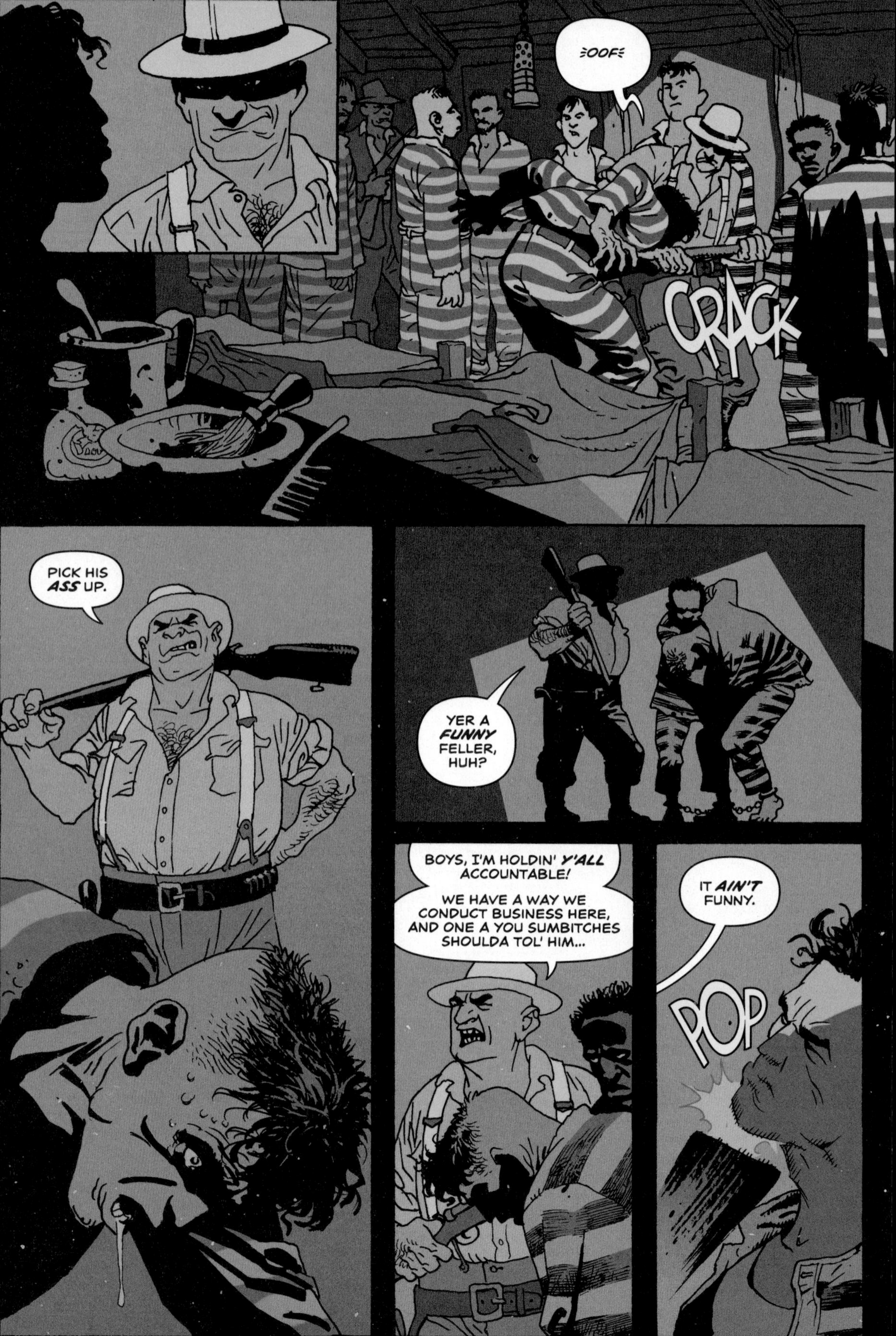

OOF
CRACK
PICK HIS ASS UP.
YER A FUNNY FELLER, HUH?
BOYS, I'M HOLDIN' Y'ALL ACCOUNTABLE!
WE HAVE A WAY WE CONDUCT BUSINESS HERE, AND ONE A YOU SUMBITCHES SHOULDA TOL' HIM...
IT AIN'T FUNNY.
POP

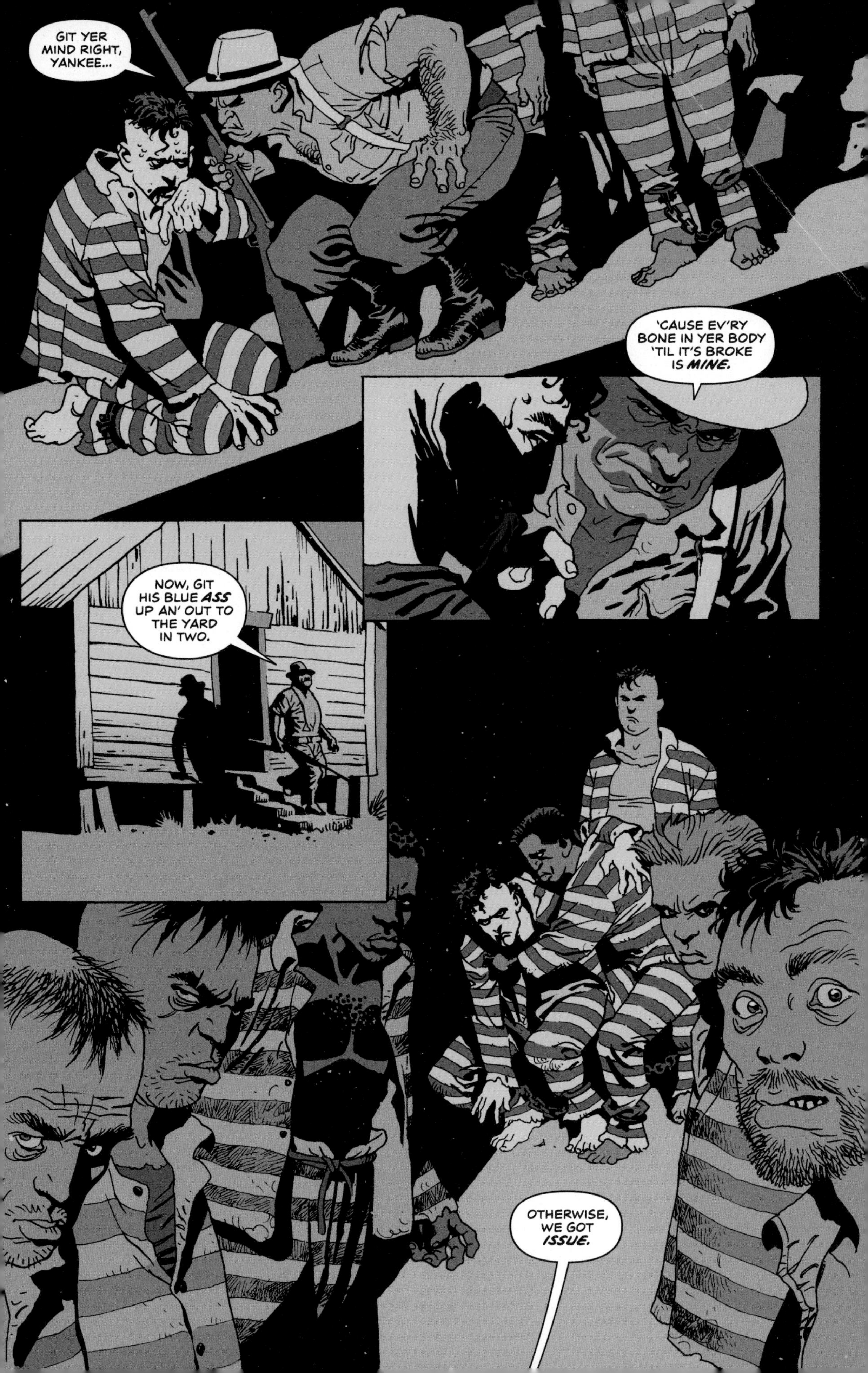
GIT YER MIND RIGHT, YANKEE...
'CAUSE EV'RY BONE IN YER BODY 'TIL IT'S BROKE IS *MINE.*
NOW, GIT HIS BLUE *ASS* UP AN' OUT TO THE YARD IN TWO.
OTHERWISE, WE GOT *ISSUE.*

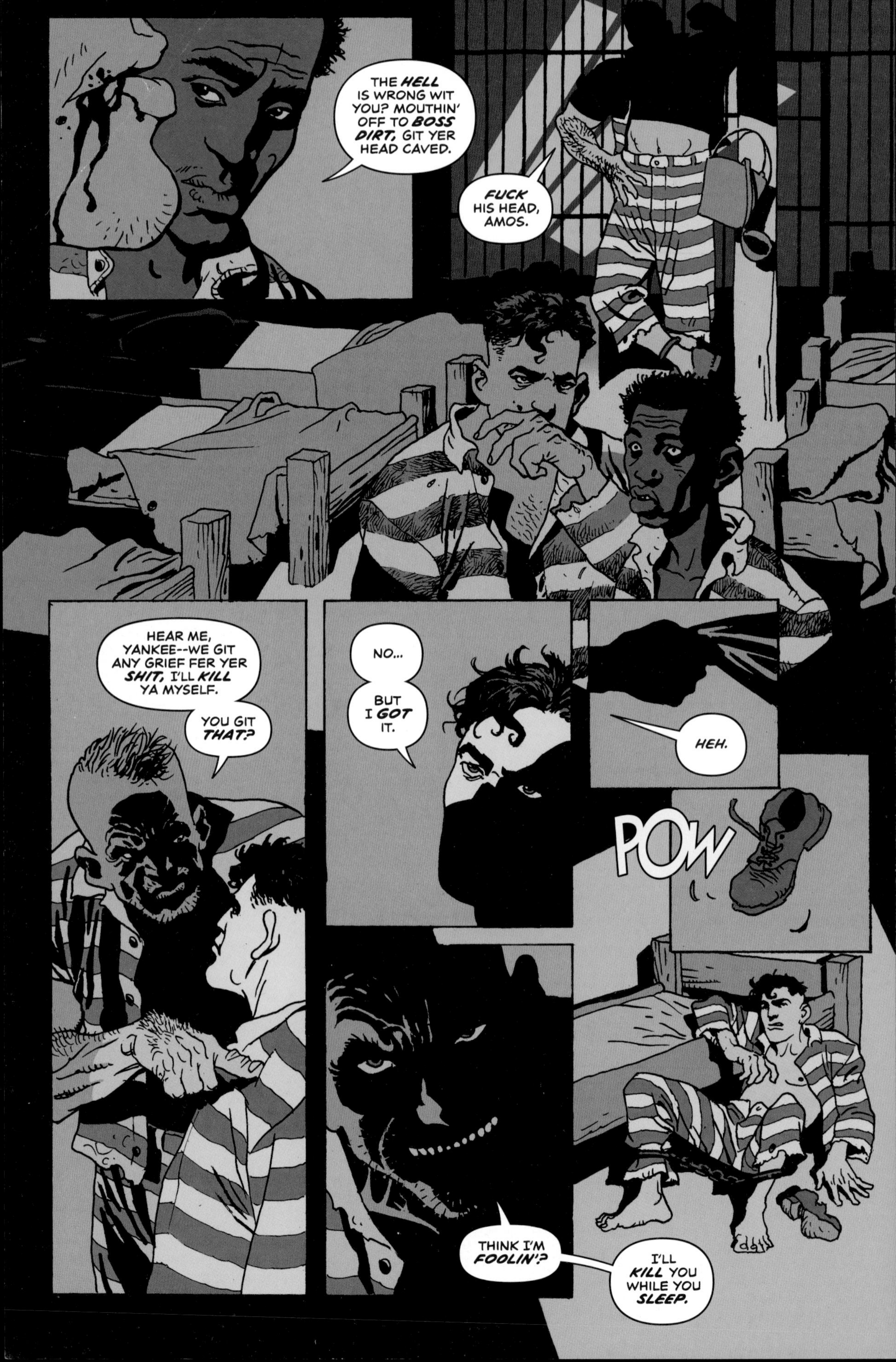

THE HELL IS WRONG WIT YOU? MOUTHIN' OFF TO BOSS DIRT, GIT YER HEAD CAVED.
FUCK HIS HEAD, AMOS.
HEAR ME, YANKEE--WE GIT ANY GRIEF FER YER SHIT, I'LL KILL YA MYSELF.
YOU GIT THAT?
NO...
BUT I GOT IT.
HEH.
POW
THINK I'M FOOLIN'?
I'LL KILL YOU WHILE YOU SLEEP.

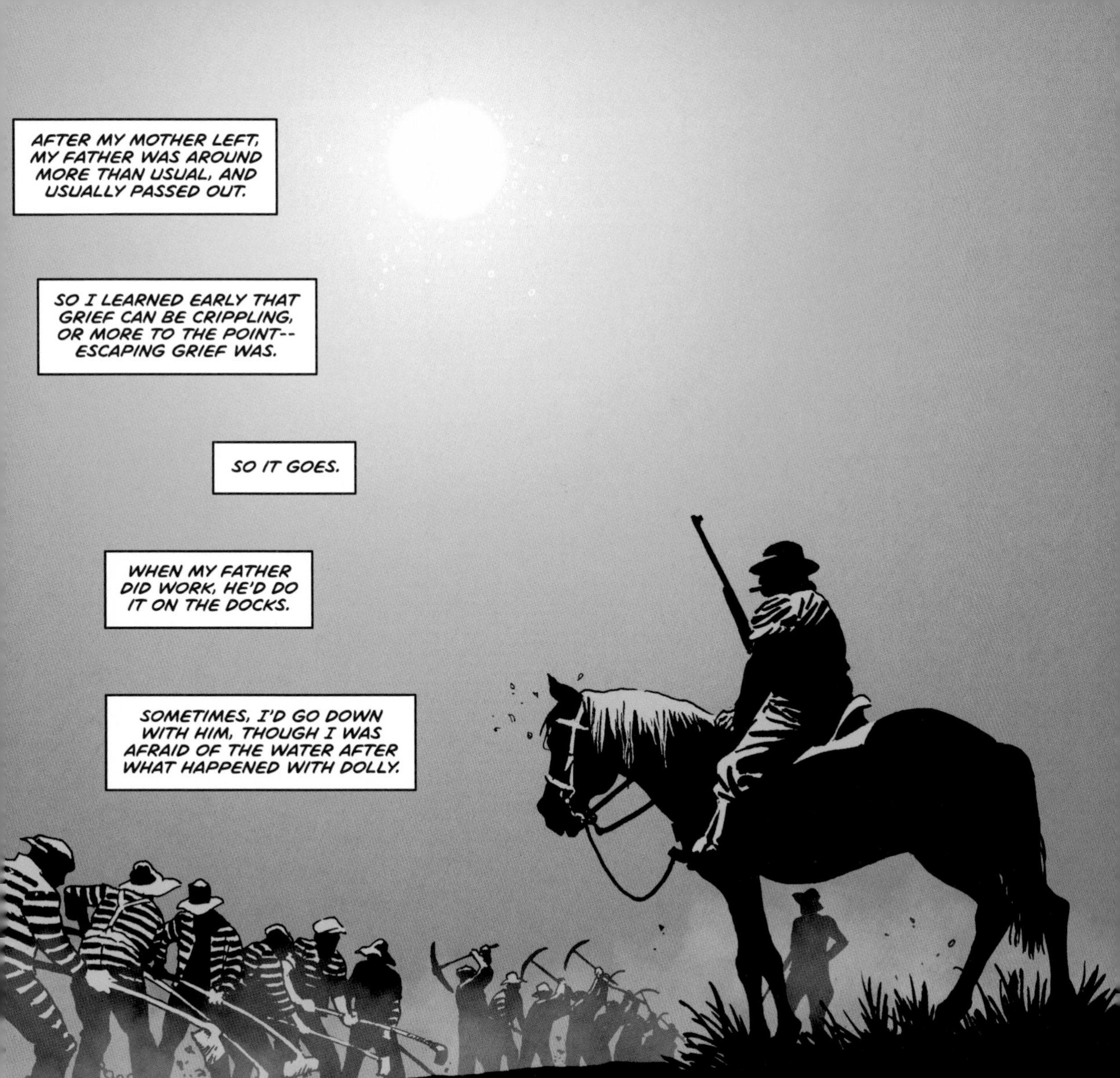
AFTER MY MOTHER LEFT, MY FATHER WAS AROUND MORE THAN USUAL, AND USUALLY PASSED OUT.
SO I LEARNED EARLY THAT GRIEF CAN BE CRIPPLING, OR MORE TO THE POINT-- ESCAPING GRIEF WAS.
SO IT GOES.
WHEN MY FATHER DID WORK, HE'D DO IT ON THE DOCKS.
SOMETIMES, I'D GO DOWN WITH HIM, THOUGH I WAS AFRAID OF THE WATER AFTER WHAT HAPPENED WITH DOLLY.

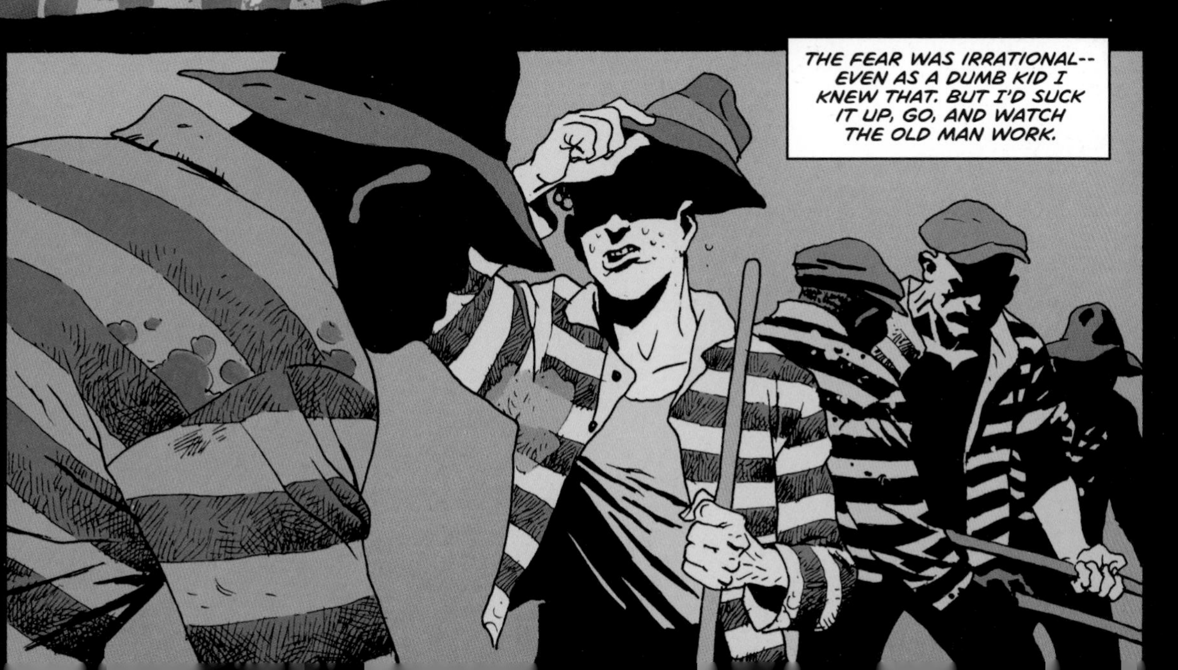
THE FEAR WAS IRRATIONAL-- EVEN AS A DUMB KID I KNEW THAT. BUT I'D SUCK IT UP, GO, AND WATCH THE OLD MAN WORK.

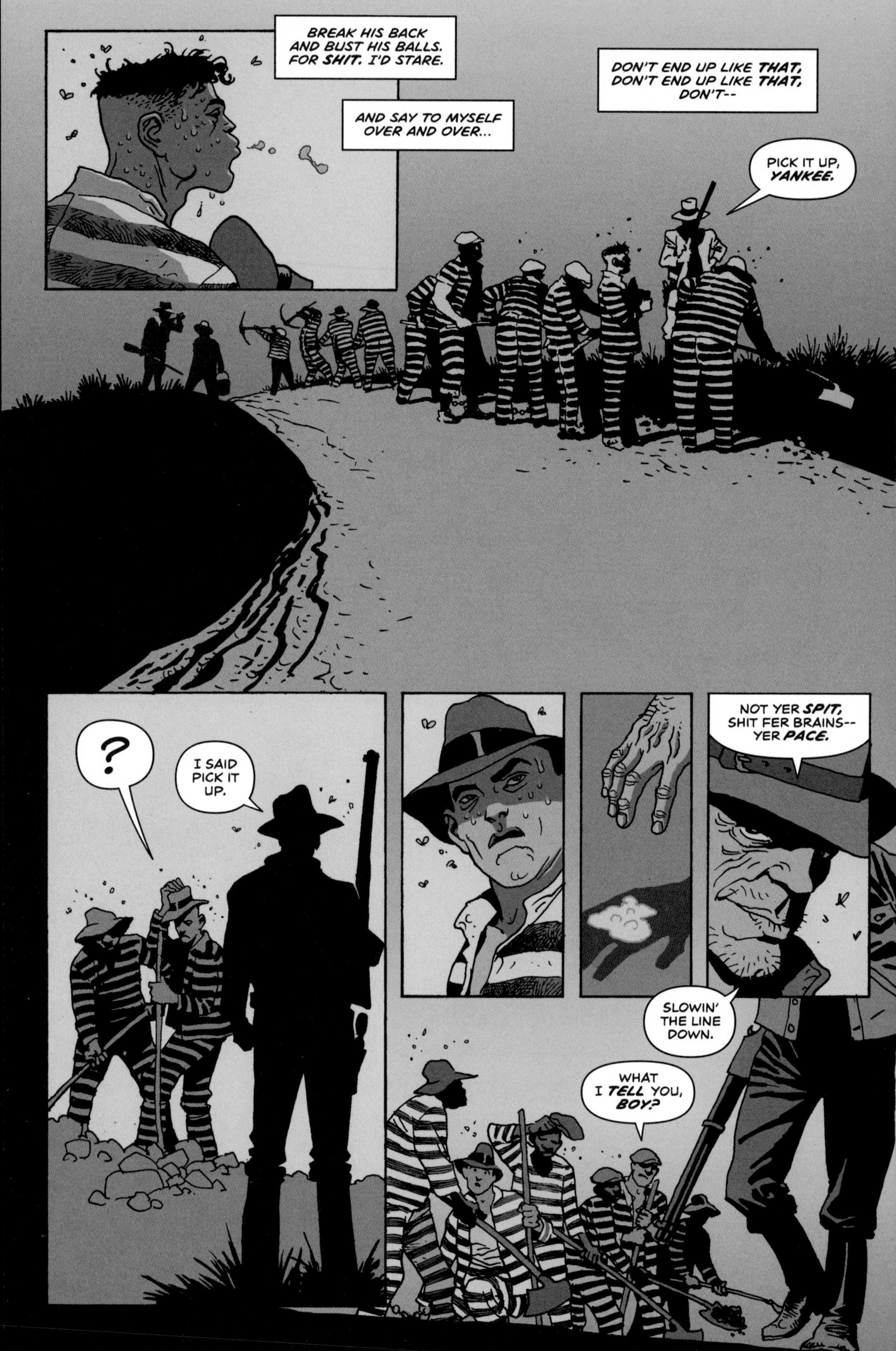
BREAK HIS BACK AND BUST HIS BALLS. FOR SHIT. I'D STARE.
AND SAY TO MYSELF OVER AND OVER...
DON'T END UP LIKE THAT, DON'T END UP LIKE THAT, DON'T--
PICK IT UP, YANKEE.
?
I SAID PICK IT UP.
NOT YER SPIT, SHIT FER BRAINS-- YER PACE.
SLOWIN' THE LINE DOWN.
WHAT I TELL YOU, BOY?

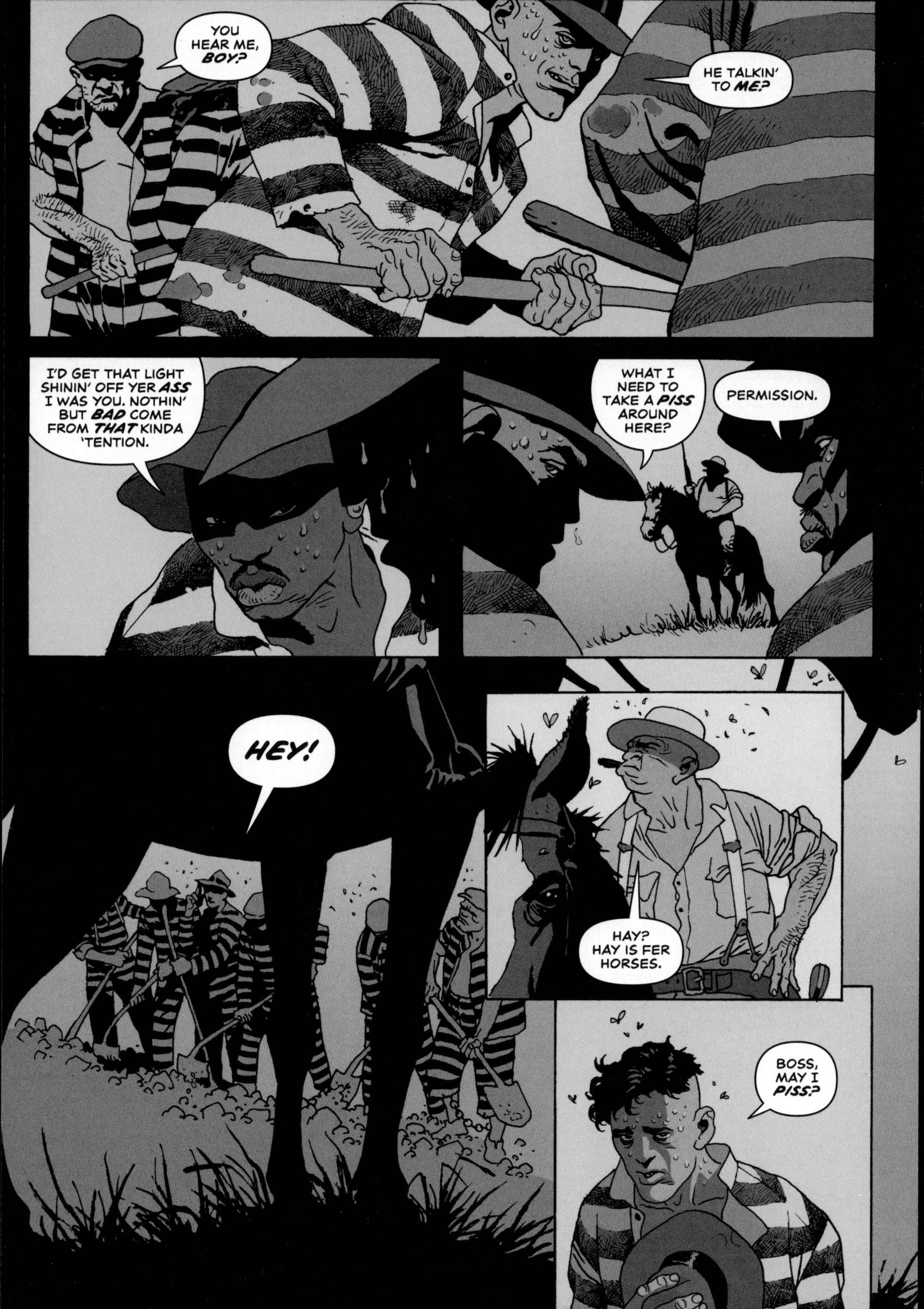

YOU HEAR ME, BOY?
HE TALKIN' TO ME?
I'D GET THAT LIGHT SHININ' OFF YER ASS I WAS YOU. NOTHIN' BUT BAD COME FROM THAT KINDA 'TENTION.
WHAT I NEED TO TAKE A PISS AROUND HERE?
PERMISSION.
HEY!
HAY? HAY IS FER HORSES.
BOSS, MAY I PISS?

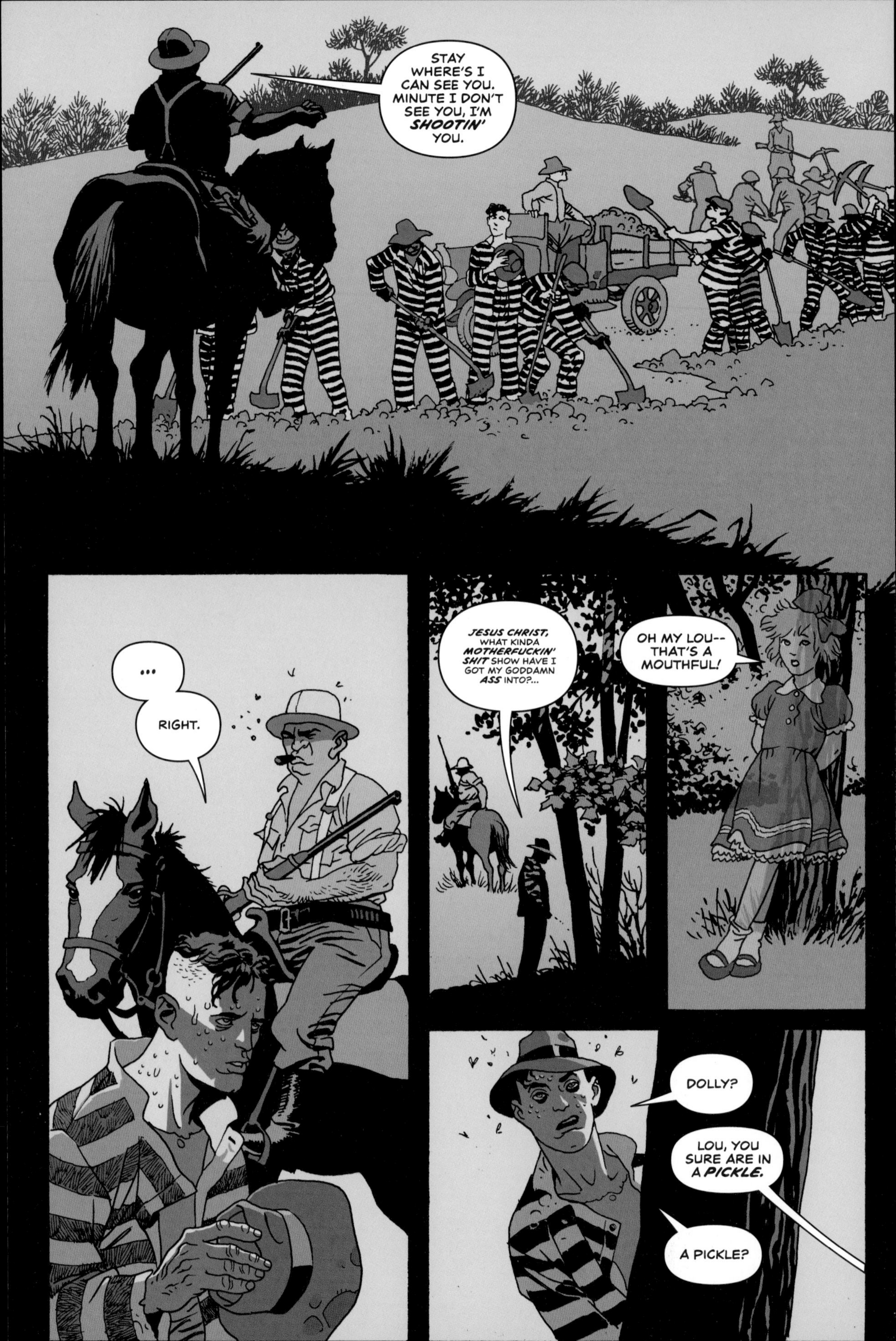
STAY WHERE'S I CAN SEE YOU. MINUTE I DON'T SEE YOU, I'M SHOOTIN' YOU.
...
RIGHT.
JESUS CHRIST, WHAT KINDA MOTHERFUCKIN' SHIT SHOW HAVE I GOT MY GODDAMN ASS INTO?...
OH MY LOU-- THAT'S A MOUTHFUL!
DOLLY?
LOU, YOU SURE ARE IN A PICKLE.
A PICKLE?

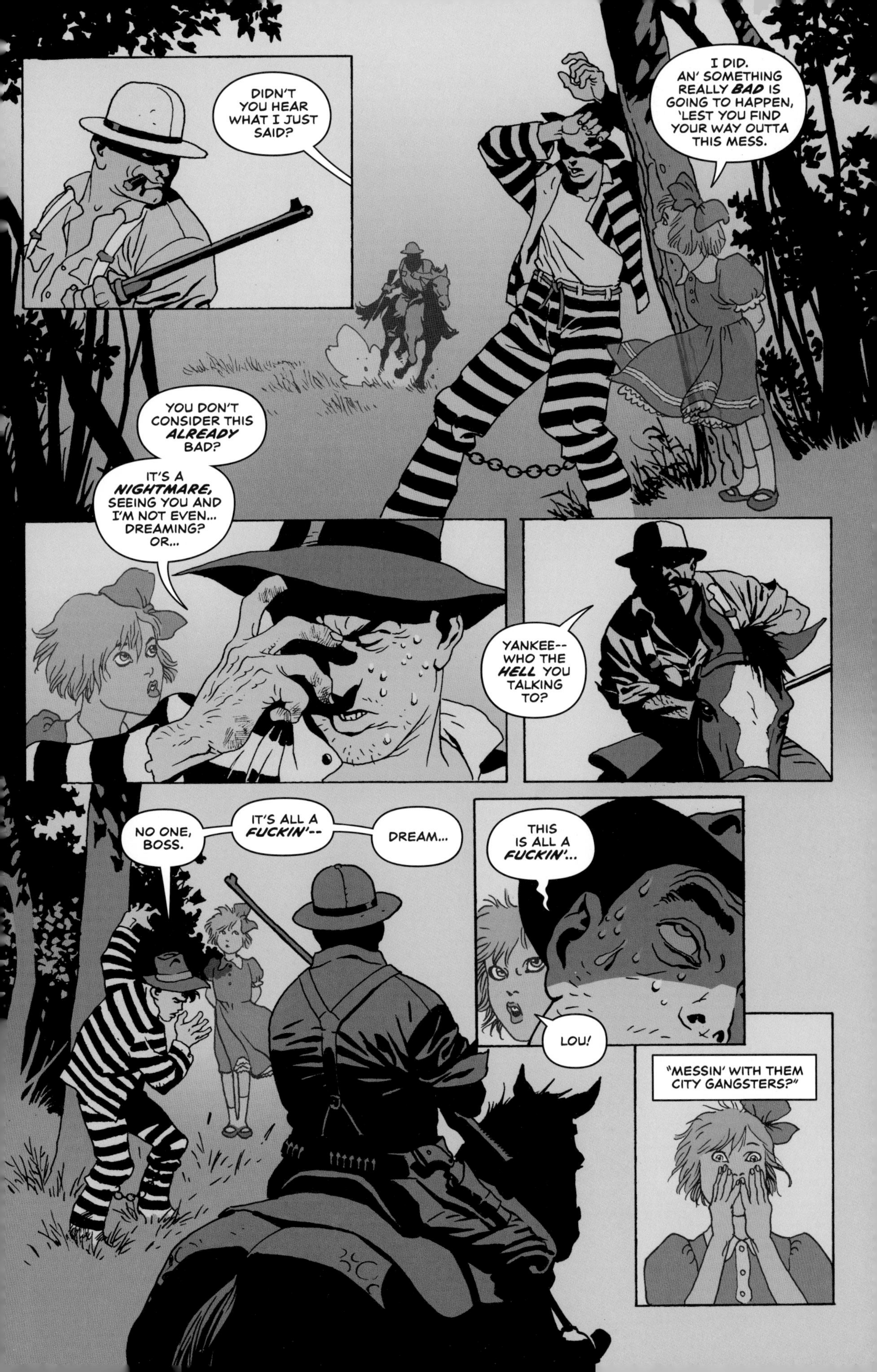

DIDN'T YOU HEAR WHAT I JUST SAID?
I DID. AN' SOMETHING REALLY BAD IS GOING TO HAPPEN, 'LEST YOU FIND YOUR WAY OUTTA THIS MESS.
YOU DON'T CONSIDER THIS ALREADY BAD?
IT'S A NIGHTMARE, SEEING YOU AND I'M NOT EVEN... DREAMING? OR...
YANKEE-- WHO THE HELL YOU TALKING TO?
NO ONE, BOSS.
IT'S ALL A FUCKIN'--
DREAM...
THIS IS ALL A FUCKIN'...
LOU!
"MESSIN' WITH THEM CITY GANGSTERS?"

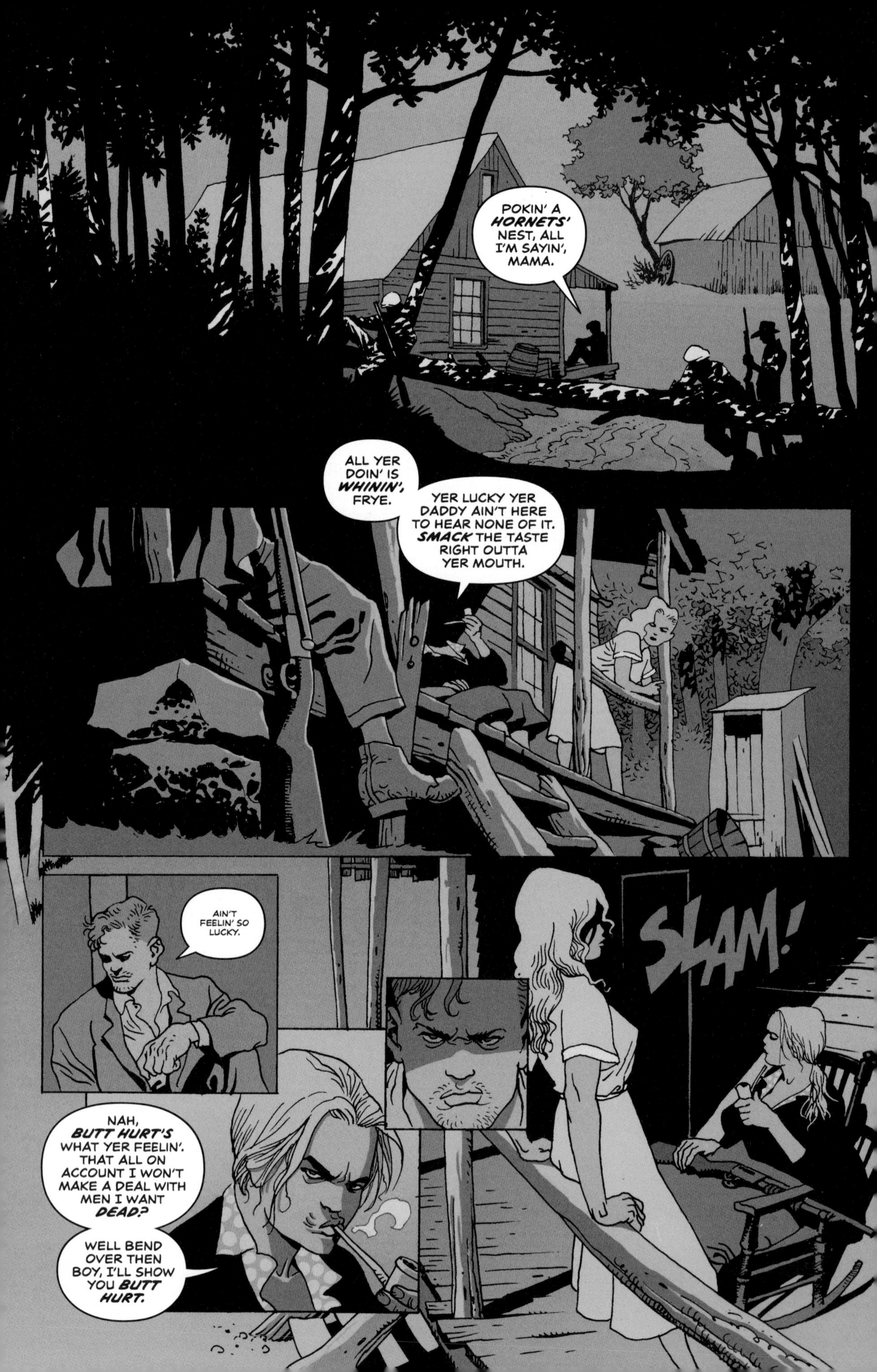
POKIN' A HORNETS' NEST, ALL I'M SAYIN', MAMA.
ALL YER DOIN' IS WHININ', FRYE.
YER LUCKY YER DADDY AIN'T HERE TO HEAR NONE OF IT. SMACK THE TASTE RIGHT OUTTA YER MOUTH.
AIN'T FEELIN' SO LUCKY.
SLAM!
NAH, BUTT HURT'S WHAT YER FEELIN'. THAT ALL ON ACCOUNT I WON'T MAKE A DEAL WITH MEN I WANT DEAD?
WELL BEND OVER THEN BOY, I'LL SHOW YOU BUTT HURT.

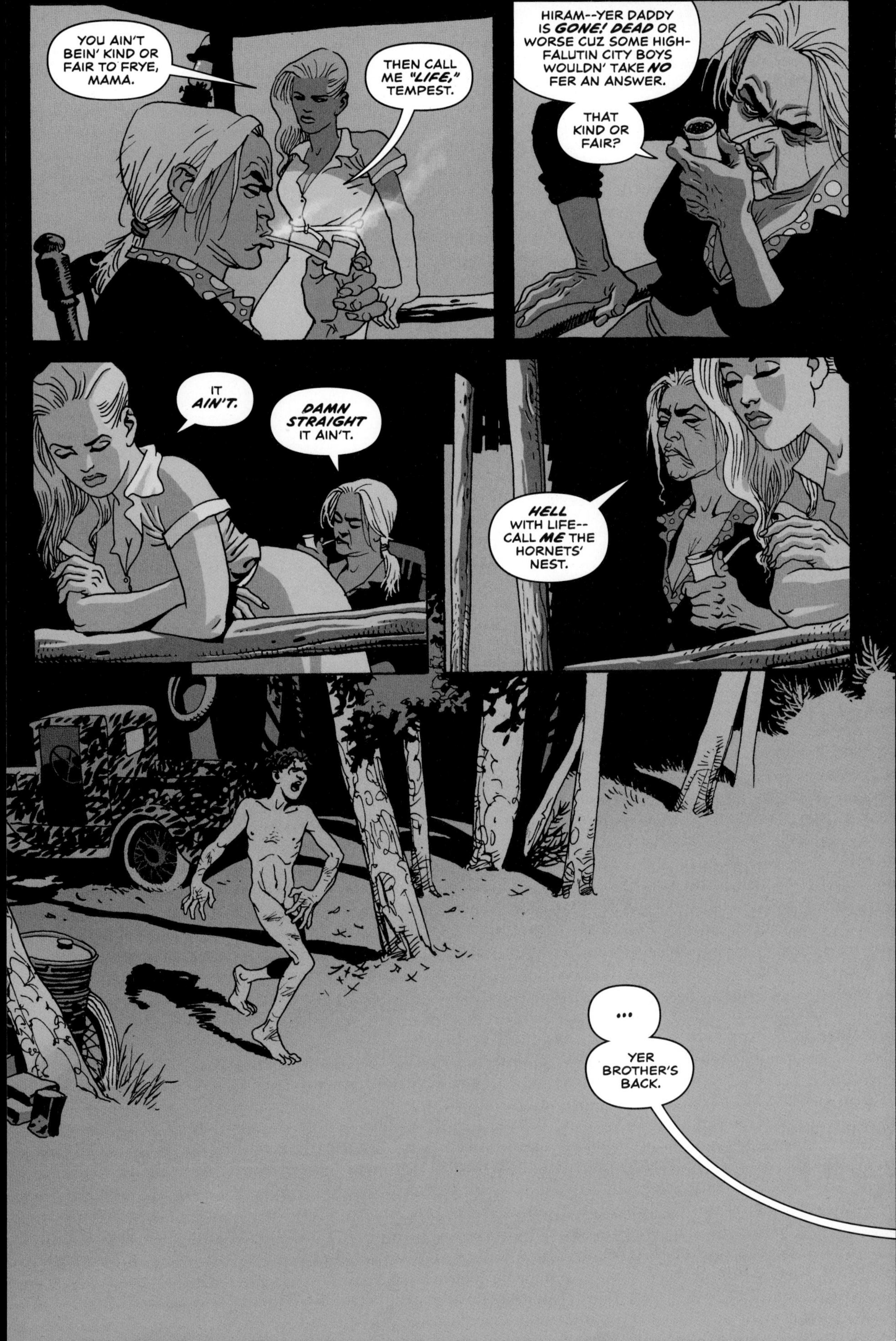
YOU AIN'T BEIN' KIND OR FAIR TO FRYE, MAMA.
THEN CALL ME "LIFE," TEMPEST.
HIRAM--YER DADDY IS GONE! DEAD OR WORSE CUZ SOME HIGH-FALUTIN CITY BOYS WOULDN' TAKE NO FER AN ANSWER.
THAT KIND OR FAIR?
IT AIN'T.
DAMN STRAIGHT IT AIN'T.
HELL WITH LIFE--CALL ME THE HORNETS' NEST.
...
YER BROTHER'S BACK.

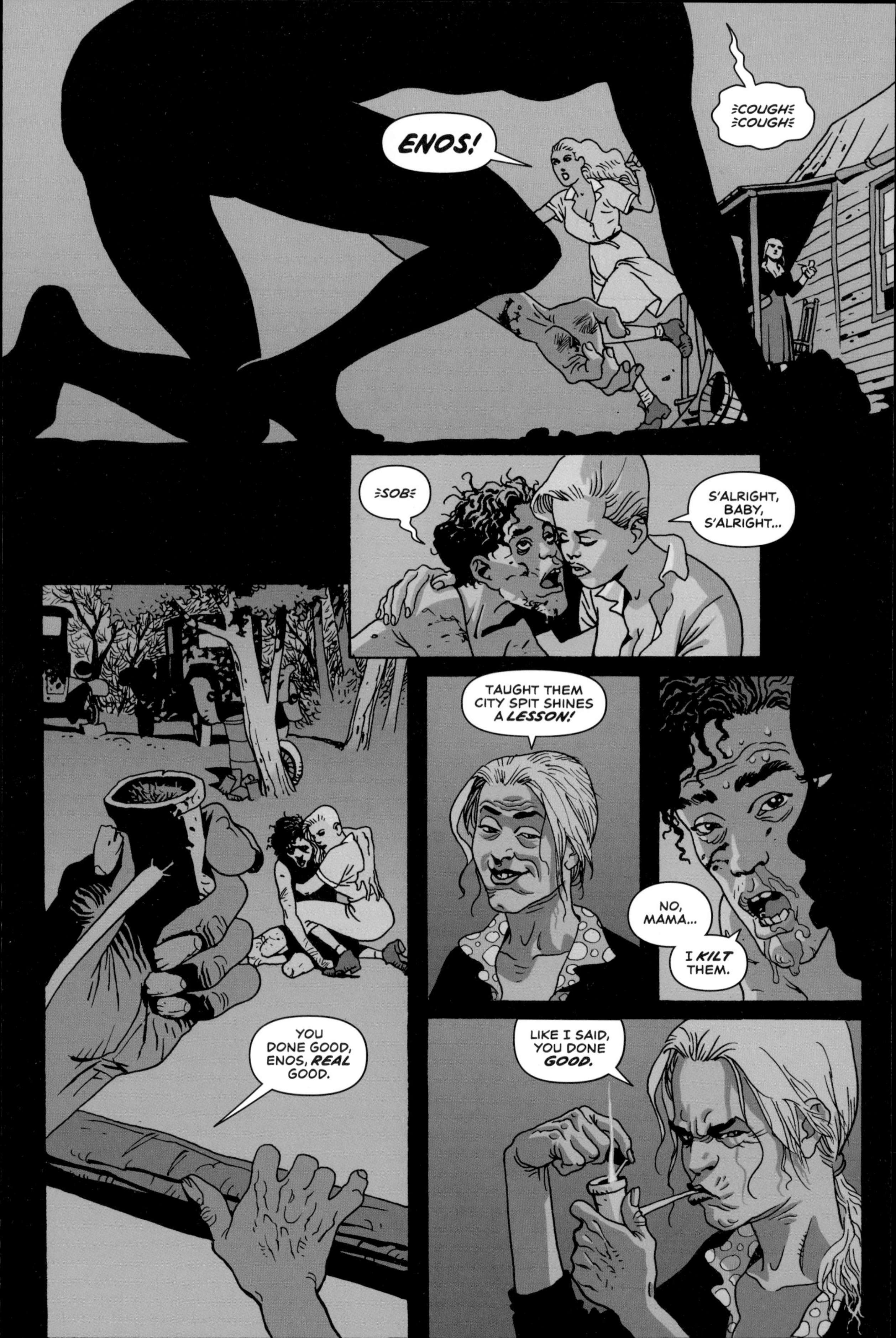
COUGH COUGH
ENOS!
SOB
S'ALRIGHT, BABY, S'ALRIGHT...
TAUGHT THEM CITY SPIT SHINES A LESSON!
NO, MAMA...
I KILT THEM.
YOU DONE GOOD, ENOS, REAL GOOD.
LIKE I SAID, YOU DONE GOOD.

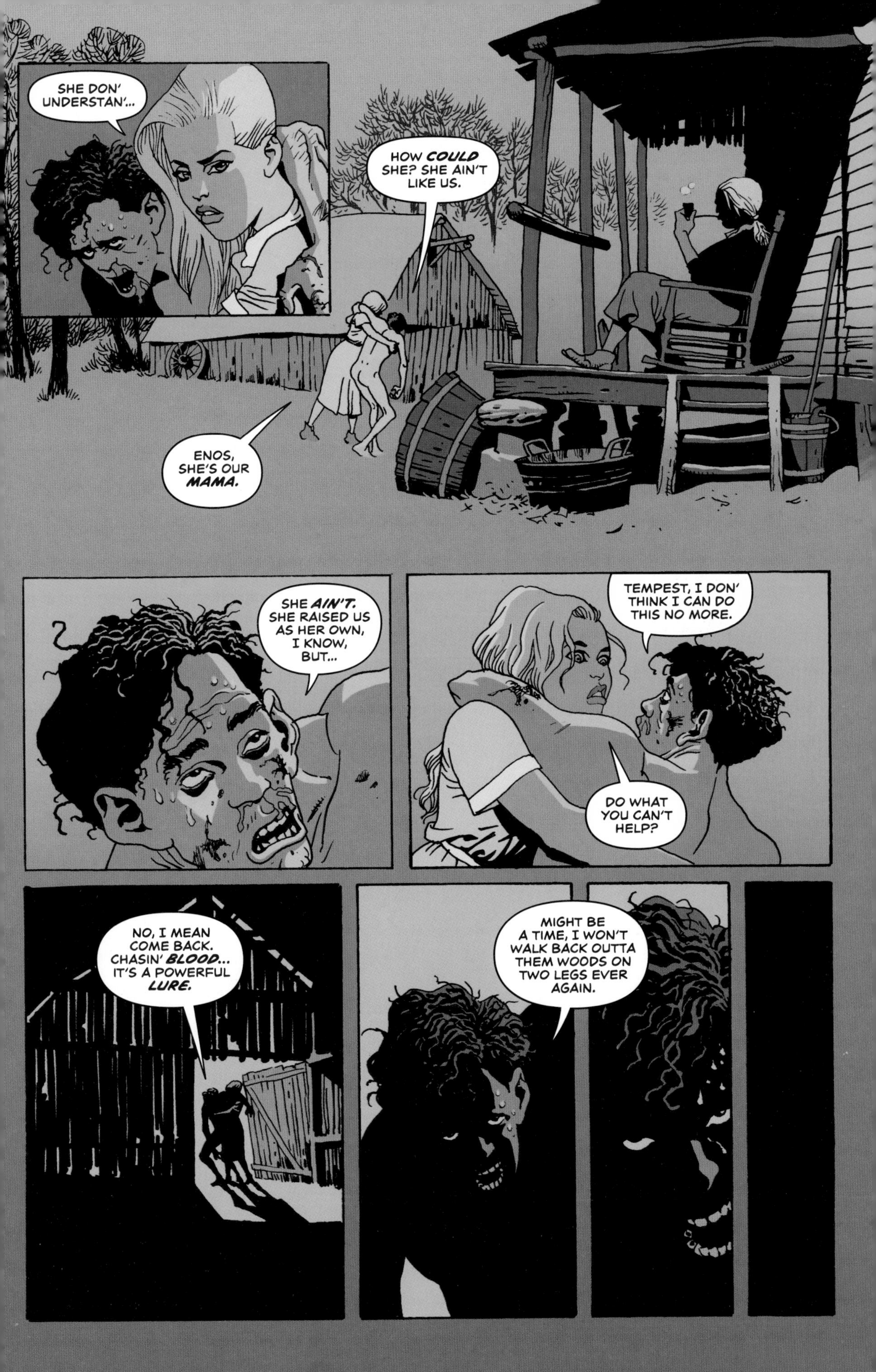
SHE DON' UNDERSTAN'...
HOW *COULD* SHE? SHE AIN'T LIKE US.
ENOS, SHE'S OUR *MAMA.*
SHE *AIN'T.* SHE RAISED US AS HER OWN, I KNOW, BUT...
TEMPEST, I DON' THINK I CAN DO THIS NO MORE.
DO WHAT YOU CAN'T HELP?
NO, I MEAN COME BACK. CHASIN' *BLOOD*... IT'S A POWERFUL *LURE.*
MIGHT BE A TIME, I WON'T WALK BACK OUTTA THEM WOODS ON TWO LEGS EVER AGAIN.

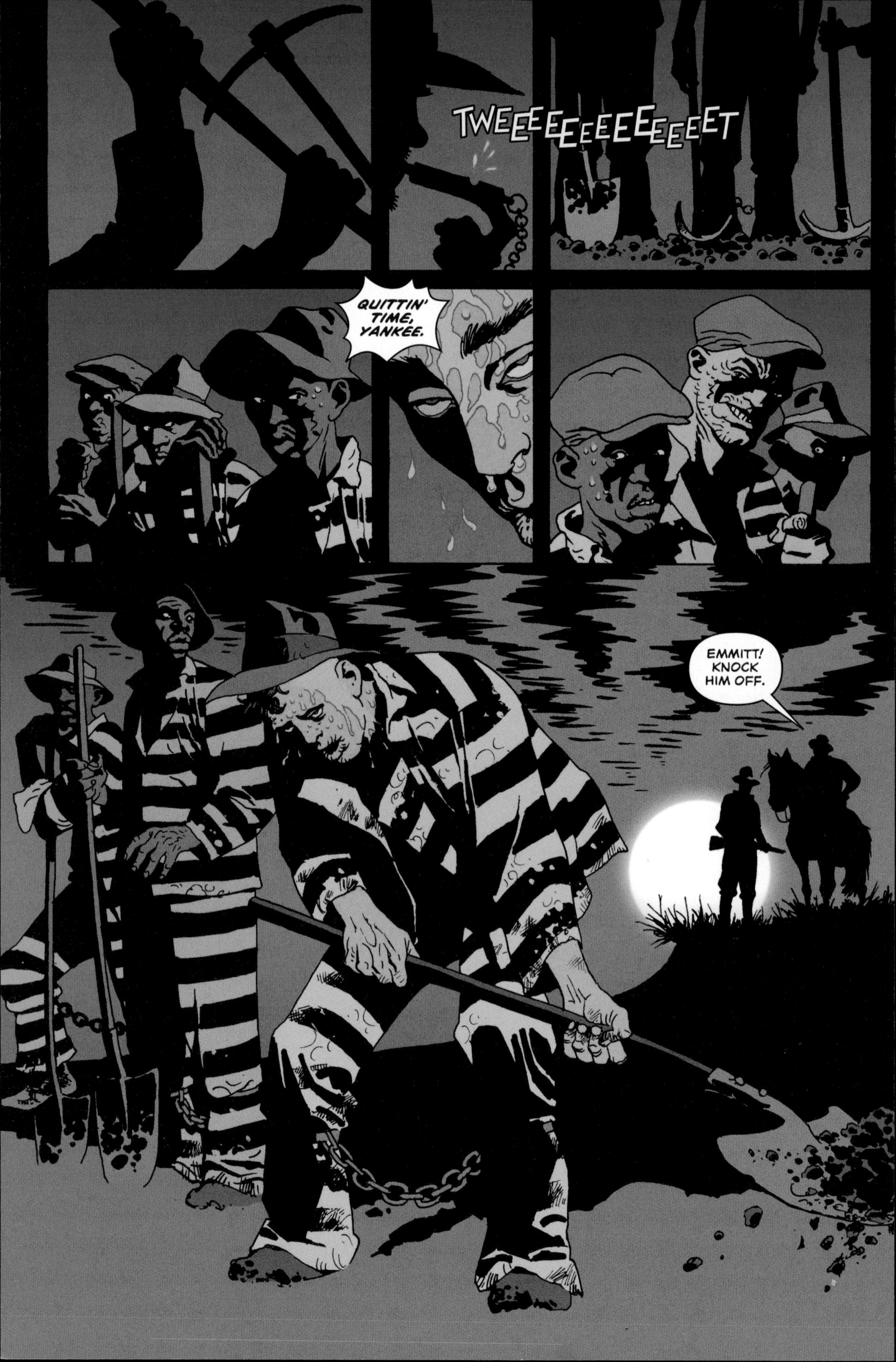
TWEEEEEEEEEEEEET
QUITTIN' TIME, YANKEE.
EMMITT! KNOCK HIM OFF.

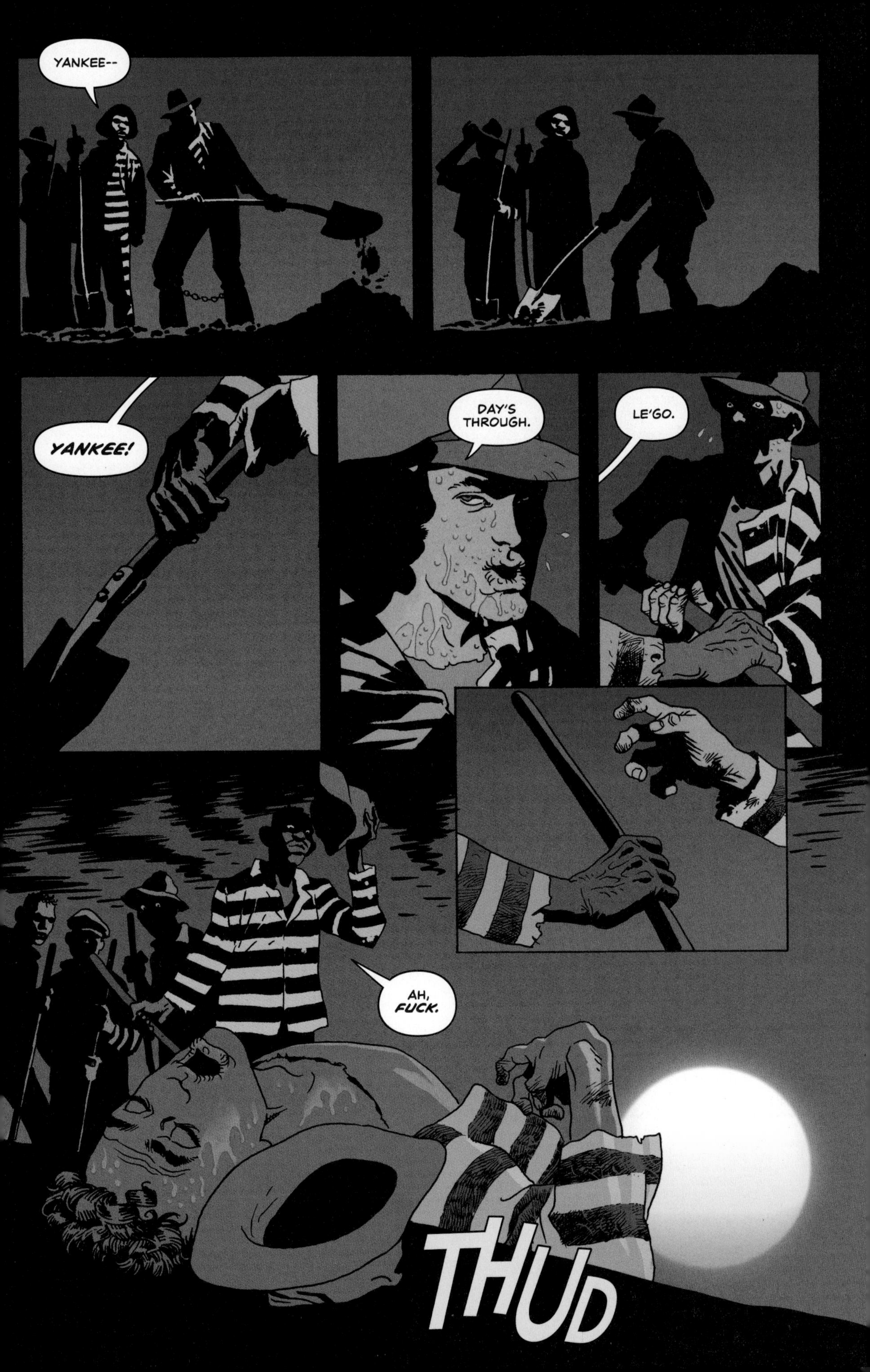
YANKEE--
YANKEE!
DAY'S THROUGH.
LE'GO.
AH, FUCK.
THUD

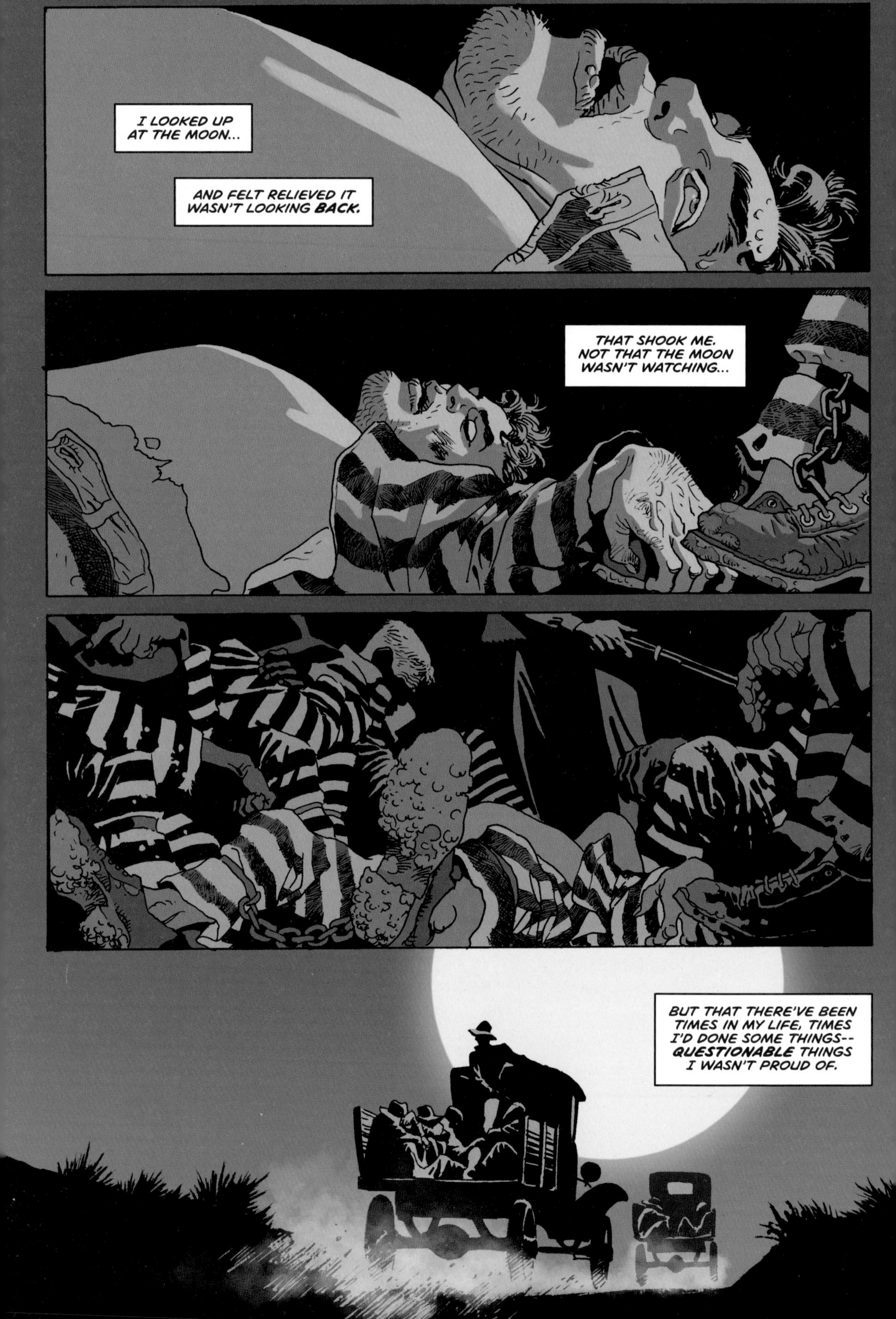
I LOOKED UP AT THE MOON...
AND FELT RELIEVED IT WASN'T LOOKING BACK.
THAT SHOOK ME. NOT THAT THE MOON WASN'T WATCHING...
BUT THAT THERE'VE BEEN TIMES IN MY LIFE, TIMES I'D DONE SOME THINGS-- QUESTIONABLE THINGS I WASN'T PROUD OF.

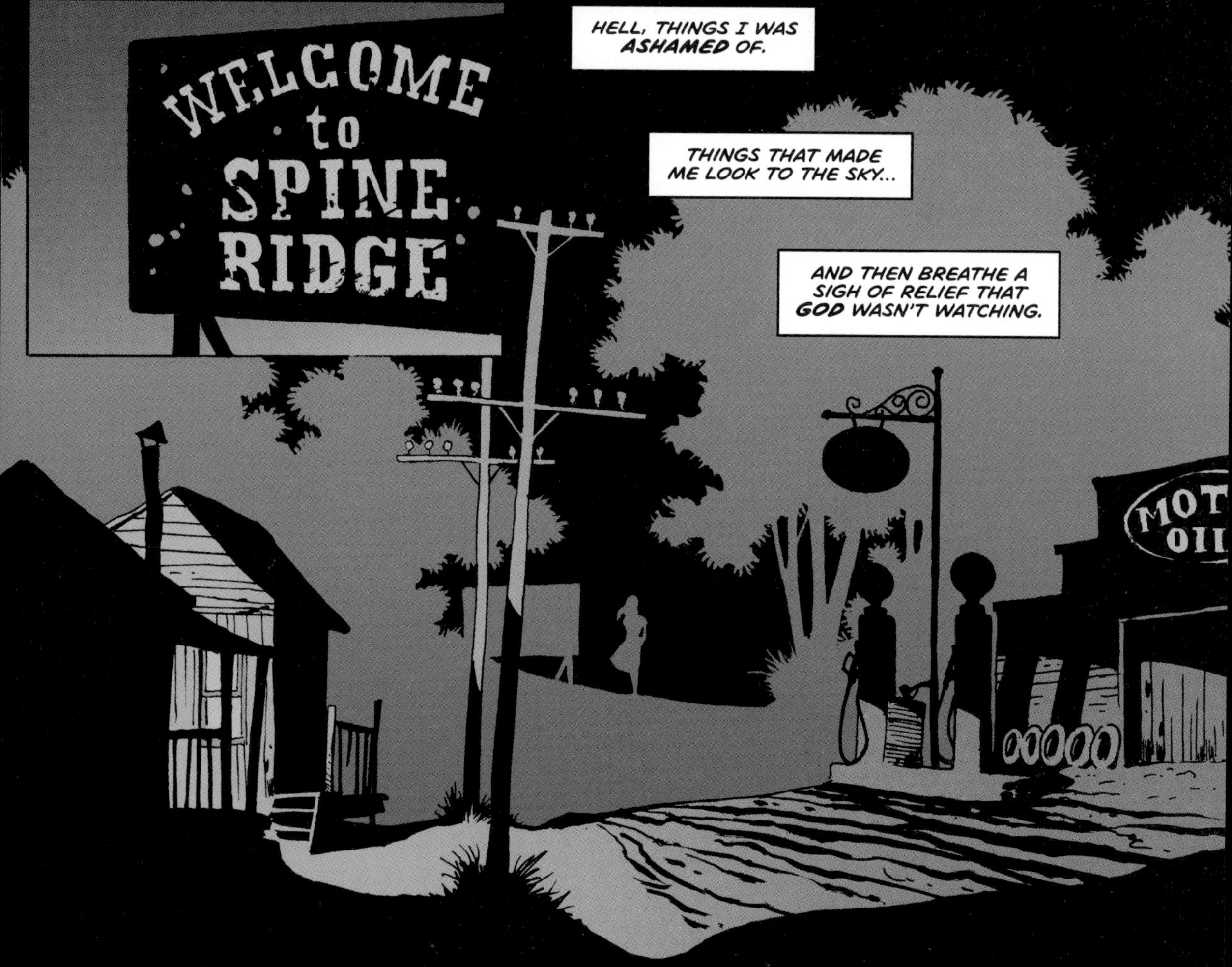
HELL, THINGS I WAS ASHAMED OF.
WELCOME to SPINE RIDGE
THINGS THAT MADE ME LOOK TO THE SKY...
AND THEN BREATHE A SIGH OF RELIEF THAT GOD WASN'T WATCHING.
MOTO OIL

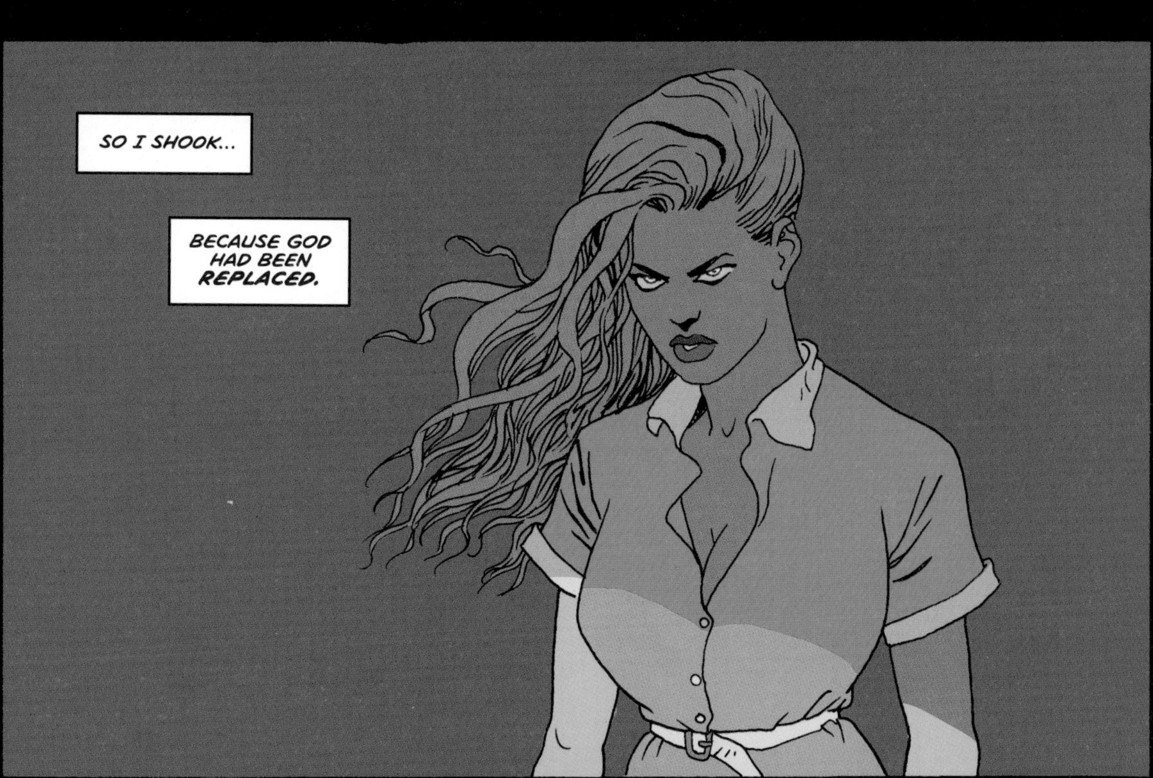
SO I SHOOK...
BECAUSE GOD HAD BEEN REPLACED.

Chapter NINE

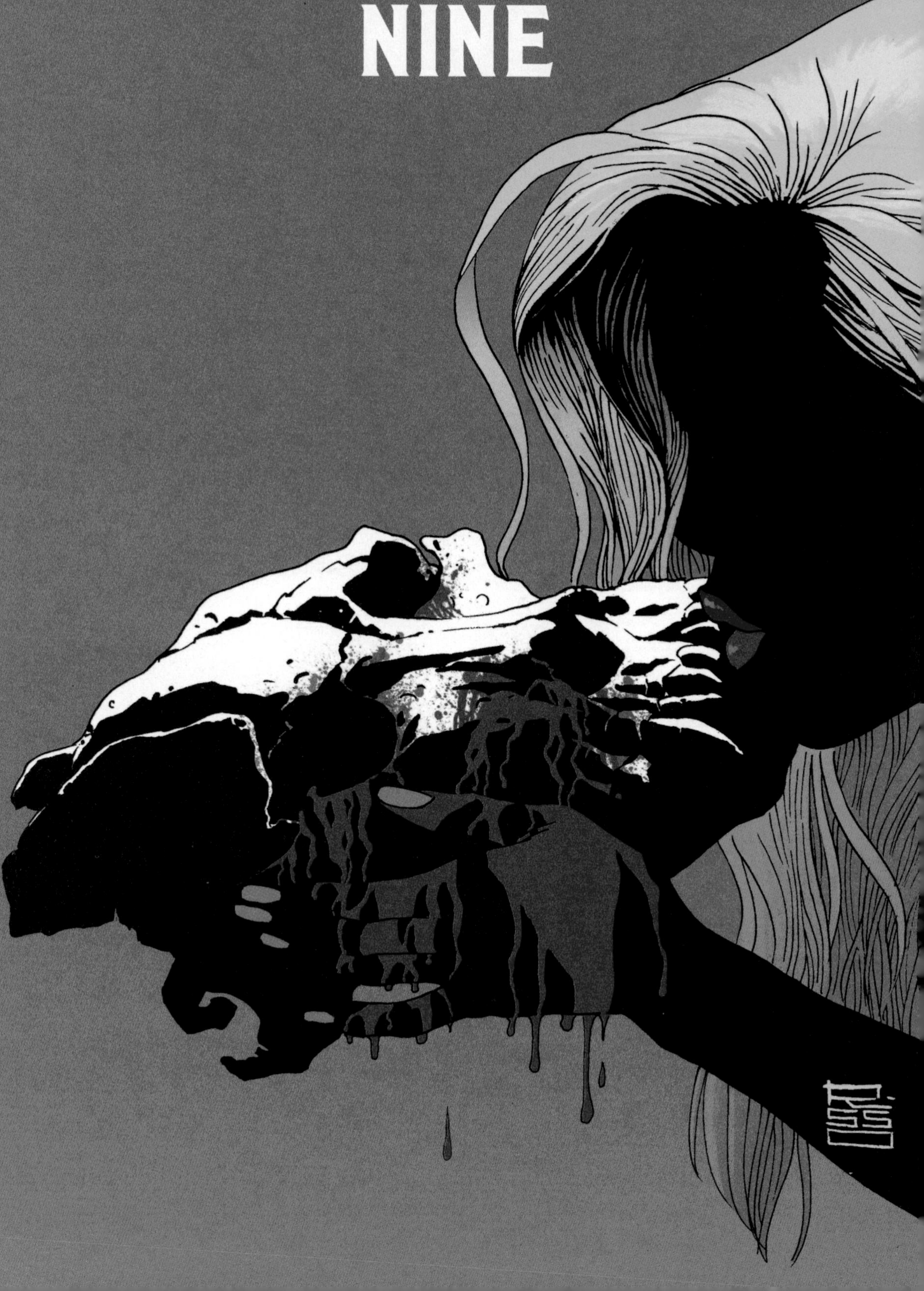

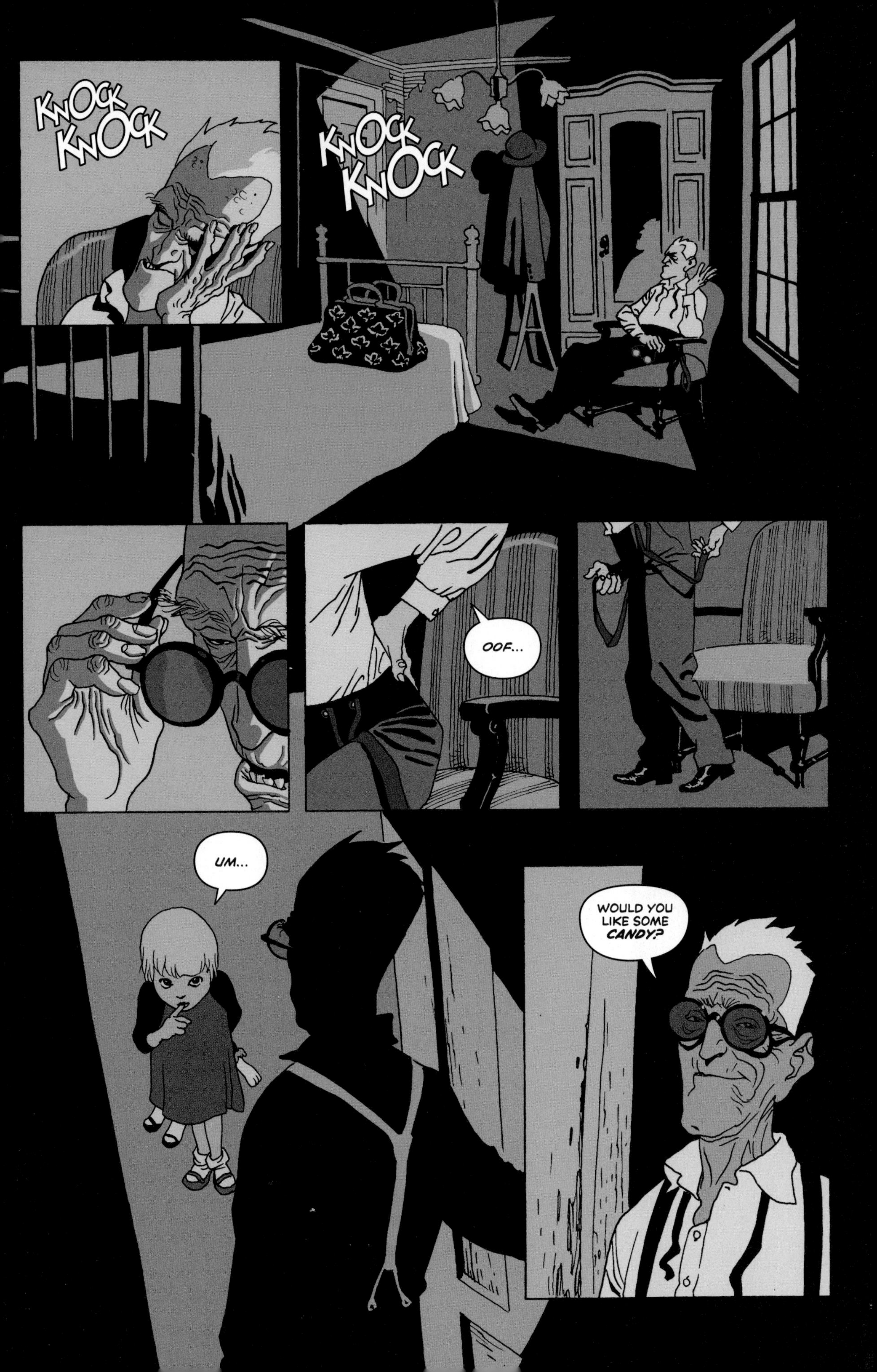
KNOCK KNOCK
KNOCK KNOCK
OOF...
UM...
WOULD YOU LIKE SOME CANDY?

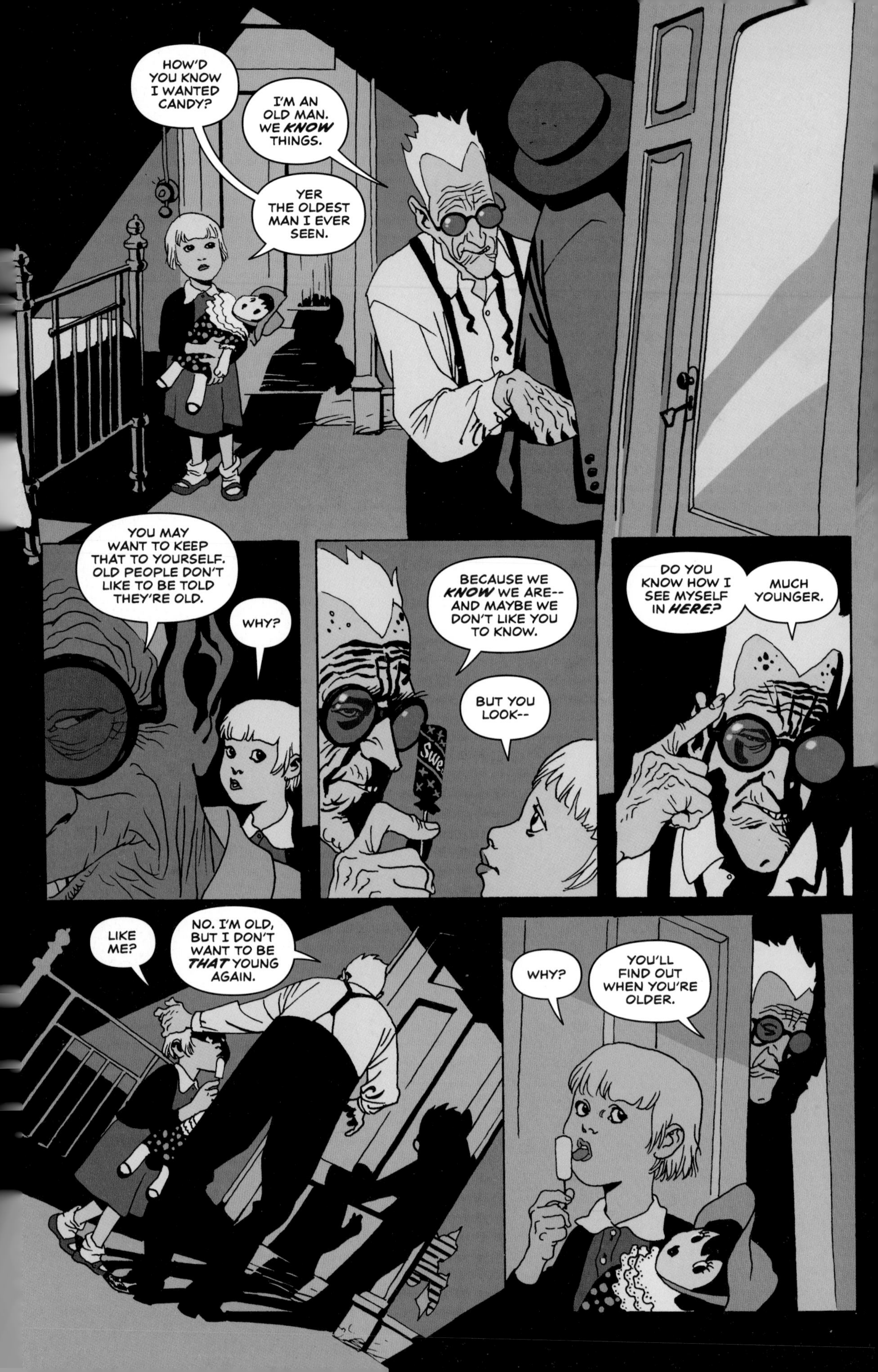
HOW'D YOU KNOW I WANTED CANDY?
I'M AN OLD MAN. WE KNOW THINGS.
YER THE OLDEST MAN I EVER SEEN.
YOU MAY WANT TO KEEP THAT TO YOURSELF. OLD PEOPLE DON'T LIKE TO BE TOLD THEY'RE OLD.
WHY?
BECAUSE WE KNOW WE ARE-- AND MAYBE WE DON'T LIKE YOU TO KNOW.
BUT YOU LOOK--
DO YOU KNOW HOW I SEE MYSELF IN HERE?
MUCH YOUNGER.
LIKE ME?
NO. I'M OLD, BUT I DON'T WANT TO BE THAT YOUNG AGAIN.
WHY?
YOU'LL FIND OUT WHEN YOU'RE OLDER.

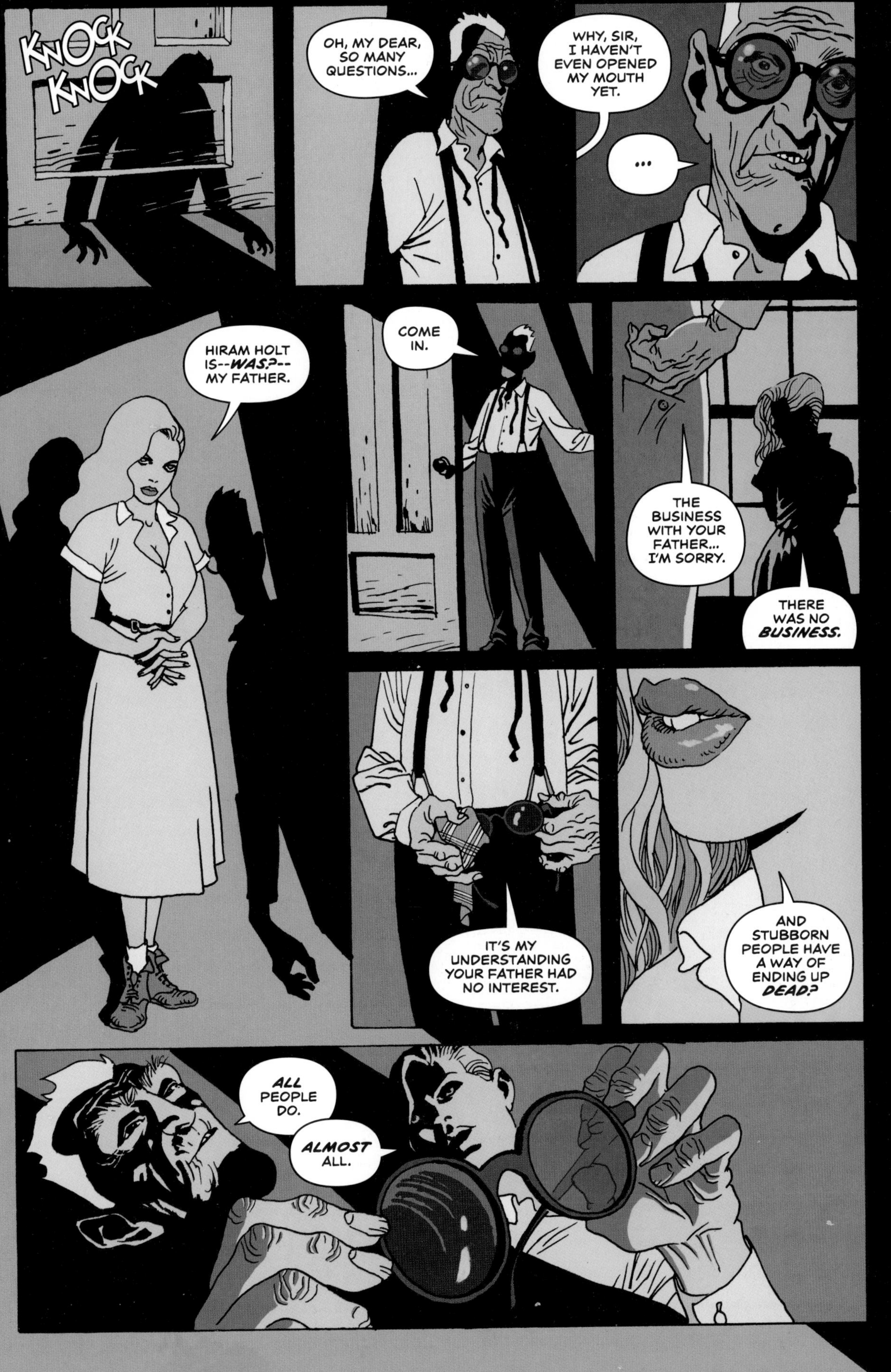
KNOCK KNOCK
OH, MY DEAR, SO MANY QUESTIONS...
WHY, SIR, I HAVEN'T EVEN OPENED MY MOUTH YET.
...
HIRAM HOLT IS--*WAS?*-- MY FATHER.
COME IN.
THE BUSINESS WITH YOUR FATHER... I'M SORRY.
THERE WAS NO *BUSINESS.*
IT'S MY UNDERSTANDING YOUR FATHER HAD NO INTEREST.
AND STUBBORN PEOPLE HAVE A WAY OF ENDING UP *DEAD?*
ALL PEOPLE DO.
ALMOST ALL.

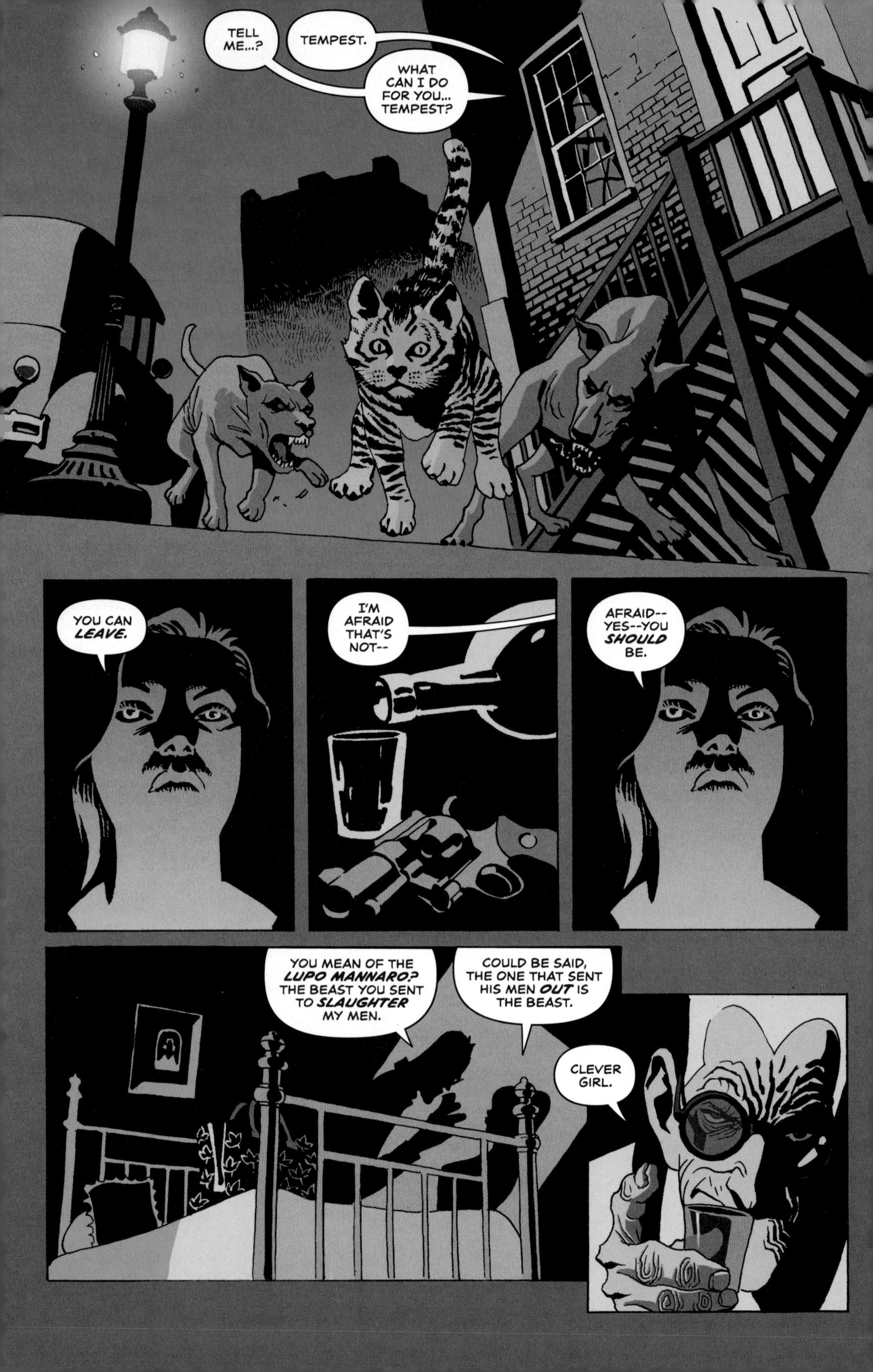
TELL ME...?
TEMPEST.
WHAT CAN I DO FOR YOU... TEMPEST?
YOU CAN *LEAVE.*
I'M AFRAID THAT'S NOT--
AFRAID--YES--YOU *SHOULD* BE.
YOU MEAN OF THE *LUPO MANNARO?* THE BEAST YOU SENT TO *SLAUGHTER* MY MEN.
COULD BE SAID, THE ONE THAT SENT HIS MEN *OUT* IS THE BEAST.
CLEVER GIRL.

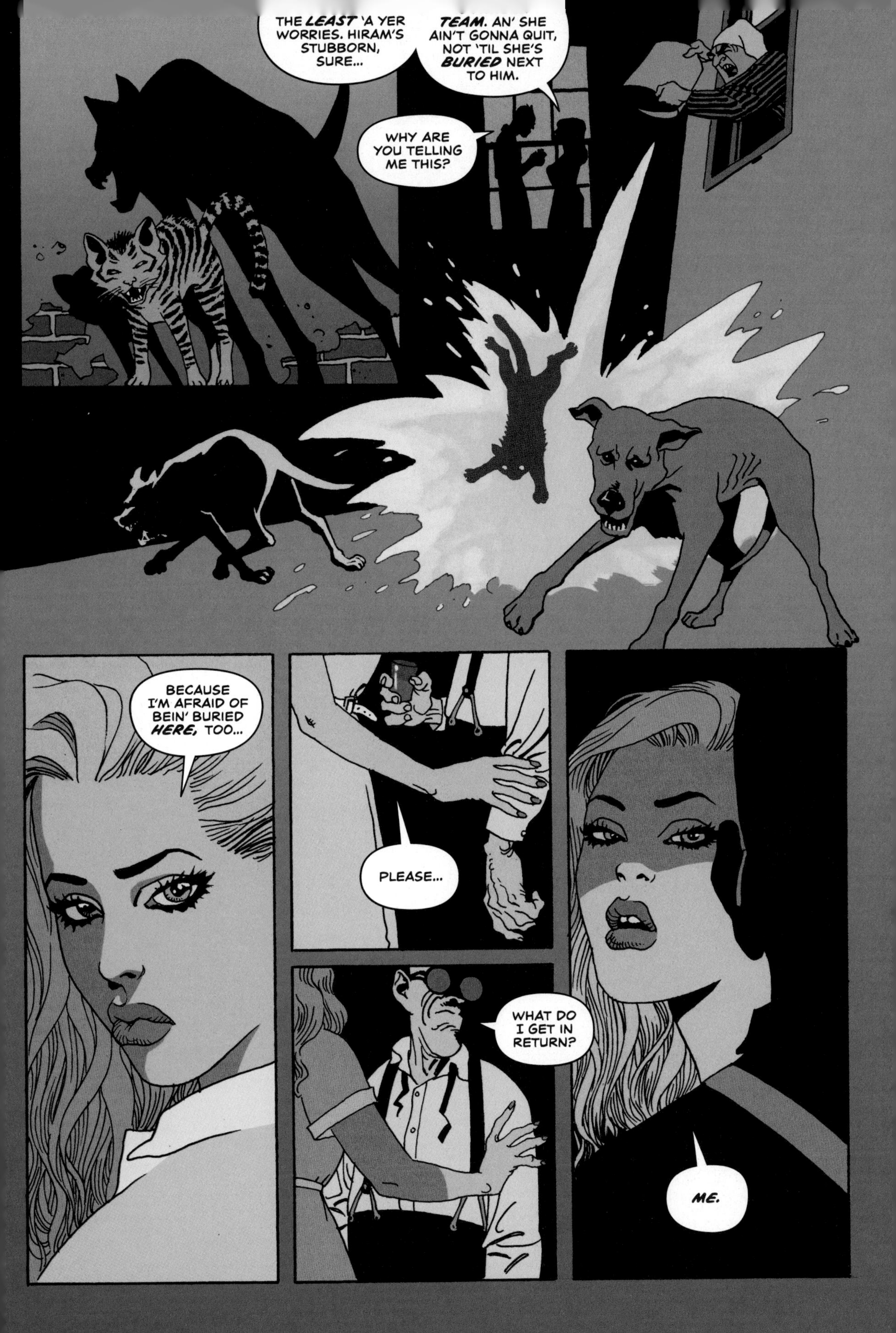
THE LEAST 'A YER WORRIES. HIRAM'S STUBBORN, SURE...
TEAM. AN' SHE AIN'T GONNA QUIT, NOT 'TIL SHE'S BURIED NEXT TO HIM.
WHY ARE YOU TELLING ME THIS?
BECAUSE I'M AFRAID OF BEIN' BURIED HERE, TOO...
PLEASE...
WHAT DO I GET IN RETURN?
ME.

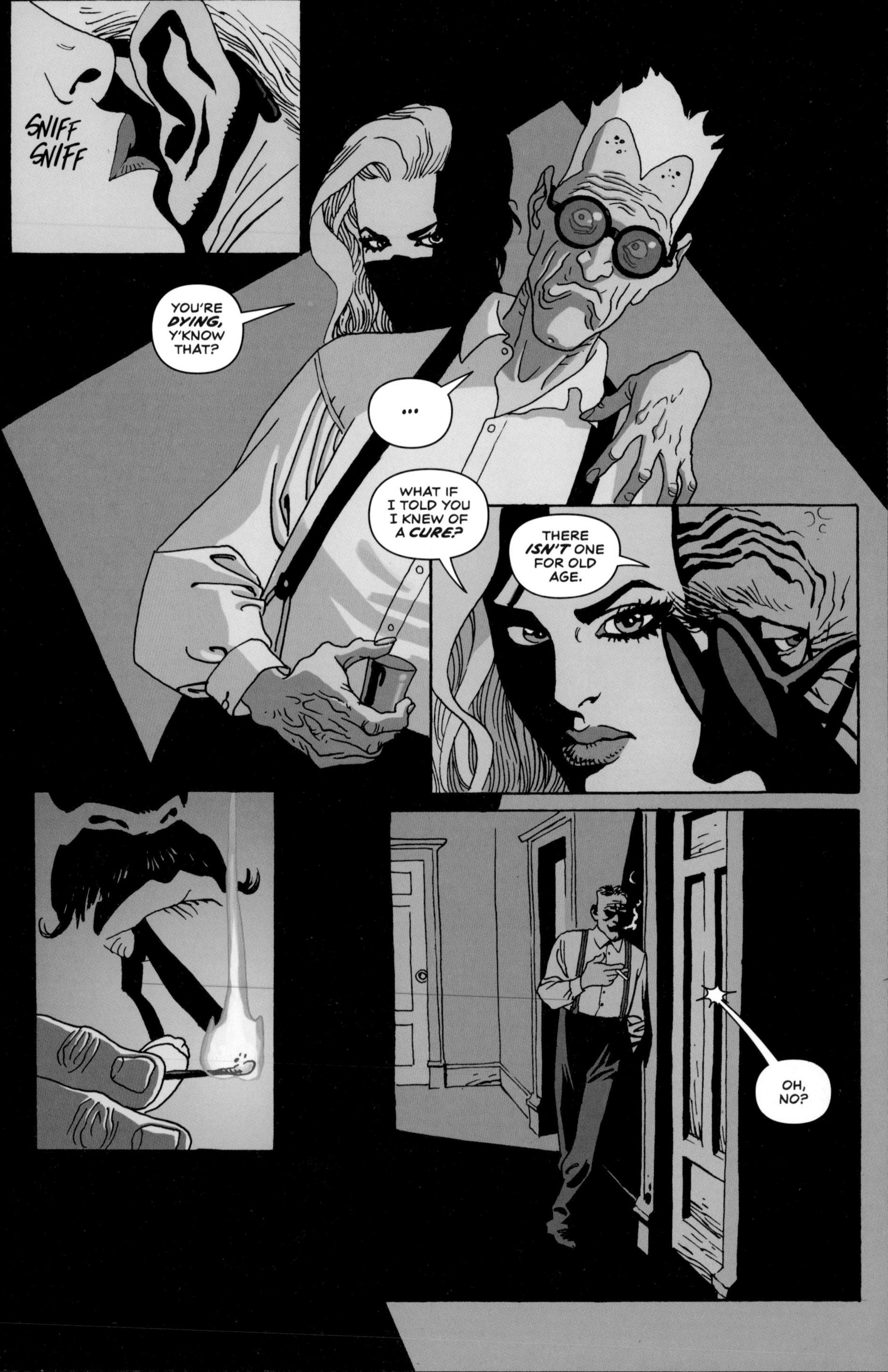
SNIFF SNIFF
YOU'RE *DYING,* Y'KNOW THAT?
...
WHAT IF I TOLD YOU I KNEW OF A *CURE?*
THERE *ISN'T* ONE FOR OLD AGE.
OH, NO?

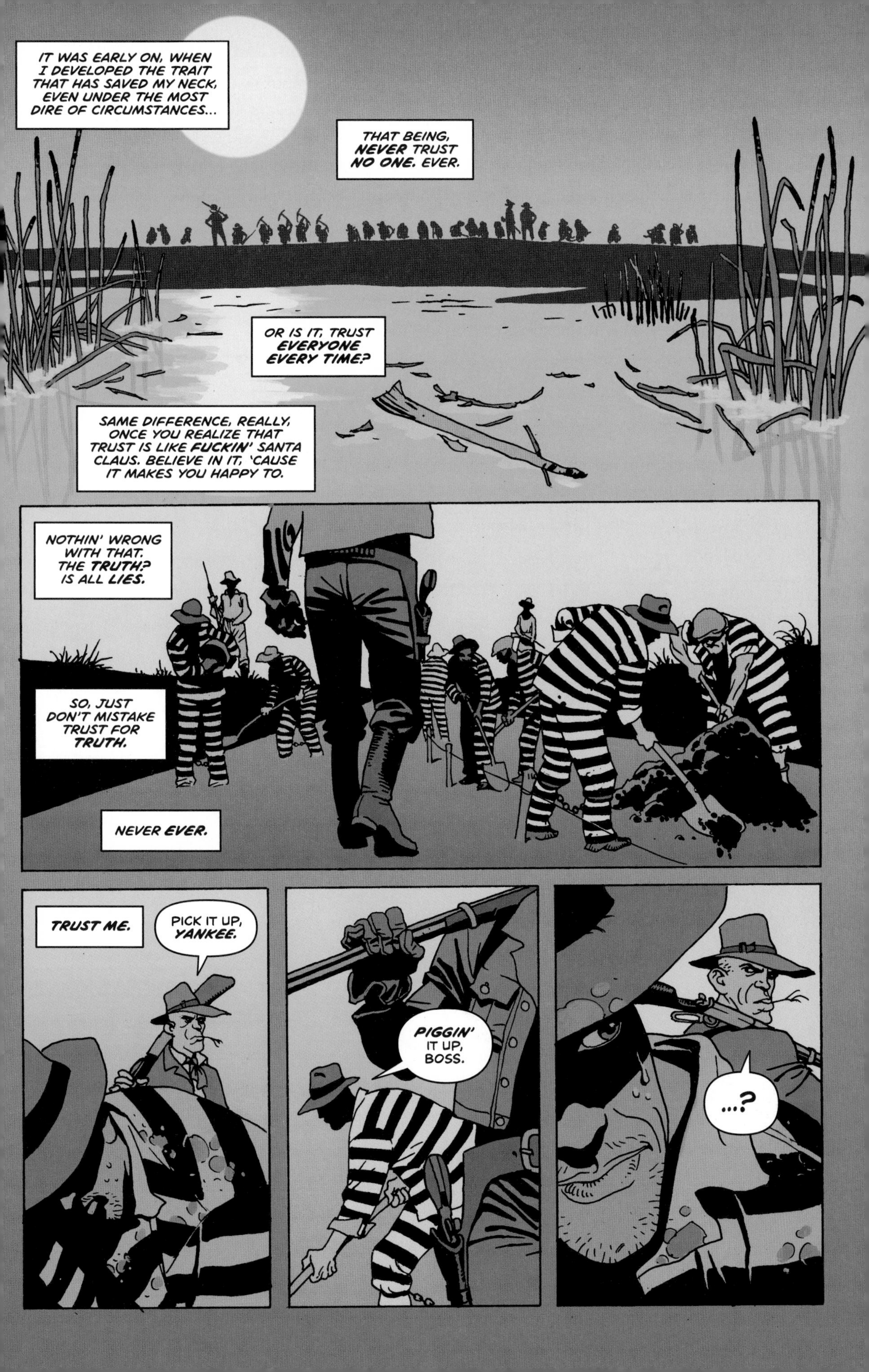
IT WAS EARLY ON, WHEN I DEVELOPED THE TRAIT THAT HAS SAVED MY NECK, EVEN UNDER THE MOST DIRE OF CIRCUMSTANCES...
THAT BEING, NEVER TRUST NO ONE. EVER.
OR IS IT, TRUST EVERYONE EVERY TIME?
SAME DIFFERENCE, REALLY, ONCE YOU REALIZE THAT TRUST IS LIKE FUCKIN' SANTA CLAUS. BELIEVE IN IT, 'CAUSE IT MAKES YOU HAPPY TO.
NOTHIN' WRONG WITH THAT. THE TRUTH? IS ALL LIES.
SO, JUST DON'T MISTAKE TRUST FOR TRUTH.
NEVER EVER.
TRUST ME.
PICK IT UP, YANKEE.
PIGGIN' IT UP, BOSS.
...?

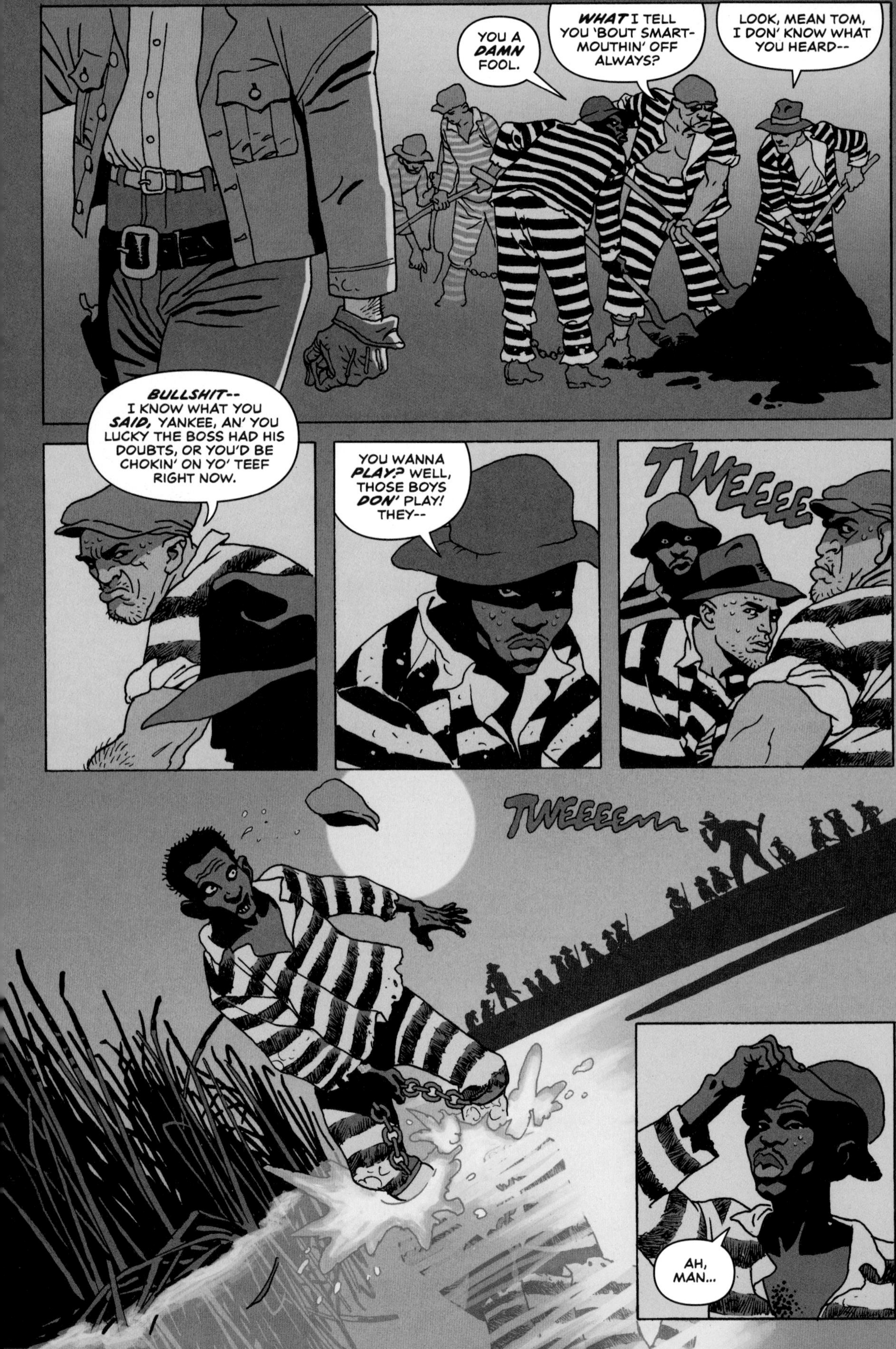

YOU A *DAMN* FOOL.
WHAT I TELL YOU 'BOUT SMART-MOUTHIN' OFF ALWAYS?
LOOK, MEAN TOM, I DON' KNOW WHAT YOU HEARD--
BULLSHIT-- I KNOW WHAT YOU *SAID,* YANKEE, AN' YOU LUCKY THE BOSS HAD HIS DOUBTS, OR YOU'D BE CHOKIN' ON YO' TEEF RIGHT NOW.
YOU WANNA *PLAY?* WELL, THOSE BOYS *DON'* PLAY! THEY--
TWEEEEE
TWEEEEm
AH, MAN...

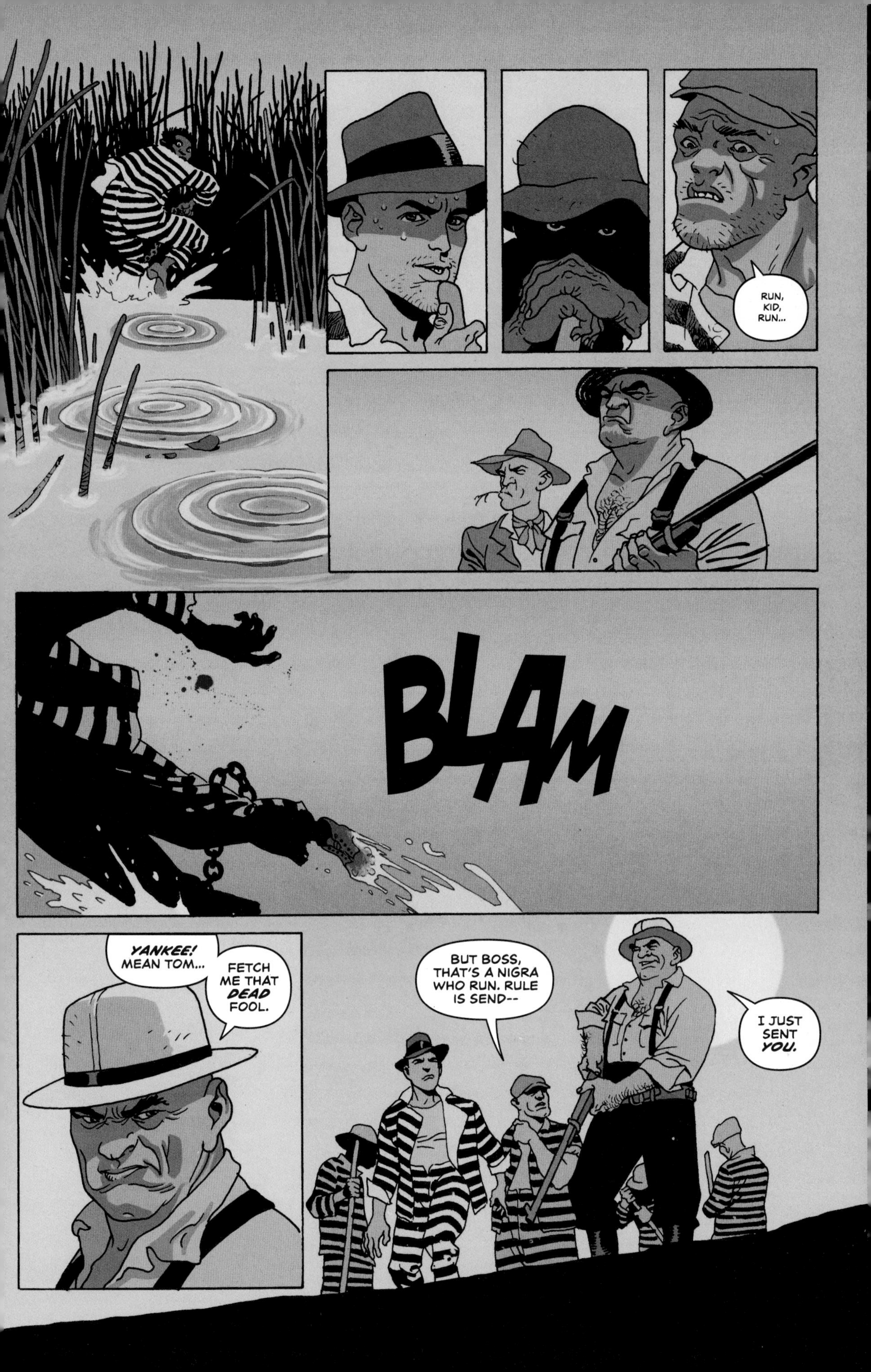
RUN, KID, RUN...
BLAM
YANKEE! MEAN TOM...
FETCH ME THAT *DEAD* FOOL.
BUT BOSS, THAT'S A NIGRA WHO RUN. RULE IS SEND--
I JUST SENT *YOU.*

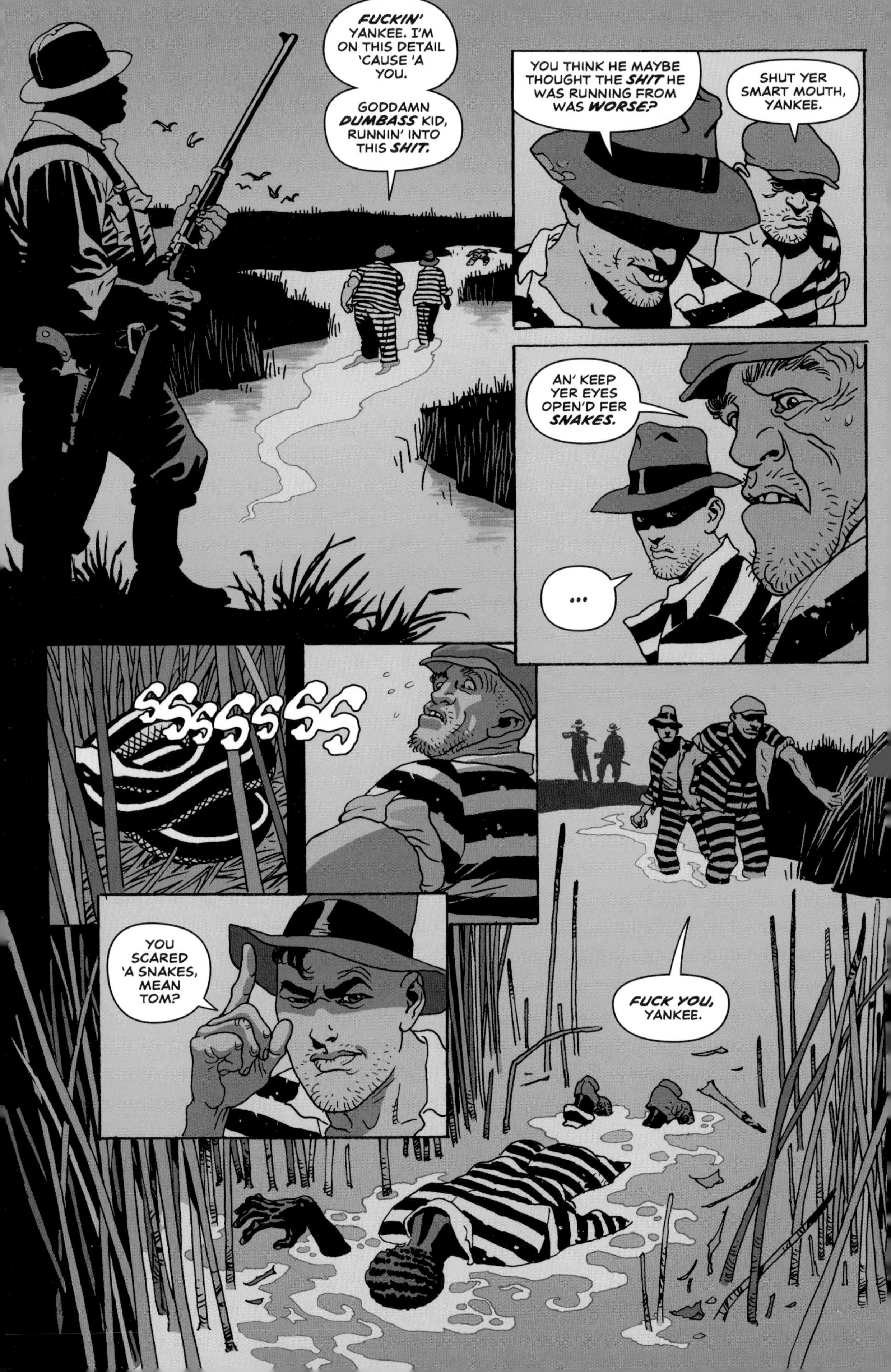
FUCKIN' YANKEE. I'M ON THIS DETAIL 'CAUSE 'A YOU.
GODDAMN DUMBASS KID, RUNNIN' INTO THIS SHIT.
YOU THINK HE MAYBE THOUGHT THE SHIT HE WAS RUNNING FROM WAS WORSE?
SHUT YER SMART MOUTH, YANKEE.
AN' KEEP YER EYES OPEN'D FER SNAKES.
...
SSSSSSS
YOU SCARED 'A SNAKES, MEAN TOM?
FUCK YOU, YANKEE.

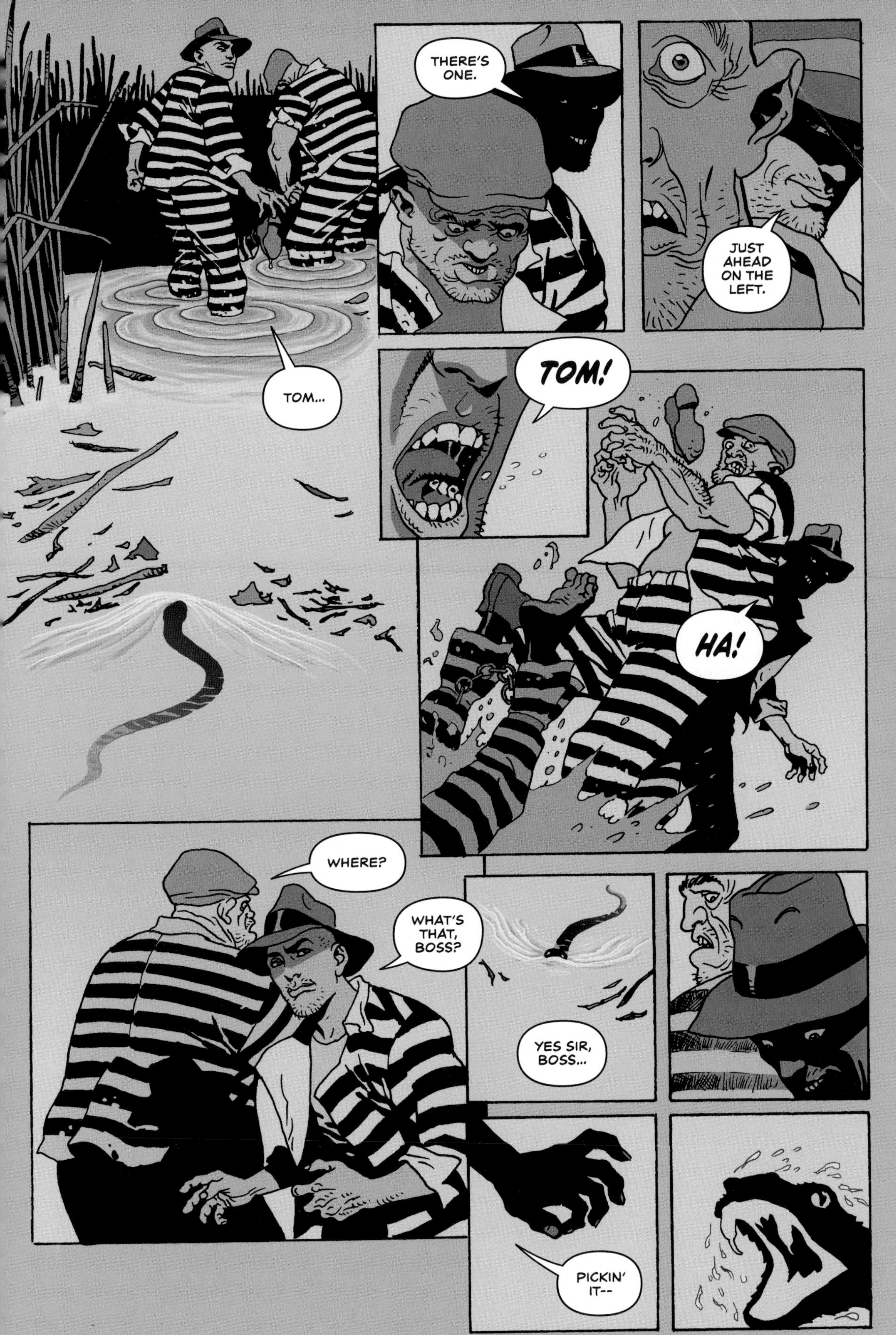
THERE'S ONE.
JUST AHEAD ON THE LEFT.
TOM...
TOM!
HA!
WHERE?
WHAT'S THAT, BOSS?
YES SIR, BOSS...
PICKIN' IT--

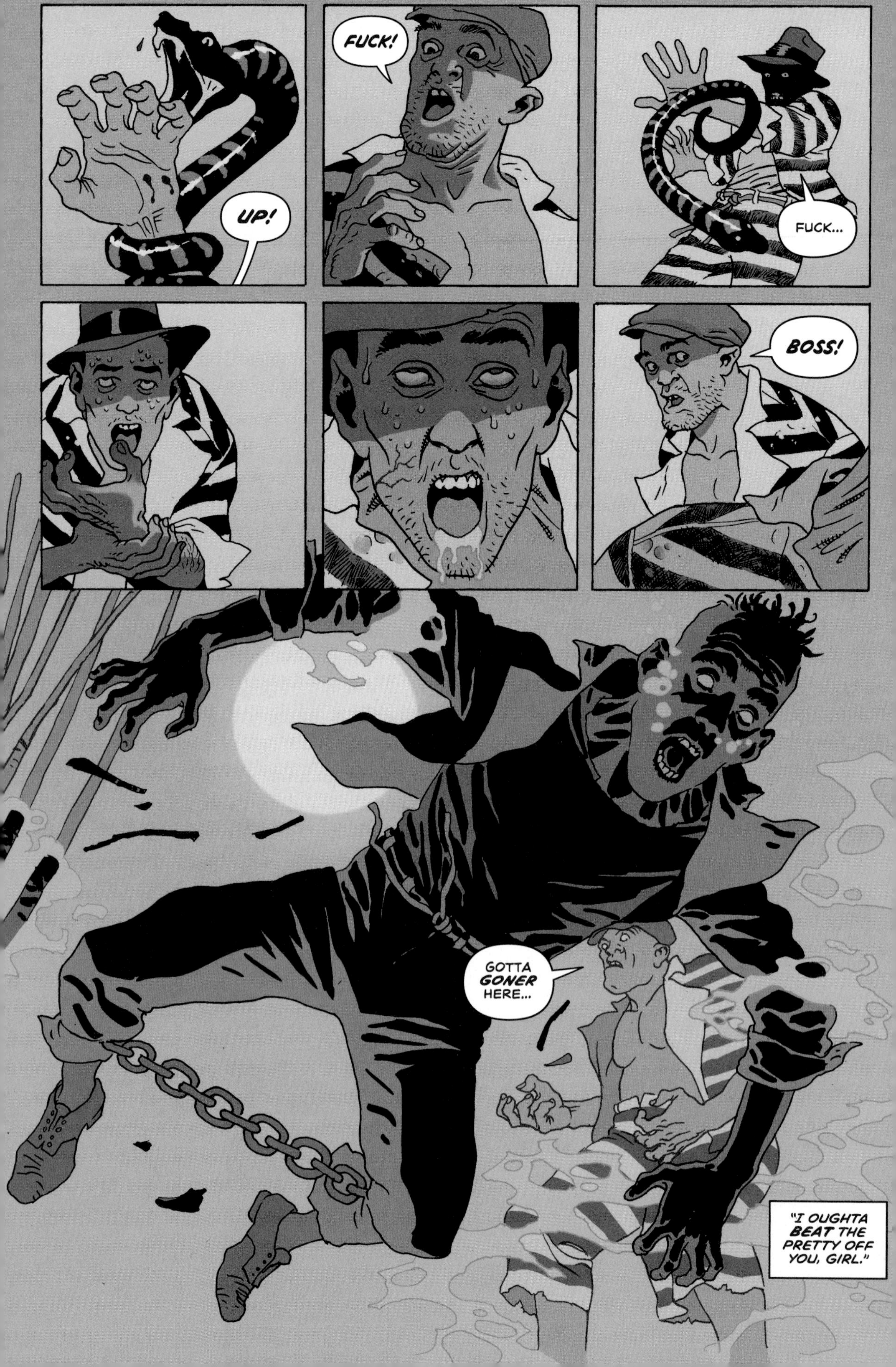
UP!
FUCK!
FUCK...
BOSS!
GOTTA GONER HERE...
"I OUGHTA BEAT THE PRETTY OFF YOU, GIRL."

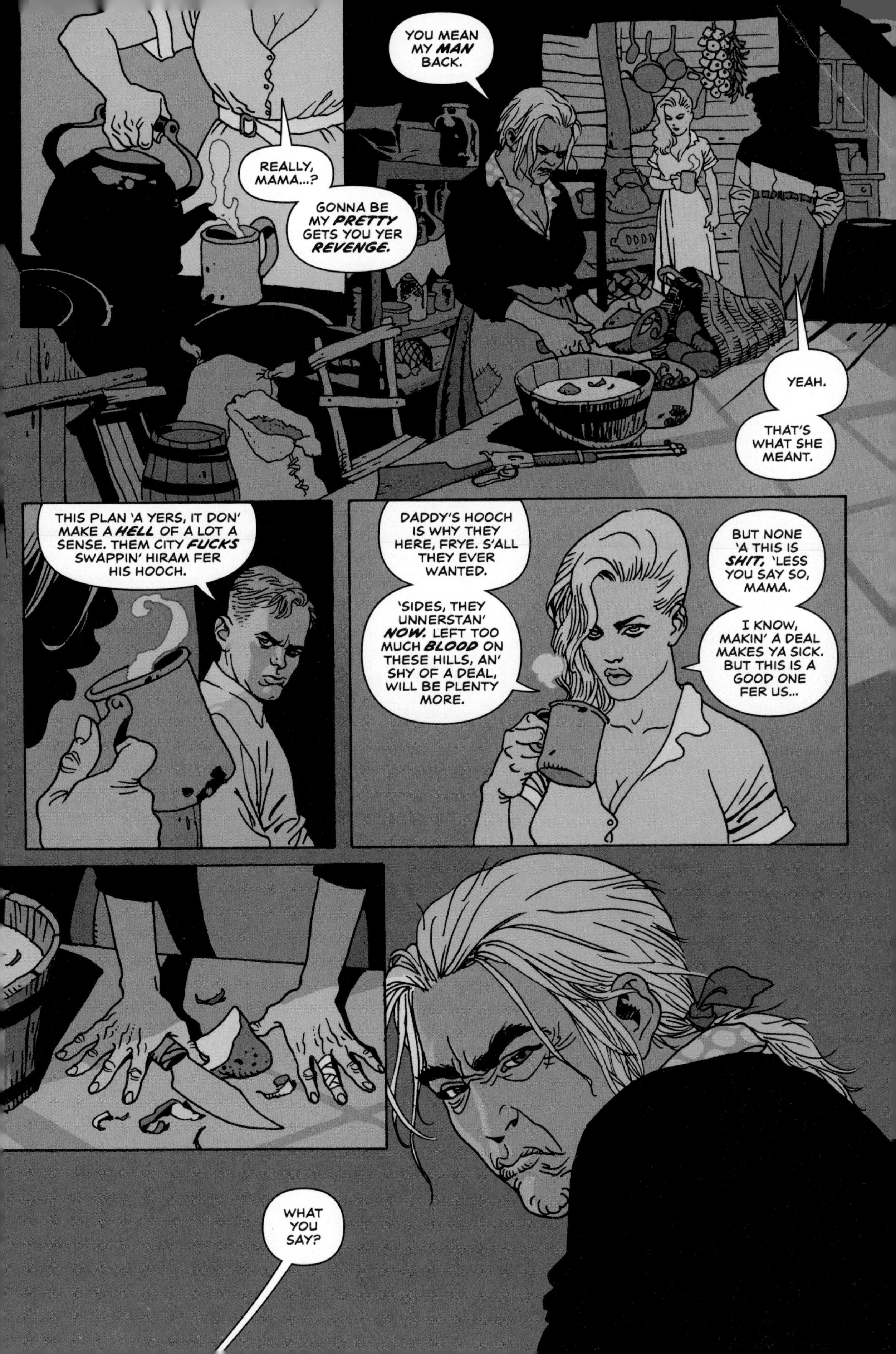
YOU MEAN MY MAN BACK.
REALLY, MAMA...?
GONNA BE MY PRETTY GETS YOU YER REVENGE.
YEAH.
THAT'S WHAT SHE MEANT.
THIS PLAN 'A YERS, IT DON' MAKE A HELL OF A LOT A SENSE. THEM CITY FUCKS SWAPPIN' HIRAM FER HIS HOOCH.
DADDY'S HOOCH IS WHY THEY HERE, FRYE. S'ALL THEY EVER WANTED.
'SIDES, THEY UNNERSTAN' NOW. LEFT TOO MUCH BLOOD ON THESE HILLS, AN' SHY OF A DEAL, WILL BE PLENTY MORE.
BUT NONE 'A THIS IS SHIT, 'LESS YOU SAY SO, MAMA.
I KNOW, MAKIN' A DEAL MAKES YA SICK. BUT THIS IS A GOOD ONE FER US...
WHAT YOU SAY?

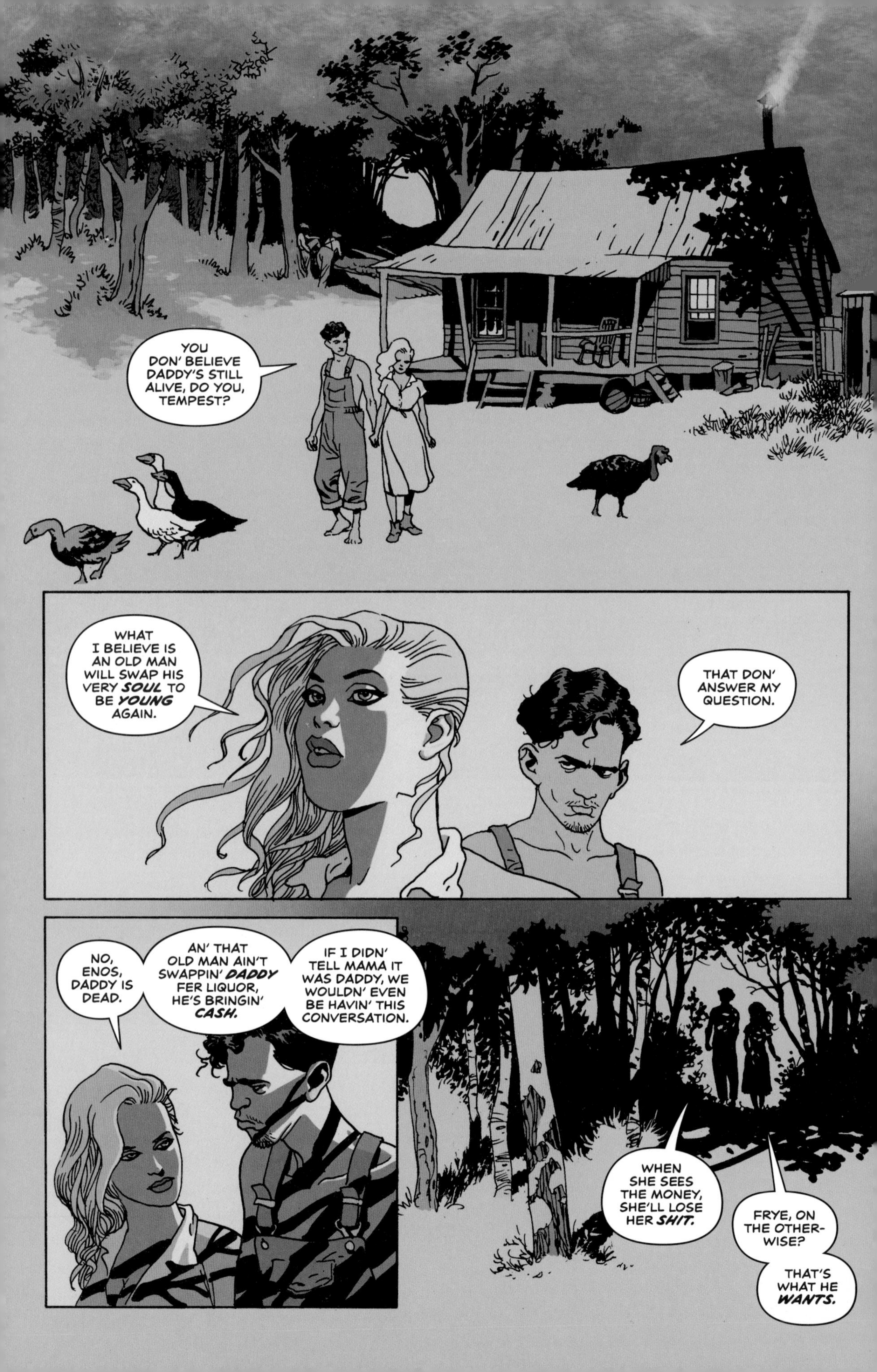
YOU DON' BELIEVE DADDY'S STILL ALIVE, DO YOU, TEMPEST?
WHAT I BELIEVE IS AN OLD MAN WILL SWAP HIS VERY *SOUL* TO BE *YOUNG* AGAIN.
THAT DON' ANSWER MY QUESTION.
NO, ENOS, DADDY IS DEAD.
AN' THAT OLD MAN AIN'T SWAPPIN' *DADDY* FER LIQUOR, HE'S BRINGIN' *CASH.*
IF I DIDN' TELL MAMA IT WAS DADDY, WE WOULDN' EVEN BE HAVIN' THIS CONVERSATION.
WHEN SHE SEES THE MONEY, SHE'LL LOSE HER *SHIT.*
FRYE, ON THE OTHER-WISE?
THAT'S WHAT HE *WANTS.*

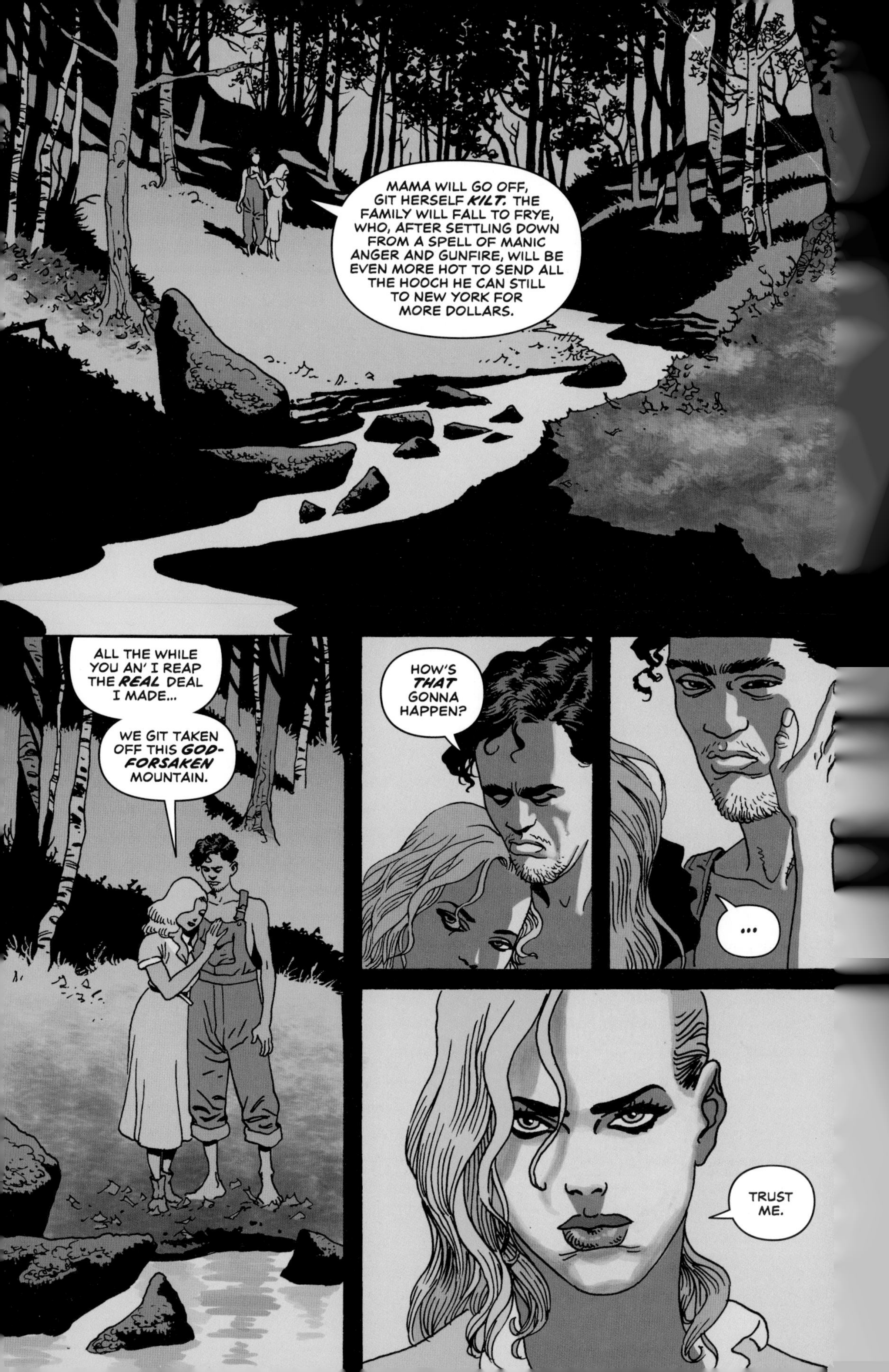
MAMA WILL GO OFF, GIT HERSELF KILT. THE FAMILY WILL FALL TO FRYE, WHO, AFTER SETTLING DOWN FROM A SPELL OF MANIC ANGER AND GUNFIRE, WILL BE EVEN MORE HOT TO SEND ALL THE HOOCH HE CAN STILL TO NEW YORK FOR MORE DOLLARS.
ALL THE WHILE YOU AN' I REAP THE REAL DEAL I MADE...
WE GIT TAKEN OFF THIS GOD-FORSAKEN MOUNTAIN.
HOW'S THAT GONNA HAPPEN?
...
TRUST ME.

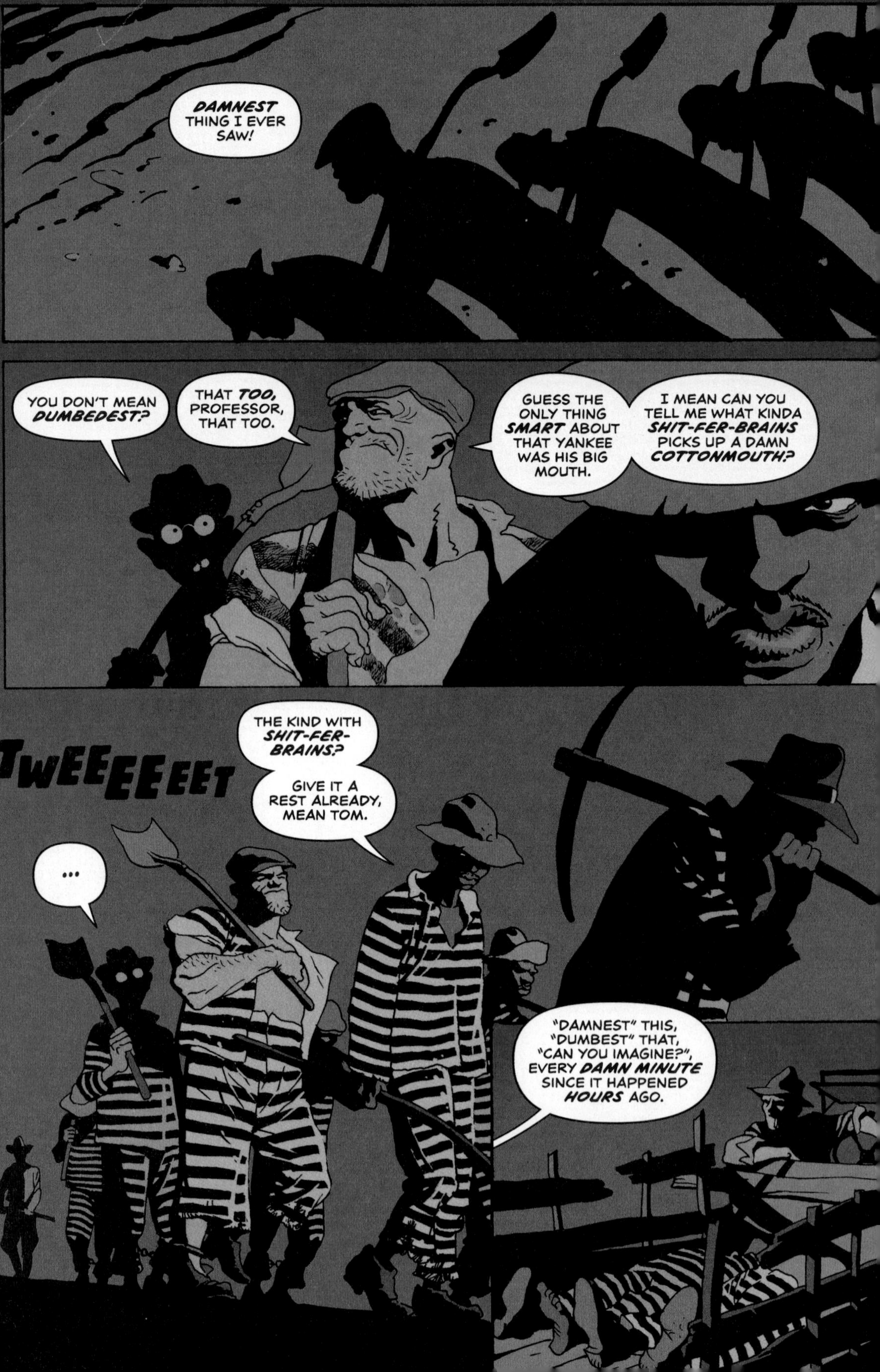
DAMNEST THING I EVER SAW!
YOU DON'T MEAN DUMBEDEST?
THAT TOO, PROFESSOR, THAT TOO.
GUESS THE ONLY THING SMART ABOUT THAT YANKEE WAS HIS BIG MOUTH.
I MEAN CAN YOU TELL ME WHAT KINDA SHIT-FER-BRAINS PICKS UP A DAMN COTTONMOUTH?
TWEEEEEET
THE KIND WITH SHIT-FER-BRAINS?
GIVE IT A REST ALREADY, MEAN TOM.
...
"DAMNEST" THIS, "DUMBEST" THAT, "CAN YOU IMAGINE?", EVERY DAMN MINUTE SINCE IT HAPPENED HOURS AGO.

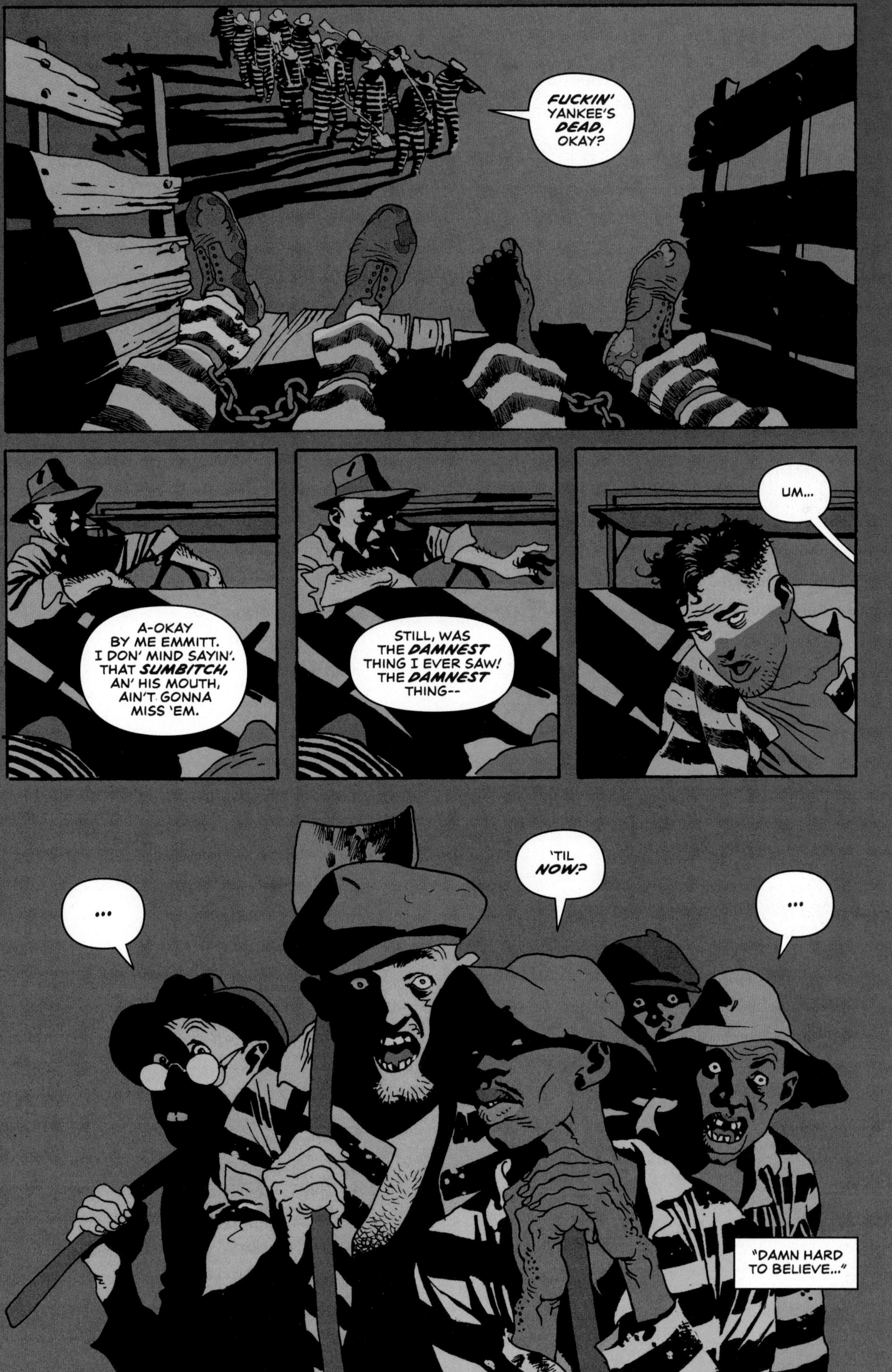
FUCKIN' YANKEE'S DEAD, OKAY?
A-OKAY BY ME EMMITT. I DON' MIND SAYIN'. THAT SUMBITCH, AN' HIS MOUTH, AIN'T GONNA MISS 'EM.
STILL, WAS THE DAMNEST THING I EVER SAW! THE DAMNEST THING--
UM...
...
'TIL NOW?
...
"DAMN HARD TO BELIEVE..."

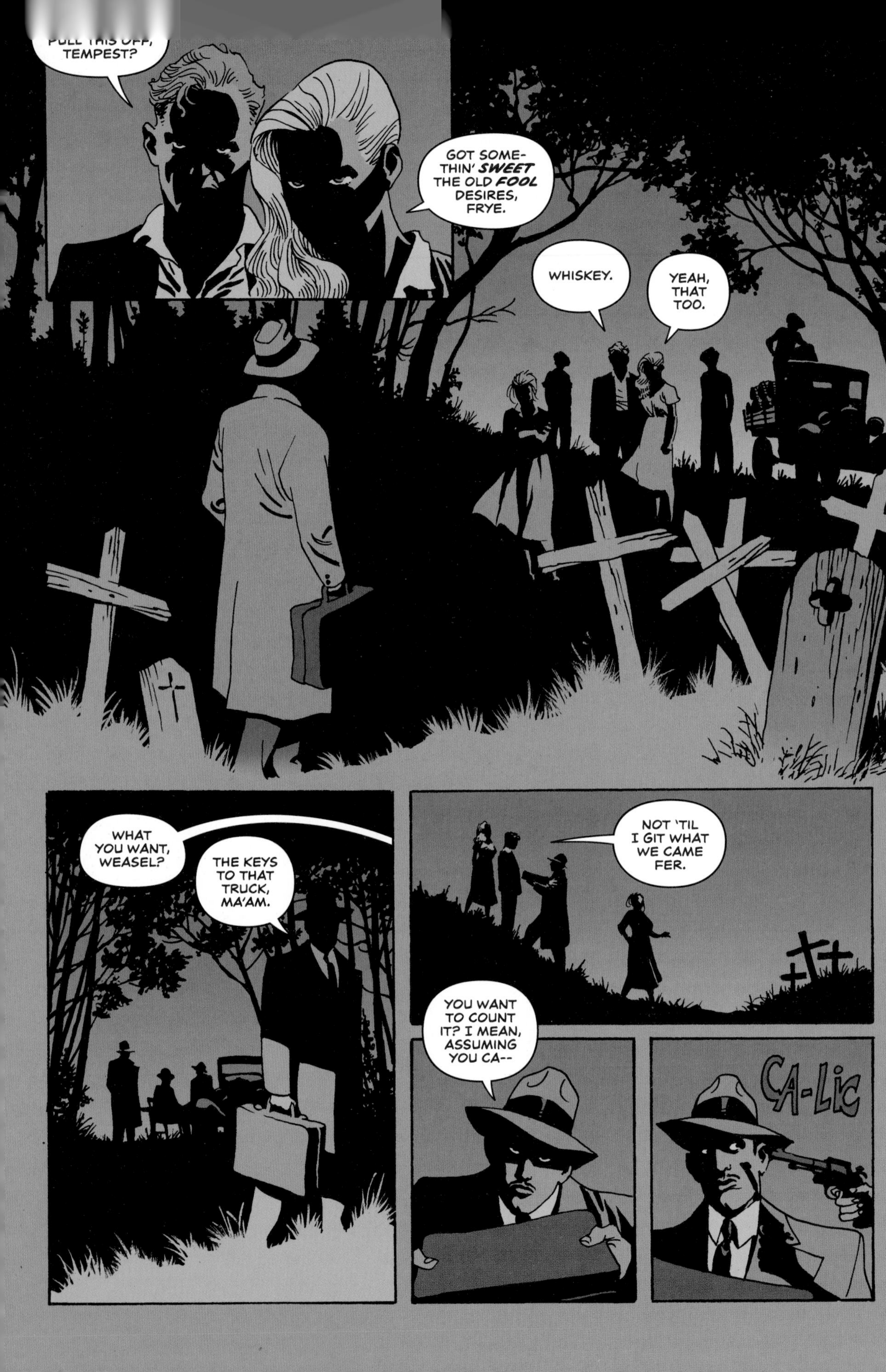
PULL THIS OFF, TEMPEST?
GOT SOMETHIN' SWEET THE OLD FOOL DESIRES, FRYE.
WHISKEY.
YEAH, THAT TOO.
WHAT YOU WANT, WEASEL?
THE KEYS TO THAT TRUCK, MA'AM.
NOT 'TIL I GIT WHAT WE CAME FER.
YOU WANT TO COUNT IT? I MEAN, ASSUMING YOU CA--
CA-LIC

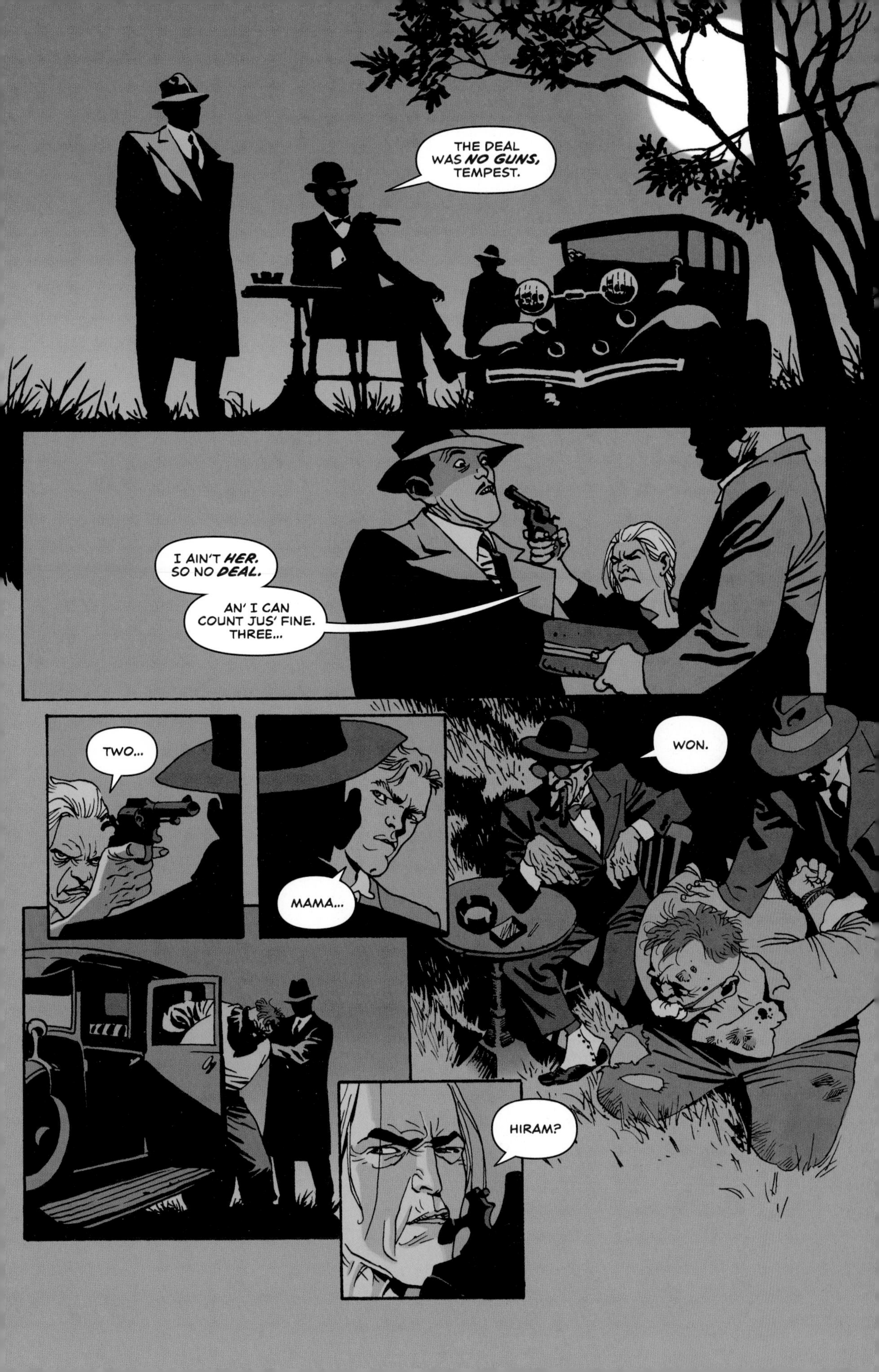
THE DEAL WAS NO GUNS, TEMPEST.
I AIN'T HER. SO NO DEAL.
AN' I CAN COUNT JUS' FINE. THREE...
TWO...
MAMA...
WON.
HIRAM?

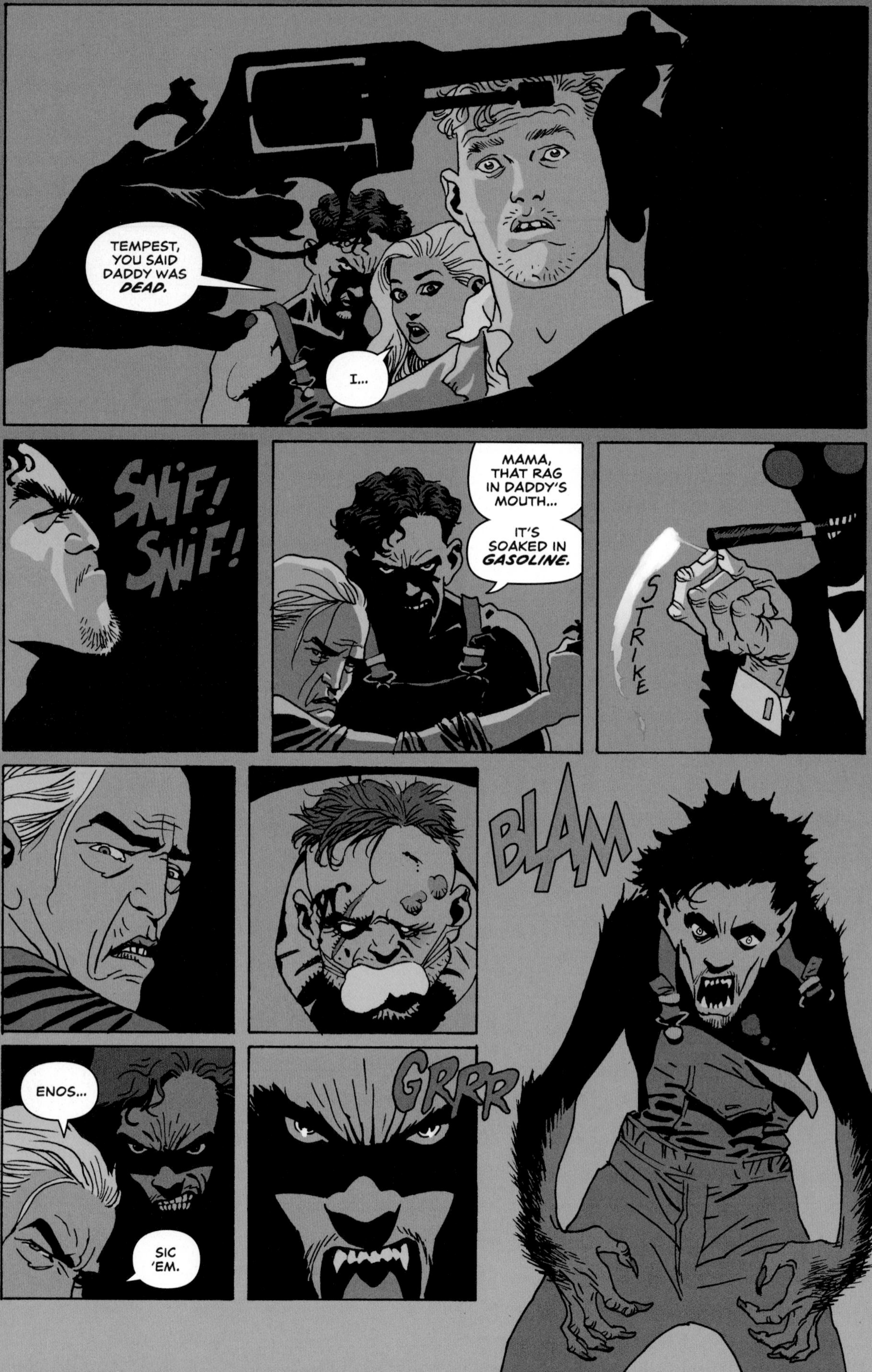
TEMPEST, YOU SAID DADDY WAS *DEAD.*
I...
SNIF! SNIF!
MAMA, THAT RAG IN DADDY'S MOUTH...
IT'S SOAKED IN *GASOLINE.*
STRIKE
BLAM
ENOS...
SIC 'EM.
GRRR

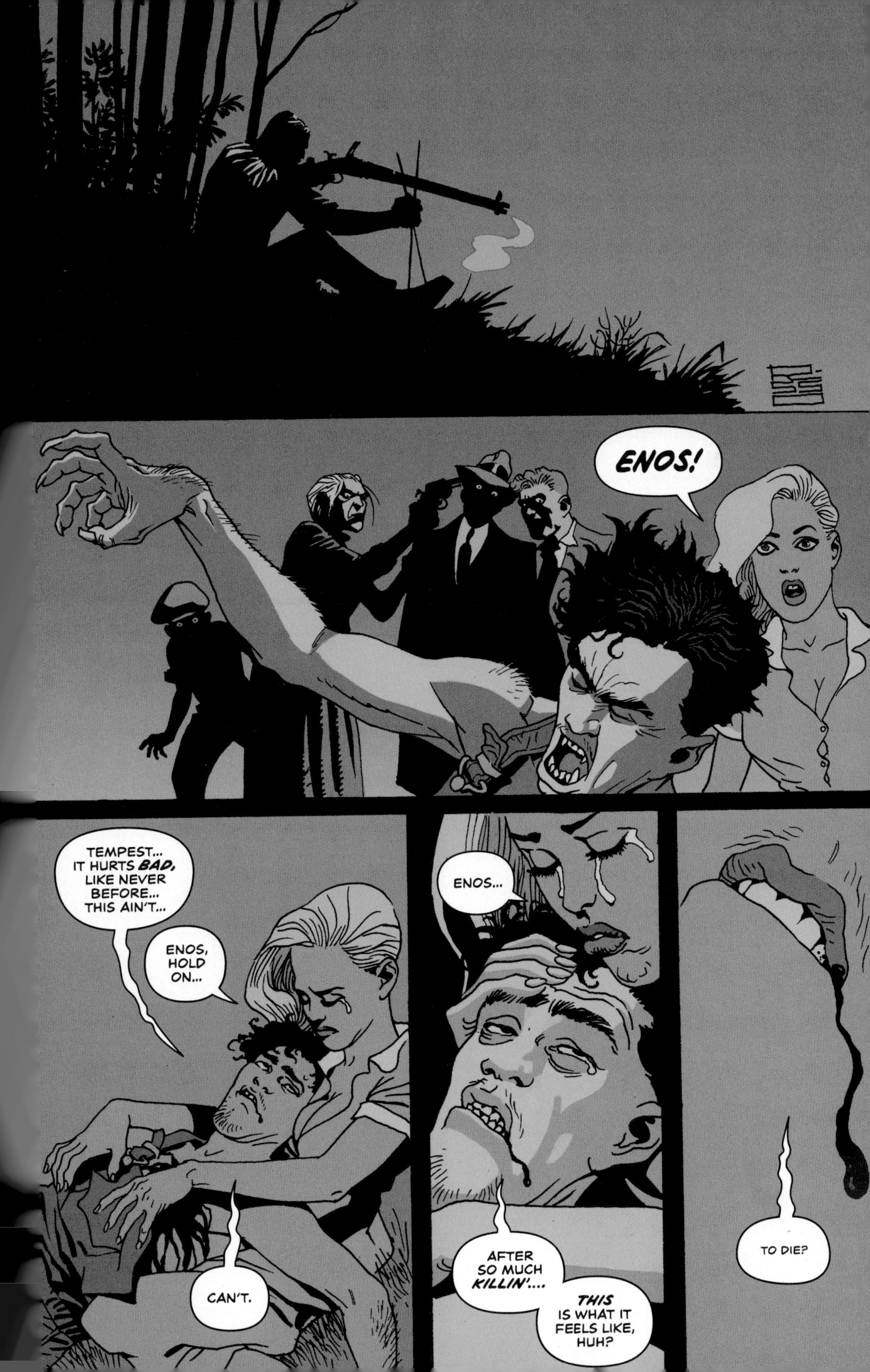
ENOS!
TEMPEST... IT HURTS BAD, LIKE NEVER BEFORE... THIS AIN'T...
ENOS, HOLD ON...
CAN'T.
ENOS...
AFTER SO MUCH KILLIN'....
THIS IS WHAT IT FEELS LIKE, HUH?
TO DIE?

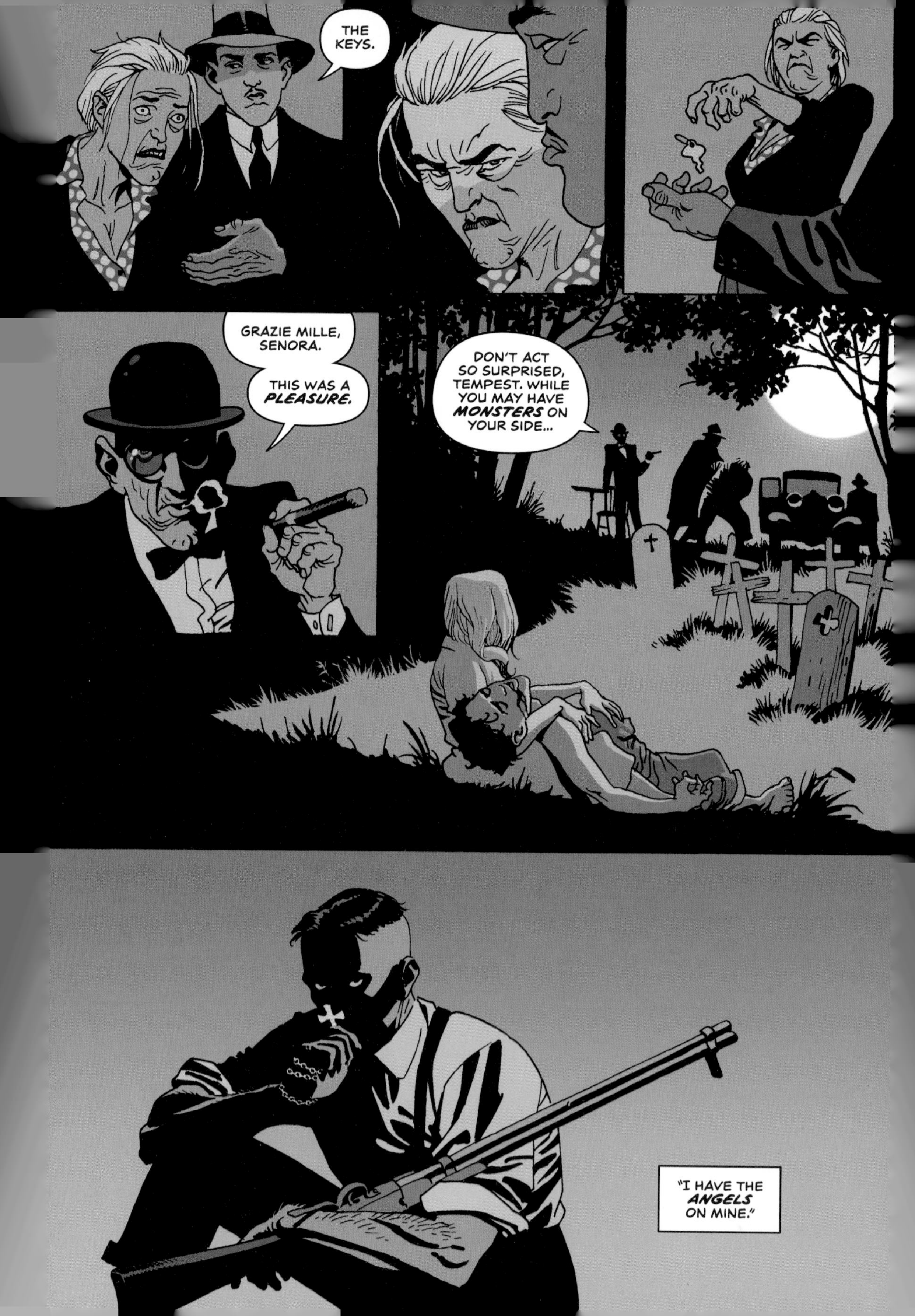
THE KEYS.
GRAZIE MILLE, SENORA.
THIS WAS A *PLEASURE.*
DON'T ACT SO SURPRISED, TEMPEST. WHILE YOU MAY HAVE *MONSTERS* ON YOUR SIDE...
"I HAVE THE *ANGELS* ON MINE."

Chapter TEN

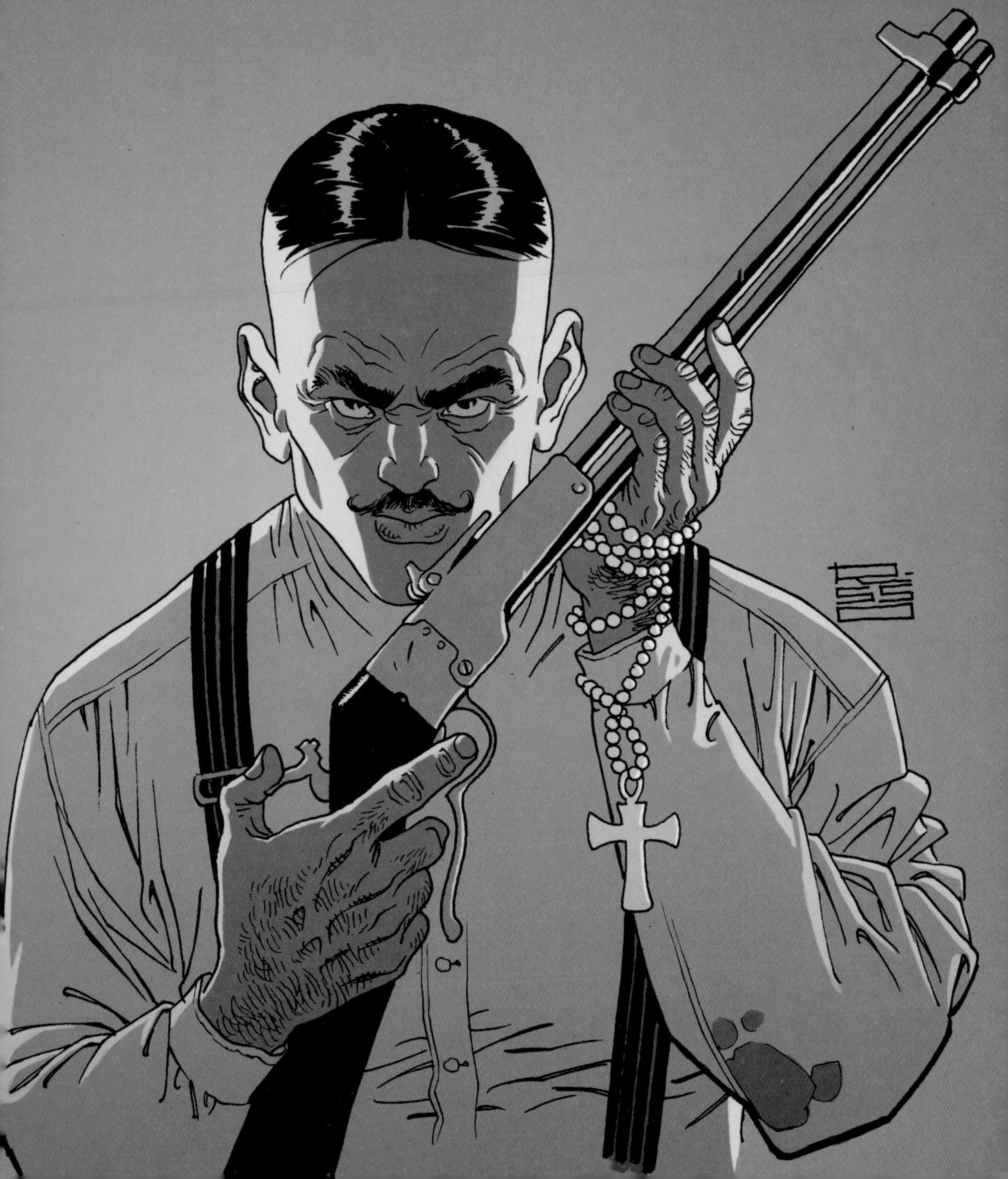

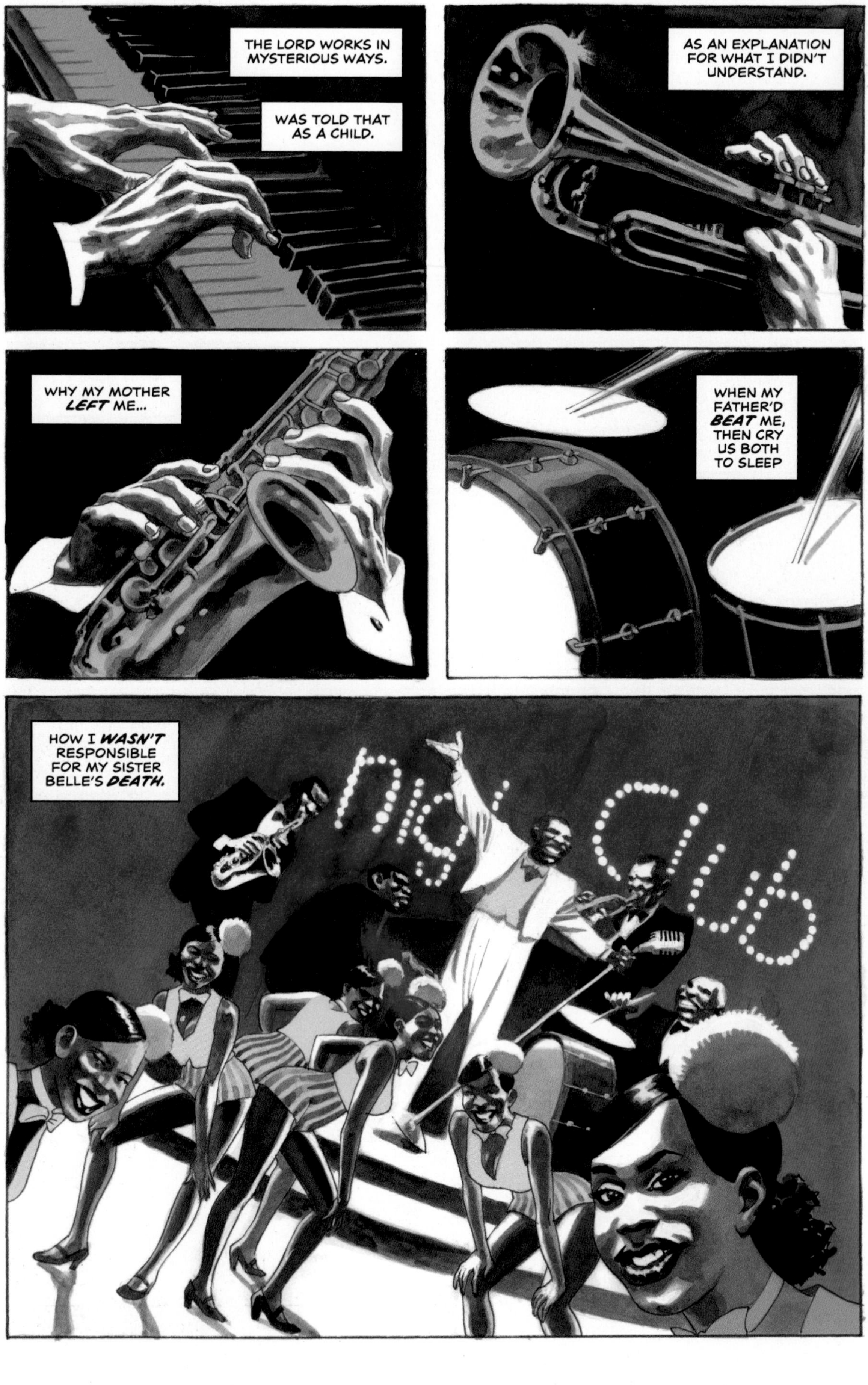
THE LORD WORKS IN MYSTERIOUS WAYS.
WAS TOLD THAT AS A CHILD.
AS AN EXPLANATION FOR WHAT I DIDN'T UNDERSTAND.
WHY MY MOTHER *LEFT* ME...
WHEN MY FATHER'D *BEAT* ME, THEN CRY US BOTH TO SLEEP
HOW I *WASN'T* RESPONSIBLE FOR MY SISTER BELLE'S *DEATH.*
night club

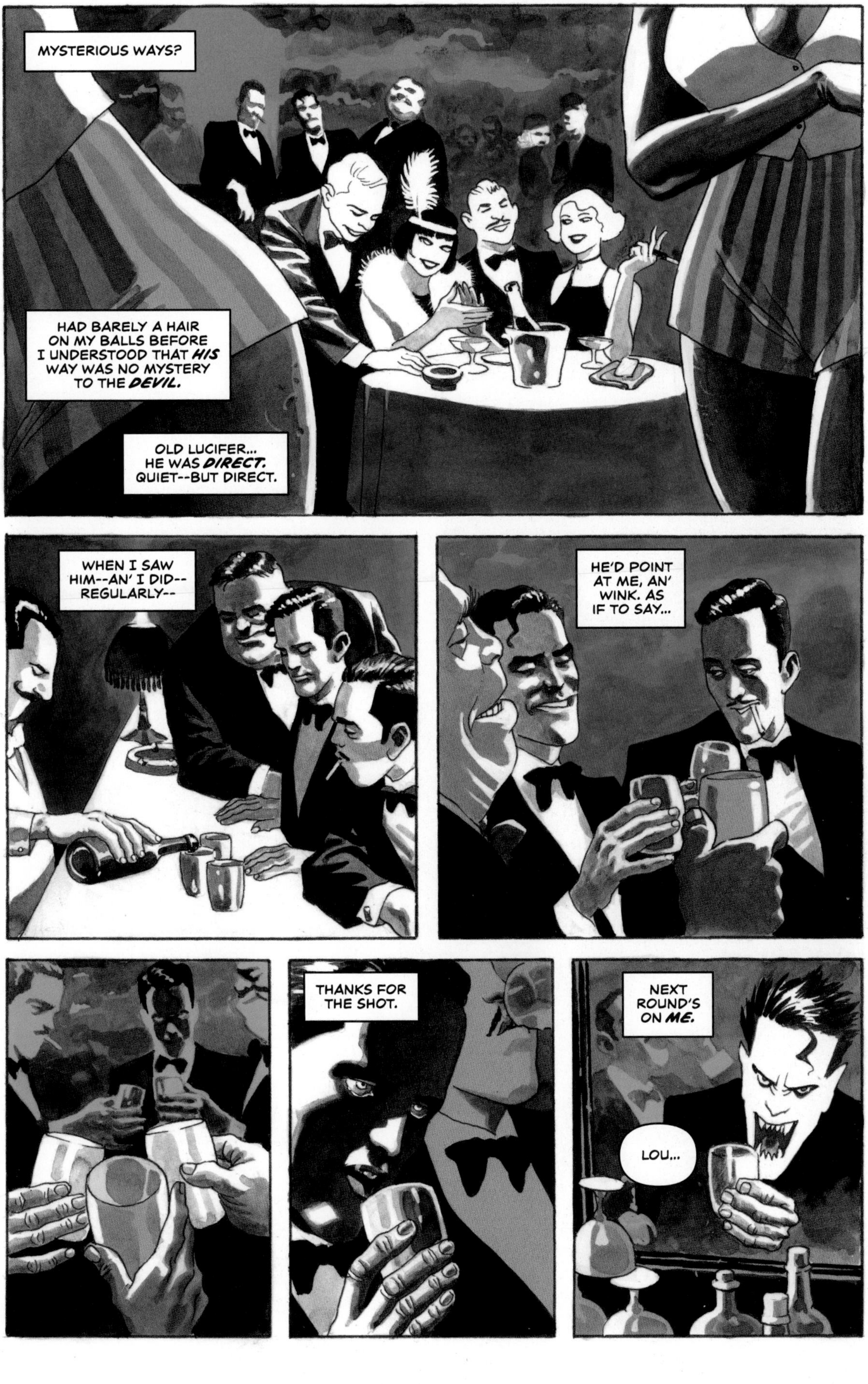
MYSTERIOUS WAYS?
HAD BARELY A HAIR ON MY BALLS BEFORE I UNDERSTOOD THAT *HIS* WAY WAS NO MYSTERY TO THE *DEVIL.*
OLD LUCIFER... HE WAS *DIRECT.* QUIET--BUT DIRECT.
WHEN I SAW HIM--AN' I DID--REGULARLY--
HE'D POINT AT ME, AN' WINK. AS IF TO SAY...
THANKS FOR THE SHOT.
NEXT ROUND'S ON *ME.*
LOU...

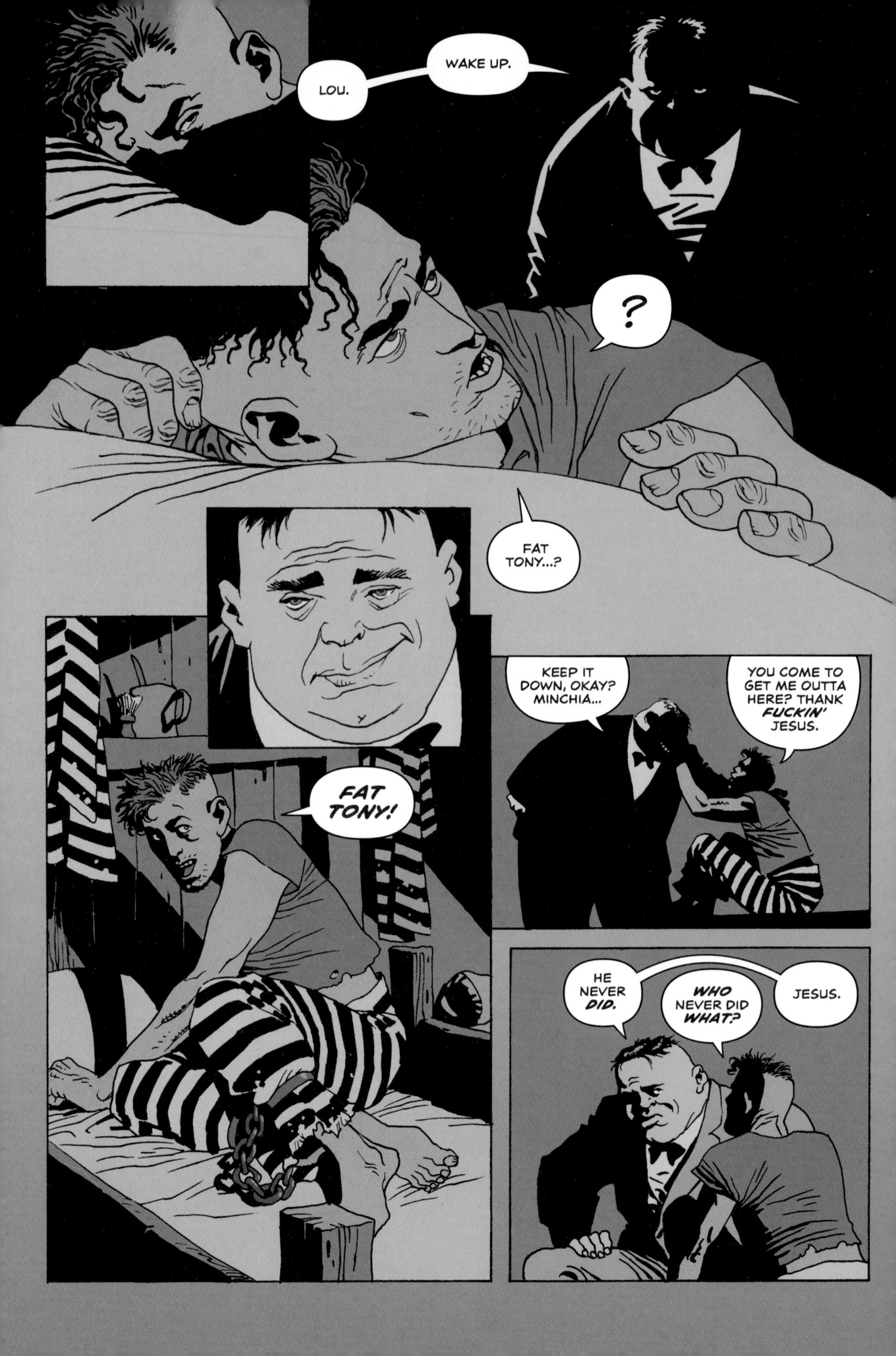

LOU.
WAKE UP.
?
FAT TONY...?
FAT TONY!
KEEP IT DOWN, OKAY? MINCHIA...
YOU COME TO GET ME OUTTA HERE? THANK FUCKIN' JESUS.
HE NEVER DID.
WHO NEVER DID WHAT?
JESUS.

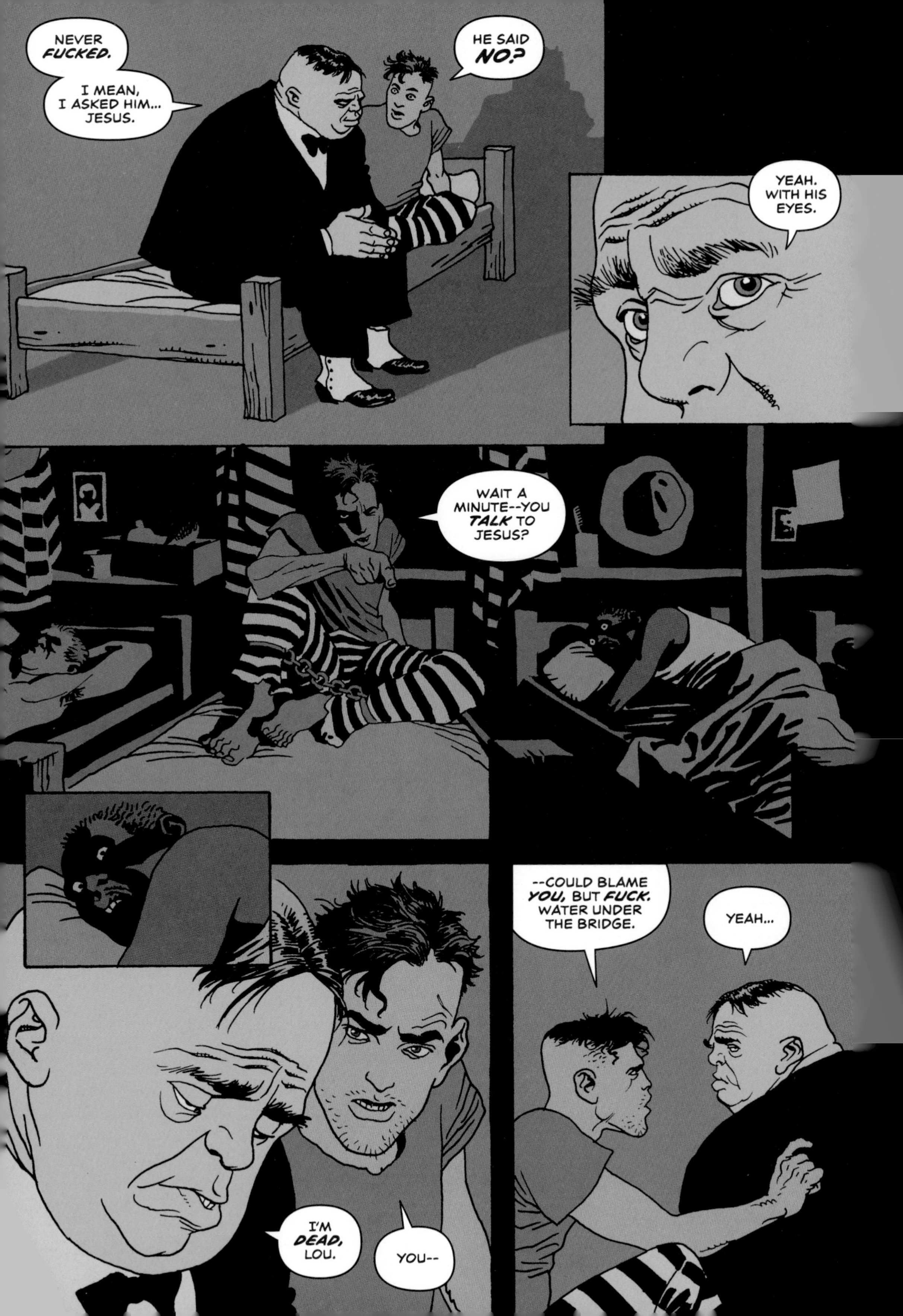

NEVER *FUCKED.*
I MEAN, I ASKED HIM... JESUS.
HE SAID *NO?*
YEAH. WITH HIS EYES.
WAIT A MINUTE--YOU *TALK* TO JESUS?
I'M *DEAD,* LOU.
YOU--
--COULD BLAME *YOU,* BUT *FUCK.* WATER UNDER THE BRIDGE.
YEAH...

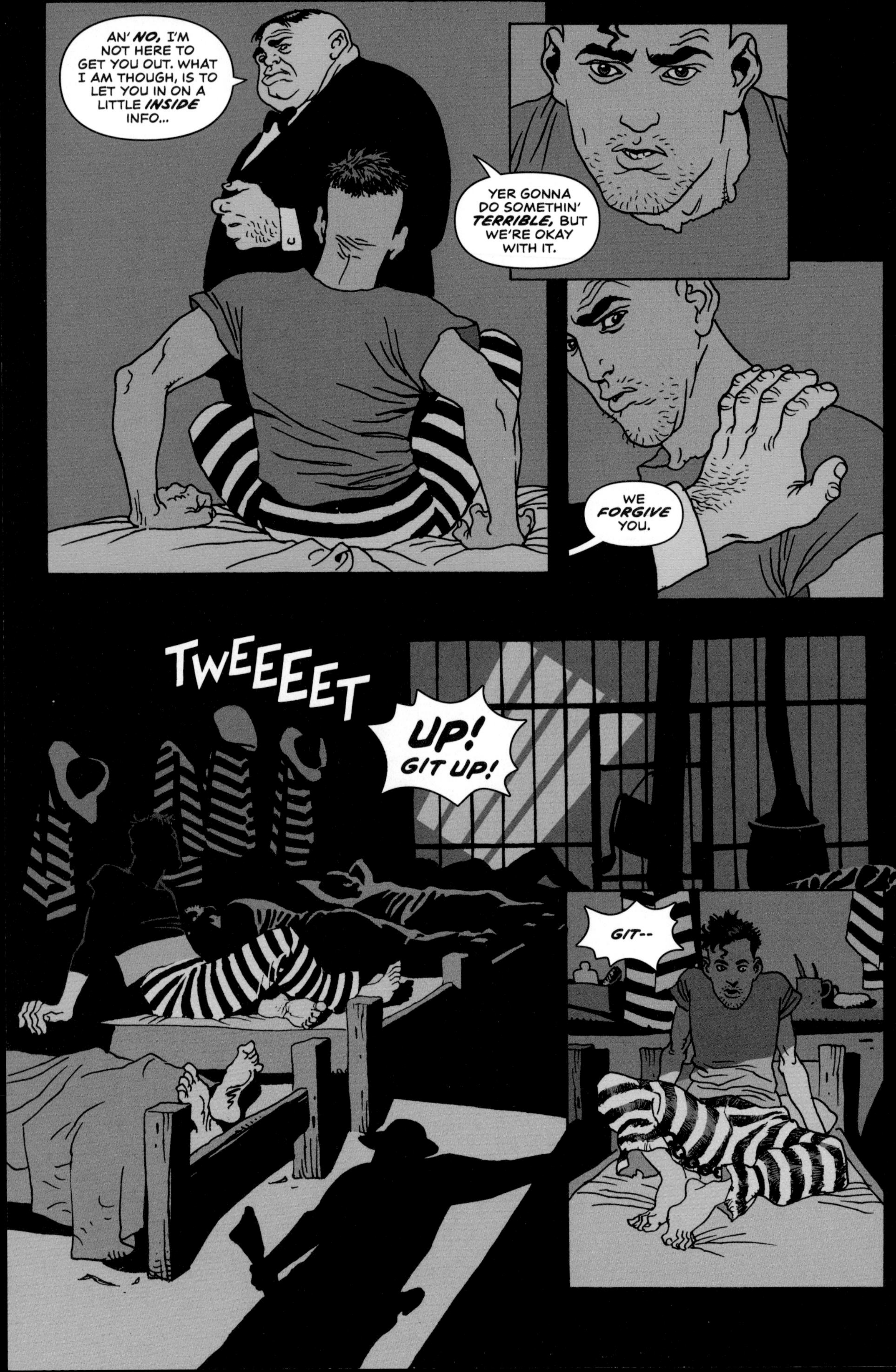
AN' NO, I'M NOT HERE TO GET YOU OUT. WHAT I AM THOUGH, IS TO LET YOU IN ON A LITTLE INSIDE INFO...
YER GONNA DO SOMETHIN' TERRIBLE, BUT WE'RE OKAY WITH IT.
WE FORGIVE YOU.
TWEEEEET
UP! GIT UP!
GIT--

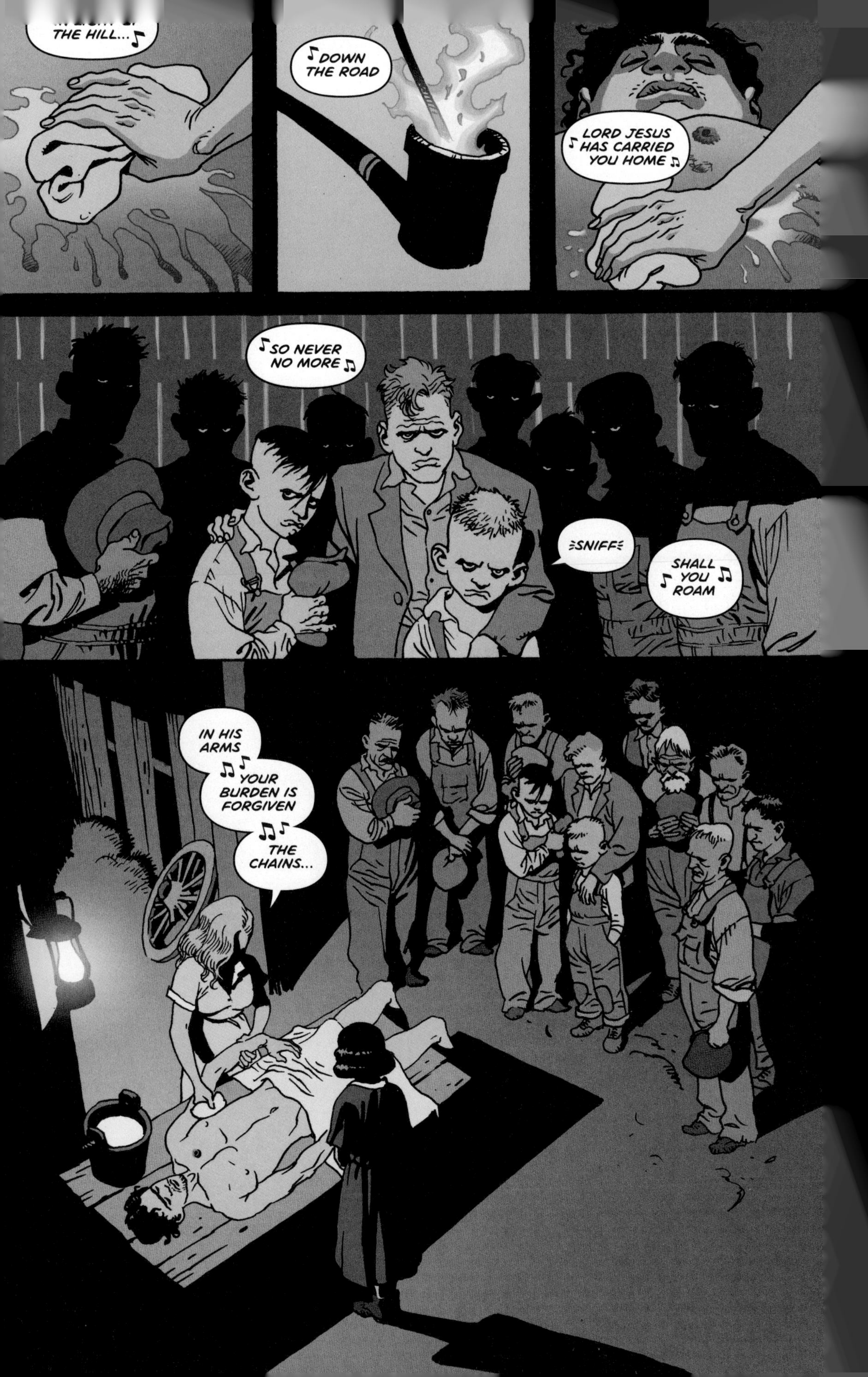
THE HILL...
DOWN THE ROAD
LORD JESUS HAS CARRIED YOU HOME
SO NEVER NO MORE
SNIFF
SHALL YOU ROAM
IN HIS ARMS
YOUR BURDEN IS FORGIVEN
THE CHAINS...

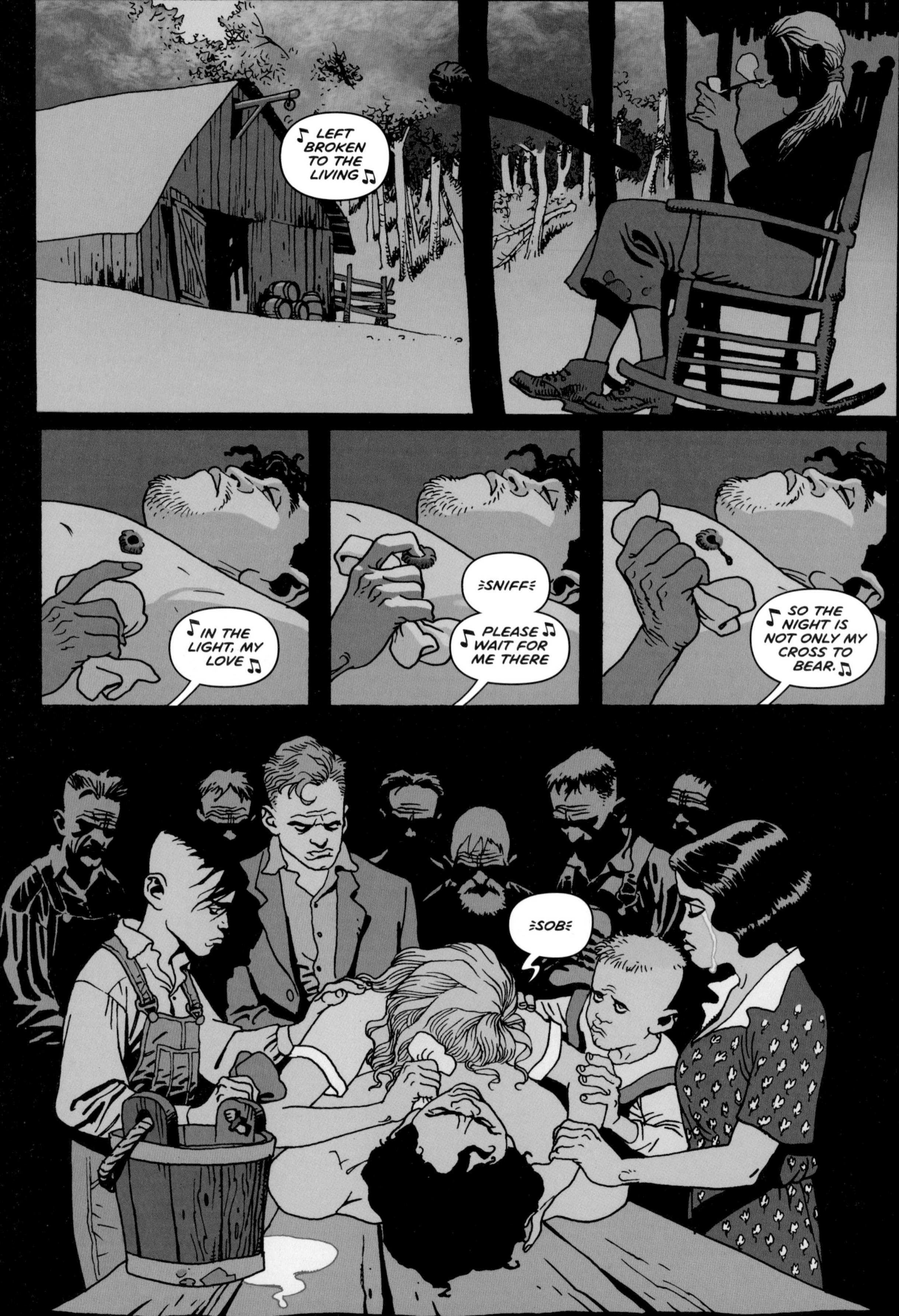
♪ LEFT BROKEN TO THE LIVING ♫
♪ IN THE LIGHT, MY LOVE ♫
SNIFF
♪ PLEASE ♫ WAIT FOR ME THERE
♪ SO THE NIGHT IS NOT ONLY MY CROSS TO BEAR. ♫
SOB

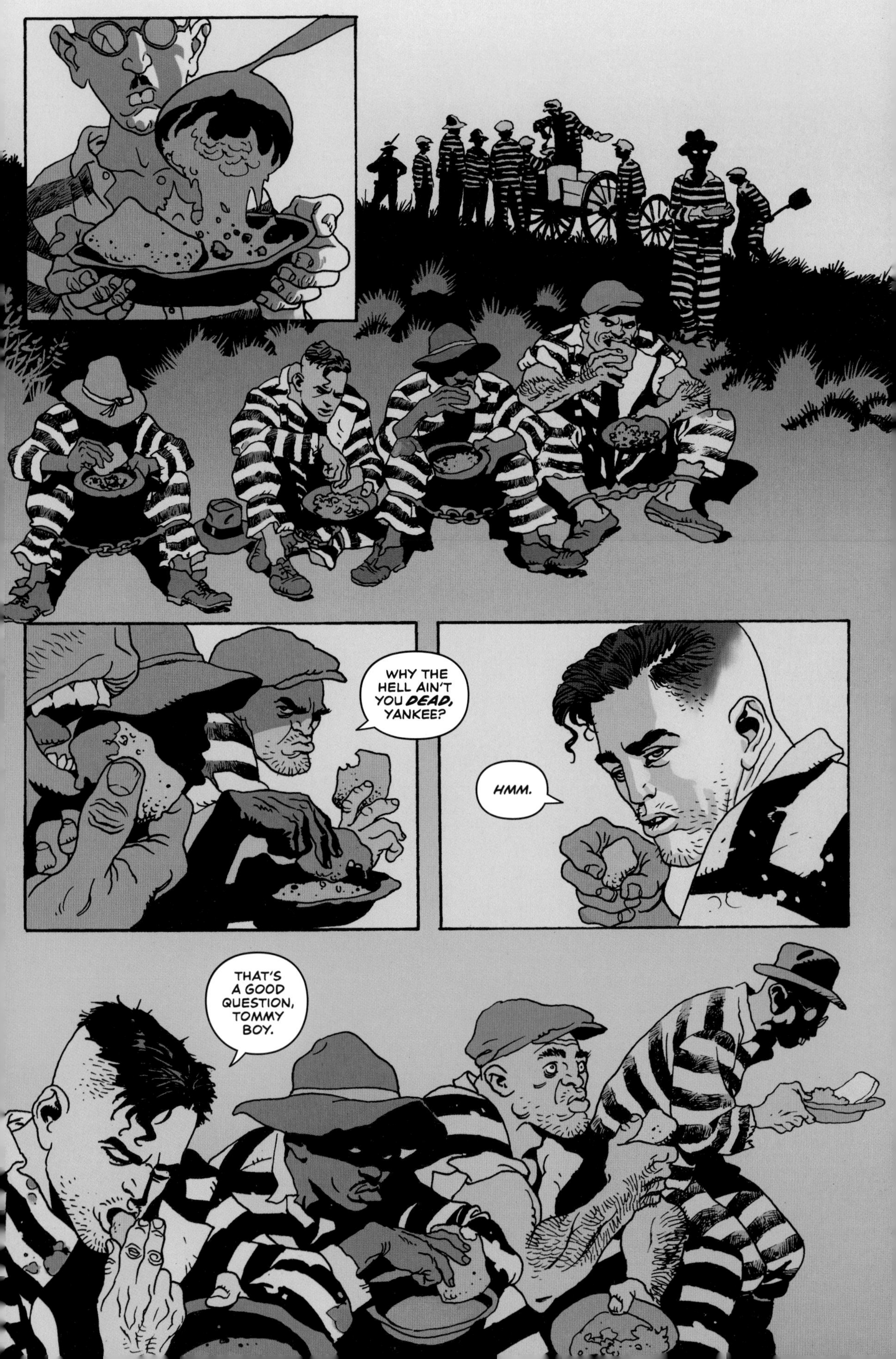
WHY THE HELL AIN'T YOU DEAD, YANKEE?
HMM.
THAT'S A GOOD QUESTION, TOMMY BOY.

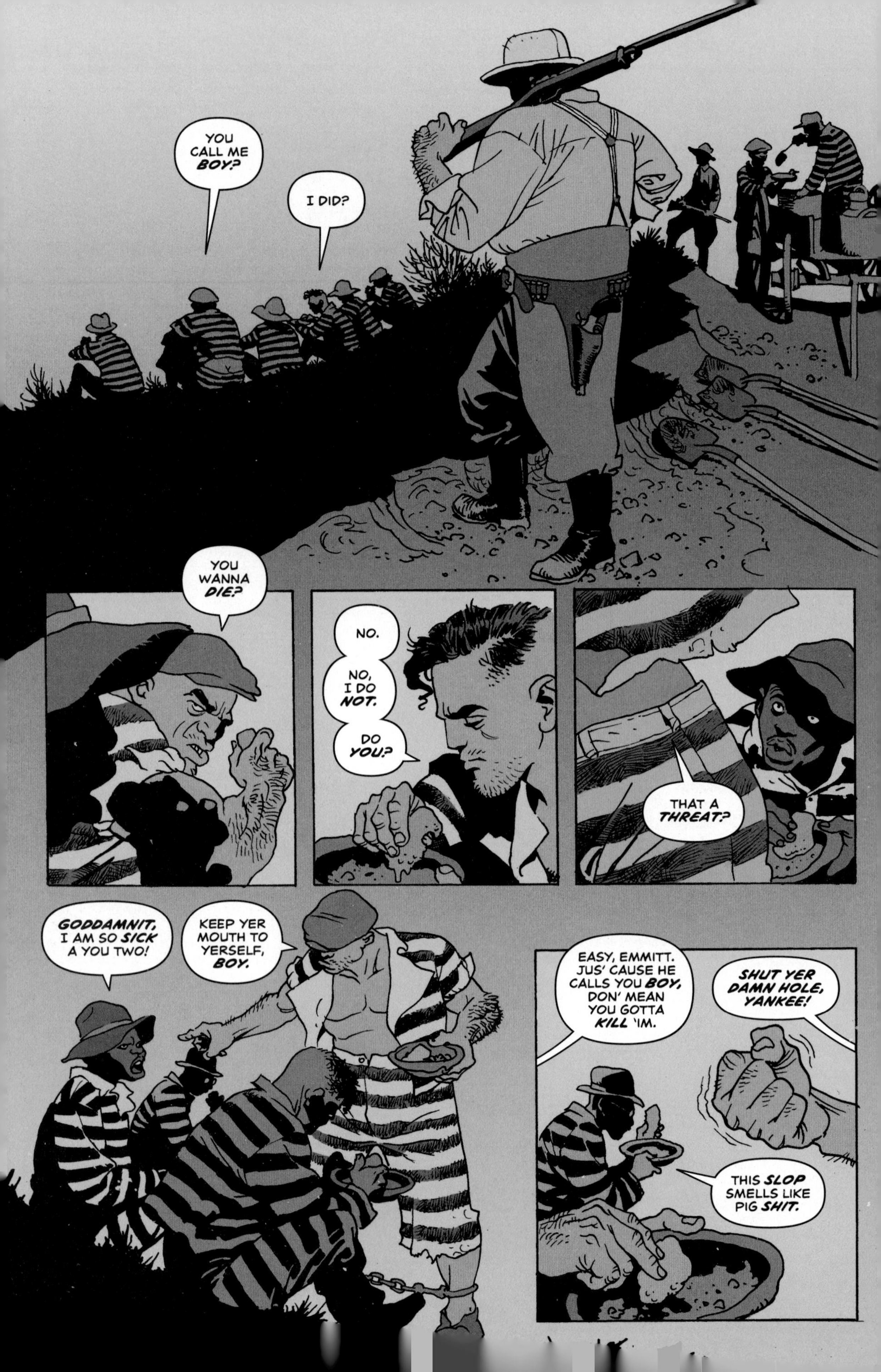
YOU CALL ME BOY?
I DID?
YOU WANNA DIE?
NO.
NO, I DO NOT.
DO YOU?
THAT A THREAT?
GODDAMNIT, I AM SO SICK A YOU TWO!
KEEP YER MOUTH TO YERSELF, BOY.
EASY, EMMITT. JUS' CAUSE HE CALLS YOU BOY, DON' MEAN YOU GOTTA KILL 'IM.
SHUT YER DAMN HOLE, YANKEE!
THIS SLOP SMELLS LIKE PIG SHIT.

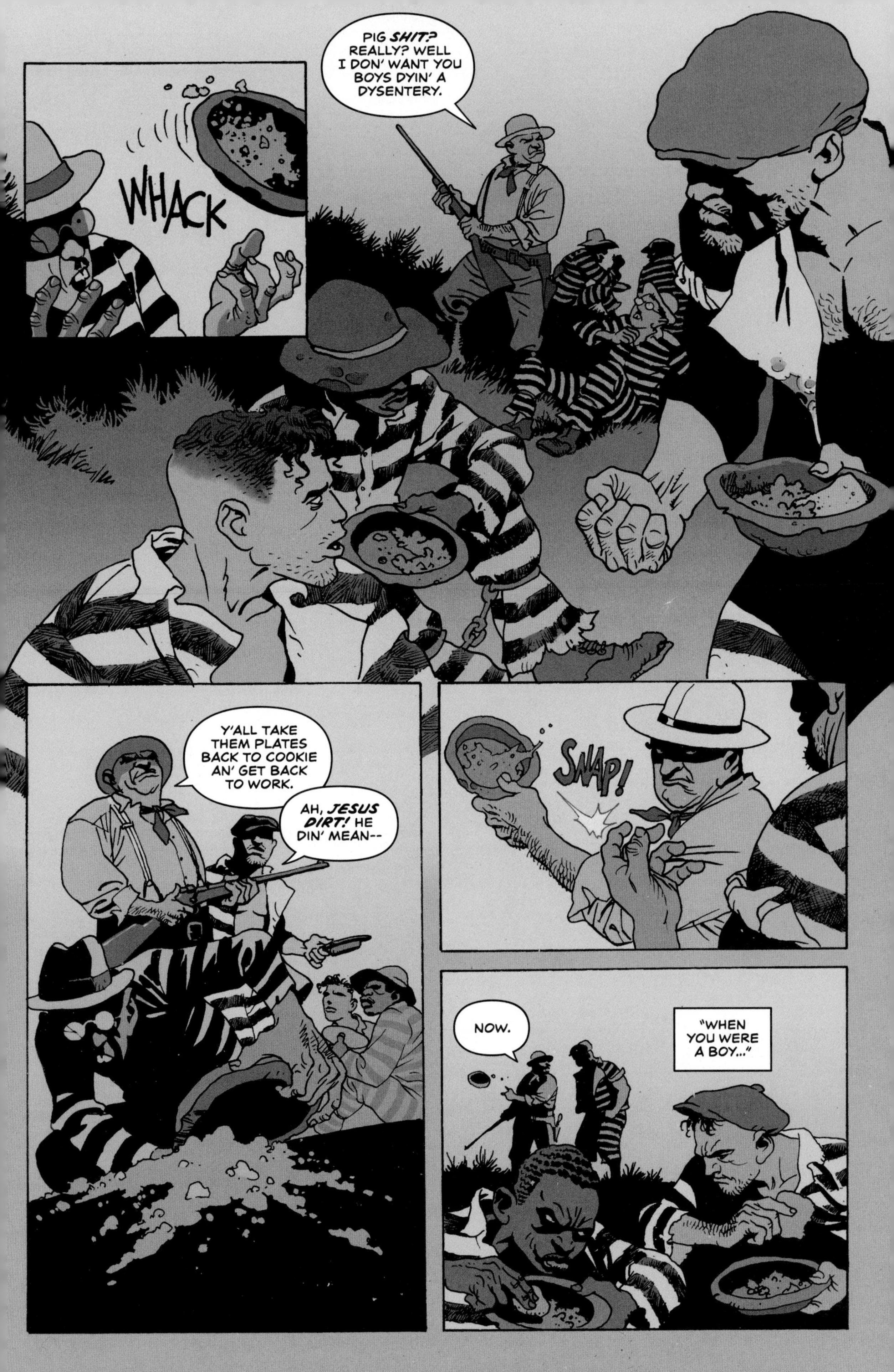
WHACK
PIG SHIT? REALLY? WELL I DON' WANT YOU BOYS DYIN' A DYSENTERY.
Y'ALL TAKE THEM PLATES BACK TO COOKIE AN' GET BACK TO WORK.
AH, JESUS DIRT! HE DIN' MEAN--
SNAP!
NOW.
"WHEN YOU WERE A BOY..."

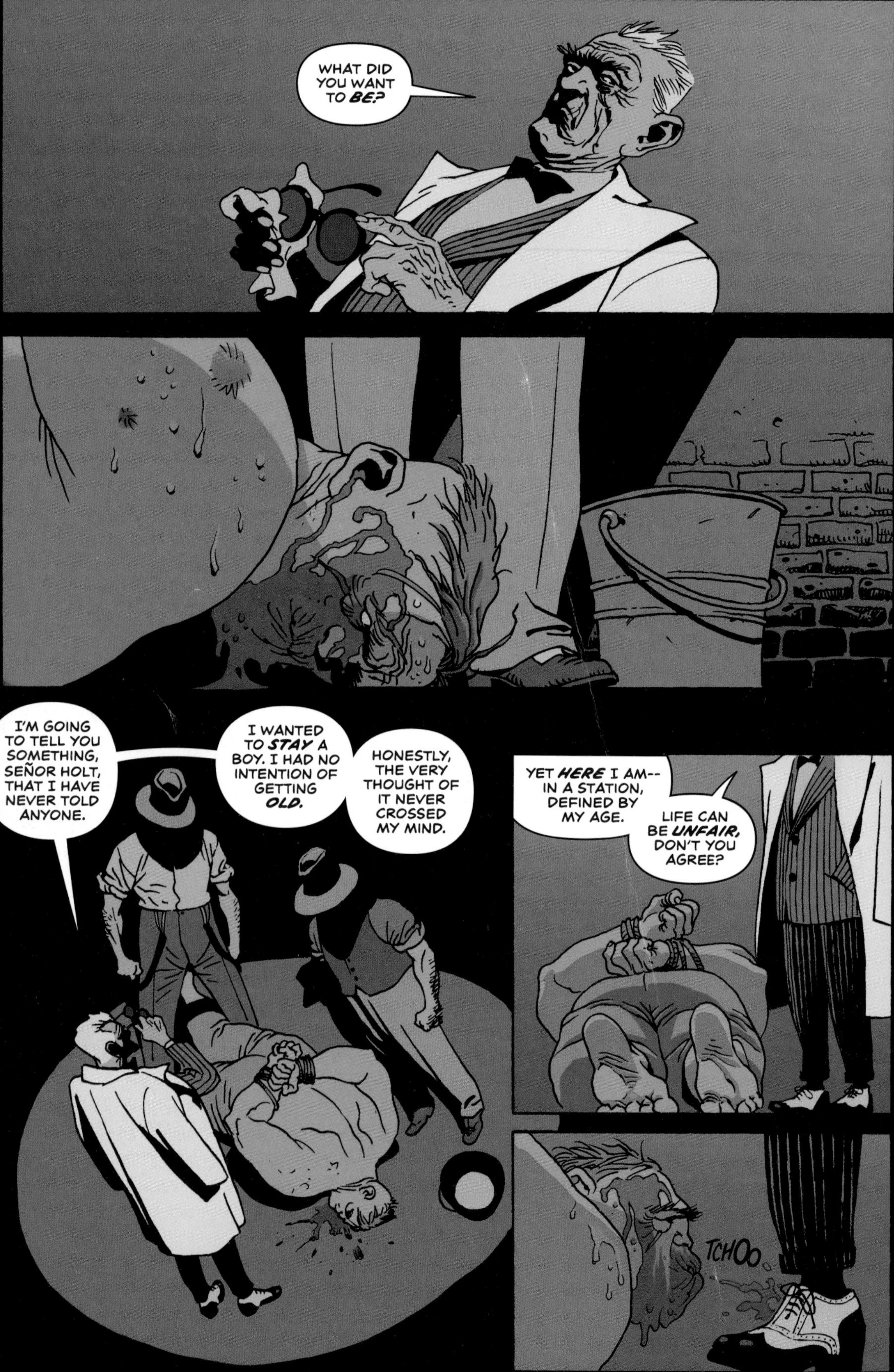
WHAT DID YOU WANT TO BE?
I'M GOING TO TELL YOU SOMETHING, SEÑOR HOLT, THAT I HAVE NEVER TOLD ANYONE.
I WANTED TO STAY A BOY. I HAD NO INTENTION OF GETTING OLD.
HONESTLY, THE VERY THOUGHT OF IT NEVER CROSSED MY MIND.
YET HERE I AM-- IN A STATION, DEFINED BY MY AGE.
LIFE CAN BE UNFAIR, DON'T YOU AGREE?
TCHOO

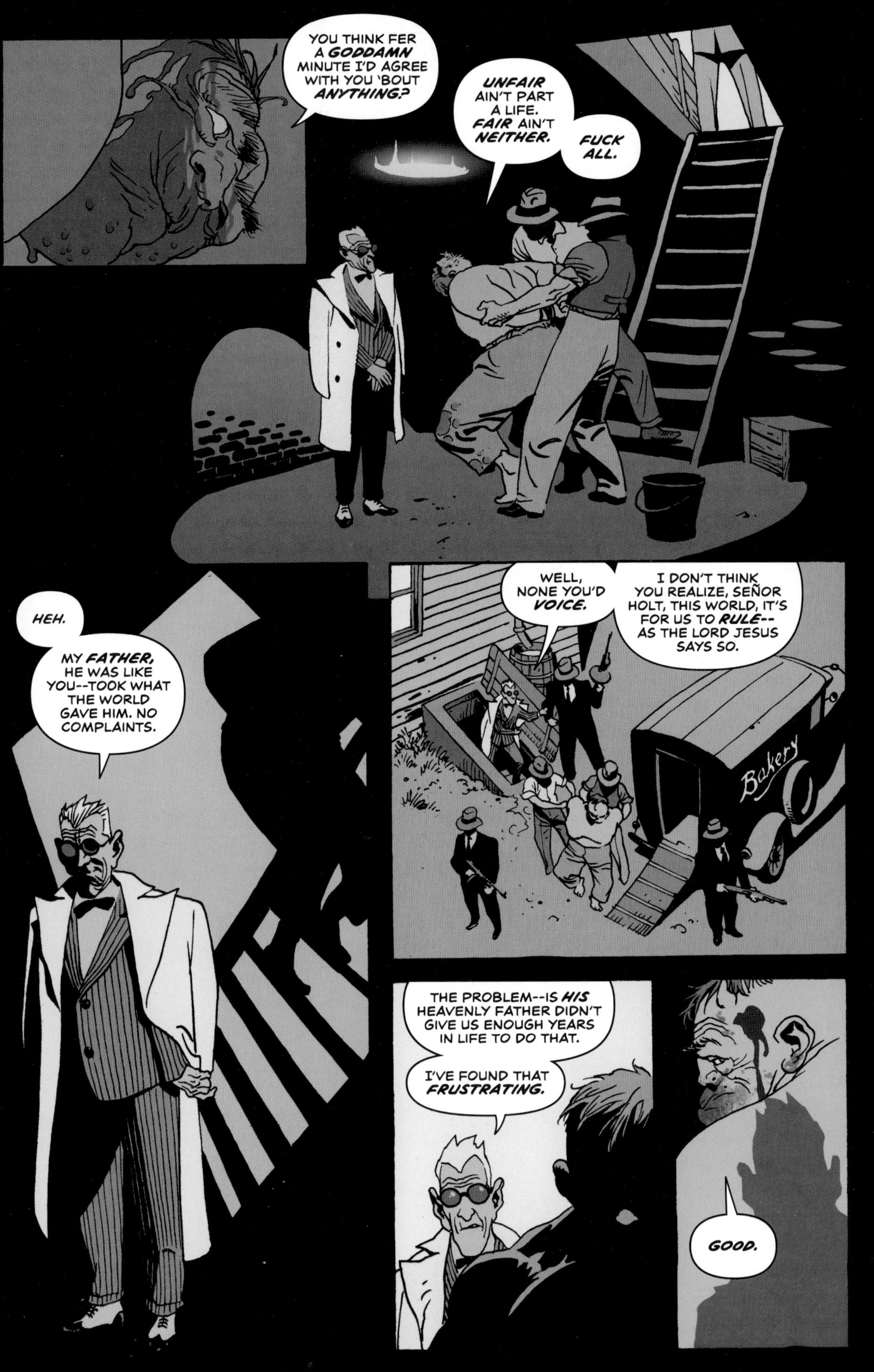
YOU THINK FER A GODDAMN MINUTE I'D AGREE WITH YOU 'BOUT ANYTHING?
UNFAIR AIN'T PART A LIFE. FAIR AIN'T NEITHER.
FUCK ALL.
HEH.
MY FATHER, HE WAS LIKE YOU--TOOK WHAT THE WORLD GAVE HIM. NO COMPLAINTS.
WELL, NONE YOU'D VOICE.
I DON'T THINK YOU REALIZE, SEÑOR HOLT, THIS WORLD, IT'S FOR US TO RULE-- AS THE LORD JESUS SAYS SO.
Bakery
THE PROBLEM--IS HIS HEAVENLY FATHER DIDN'T GIVE US ENOUGH YEARS IN LIFE TO DO THAT.
I'VE FOUND THAT FRUSTRATING.
GOOD.

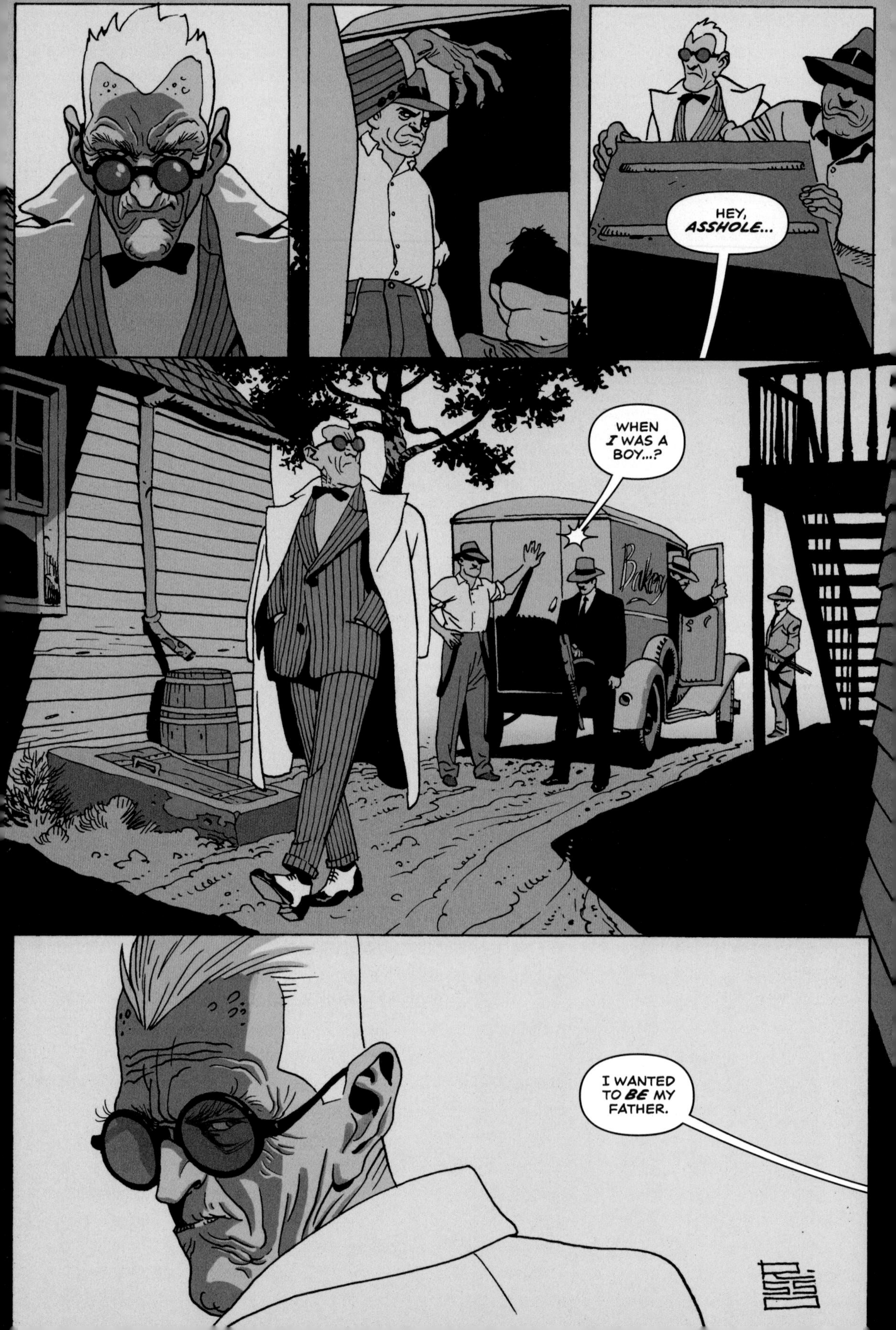
HEY, ASSHOLE...
WHEN I WAS A BOY...?
Bakery
I WANTED TO BE MY FATHER.

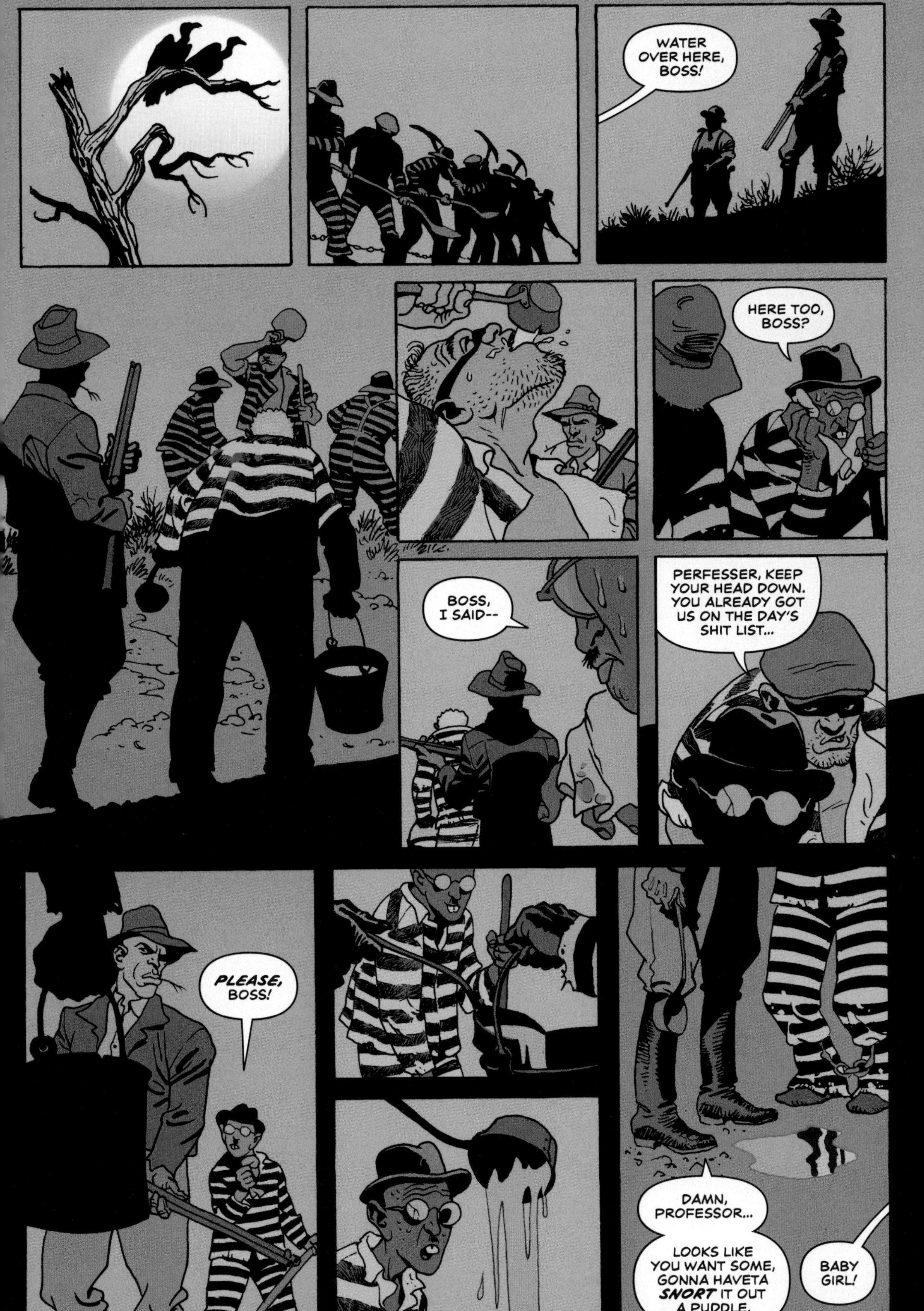
WATER OVER HERE, BOSS!
HERE TOO, BOSS?
BOSS, I SAID--
PERFESSER, KEEP YOUR HEAD DOWN. YOU ALREADY GOT US ON THE DAY'S SHIT LIST...
PLEASE, BOSS!
DAMN, PROFESSOR...
LOOKS LIKE YOU WANT SOME, GONNA HAVETA SNORT IT OUT A PUDDLE.
BABY GIRL!

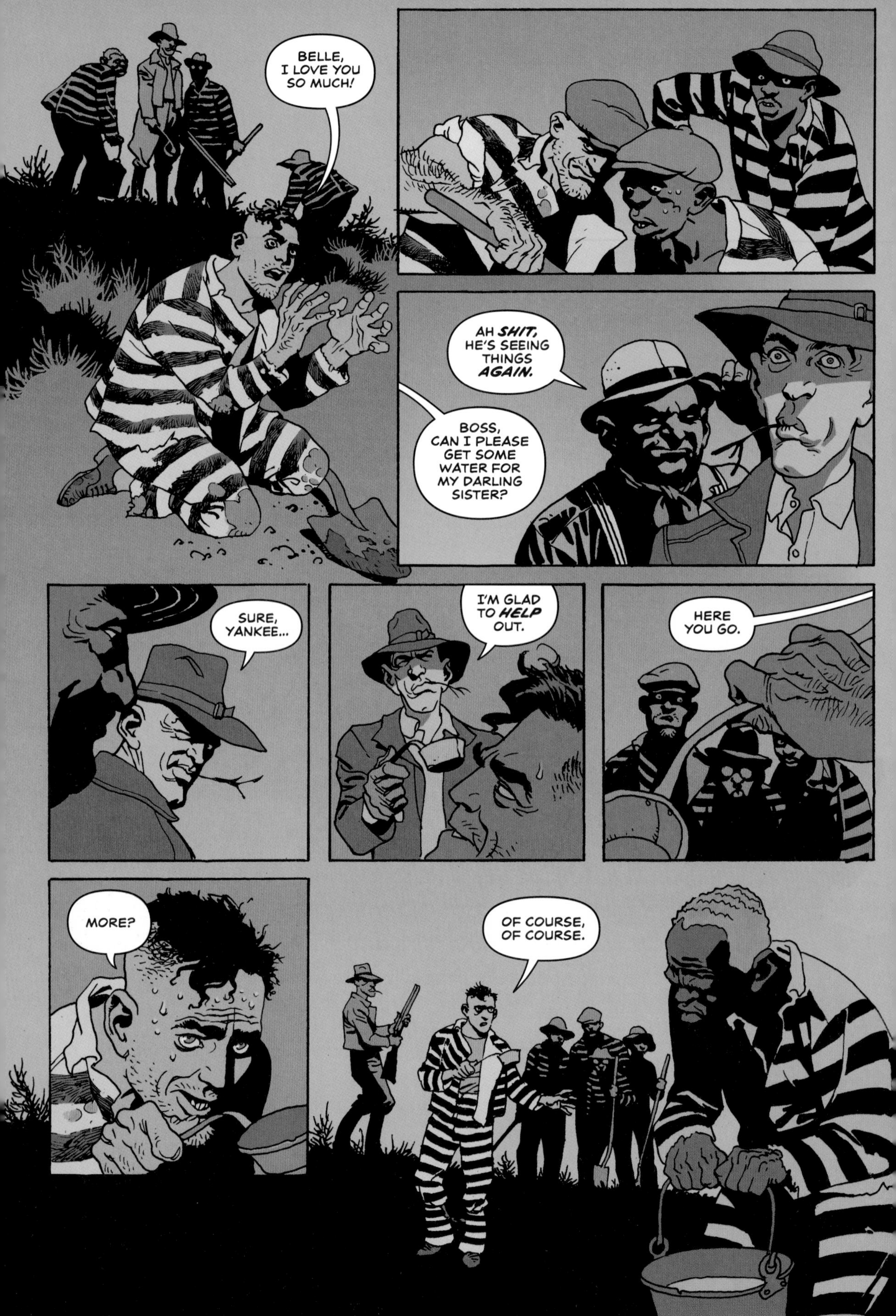
BELLE, I LOVE YOU SO MUCH!
AH *SHIT,* HE'S SEEING THINGS *AGAIN.*
BOSS, CAN I PLEASE GET SOME WATER FOR MY DARLING SISTER?
SURE, YANKEE...
I'M GLAD TO *HELP* OUT.
HERE YOU GO.
MORE?
OF COURSE, OF COURSE.

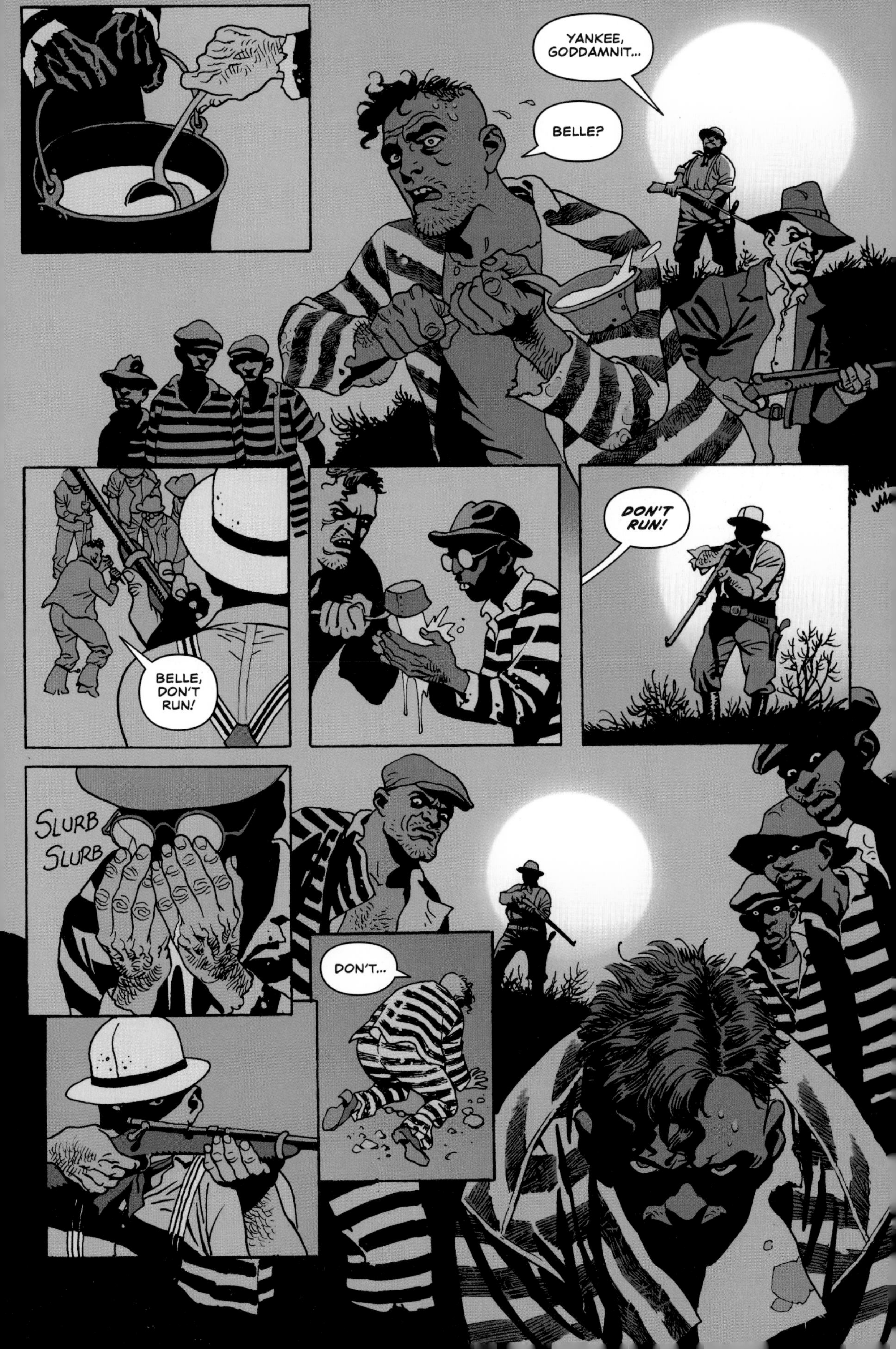
YANKEE, GODDAMNIT...
BELLE?
BELLE, DON'T RUN!
DON'T RUN!
SLURB SLURB
DON'T...

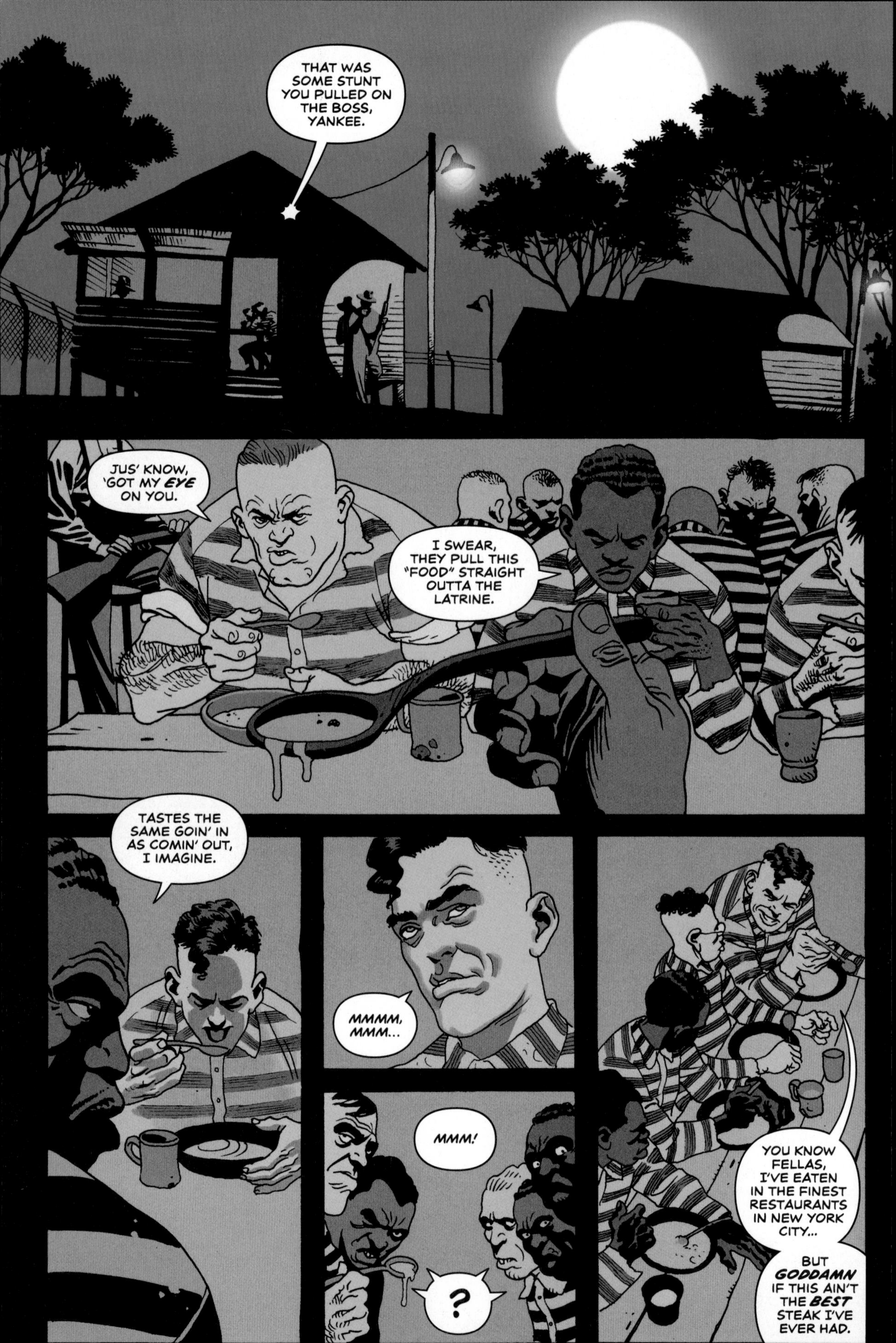
THAT WAS SOME STUNT YOU PULLED ON THE BOSS, YANKEE.
JUS' KNOW, 'GOT MY *EYE* ON YOU.
I SWEAR, THEY PULL THIS "FOOD" STRAIGHT OUTTA THE LATRINE.
TASTES THE SAME GOIN' IN AS COMIN' OUT, I IMAGINE.
MMMM, MMM...
MMM!
?
YOU KNOW FELLAS, I'VE EATEN IN THE FINEST RESTAURANTS IN NEW YORK CITY...
BUT ***GODDAMN*** IF THIS AIN'T THE ***BEST*** STEAK I'VE EVER HAD.

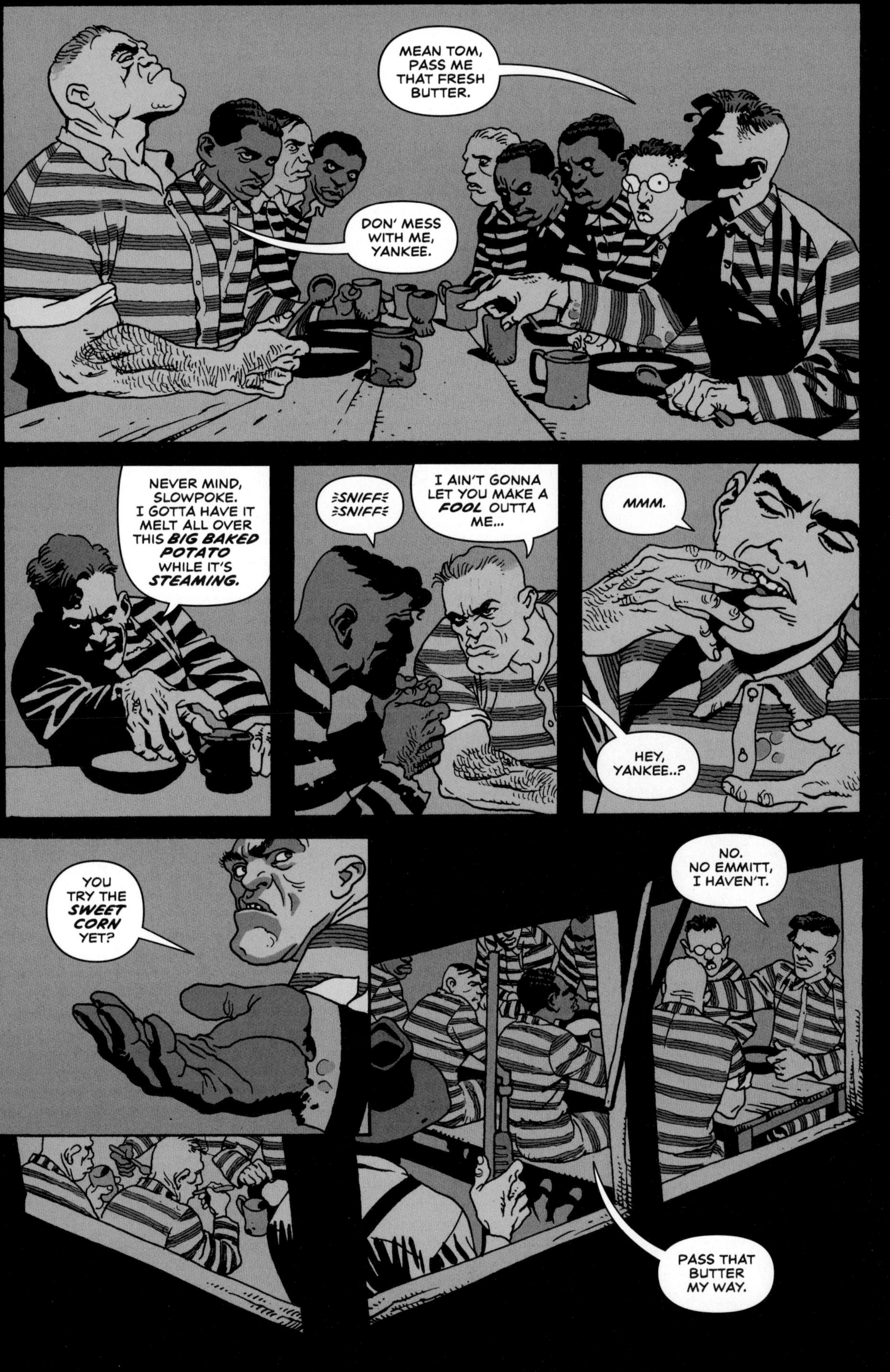
MEAN TOM, PASS ME THAT FRESH BUTTER.
DON' MESS WITH ME, YANKEE.
NEVER MIND, SLOWPOKE. I GOTTA HAVE IT MELT ALL OVER THIS BIG BAKED POTATO WHILE IT'S STEAMING.
SNIFF SNIFF
I AIN'T GONNA LET YOU MAKE A FOOL OUTTA ME...
MMM.
HEY, YANKEE..?
YOU TRY THE SWEET CORN YET?
NO. NO EMMITT, I HAVEN'T.
PASS THAT BUTTER MY WAY.

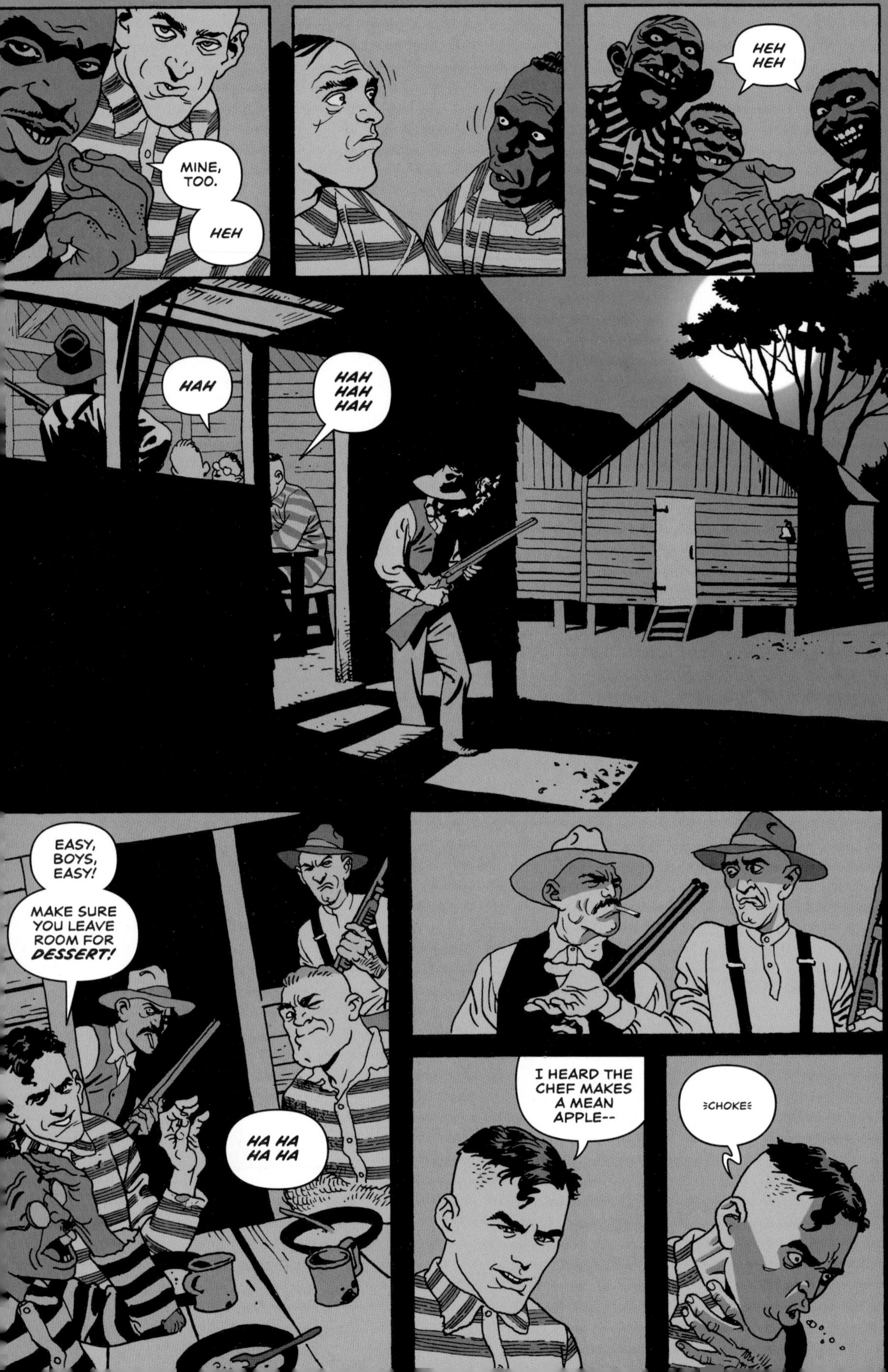
MINE, TOO.
HEH
HEH HEH
HAH
HAH HAH HAH
EASY, BOYS, EASY!
MAKE SURE YOU LEAVE ROOM FOR DESSERT!
HA HA HA HA
I HEARD THE CHEF MAKES A MEAN APPLE--
CHOKE

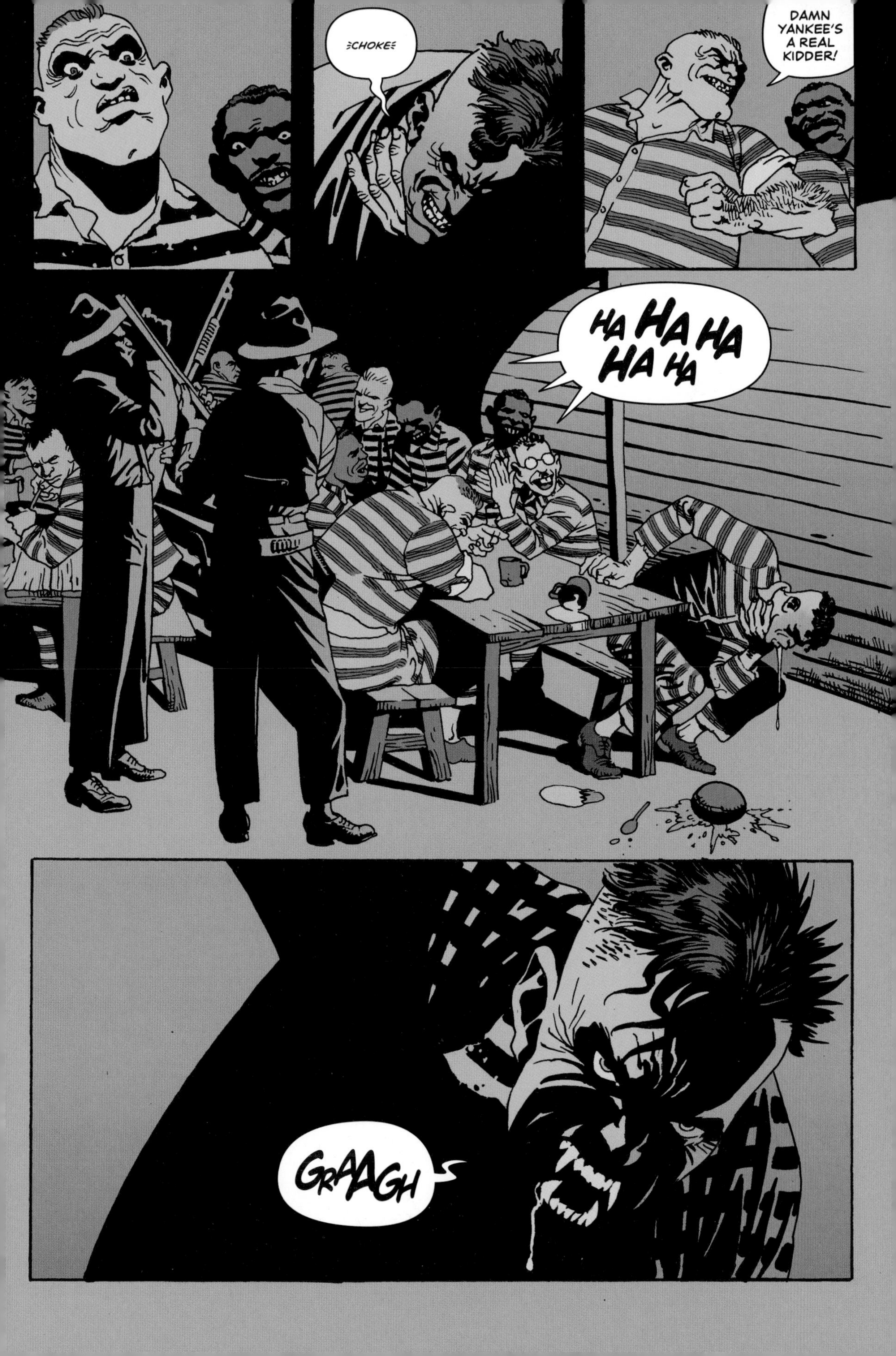

CHOKE
DAMN YANKEE'S A REAL KIDDER!
HA HA HA HA HA HA
GRAAGH

Chapter ELEVEN

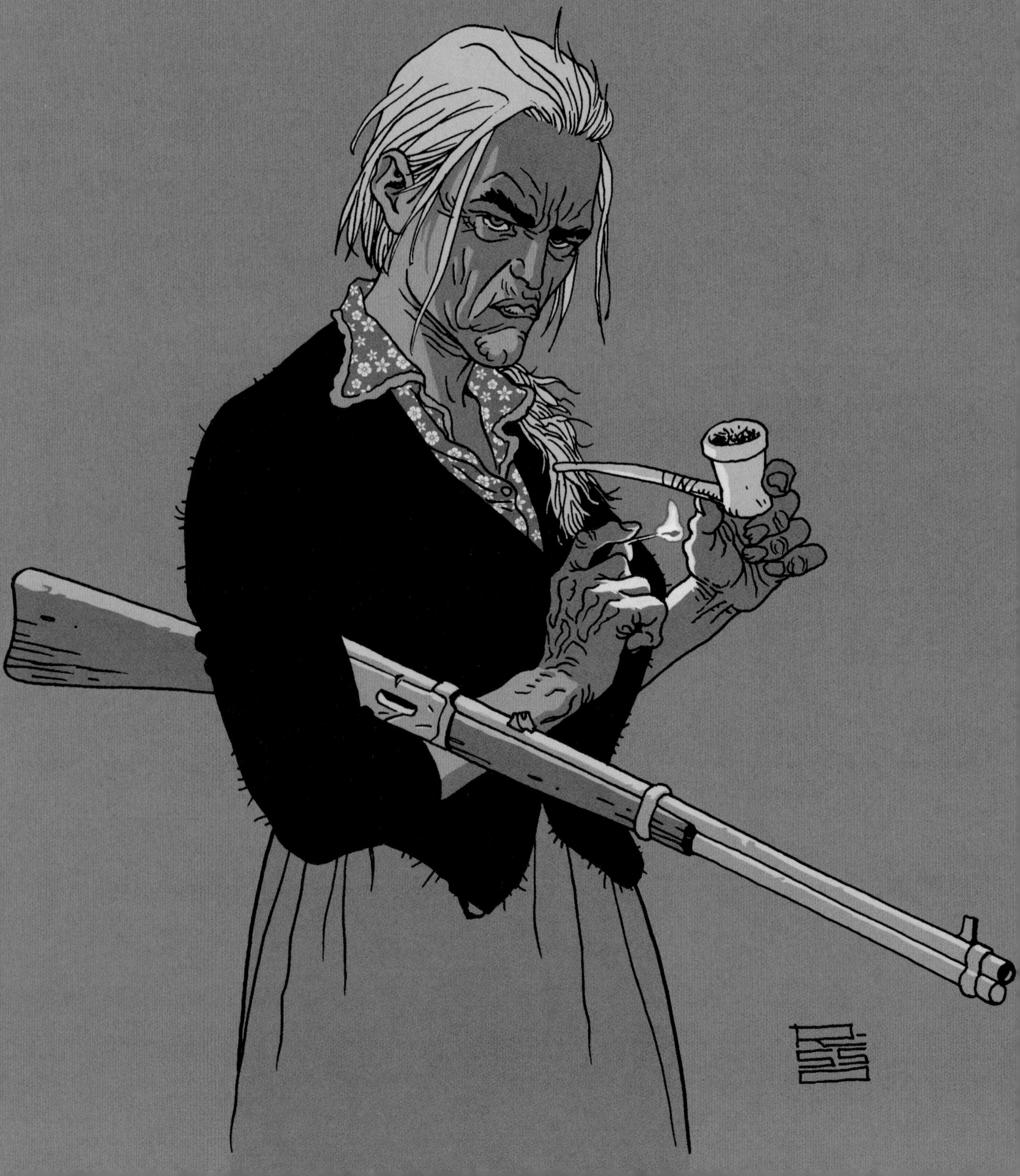

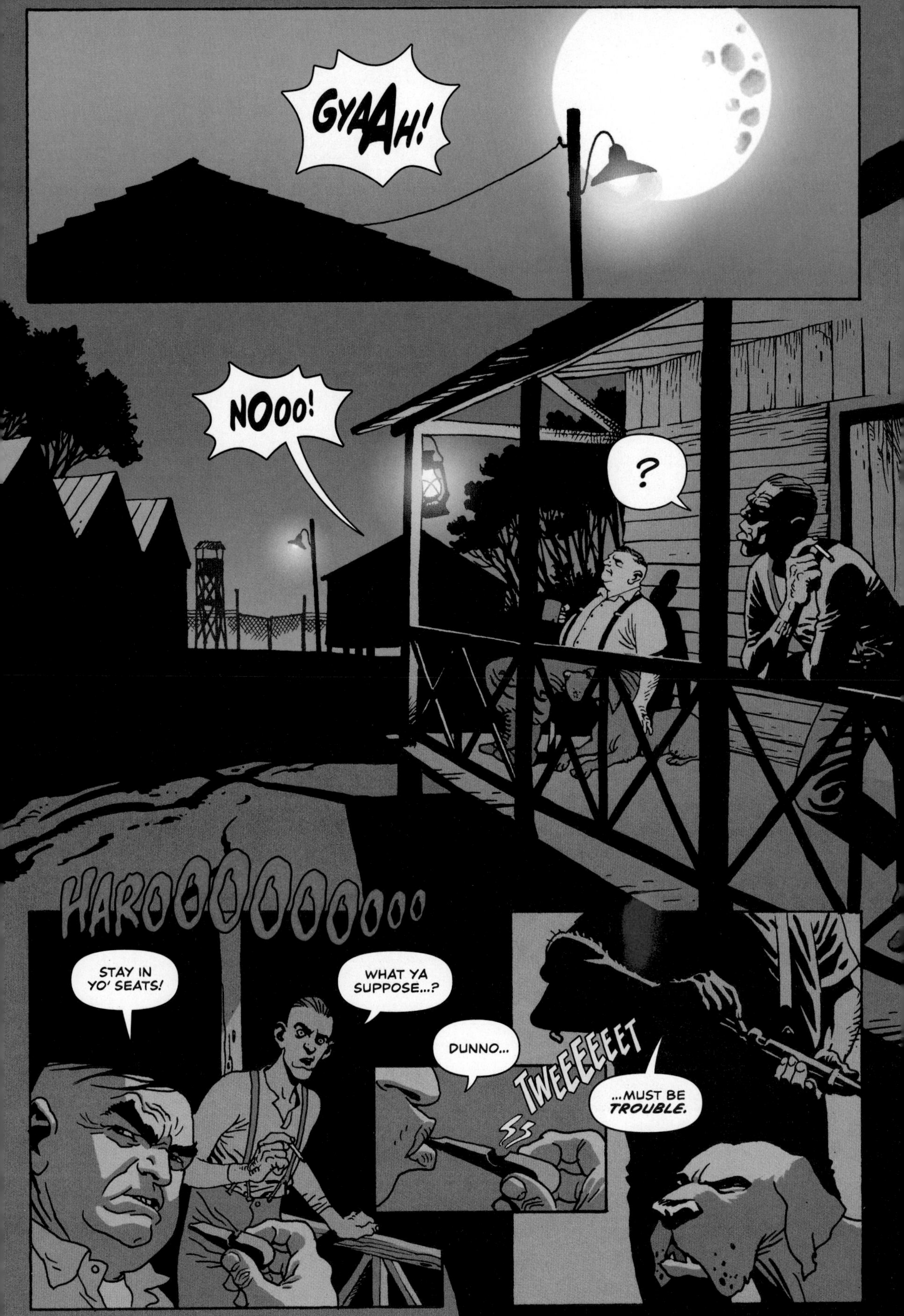
GYAAAH!
NOoo!
?
HAROOOOOOOOOO
STAY IN YO' SEATS!
WHAT YA SUPPOSE...?
DUNNO...
TWEEEEEET
...MUST BE TROUBLE.

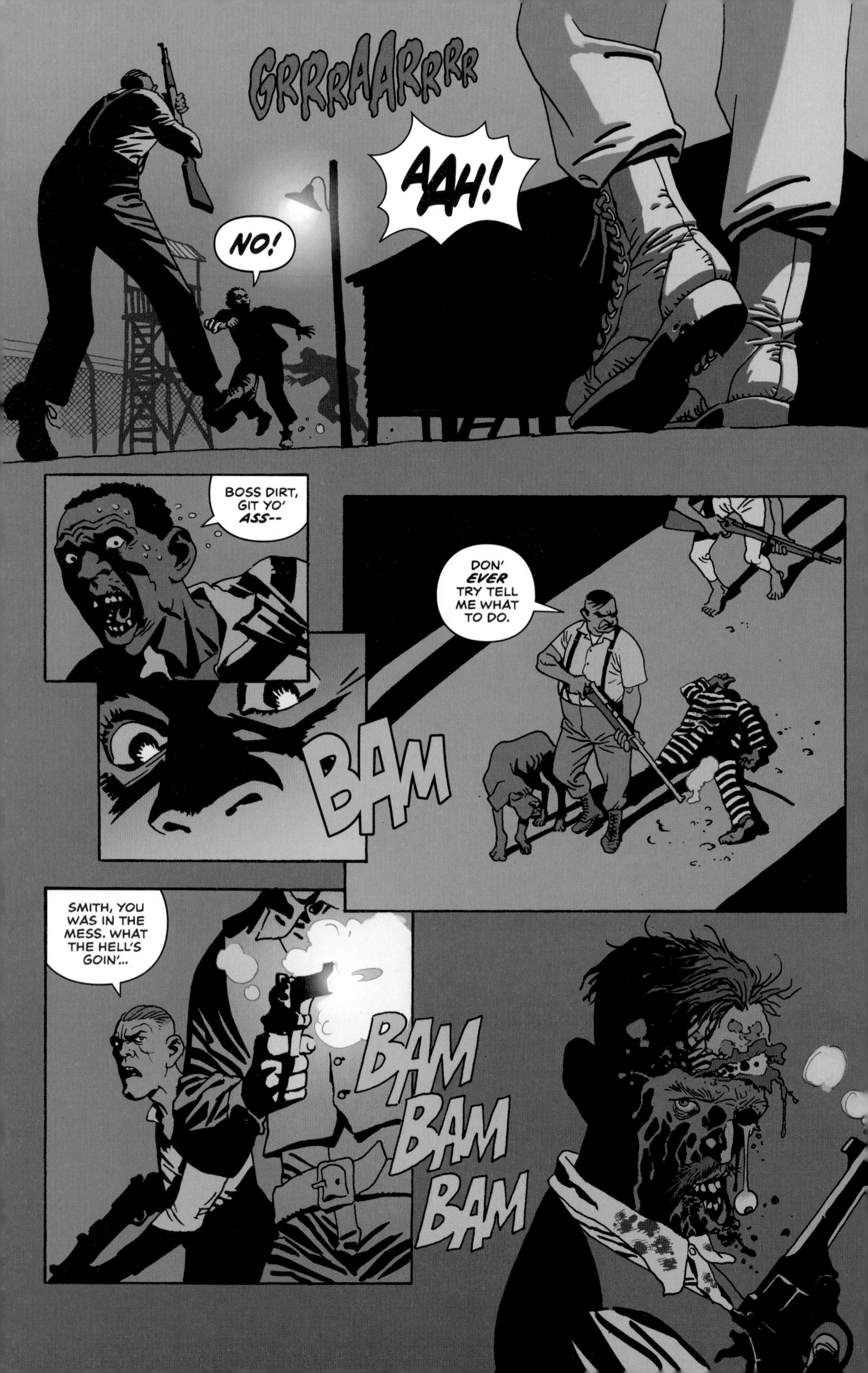
GRRRAARRRR
NO!
AAH!
BOSS DIRT, GIT YO' ASS--
DON' EVER TRY TELL ME WHAT TO DO.
BAM
SMITH, YOU WAS IN THE MESS. WHAT THE HELL'S GOIN'...
BAM
BAM
BAM

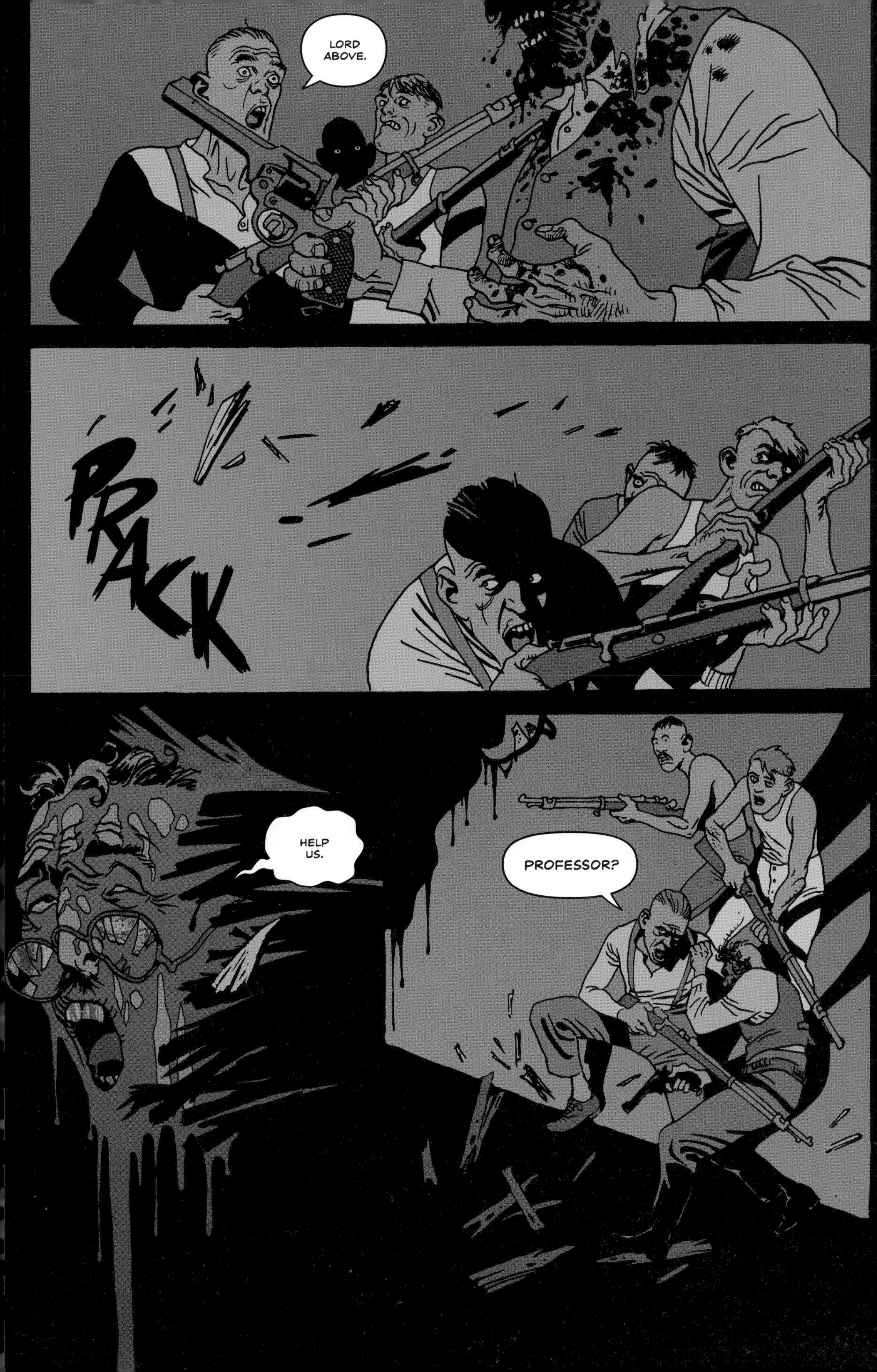
LORD ABOVE.
PRACK
HELP US.
PROFESSOR?

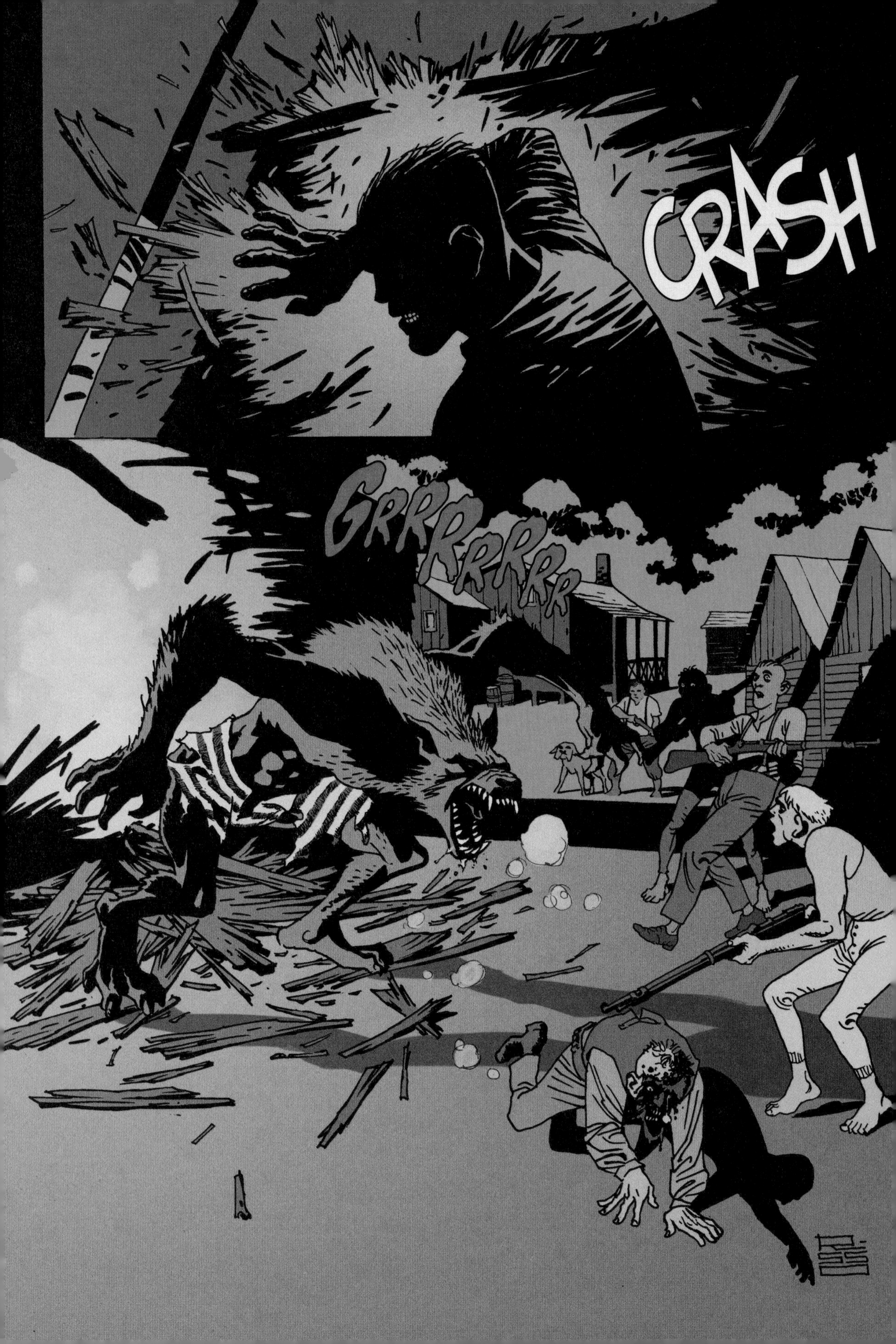
CRASH
GRRRRRRRRR

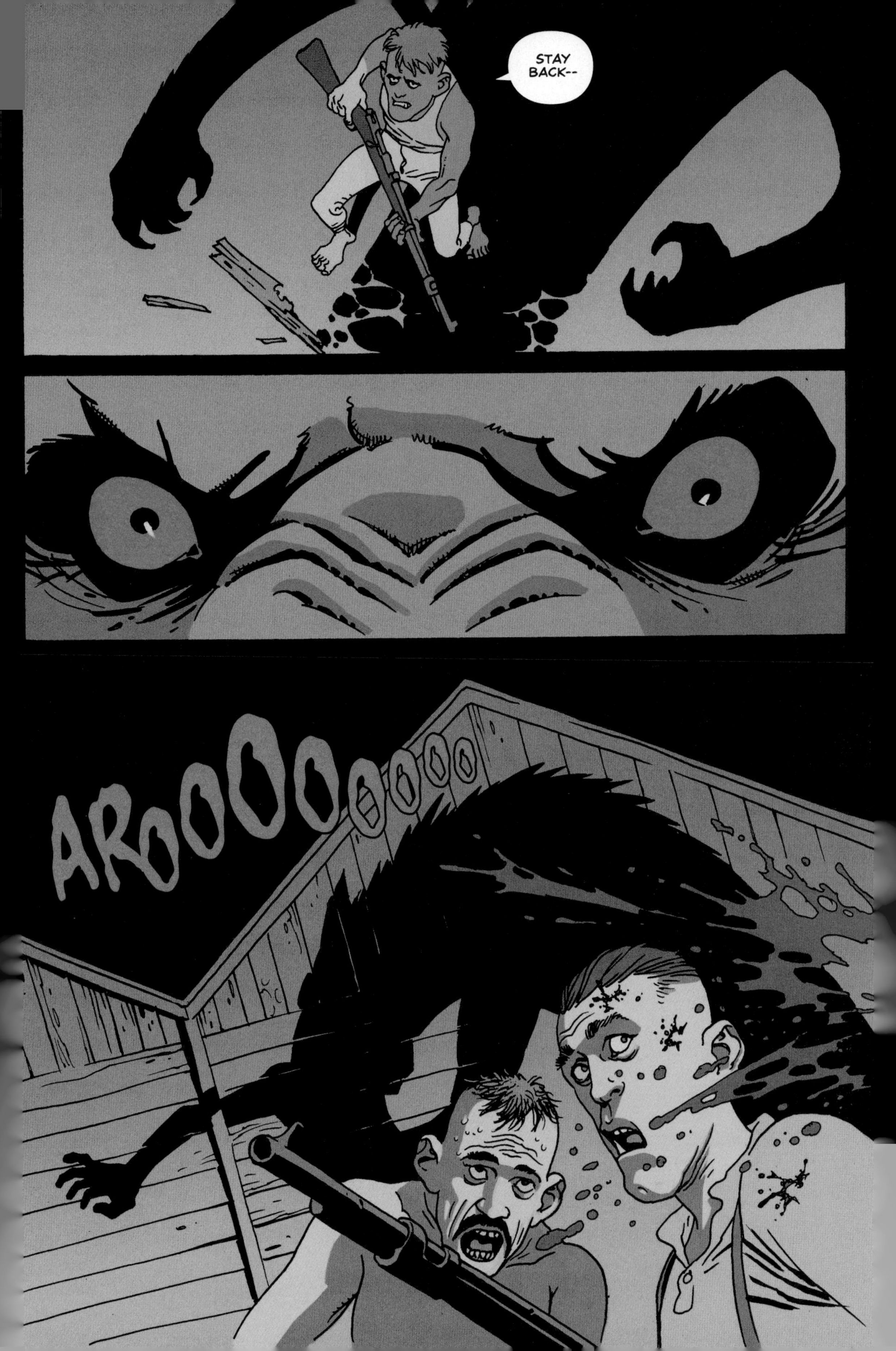
STAY BACK--
AROOOOOOOOO

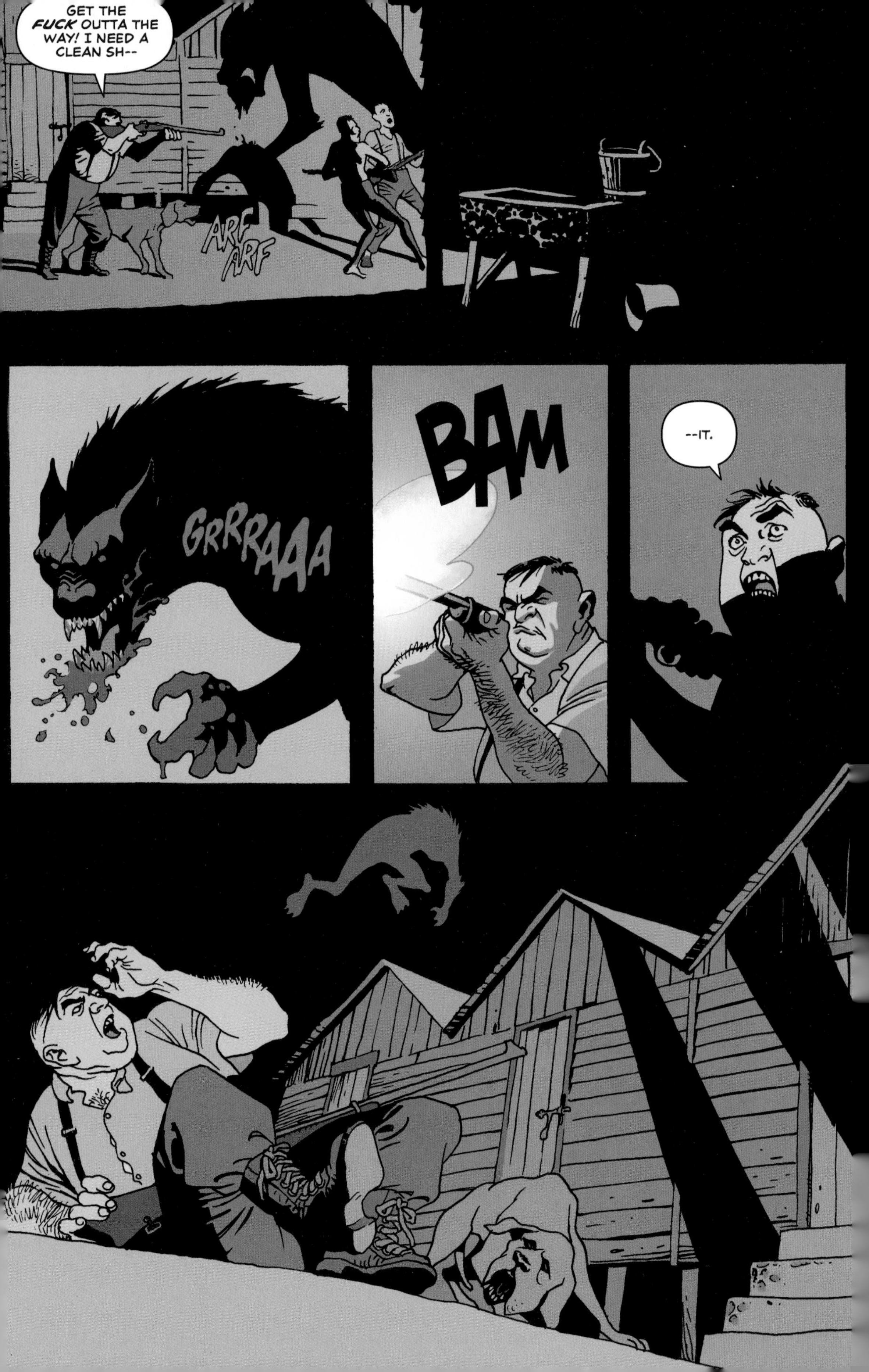
GET THE FUCK OUTTA THE WAY! I NEED A CLEAN SH--
ARF ARF
GRRRAAAA
BAM
--IT.

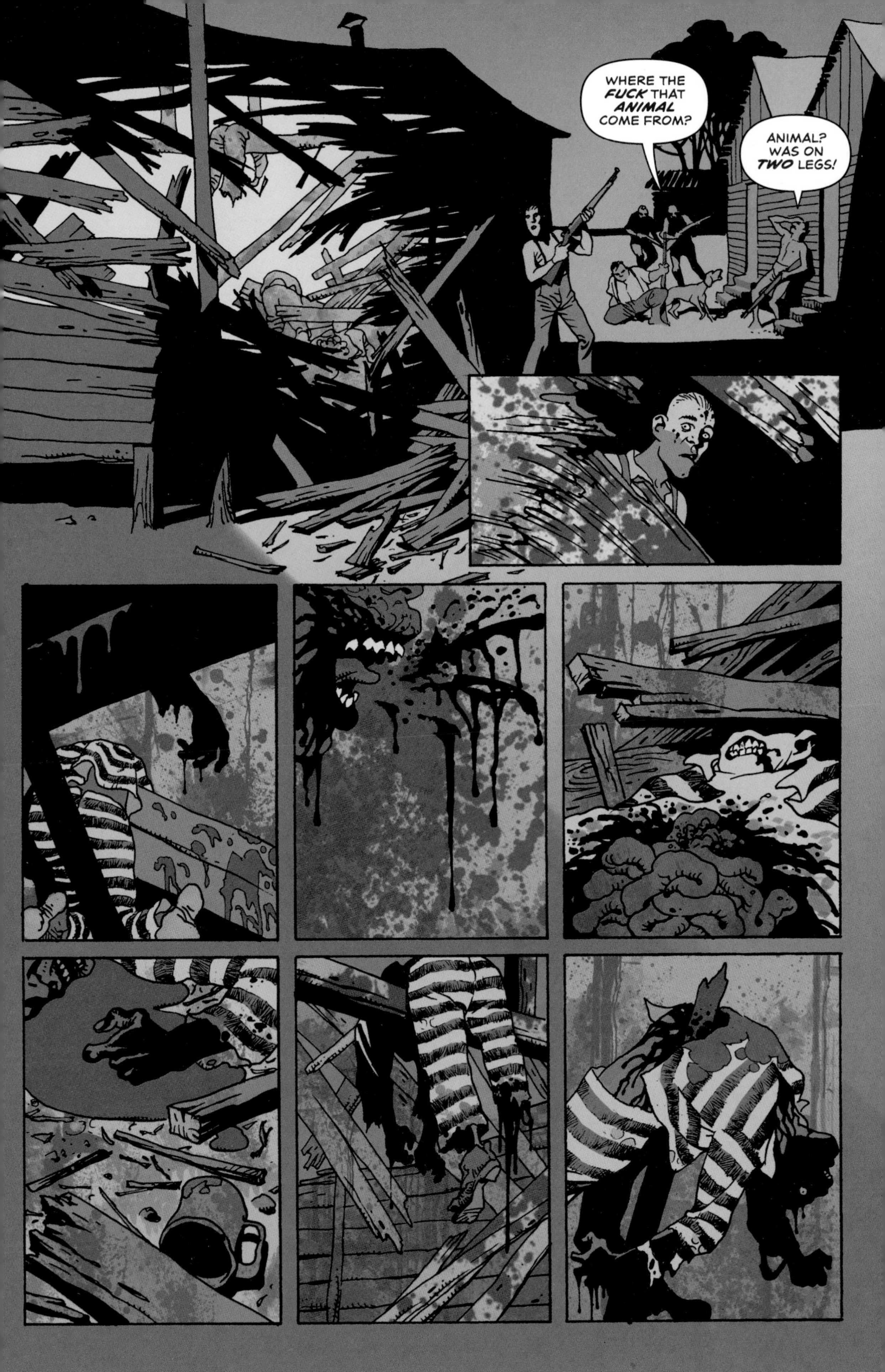
WHERE THE FUCK THAT ANIMAL COME FROM?
ANIMAL? WAS ON TWO LEGS!

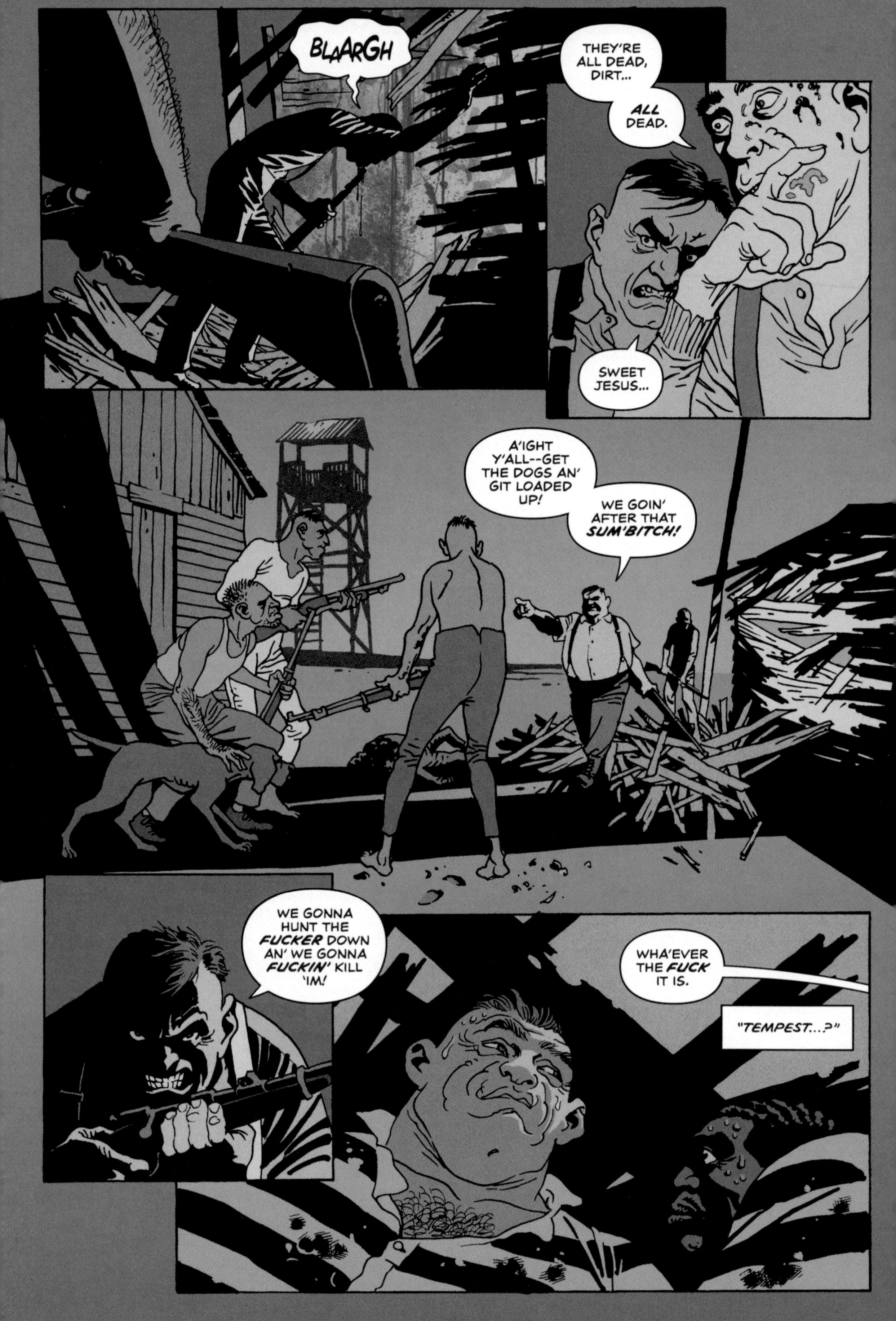
BLAARGH
THEY'RE ALL DEAD, DIRT...
ALL DEAD.
SWEET JESUS...
A'IGHT Y'ALL--GET THE DOGS AN' GIT LOADED UP!
WE GOIN' AFTER THAT SUM'BITCH!
WE GONNA HUNT THE FUCKER DOWN AN' WE GONNA FUCKIN' KILL 'IM!
WHA'EVER THE FUCK IT IS.
"TEMPEST...?"

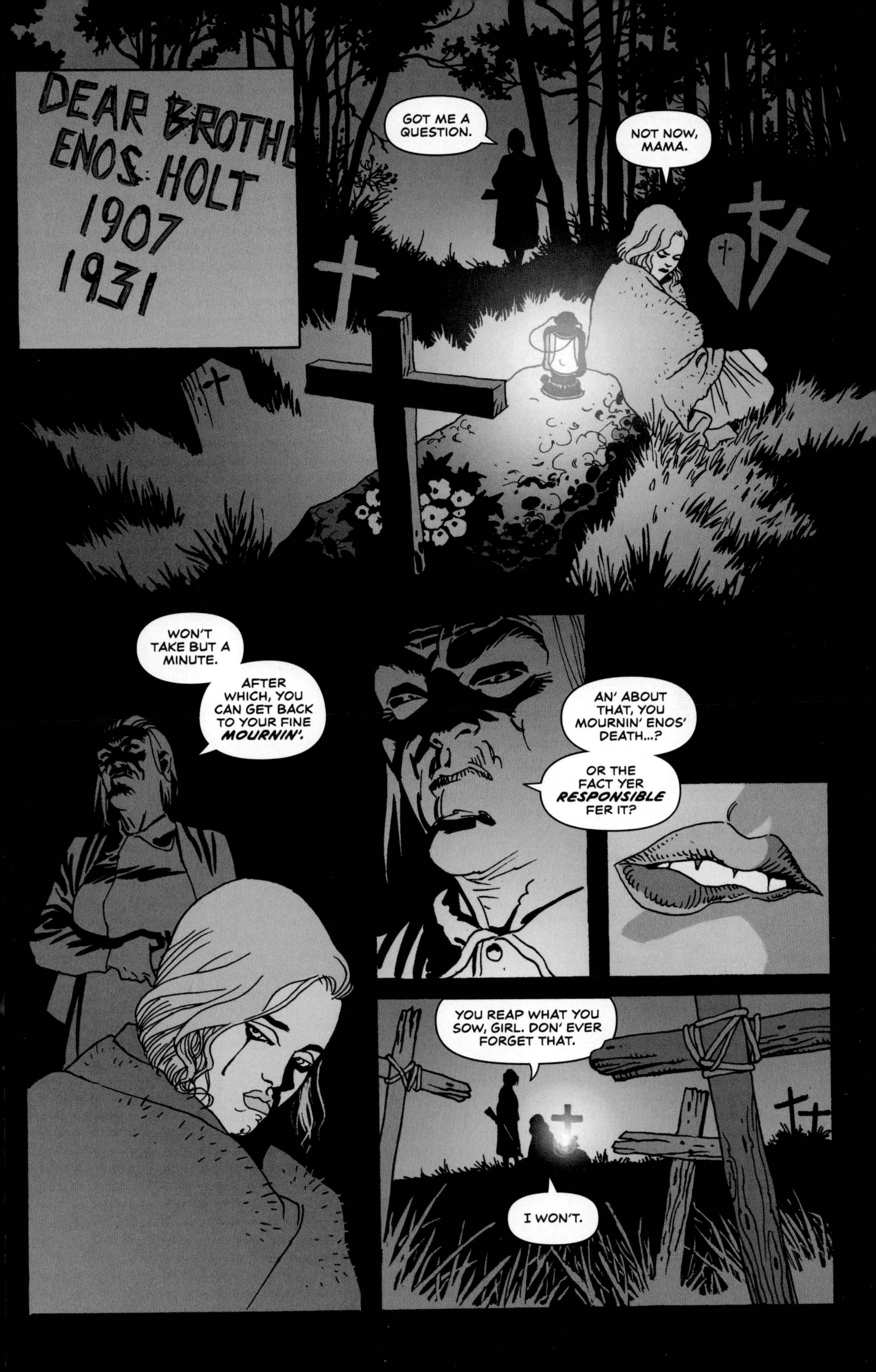
DEAR BROTHE
ENOS HOLT
1907
1931
GOT ME A QUESTION.
NOT NOW, MAMA.
WON'T TAKE BUT A MINUTE.
AFTER WHICH, YOU CAN GET BACK TO YOUR FINE MOURNIN'.
AN' ABOUT THAT, YOU MOURNIN' ENOS' DEATH...?
OR THE FACT YER RESPONSIBLE FER IT?
YOU REAP WHAT YOU SOW, GIRL. DON' EVER FORGET THAT.
I WON'T.

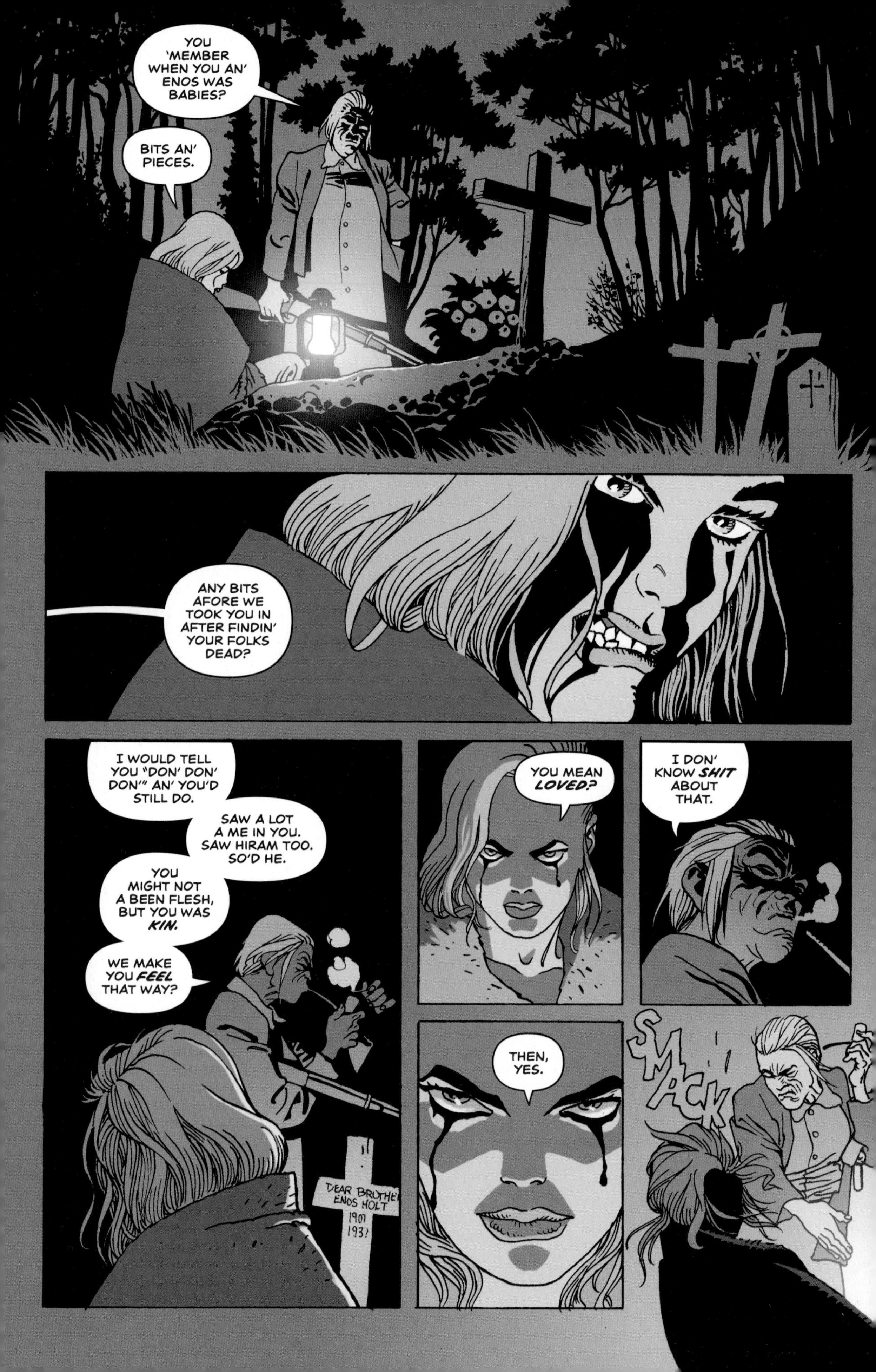
YOU 'MEMBER WHEN YOU AN' ENOS WAS BABIES?
BITS AN' PIECES.
ANY BITS AFORE WE TOOK YOU IN AFTER FINDIN' YOUR FOLKS DEAD?
I WOULD TELL YOU "DON' DON' DON'" AN' YOU'D STILL DO.
SAW A LOT A ME IN YOU. SAW HIRAM TOO. SO'D HE.
YOU MIGHT NOT A BEEN FLESH, BUT YOU WAS KIN.
WE MAKE YOU FEEL THAT WAY?
DEAR BROTHE ENOS HOLT 1907 1931
YOU MEAN LOVED?
I DON' KNOW SHIT ABOUT THAT.
THEN, YES.
SMACK

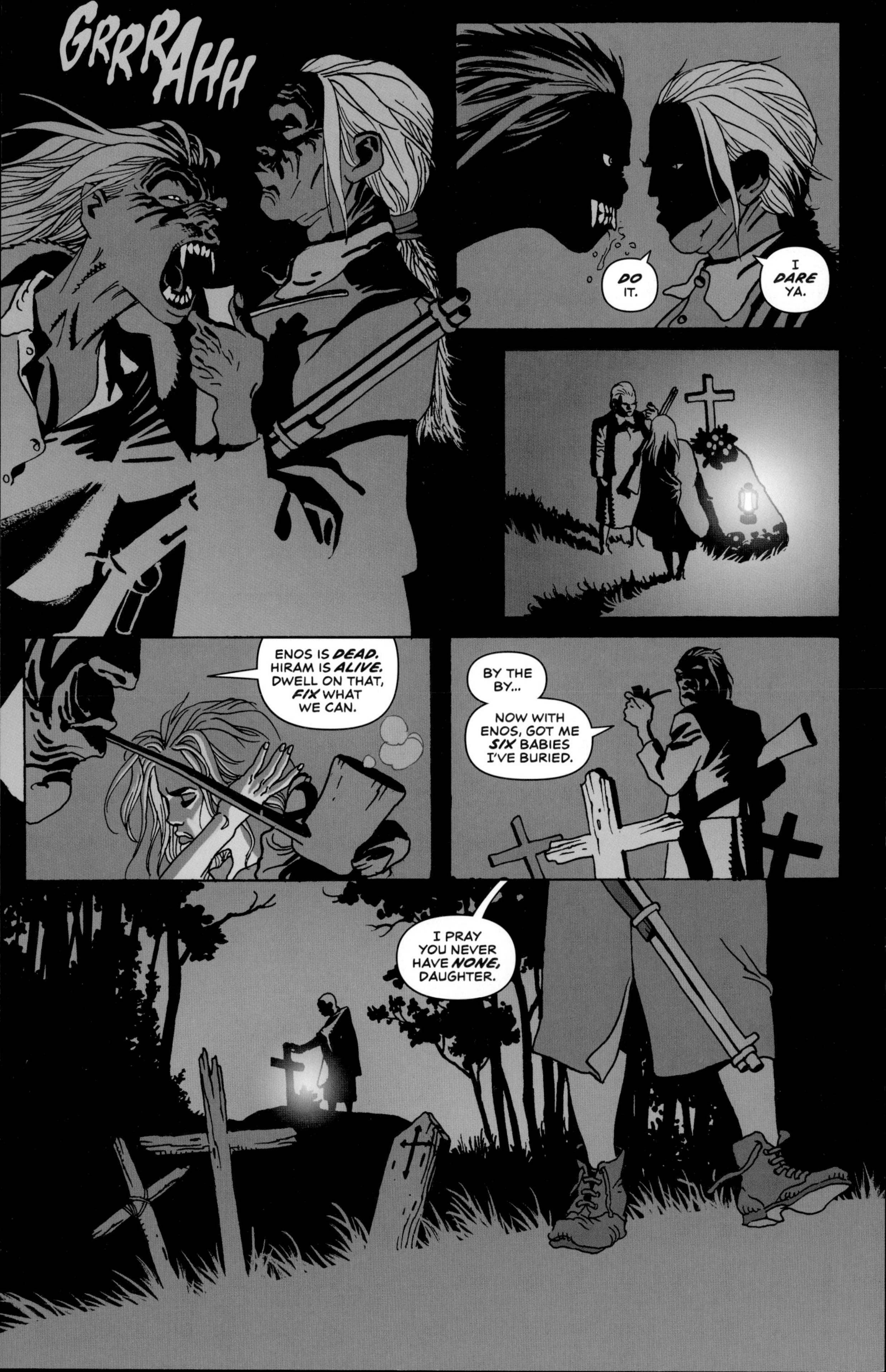
GRRRAHH
DO IT.
I DARE YA.
ENOS IS DEAD. HIRAM IS ALIVE. DWELL ON THAT, FIX WHAT WE CAN.
BY THE BY...
NOW WITH ENOS, GOT ME SIX BABIES I'VE BURIED.
I PRAY YOU NEVER HAVE NONE, DAUGHTER.

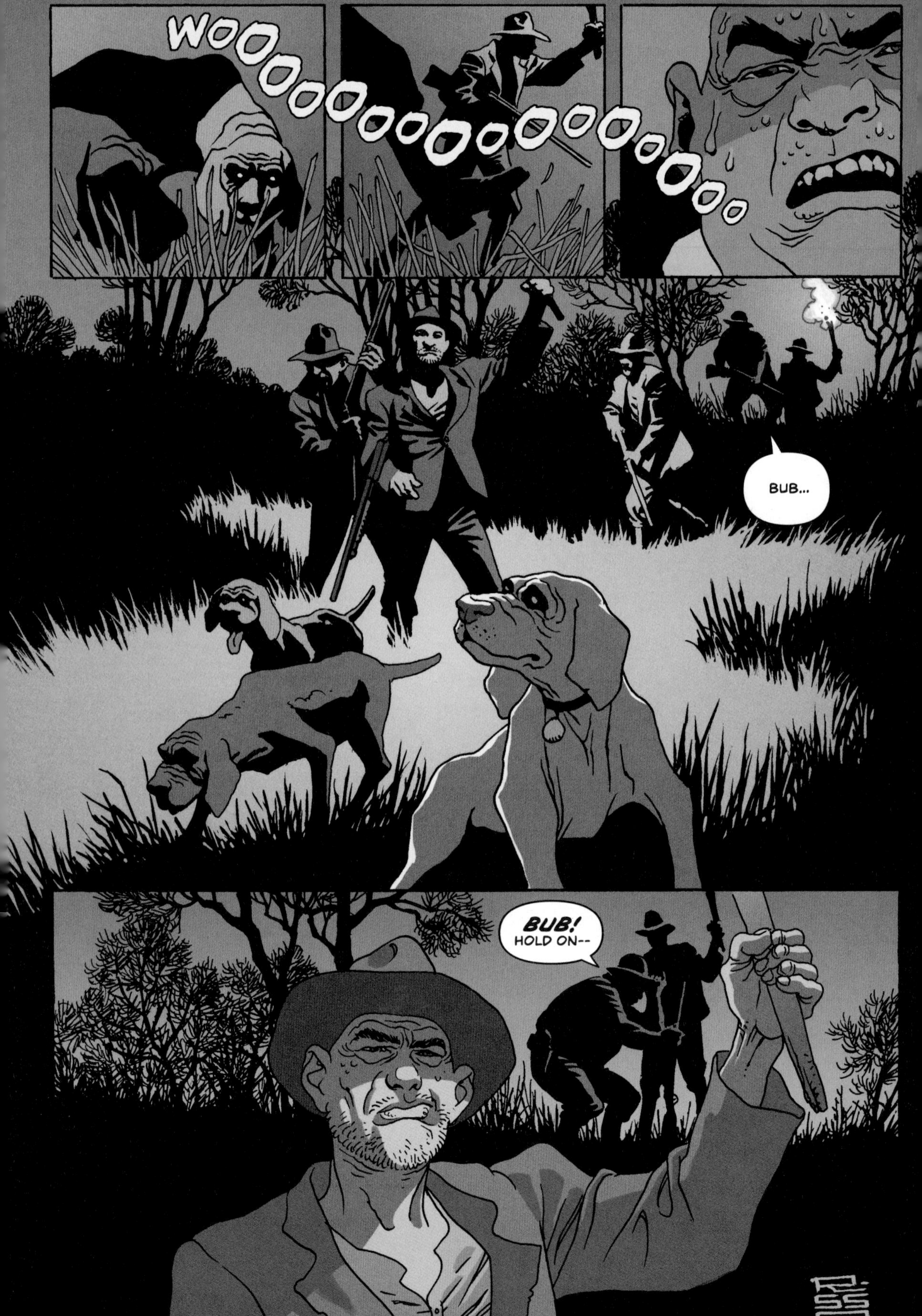
WOOOOOOOOOOOOOOOOOO
BUB...
BUB! HOLD ON--

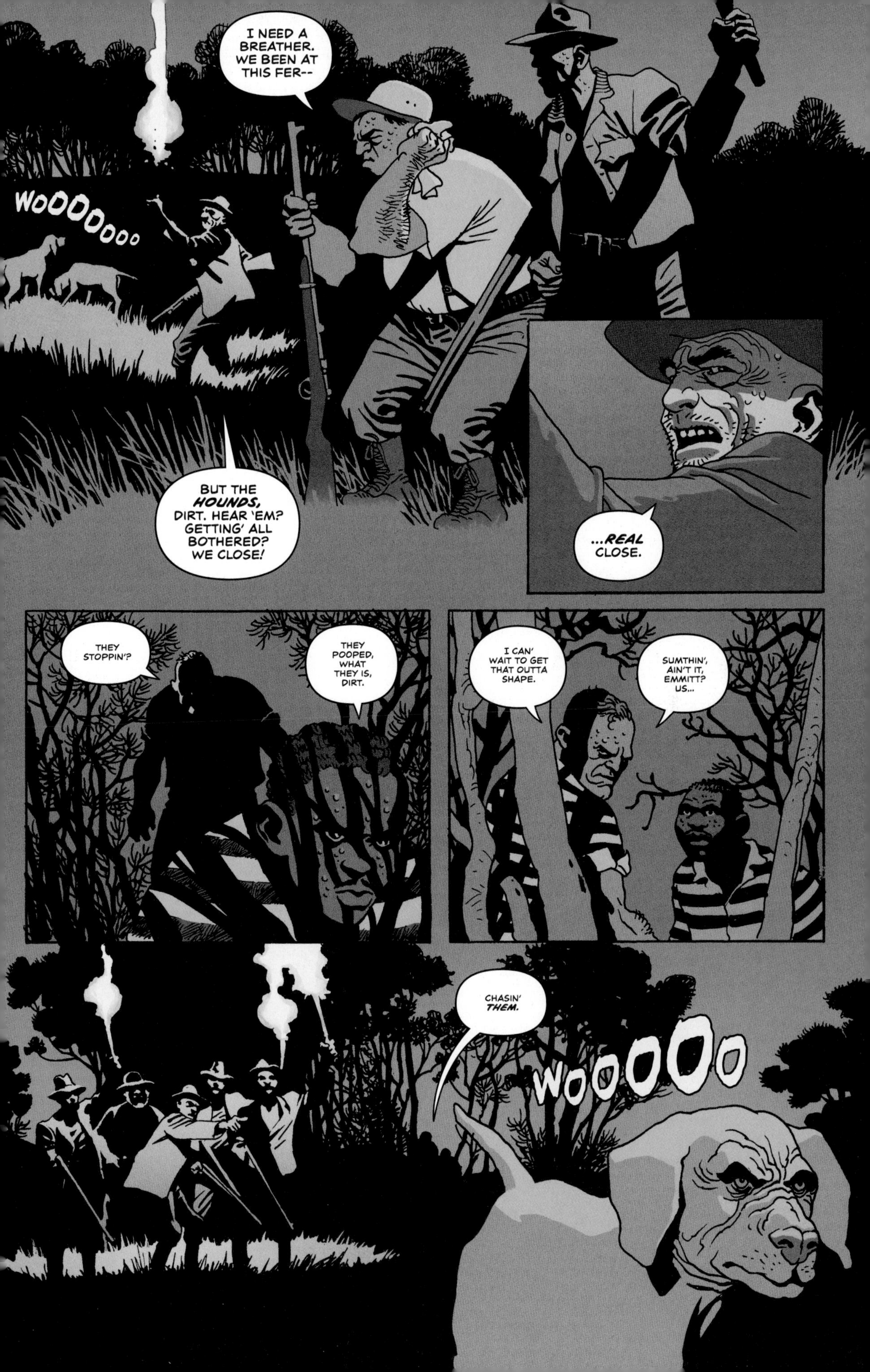
I NEED A BREATHER. WE BEEN AT THIS FER--
WOOOOOooo
BUT THE *HOUNDS,* DIRT. HEAR 'EM? GETTING' ALL BOTHERED? WE CLOSE!
...*REAL* CLOSE.
THEY STOPPIN'?
THEY POOPED, WHAT THEY IS, DIRT.
I CAN' WAIT TO GET THAT OUTTA SHAPE.
SUMTHIN', AIN'T IT, EMMITT? US...
CHASIN' *THEM.*
WOOOOO

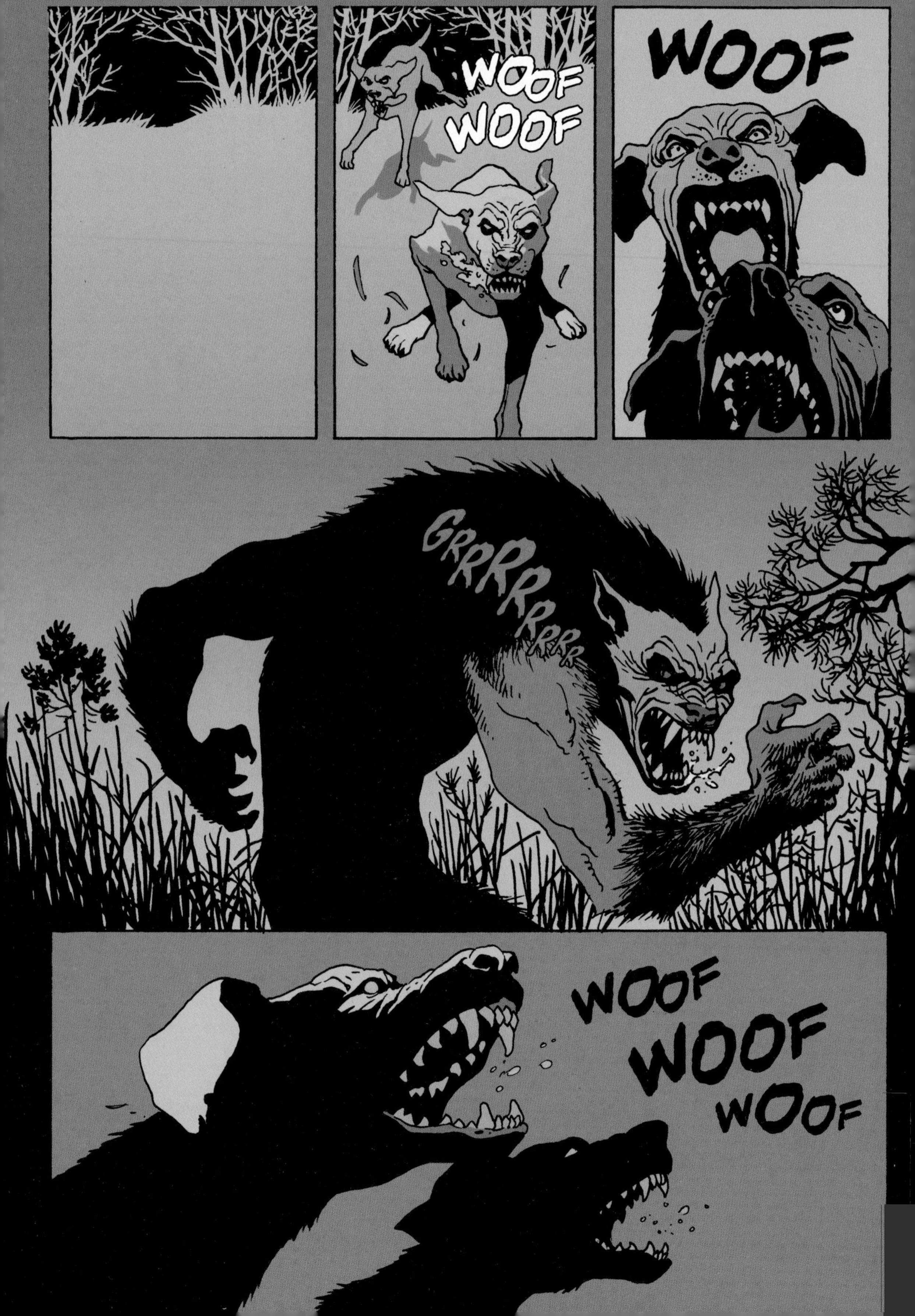
WOOF
WOOF
WOOF
GRRRRRRRR
WOOF
WOOF
WOOF

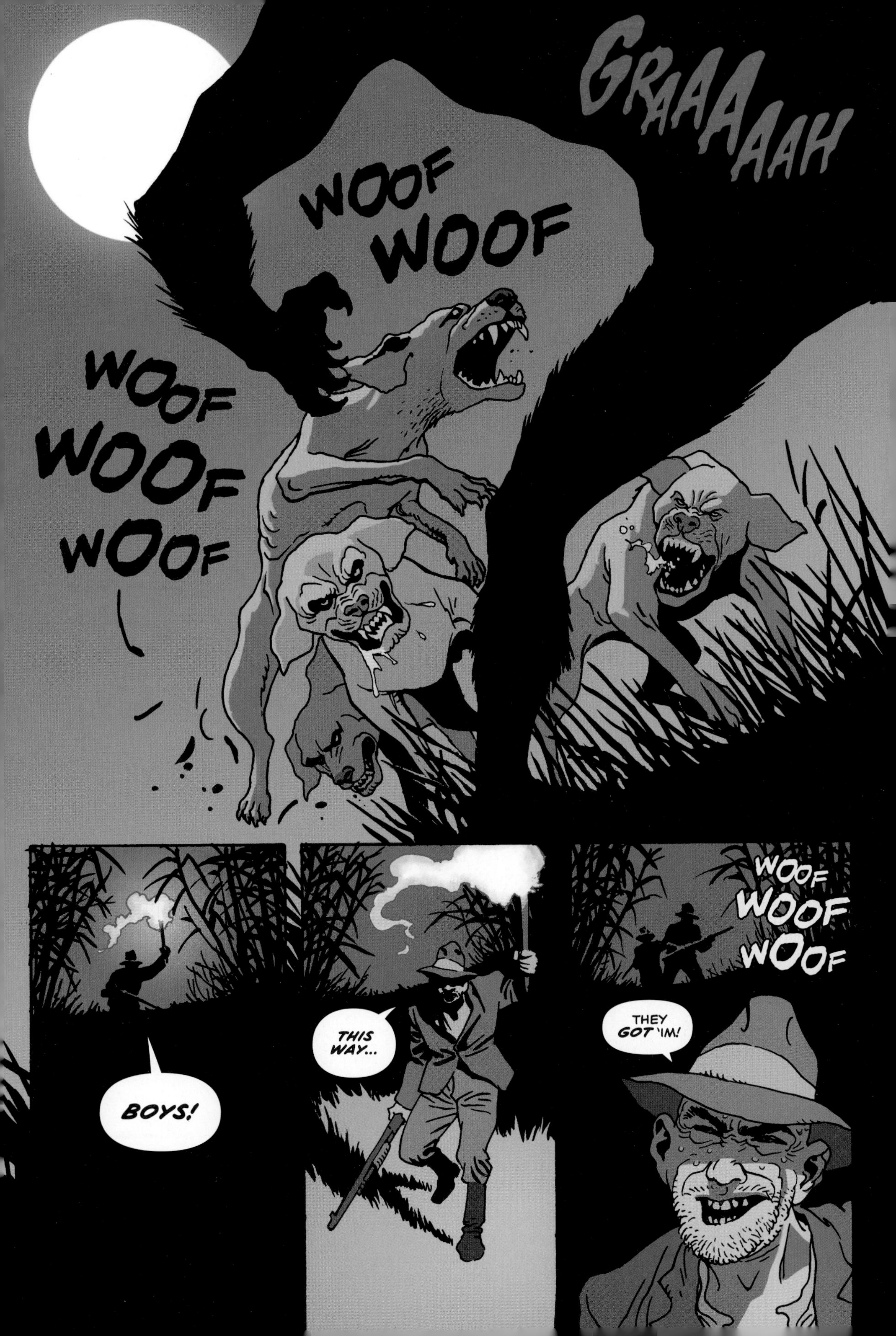

GRAAAAAAH
WOOF WOOF
WOOF WOOF WOOF
WOOF WOOF WOOF
BOYS!
THIS WAY...
THEY GOT 'IM!

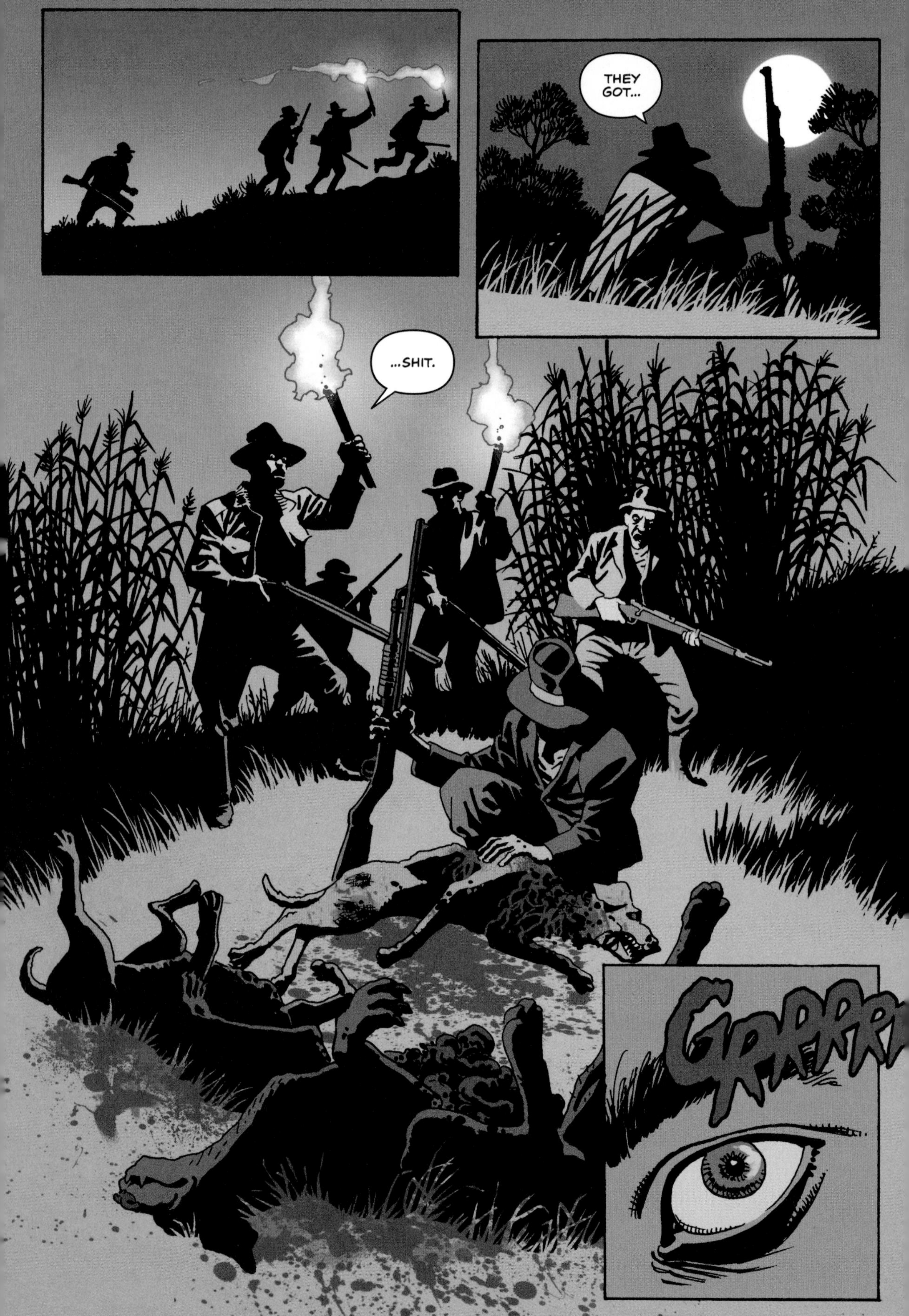
THEY GOT...
...SHIT.
GRRRR

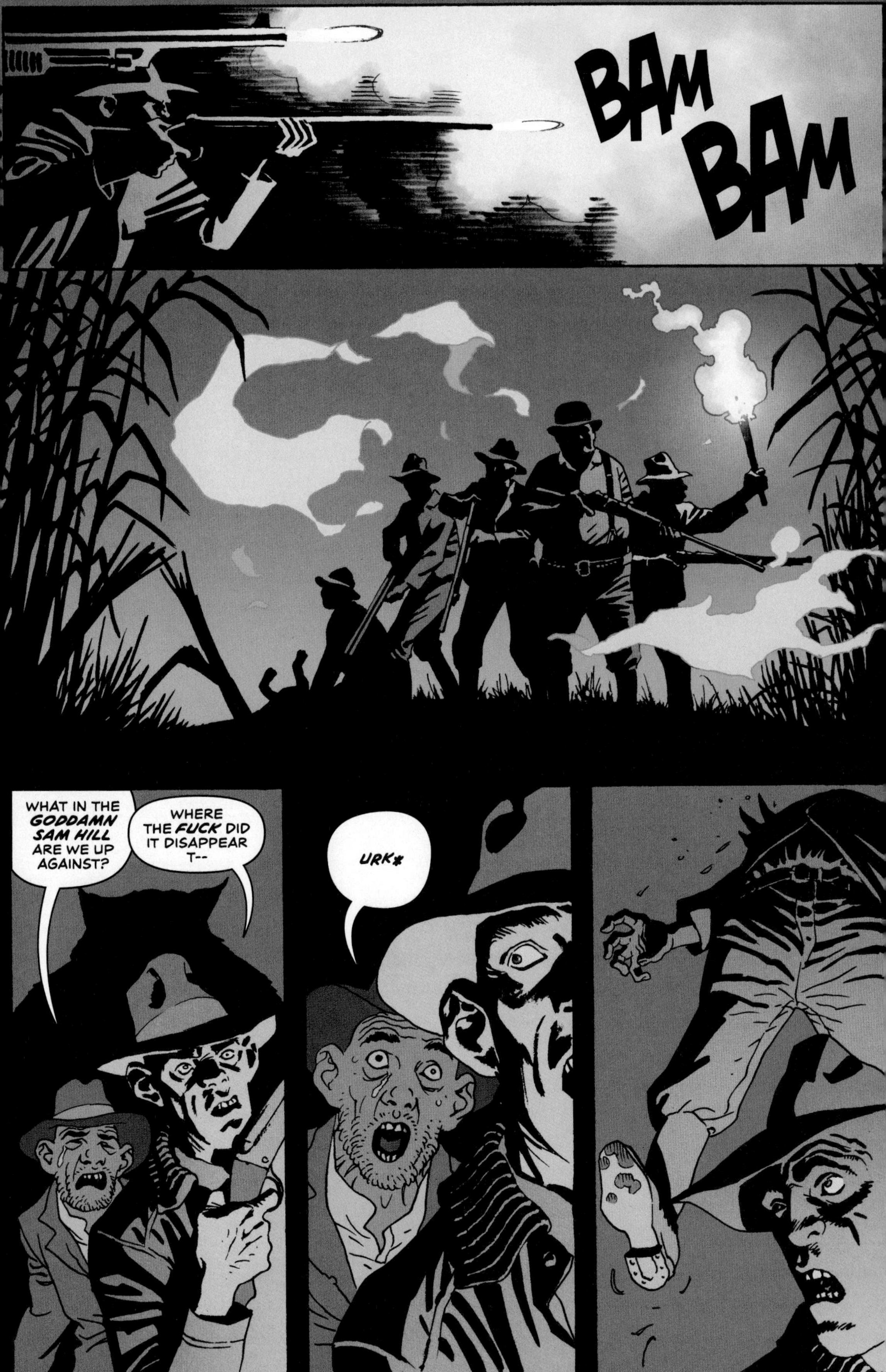
BAM
BAM
WHAT IN THE GODDAMN SAM HILL ARE WE UP AGAINST?
WHERE THE FUCK DID IT DISAPPEAR T--
URK*

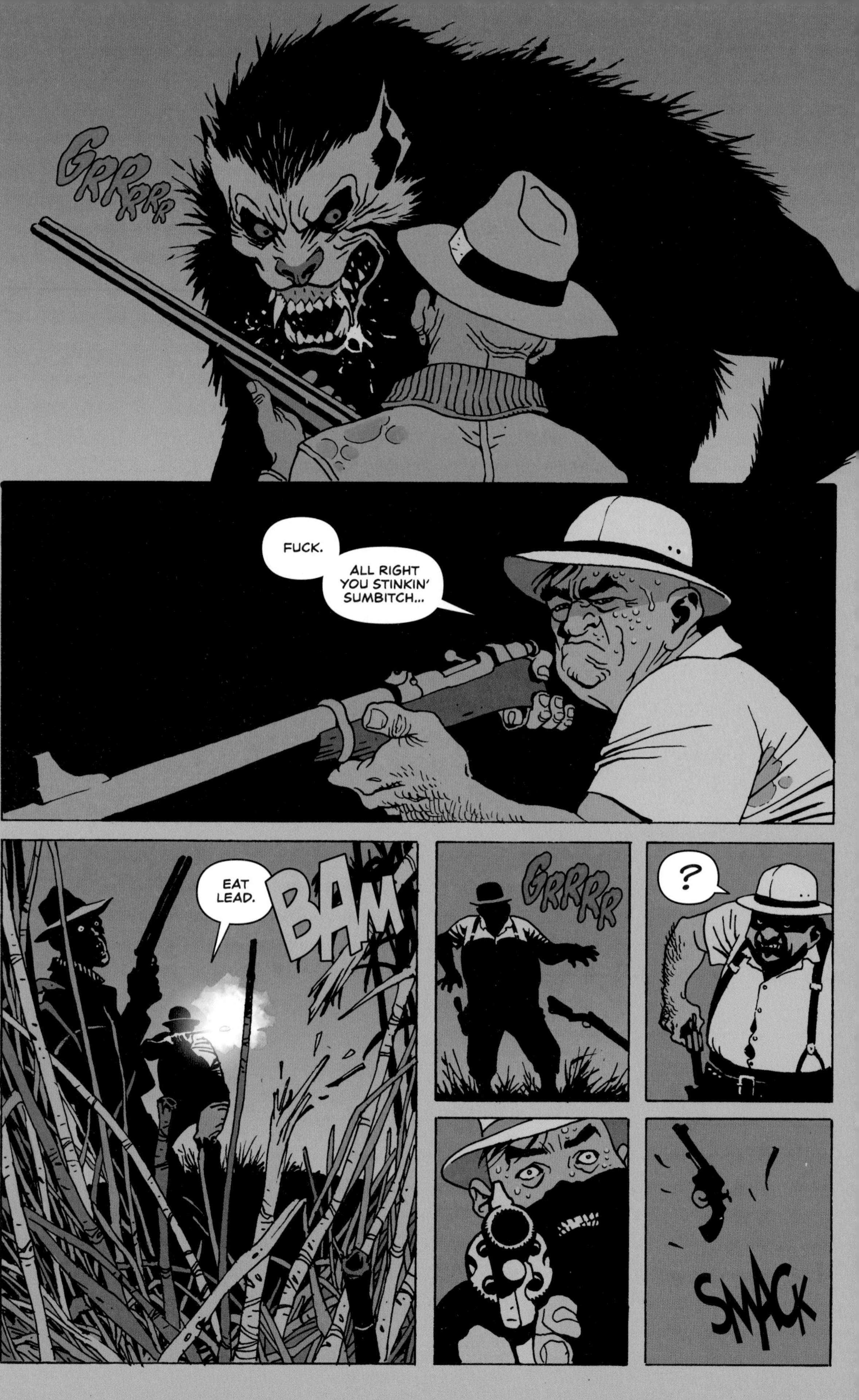
GRRRRRR
FUCK.
ALL RIGHT YOU STINKIN' SUMBITCH...
EAT LEAD.
BAM
GRRRR
?
SMACK

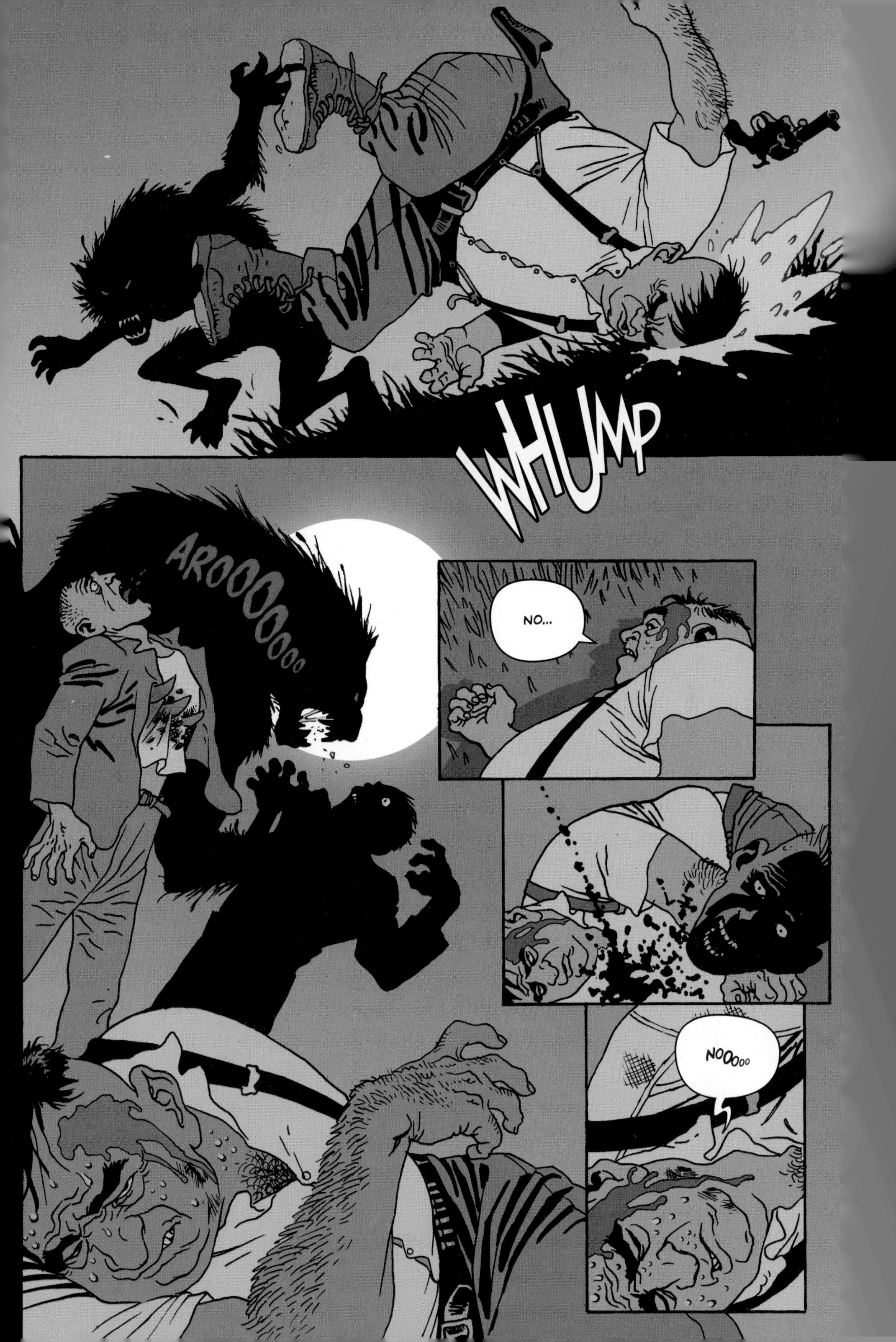
WHUMP
AROOOOOooo
NO...
NOOooo

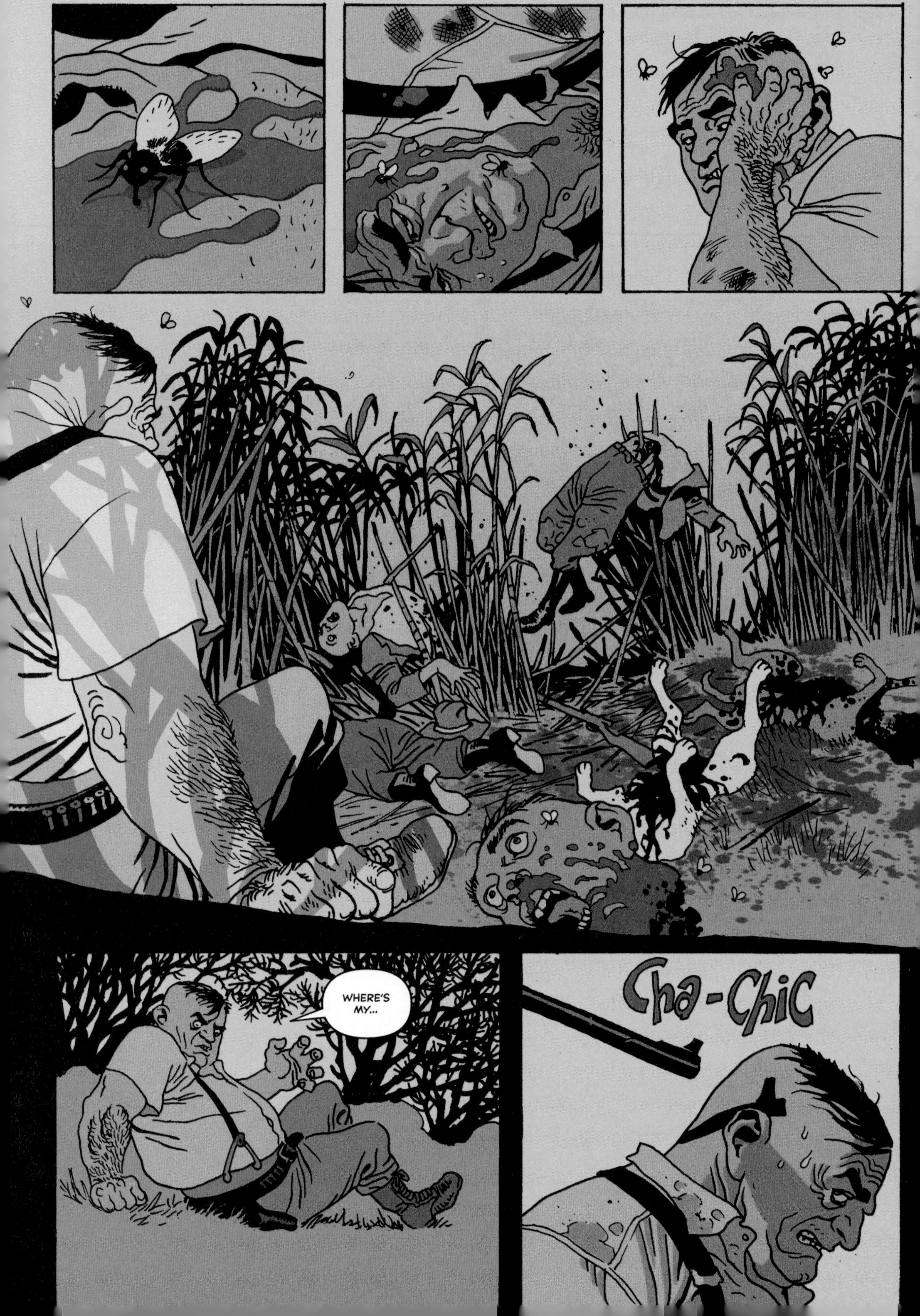
WHERE'S MY...
Cha-Chic

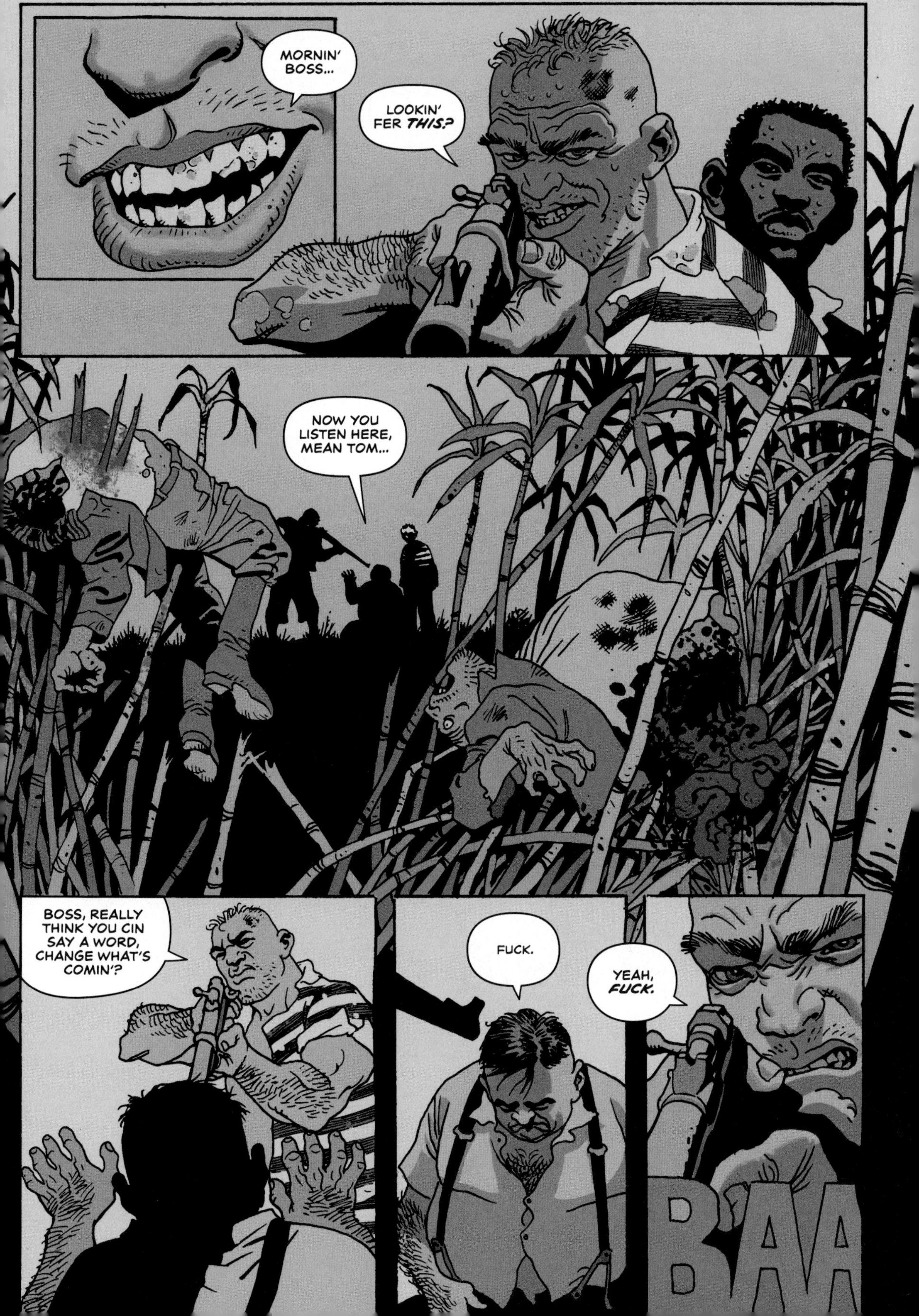
MORNIN' BOSS...
LOOKIN' FER *THIS?*
NOW YOU LISTEN HERE, MEAN TOM...
BOSS, REALLY THINK YOU CIN SAY A WORD, CHANGE WHAT'S COMIN'?
FUCK.
YEAH, *FUCK.*
BAA

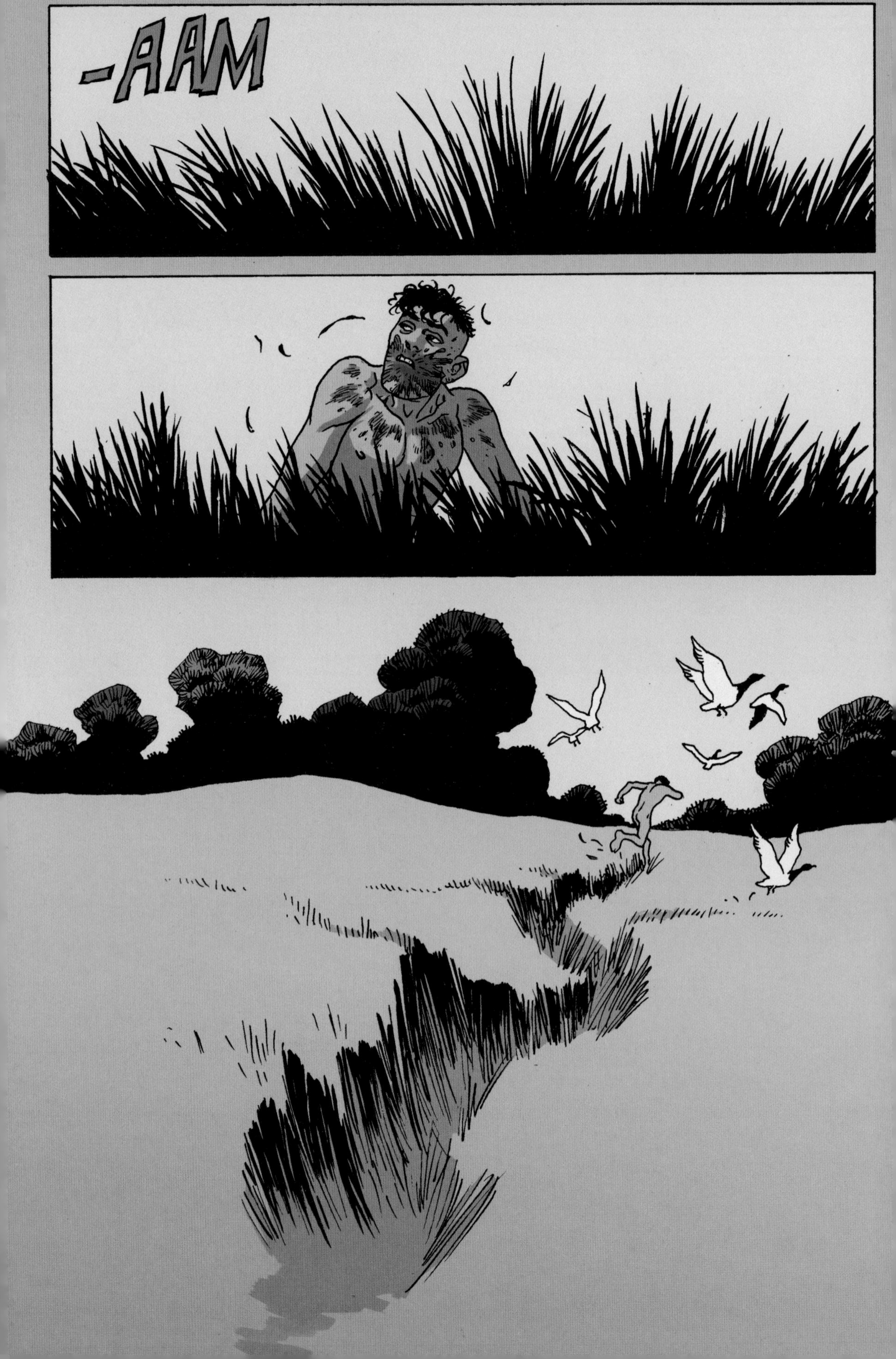
-AAM

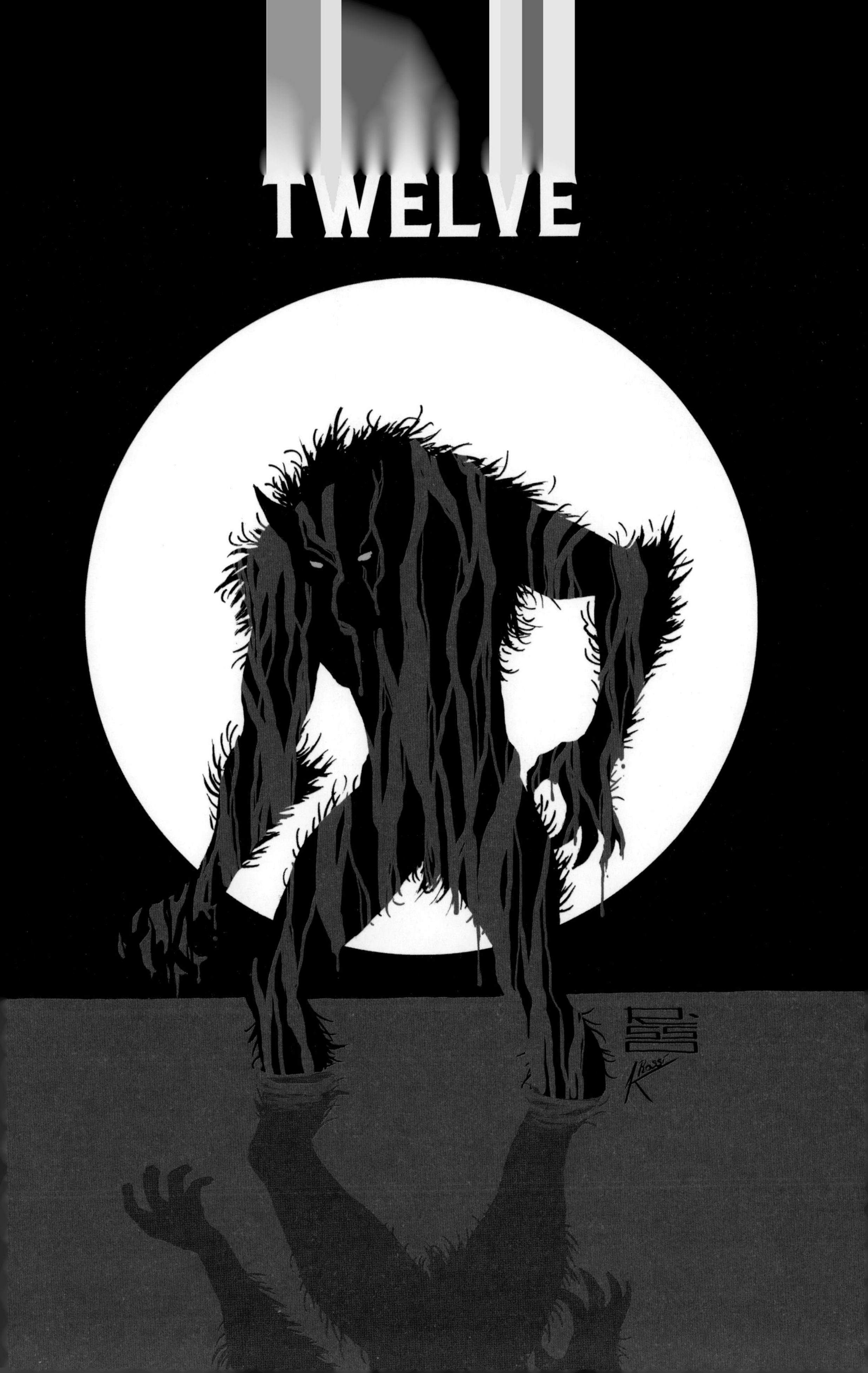
TWELVE

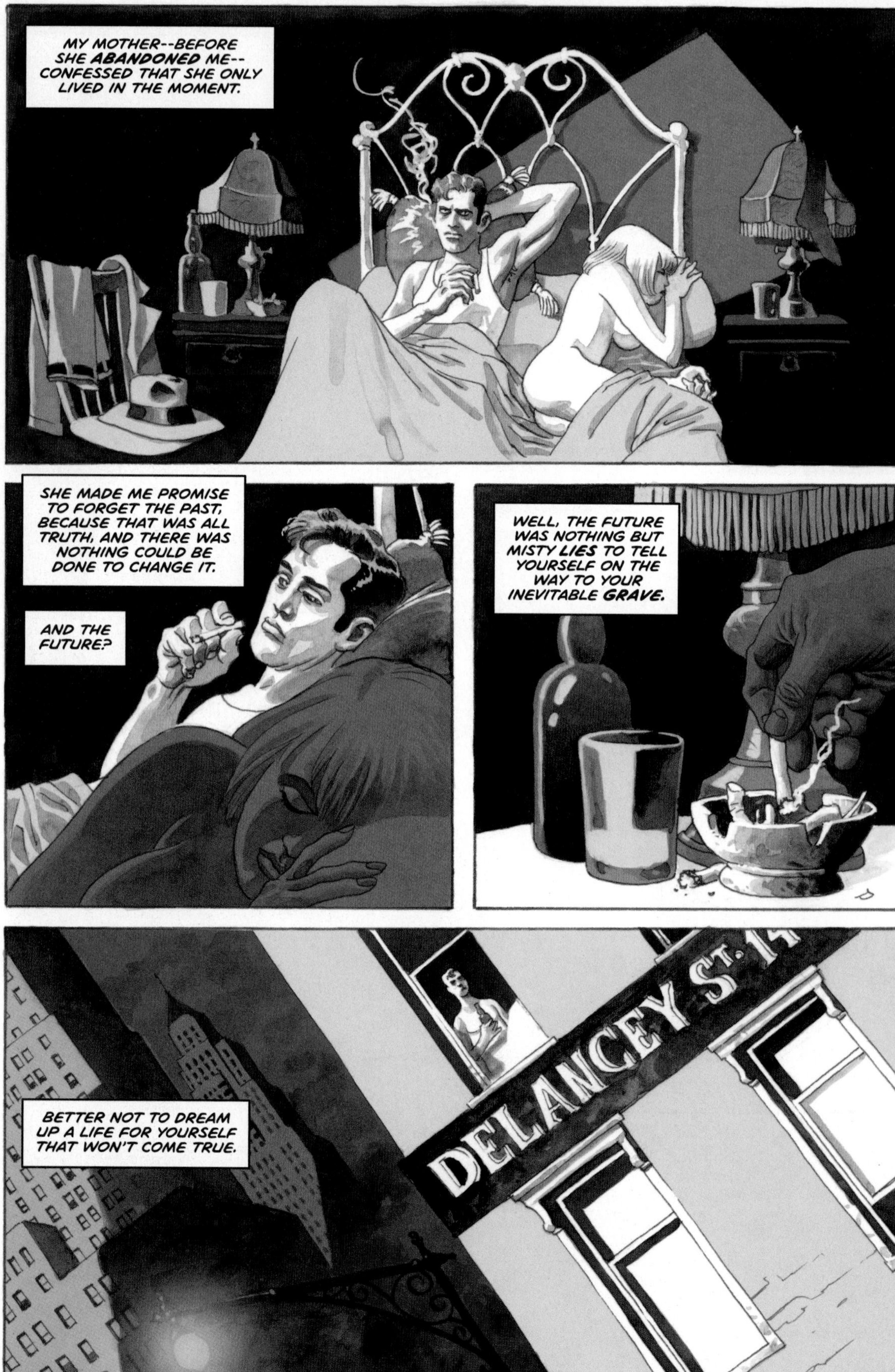
MY MOTHER--BEFORE SHE ABANDONED ME--CONFESSED THAT SHE ONLY LIVED IN THE MOMENT.
SHE MADE ME PROMISE TO FORGET THE PAST, BECAUSE THAT WAS ALL TRUTH, AND THERE WAS NOTHING COULD BE DONE TO CHANGE IT.
AND THE FUTURE?
WELL, THE FUTURE WAS NOTHING BUT MISTY LIES TO TELL YOURSELF ON THE WAY TO YOUR INEVITABLE GRAVE.
DELANCEY ST.
BETTER NOT TO DREAM UP A LIFE FOR YOURSELF THAT WON'T COME TRUE.

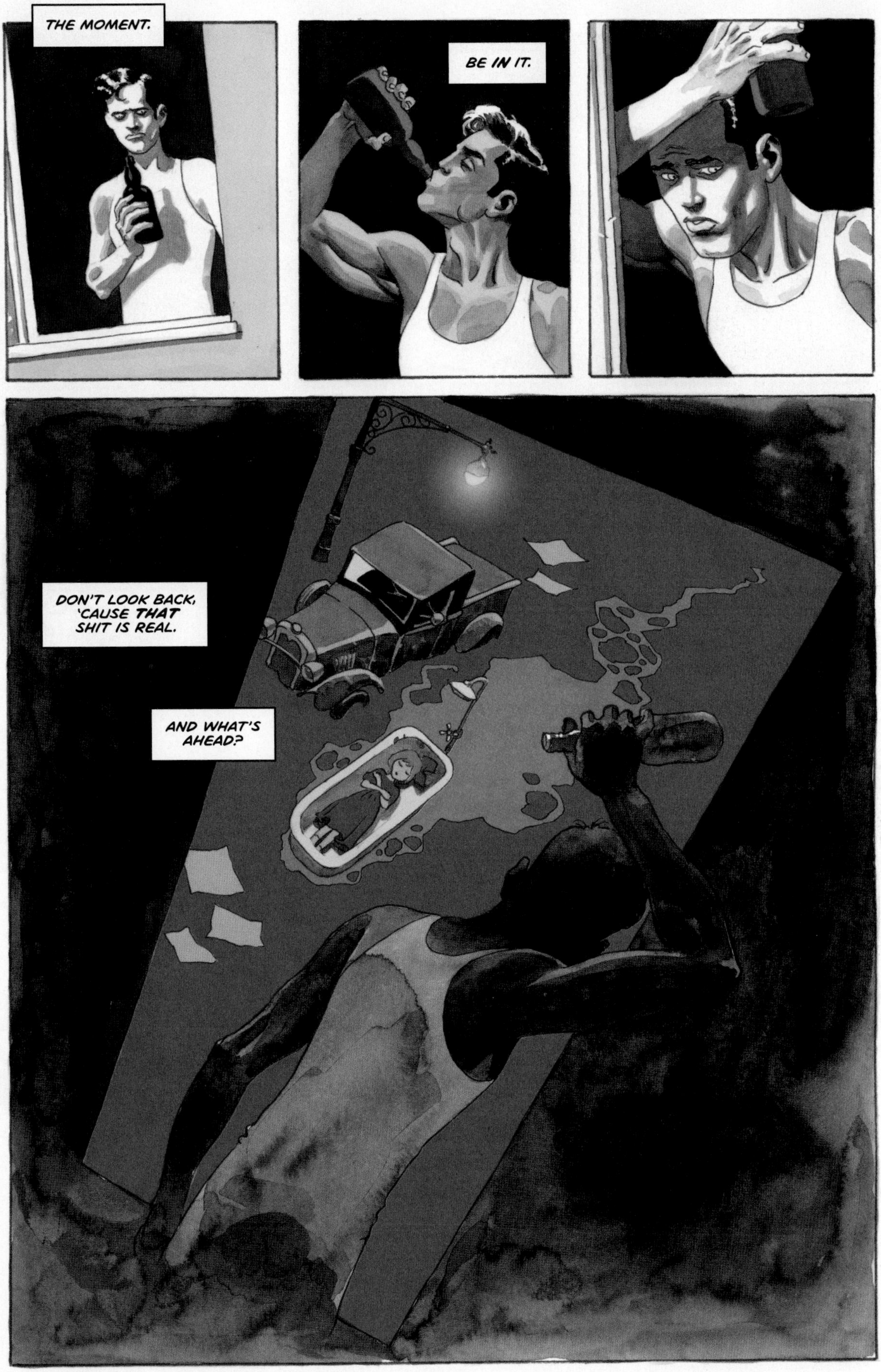
THE MOMENT.
BE IN IT.
DON'T LOOK BACK, 'CAUSE **THAT** SHIT IS REAL.
AND WHAT'S AHEAD?

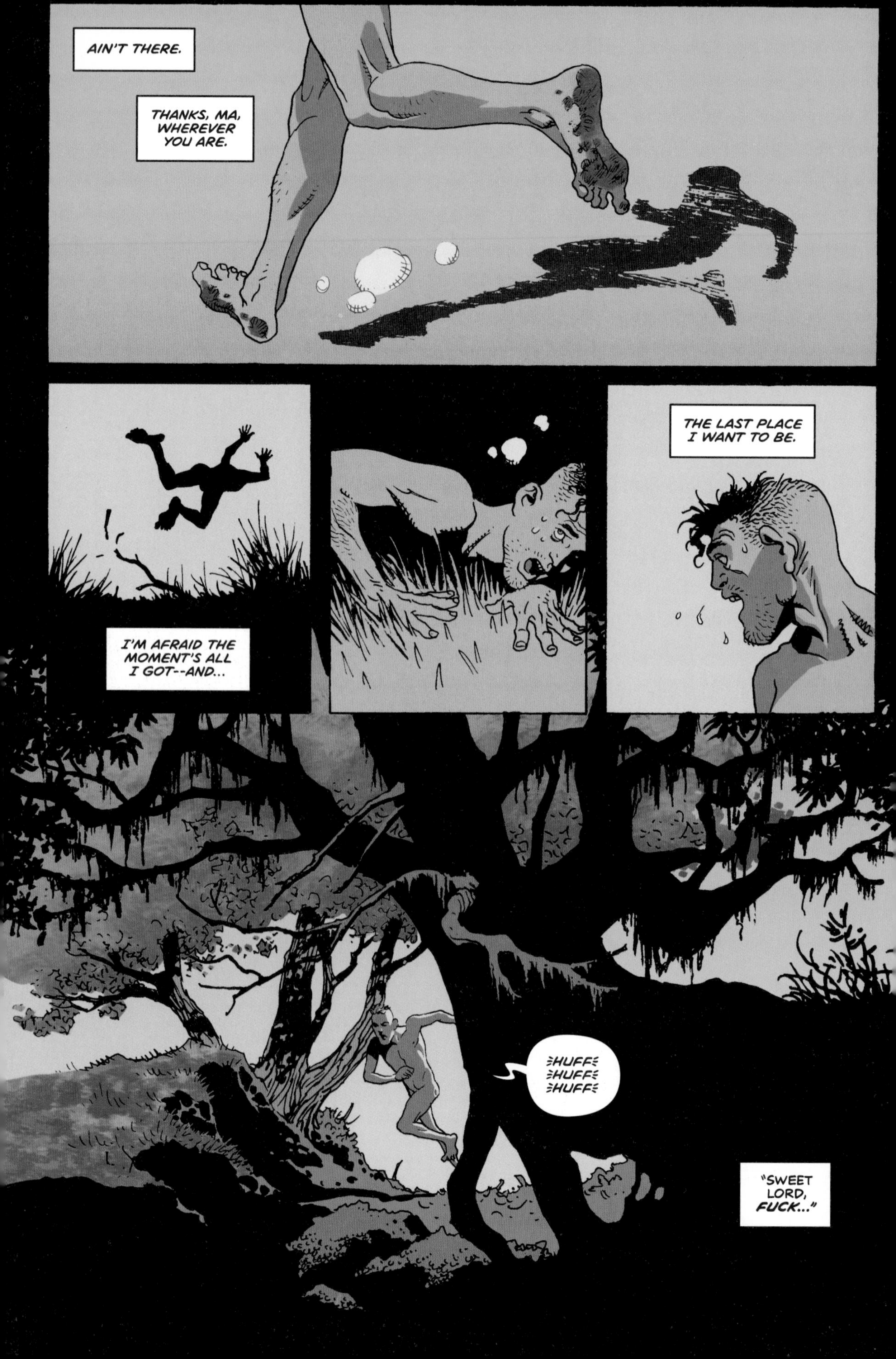
AIN'T THERE.
THANKS, MA, WHEREVER YOU ARE.
I'M AFRAID THE MOMENT'S ALL I GOT--AND...
THE LAST PLACE I WANT TO BE.
HUFF HUFF HUFF
"SWEET LORD, FUCK..."

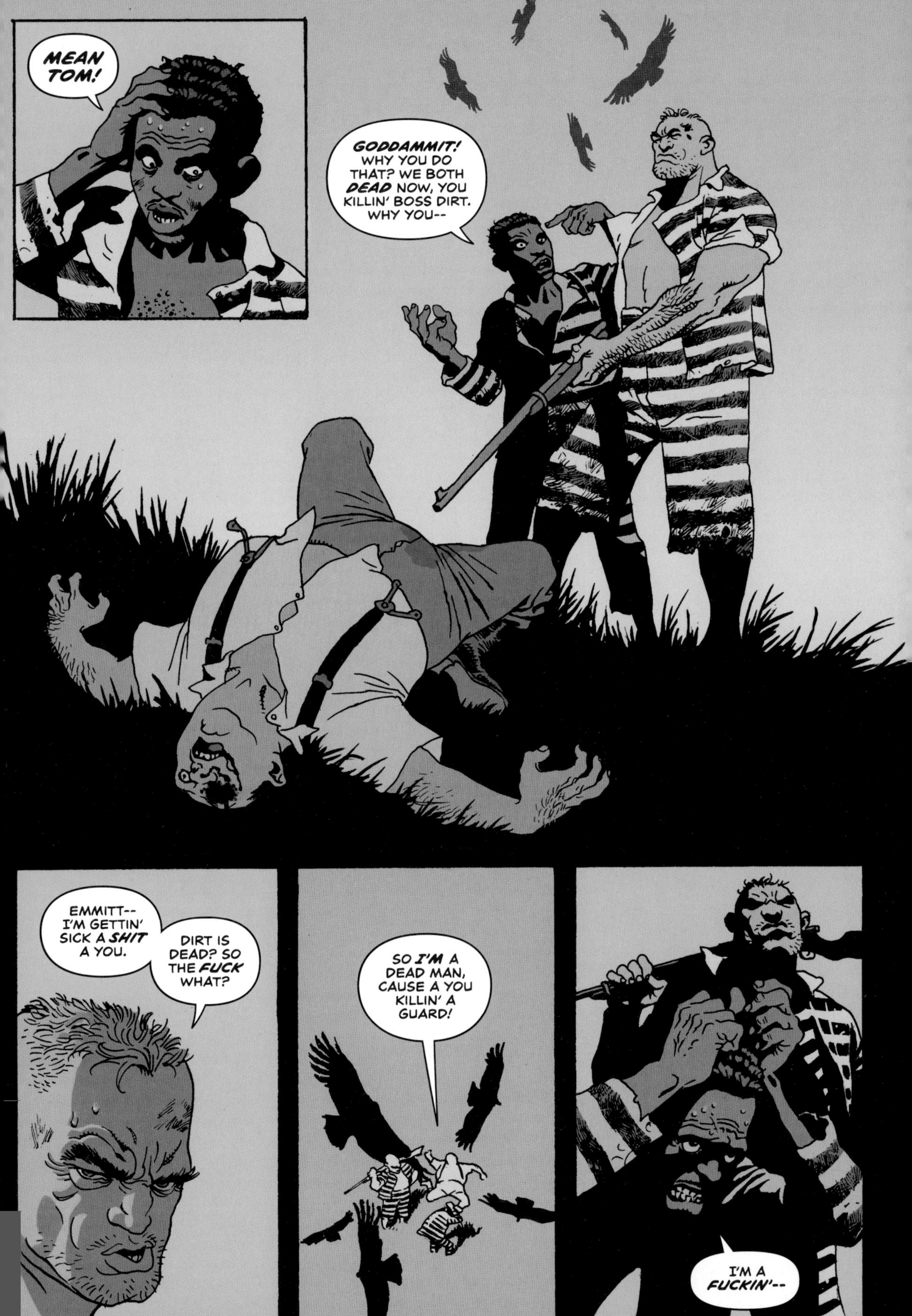
MEAN TOM!
GODDAMMIT! WHY YOU DO THAT? WE BOTH DEAD NOW, YOU KILLIN' BOSS DIRT. WHY YOU--
EMMITT-- I'M GETTIN' SICK A SHIT A YOU.
DIRT IS DEAD? SO THE FUCK WHAT?
SO I'M A DEAD MAN, CAUSE A YOU KILLIN' A GUARD!
I'M A FUCKIN'--

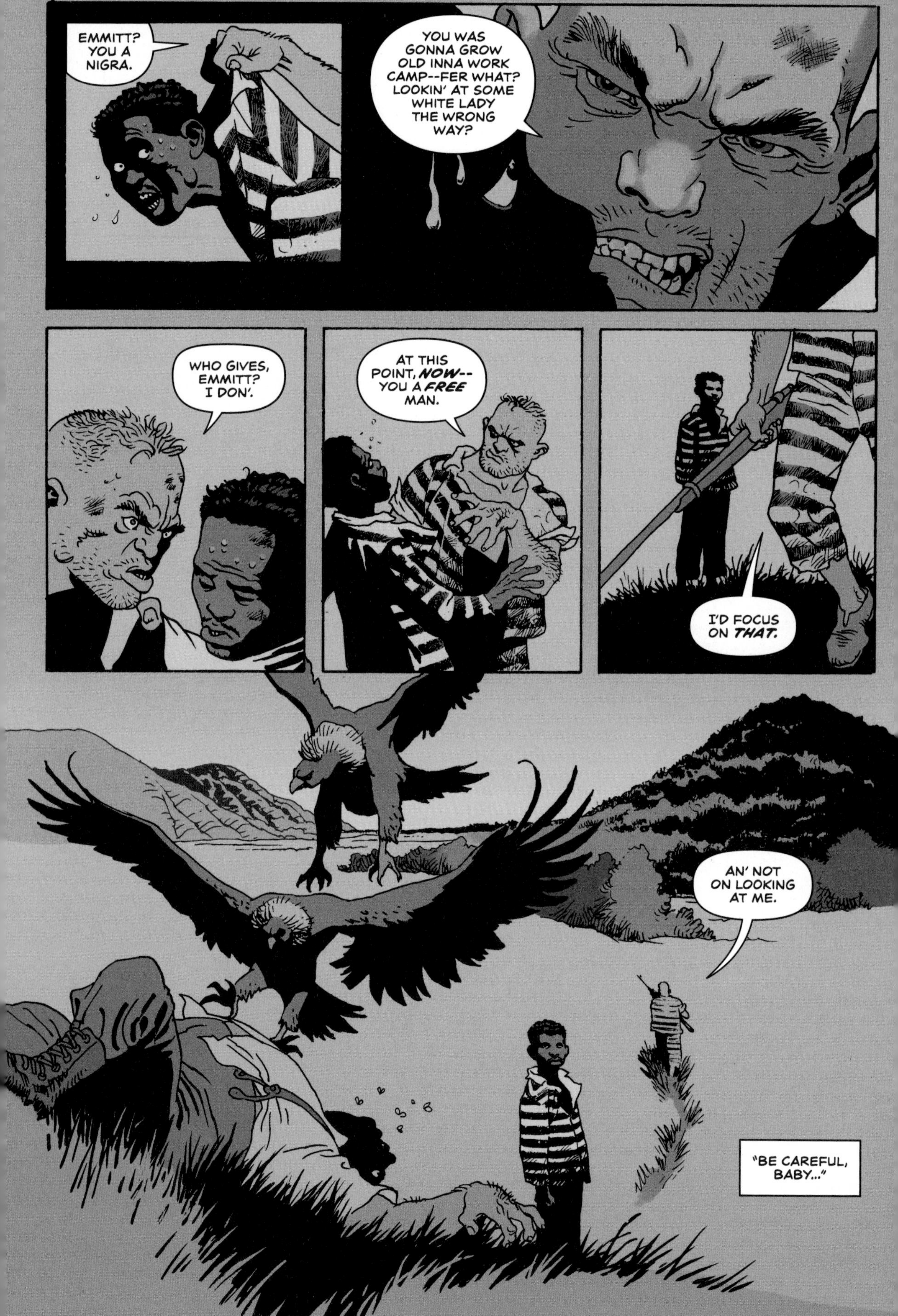
EMMITT? YOU A NIGRA.
YOU WAS GONNA GROW OLD INNA WORK CAMP--FER WHAT? LOOKIN' AT SOME WHITE LADY THE WRONG WAY?
WHO GIVES, EMMITT? I DON'.
AT THIS POINT, NOW-- YOU A FREE MAN.
I'D FOCUS ON THAT.
AN' NOT ON LOOKING AT ME.
"BE CAREFUL, BABY..."

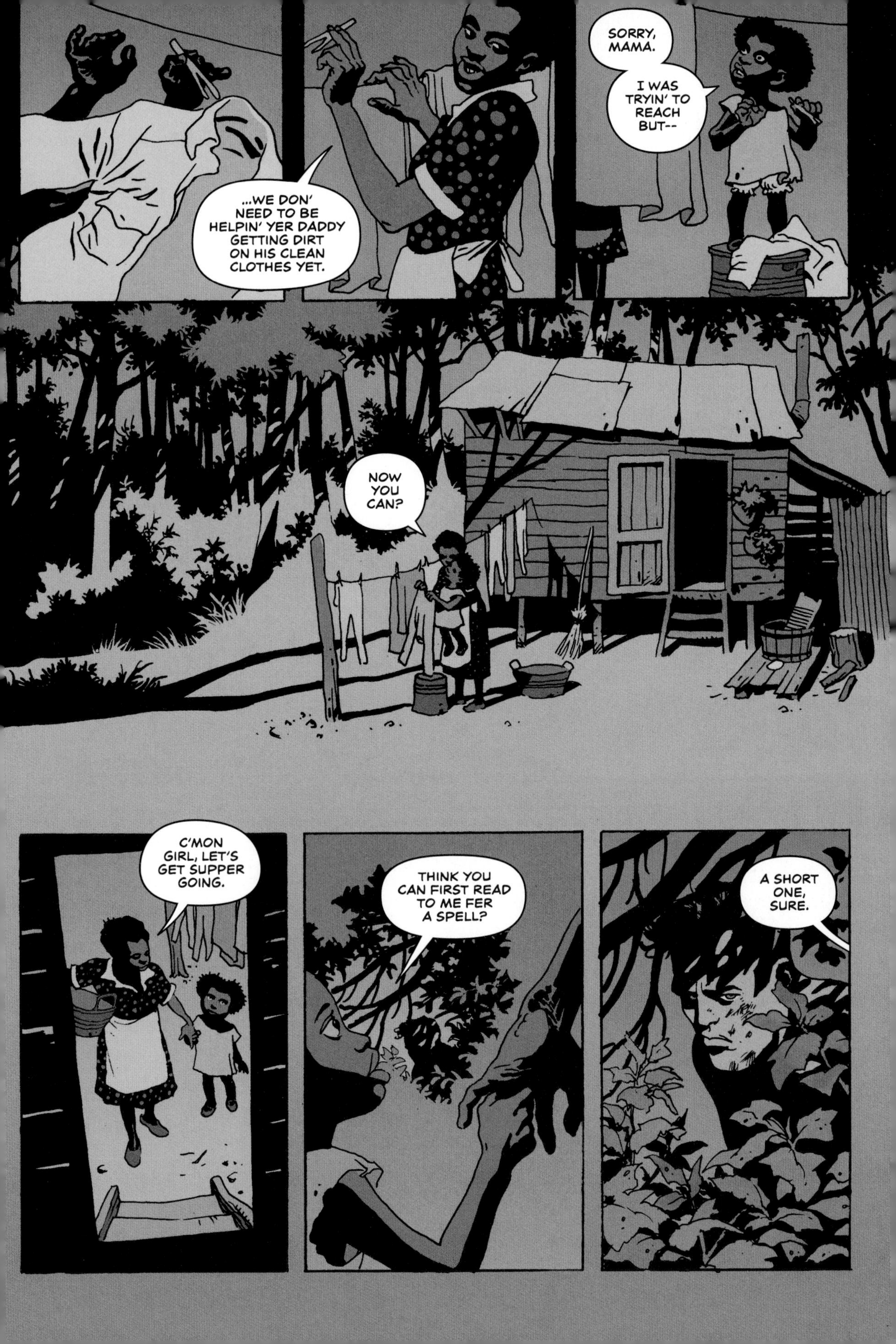
...WE DON' NEED TO BE HELPIN' YER DADDY GETTING DIRT ON HIS CLEAN CLOTHES YET.
SORRY, MAMA.
I WAS TRYIN' TO REACH BUT--
NOW YOU CAN?
C'MON GIRL, LET'S GET SUPPER GOING.
THINK YOU CAN FIRST READ TO ME FER A SPELL?
A SHORT ONE, SURE.

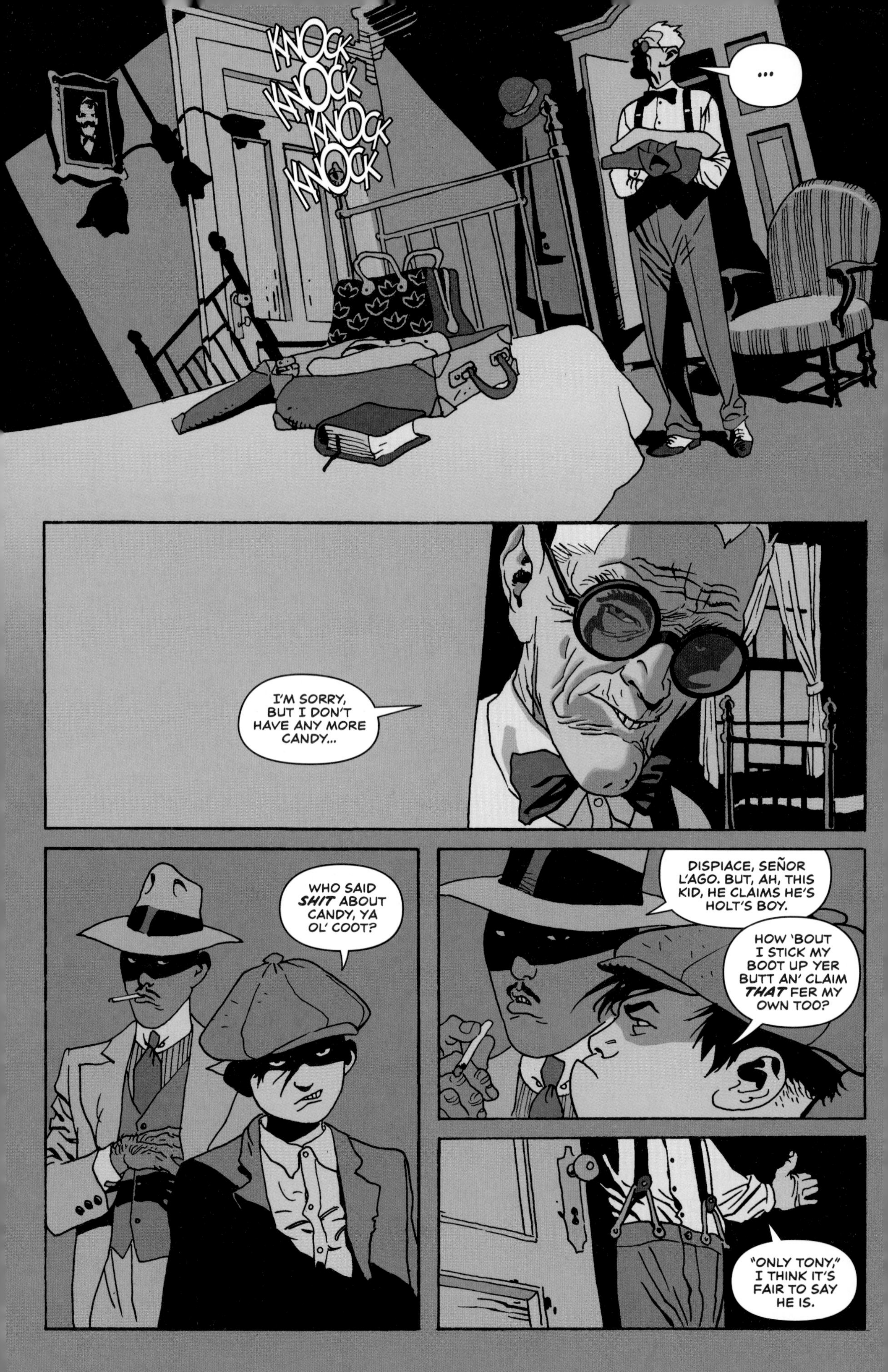
KNOCK KNOCK KNOCK KNOCK
...
I'M SORRY, BUT I DON'T HAVE ANY MORE CANDY...
WHO SAID SHIT ABOUT CANDY, YA OL' COOT?
DISPIACE, SEÑOR L'AGO. BUT, AH, THIS KID, HE CLAIMS HE'S HOLT'S BOY.
HOW 'BOUT I STICK MY BOOT UP YER BUTT AN' CLAIM THAT FER MY OWN TOO?
"ONLY TONY," I THINK IT'S FAIR TO SAY HE IS.

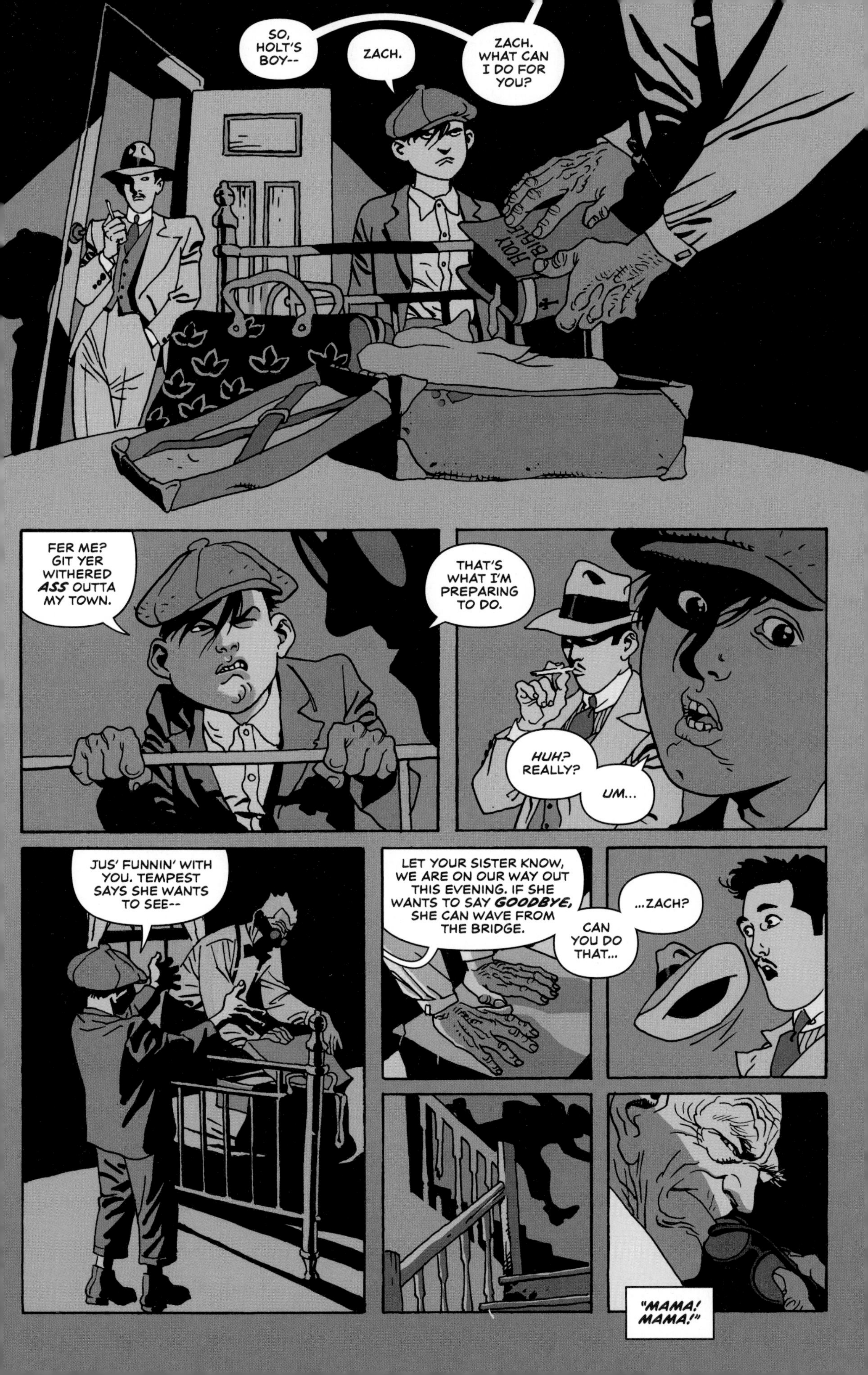
SO, HOLT'S BOY--
ZACH.
ZACH. WHAT CAN I DO FOR YOU?
HOLY BIBLE
FER ME? GIT YER WITHERED ASS OUTTA MY TOWN.
THAT'S WHAT I'M PREPARING TO DO.
HUH? REALLY?
UM...
JUS' FUNNIN' WITH YOU. TEMPEST SAYS SHE WANTS TO SEE--
LET YOUR SISTER KNOW, WE ARE ON OUR WAY OUT THIS EVENING. IF SHE WANTS TO SAY GOODBYE, SHE CAN WAVE FROM THE BRIDGE.
CAN YOU DO THAT...
...ZACH?
"MAMA! MAMA!"

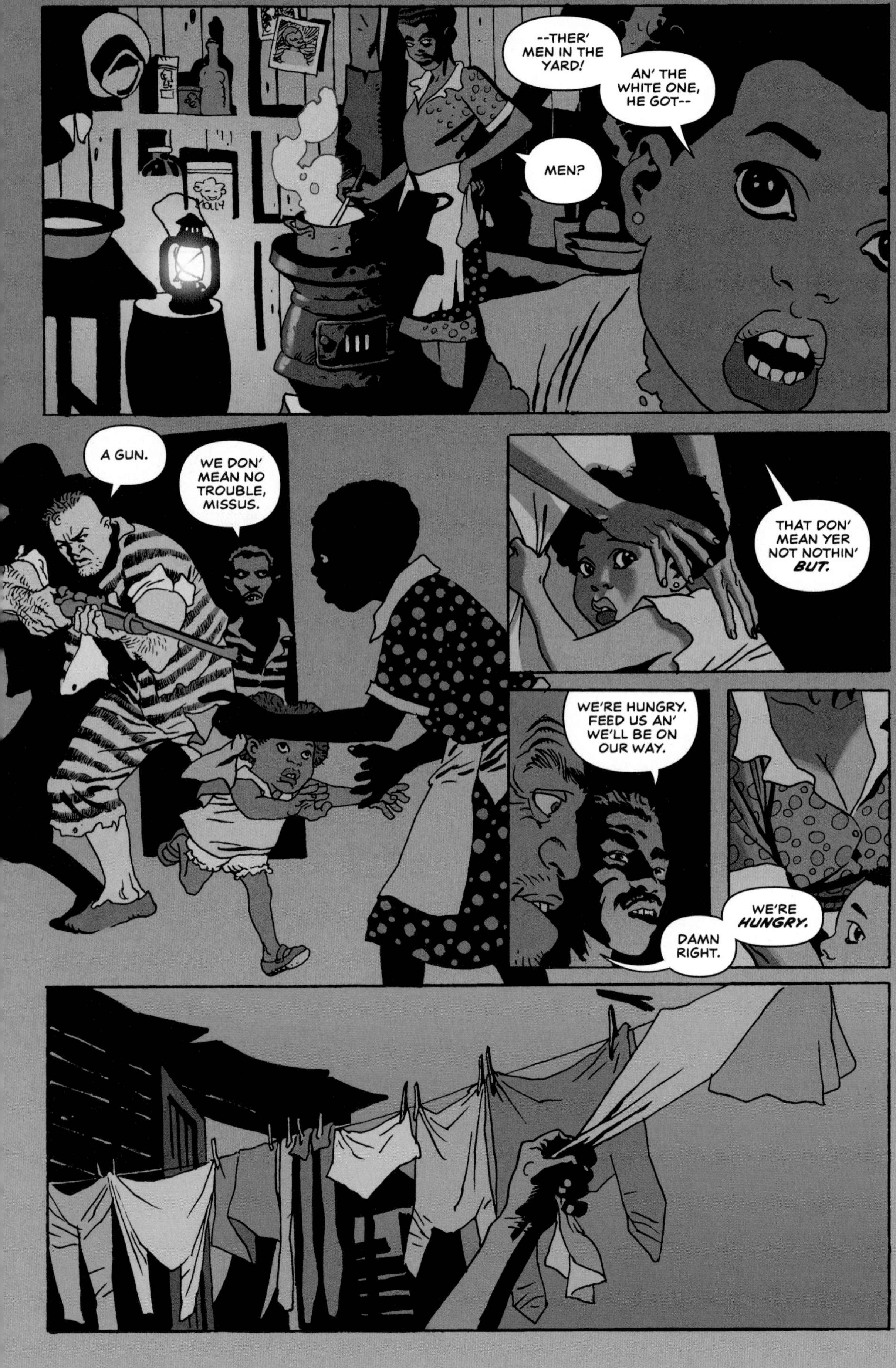
--THER' MEN IN THE YARD!
AN' THE WHITE ONE, HE GOT--
MEN?
A GUN.
WE DON' MEAN NO TROUBLE, MISSUS.
THAT DON' MEAN YER NOT NOTHIN' BUT.
WE'RE HUNGRY. FEED US AN' WE'LL BE ON OUR WAY.
WE'RE HUNGRY.
DAMN RIGHT.
MOLLY

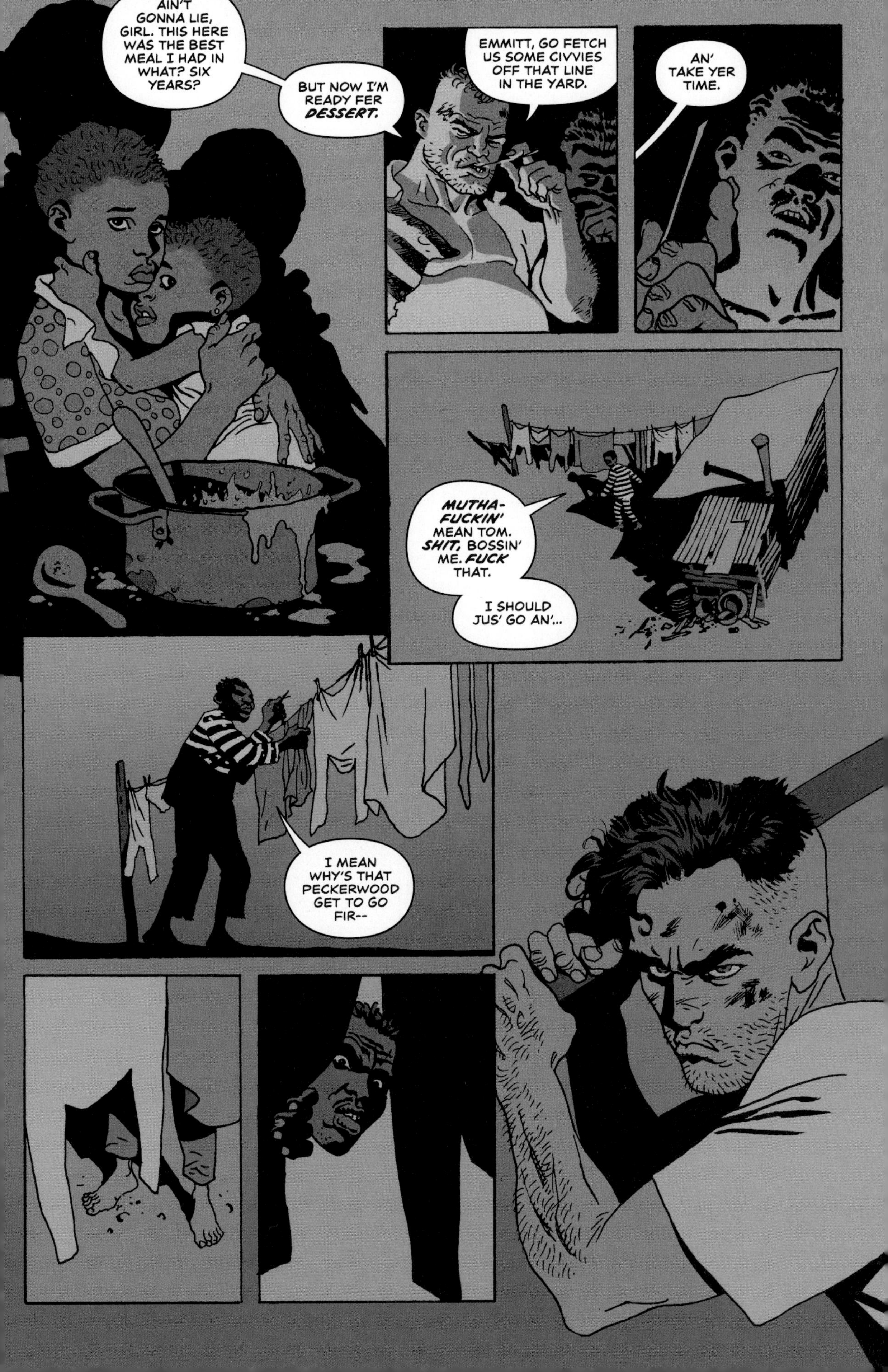
AIN'T GONNA LIE, GIRL. THIS HERE WAS THE BEST MEAL I HAD IN WHAT? SIX YEARS?
BUT NOW I'M READY FER DESSERT.
EMMITT, GO FETCH US SOME CIVVIES OFF THAT LINE IN THE YARD.
AN' TAKE YER TIME.
MUTHA-FUCKIN' MEAN TOM. SHIT, BOSSIN' ME. FUCK THAT.
I SHOULD JUS' GO AN'...
I MEAN WHY'S THAT PECKERWOOD GET TO GO FIR--

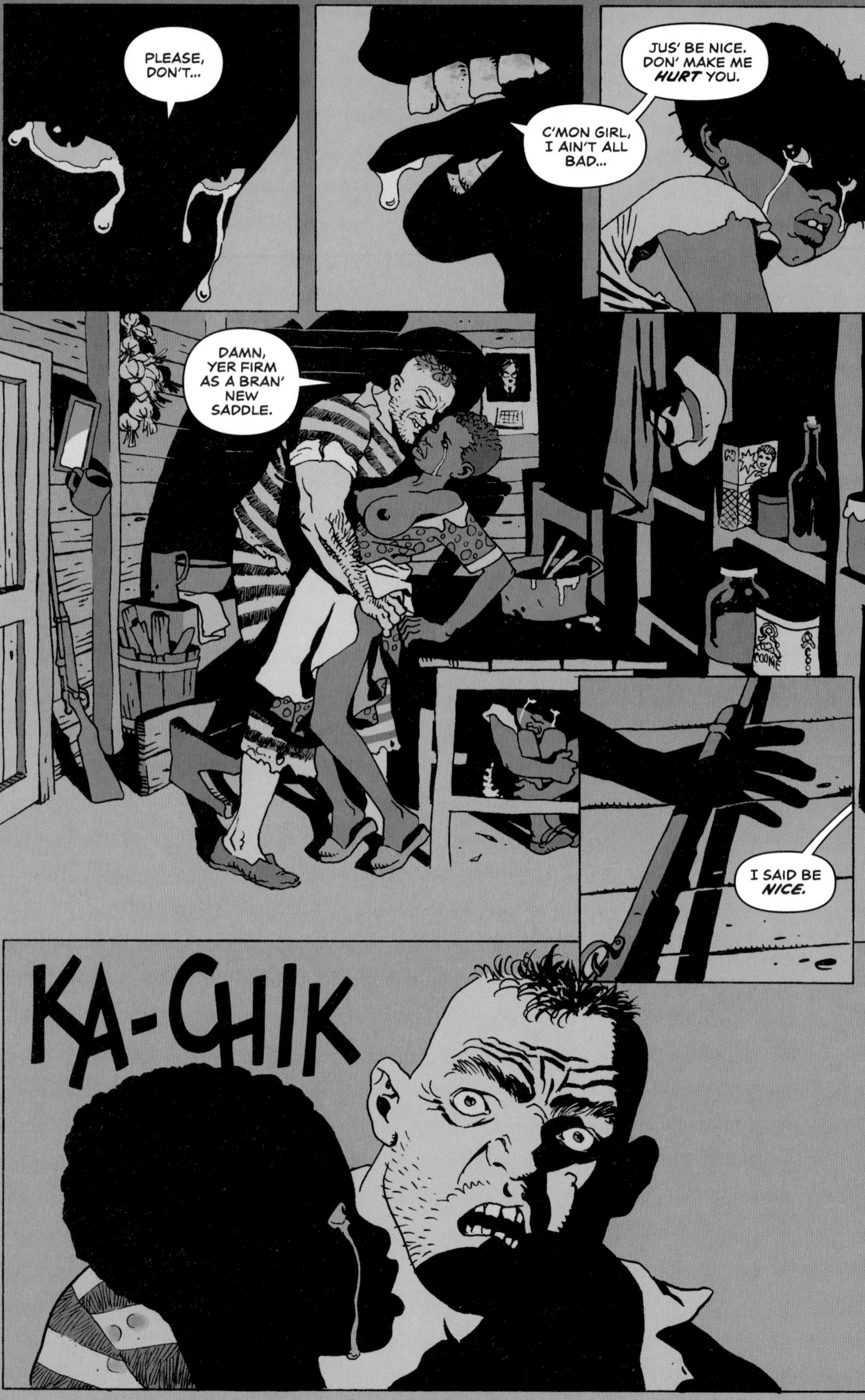
PLEASE, DON'T...
C'MON GIRL, I AIN'T ALL BAD...
JUS' BE NICE. DON' MAKE ME *HURT* YOU.
DAMN, YER FIRM AS A BRAN' NEW SADDLE.
I SAID BE *NICE.*
KA-CHIK

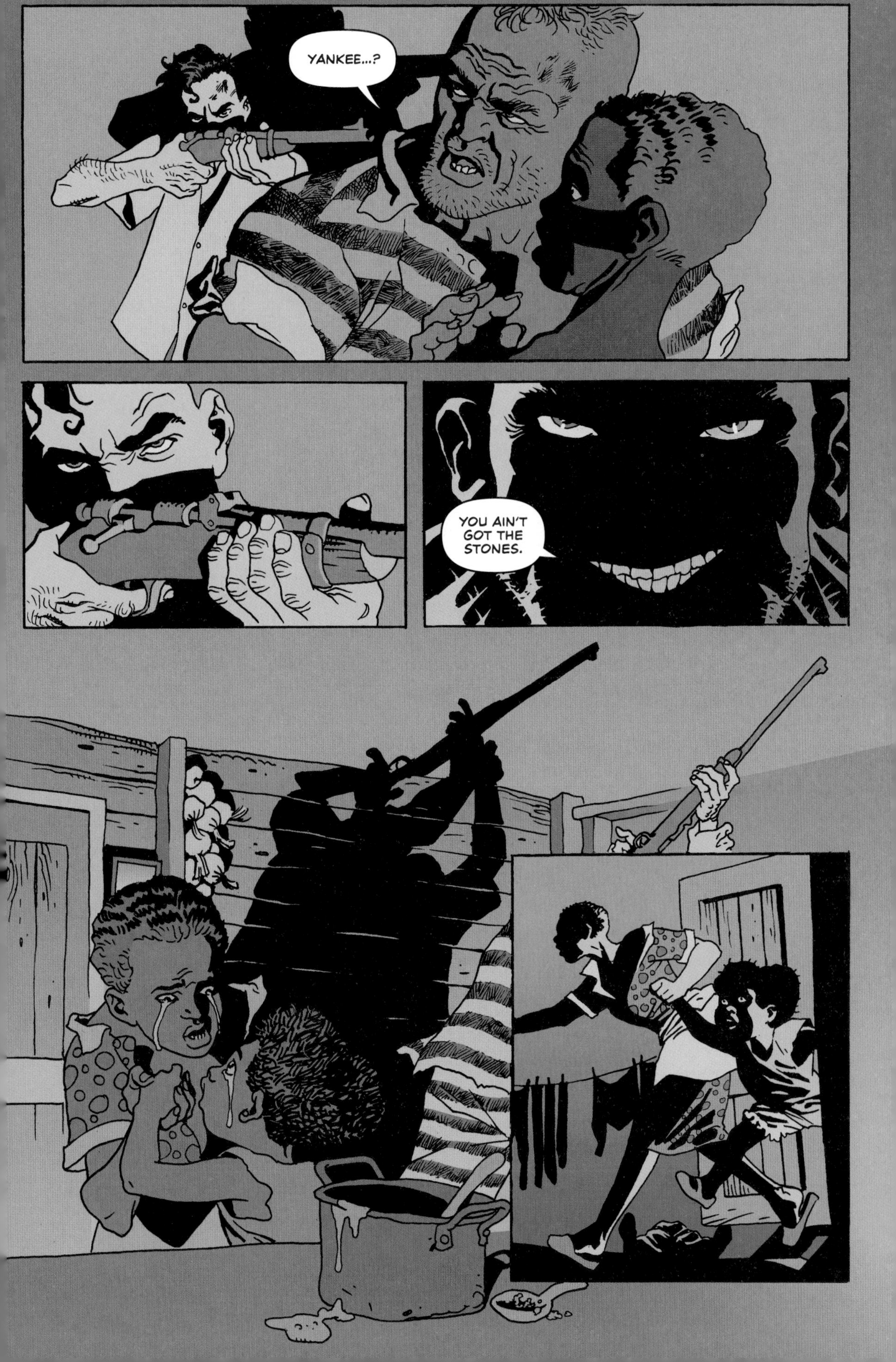
YANKEE...?
YOU AIN'T GOT THE STONES.

AR0oOOOoooo

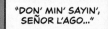
"DON' MIN' SAYIN', SEÑOR L'AGO..."

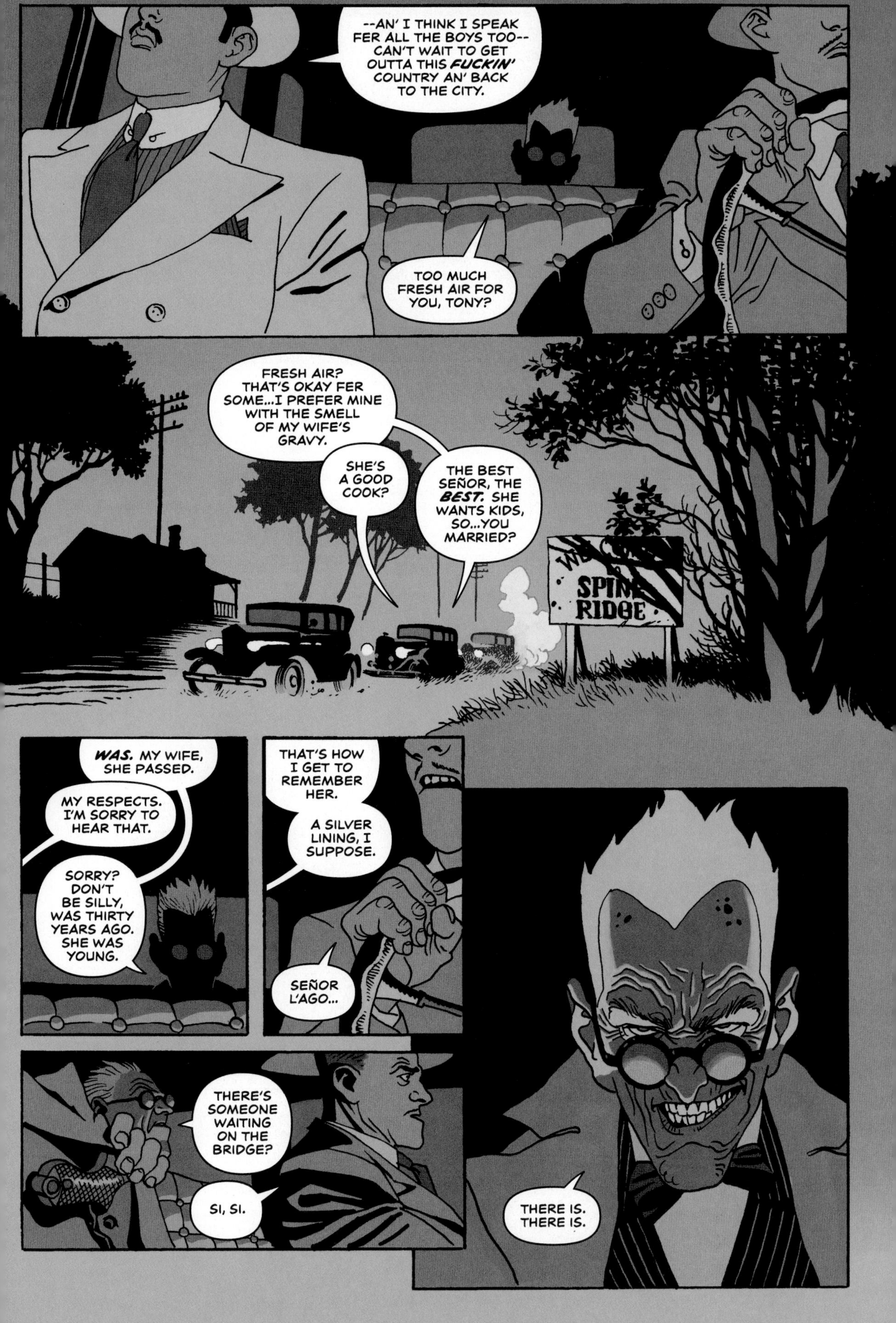
--AN' I THINK I SPEAK FER ALL THE BOYS TOO-- CAN'T WAIT TO GET OUTTA THIS ***FUCKIN'*** COUNTRY AN' BACK TO THE CITY.
TOO MUCH FRESH AIR FOR YOU, TONY?
FRESH AIR? THAT'S OKAY FER SOME...I PREFER MINE WITH THE SMELL OF MY WIFE'S GRAVY.
SHE'S A GOOD COOK?
THE BEST SEÑOR, THE ***BEST.*** SHE WANTS KIDS, SO...YOU MARRIED?
SPINE RIDGE
WAS. MY WIFE, SHE PASSED.
MY RESPECTS. I'M SORRY TO HEAR THAT.
SORRY? DON'T BE SILLY, WAS THIRTY YEARS AGO. SHE WAS YOUNG.
THAT'S HOW I GET TO REMEMBER HER.
A SILVER LINING, I SUPPOSE.
SEÑOR L'AGO...
THERE'S SOMEONE WAITING ON THE BRIDGE?
SI, SI.
THERE IS. THERE IS.

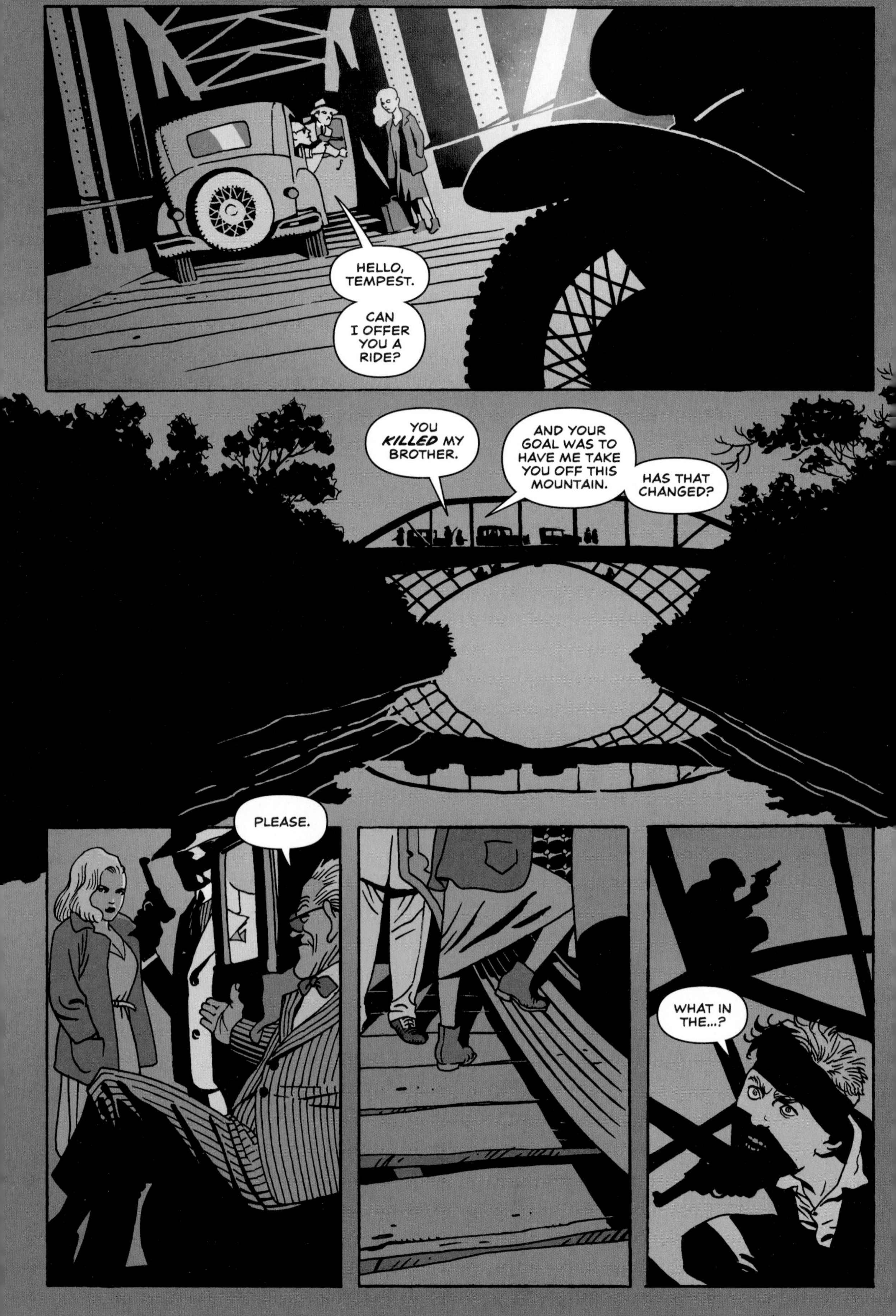
HELLO, TEMPEST.
CAN I OFFER YOU A RIDE?
YOU *KILLED* MY BROTHER.
AND YOUR GOAL WAS TO HAVE ME TAKE YOU OFF THIS MOUNTAIN.
HAS THAT CHANGED?
PLEASE.
WHAT IN THE...?

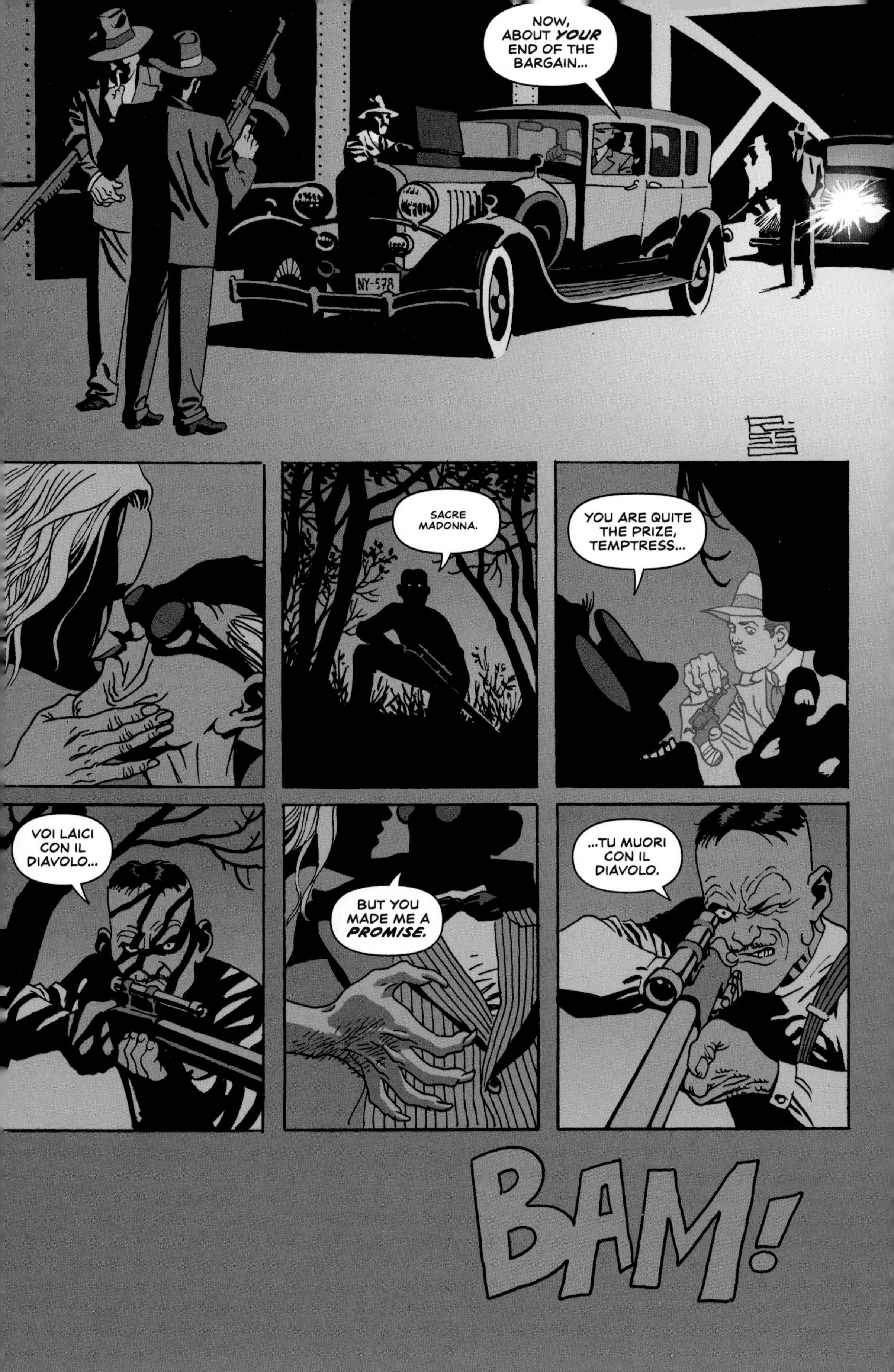
NOW, ABOUT *YOUR* END OF THE BARGAIN...
SACRE MADONNA.
YOU ARE QUITE THE PRIZE, TEMPTRESS...
VOI LAICI CON IL DIAVOLO...
BUT YOU MADE ME A *PROMISE.*
...TU MUORI CON IL DIAVOLO.
BAM!

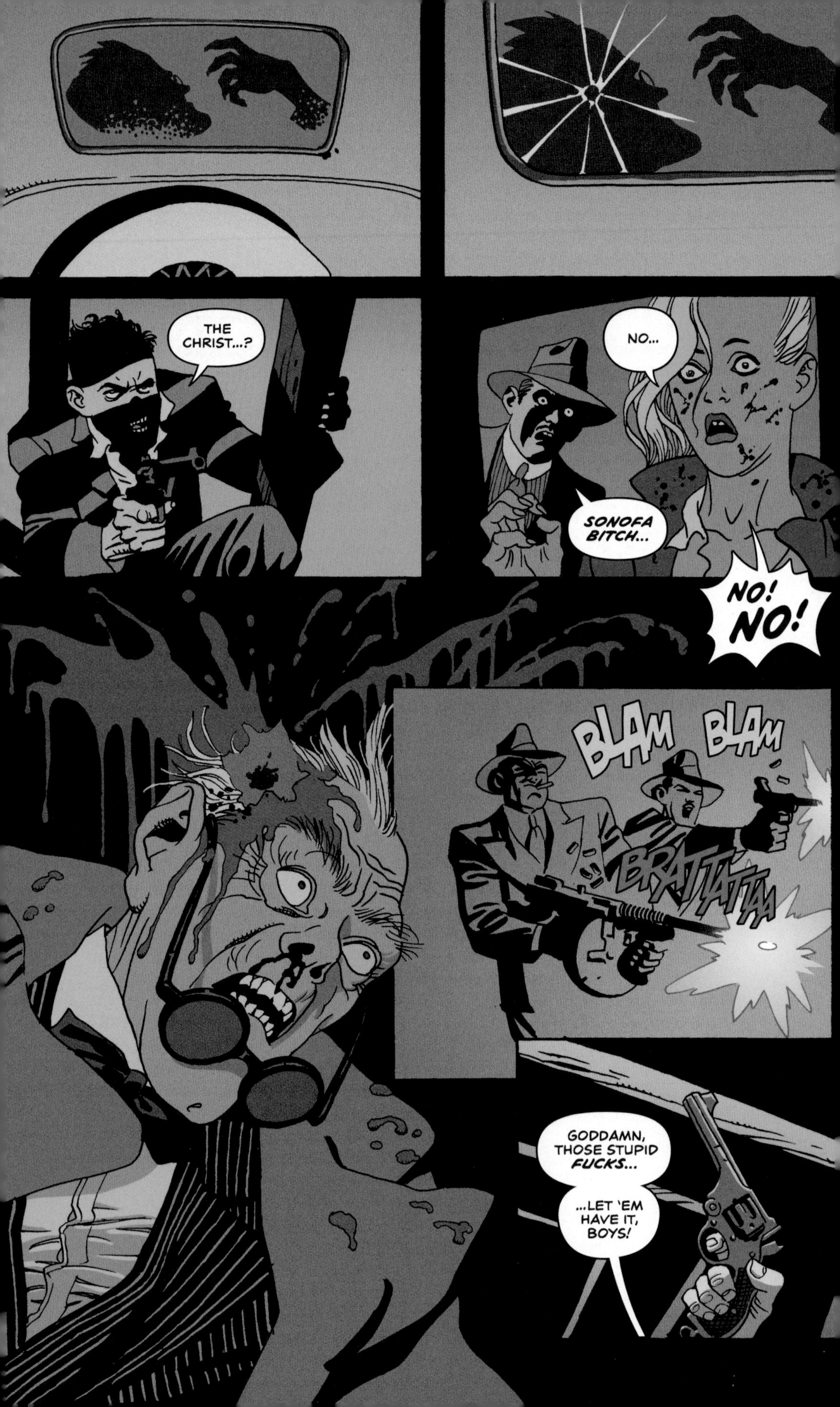
THE CHRIST...?
NO...
SONOFA BITCH...
NO! NO!
BLAM BLAM
BRATTATTAA
GODDAMN, THOSE STUPID FUCKS...
...LET 'EM HAVE IT, BOYS!

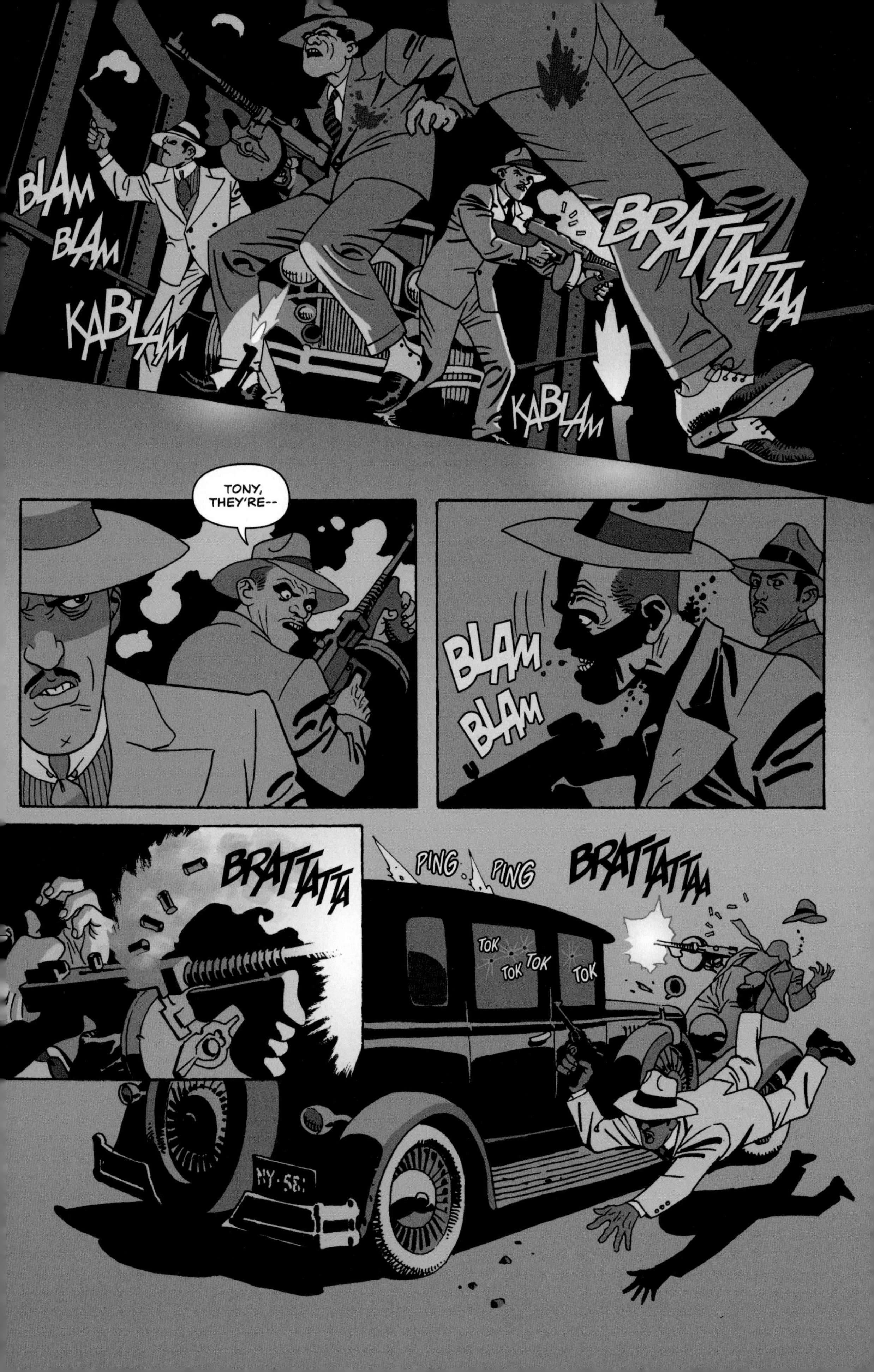
BLAM
BLAM
KABLAM
BRATTATTAA
KABLAM
TONY, THEY'RE--
BLAM
BLAM
BRATTATTA
PING
PING
BRATTATTAA
TOK
TOK
TOK
TOK
NY-581

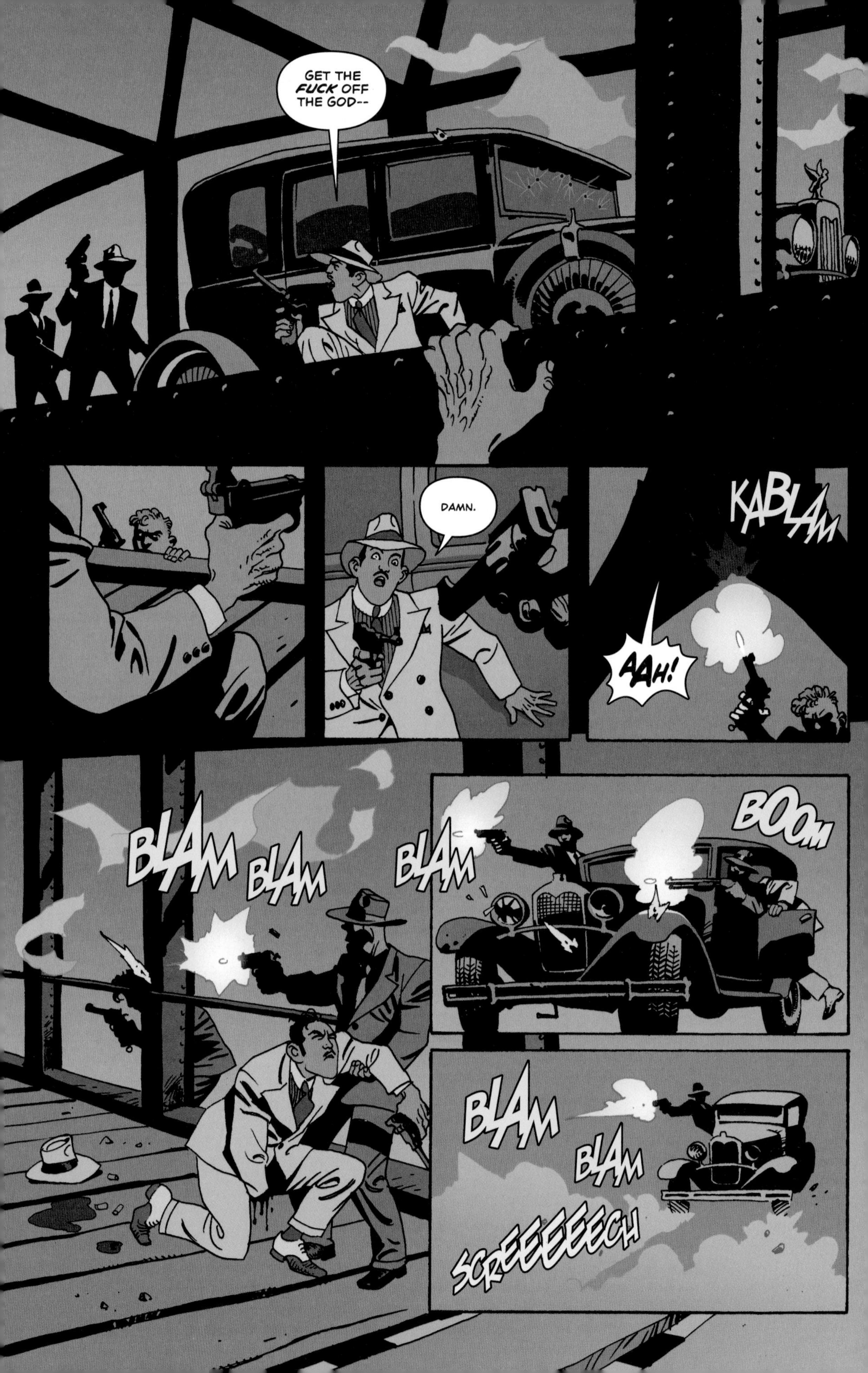
GET THE *FUCK* OFF THE GOD--
DAMN.
KABLAM
AAH!
BLAM
BLAM
BLAM
BOOM
BLAM
BLAM
SCREEEEEECH

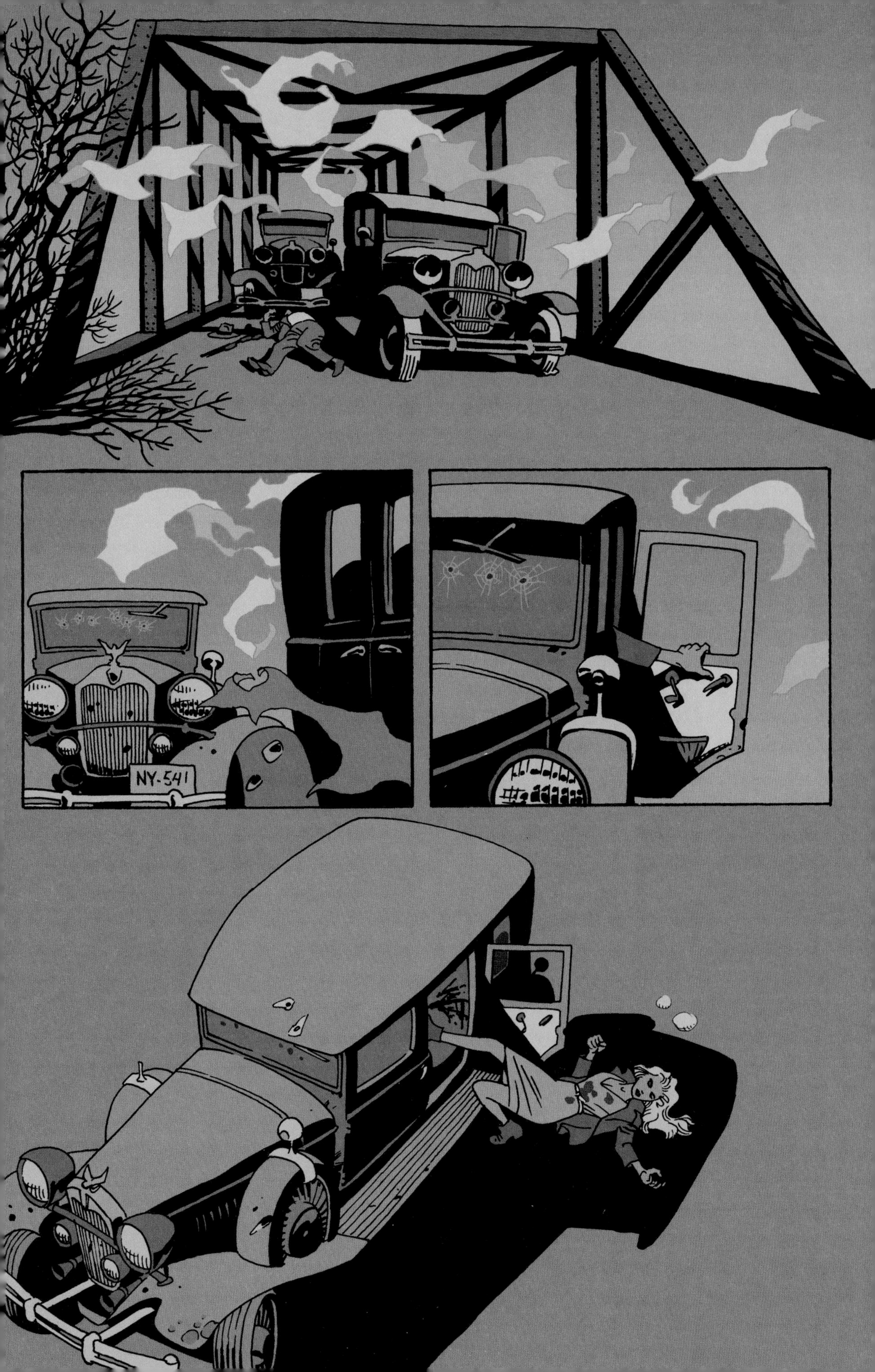
NY-541

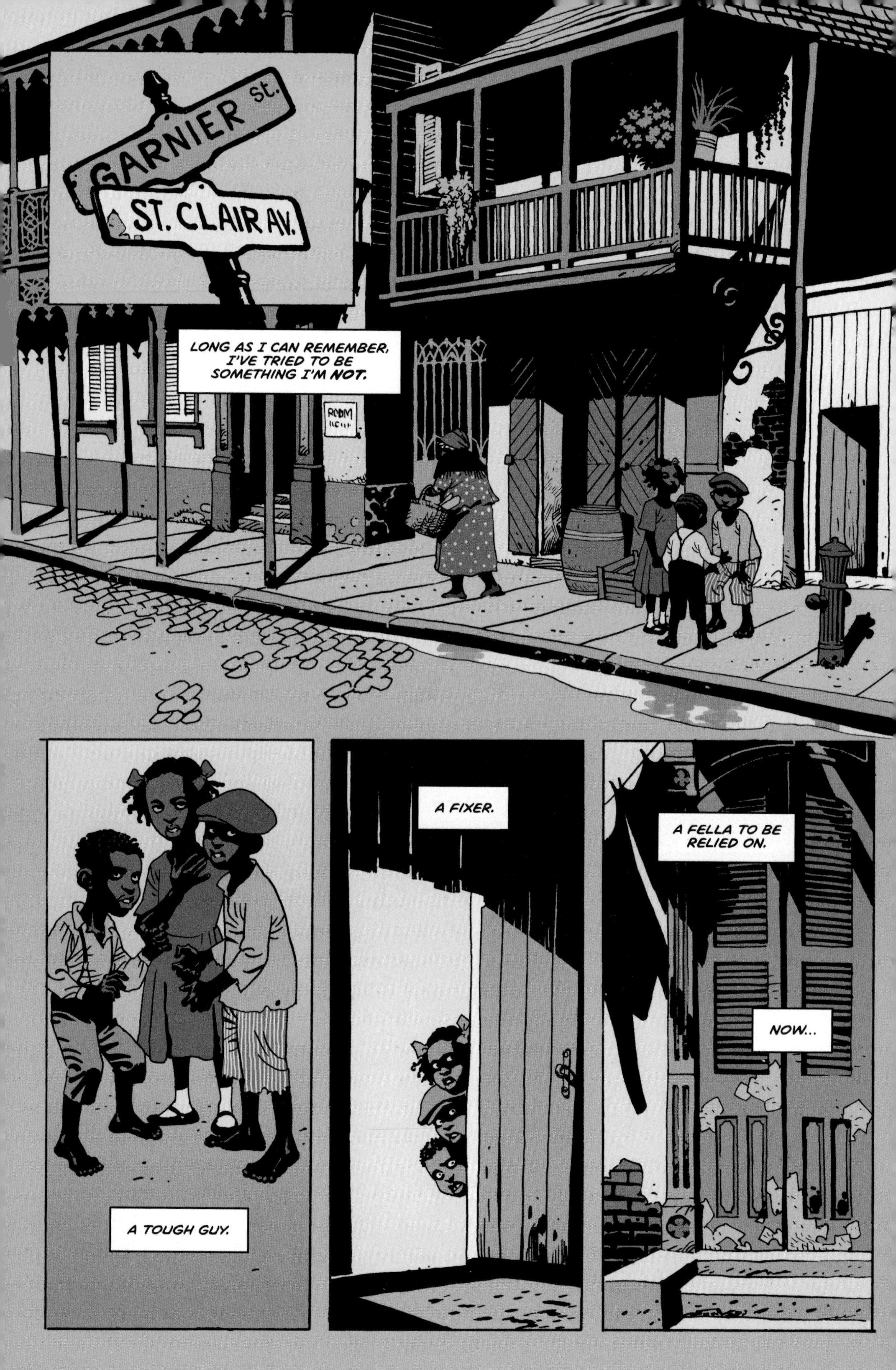
GARNIER St.
ST. CLAIR AV.
LONG AS I CAN REMEMBER, I'VE TRIED TO BE SOMETHING I'M NOT.
ROOM
A TOUGH GUY.
A FIXER.
A FELLA TO BE RELIED ON.
NOW...

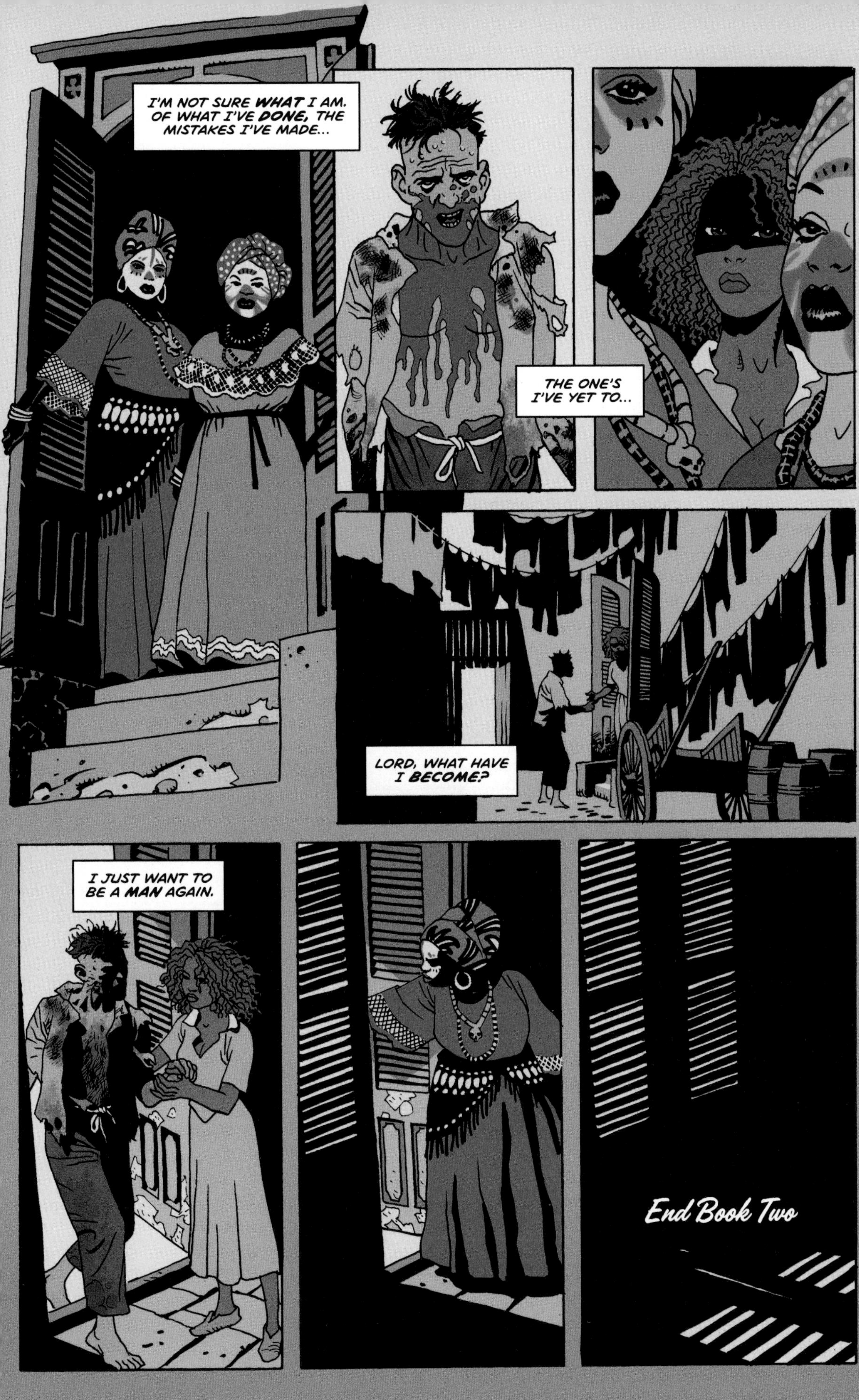
I'M NOT SURE WHAT I AM. OF WHAT I'VE DONE, THE MISTAKES I'VE MADE...
THE ONE'S I'VE YET TO...
LORD, WHAT HAVE I BECOME?
I JUST WANT TO BE A MAN AGAIN.
End Book Two

MOONSHINE

Variant Cover Gallery

GABRIEL BÁ
FÁBIO MOON
RAFAEL ALBUQUERQUE
GERARDO ZAFFINO
RAFAEL GRAMPÁ
PAUL POPE
with
LEE LOUGHRIDGE

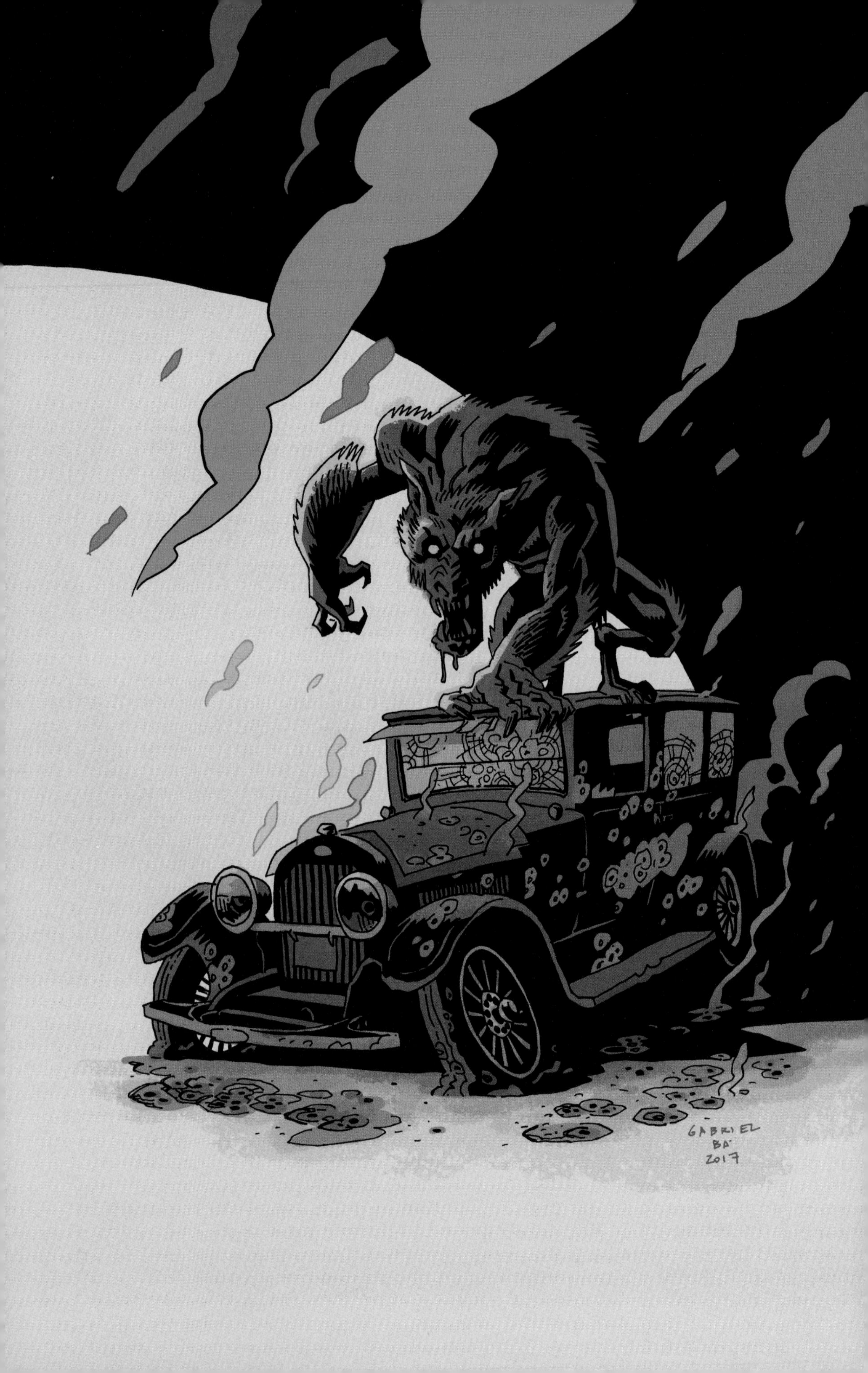
GABRIEL
BÁ
2017

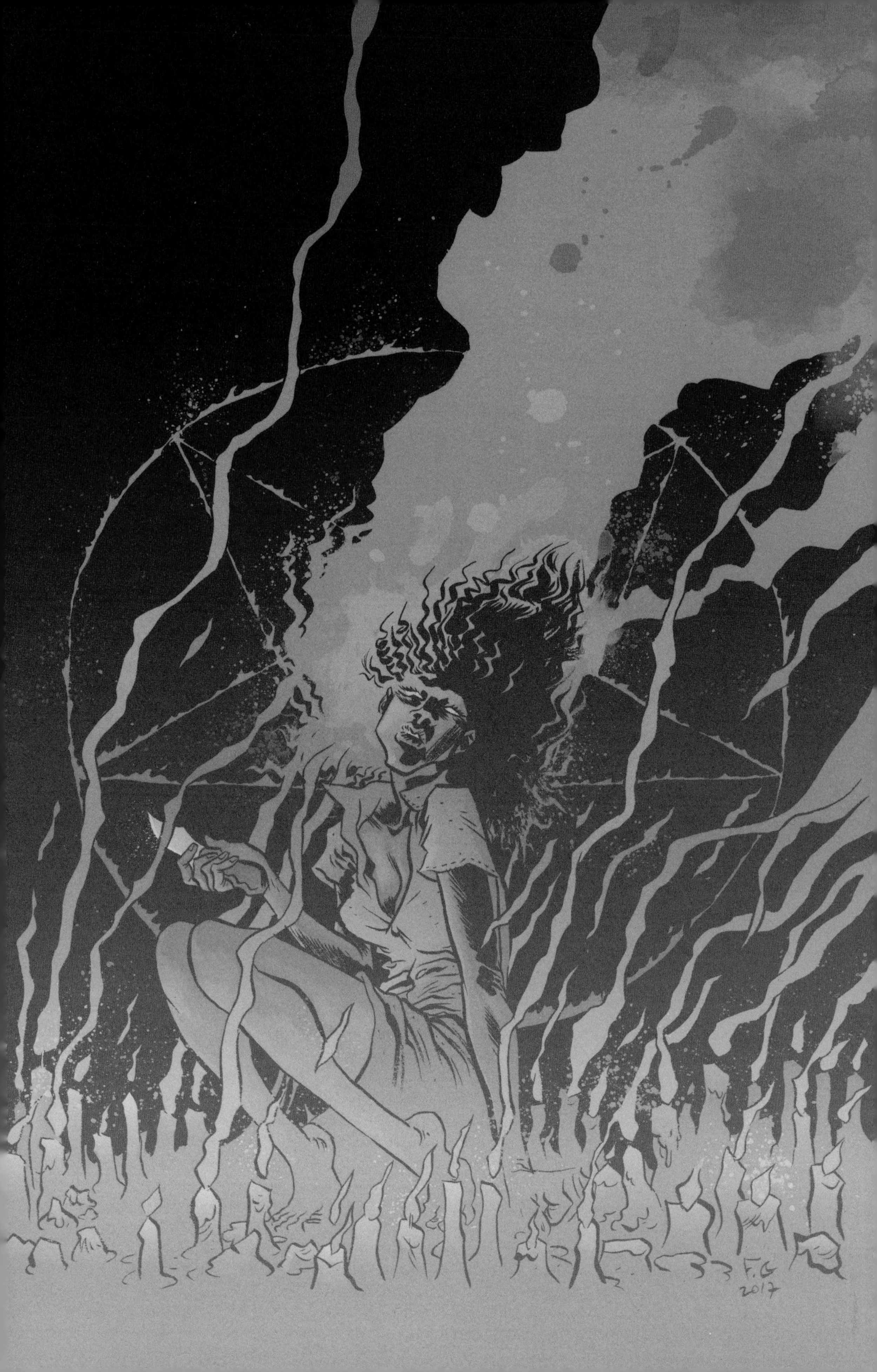
F.G
2017

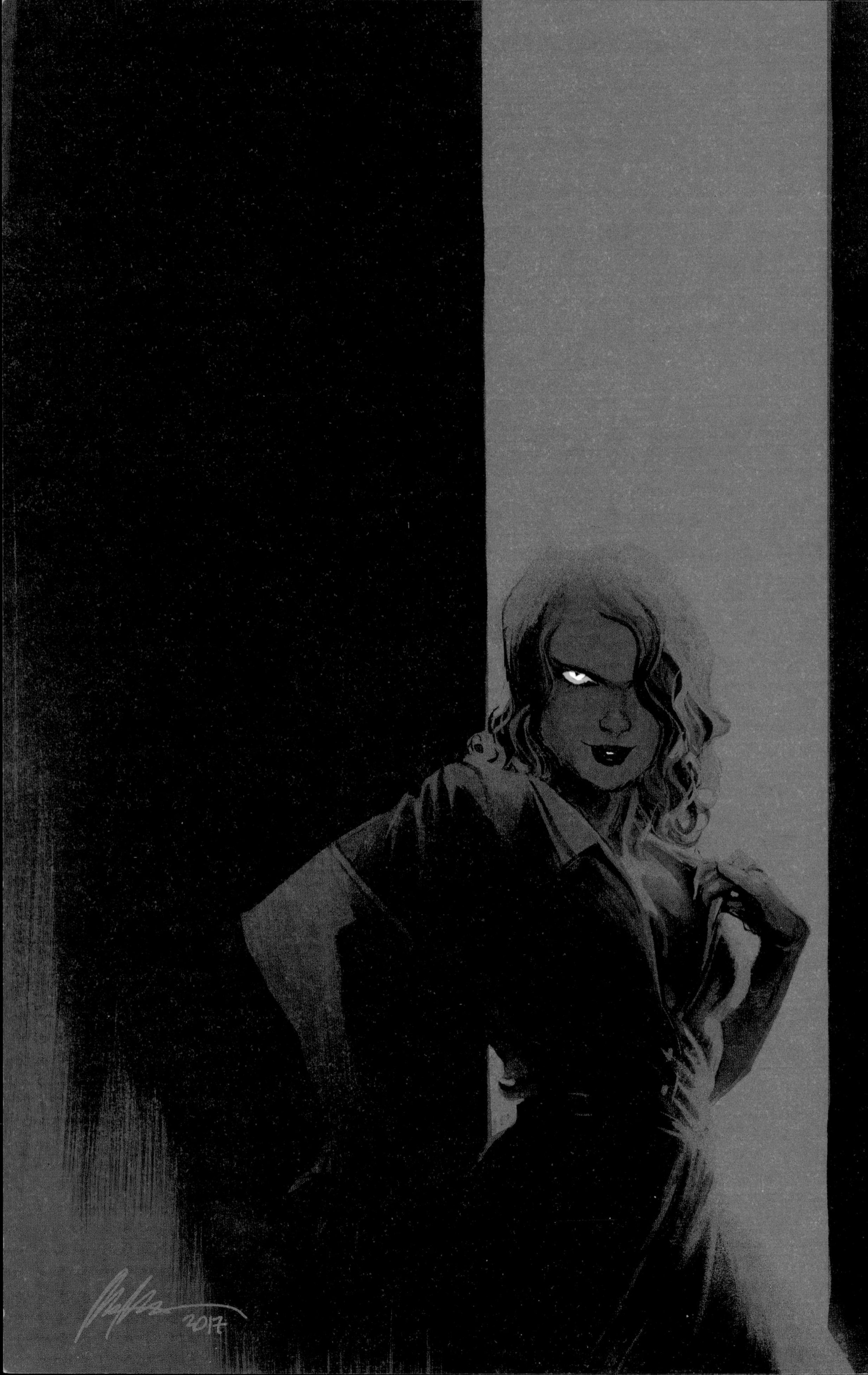

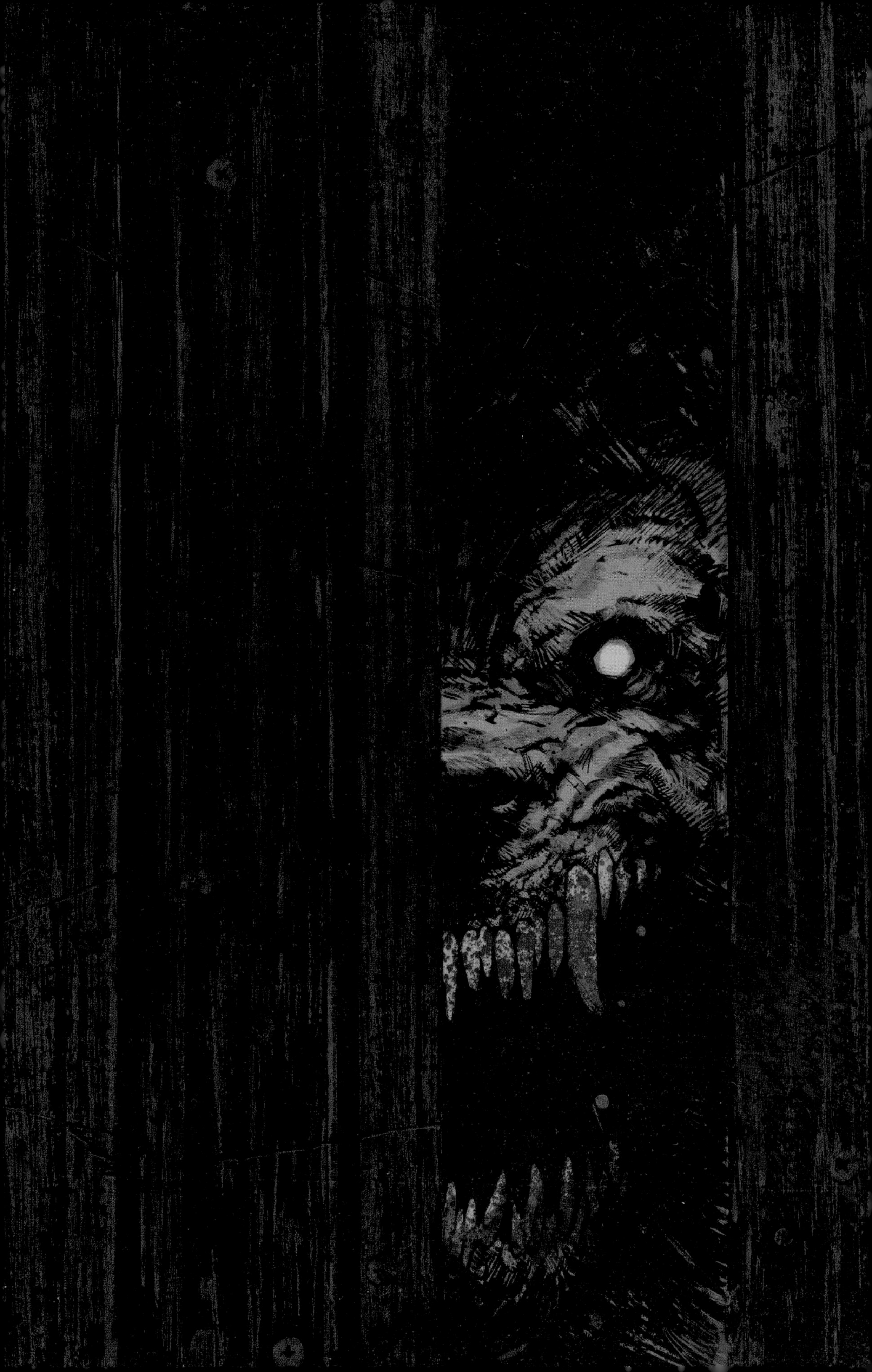

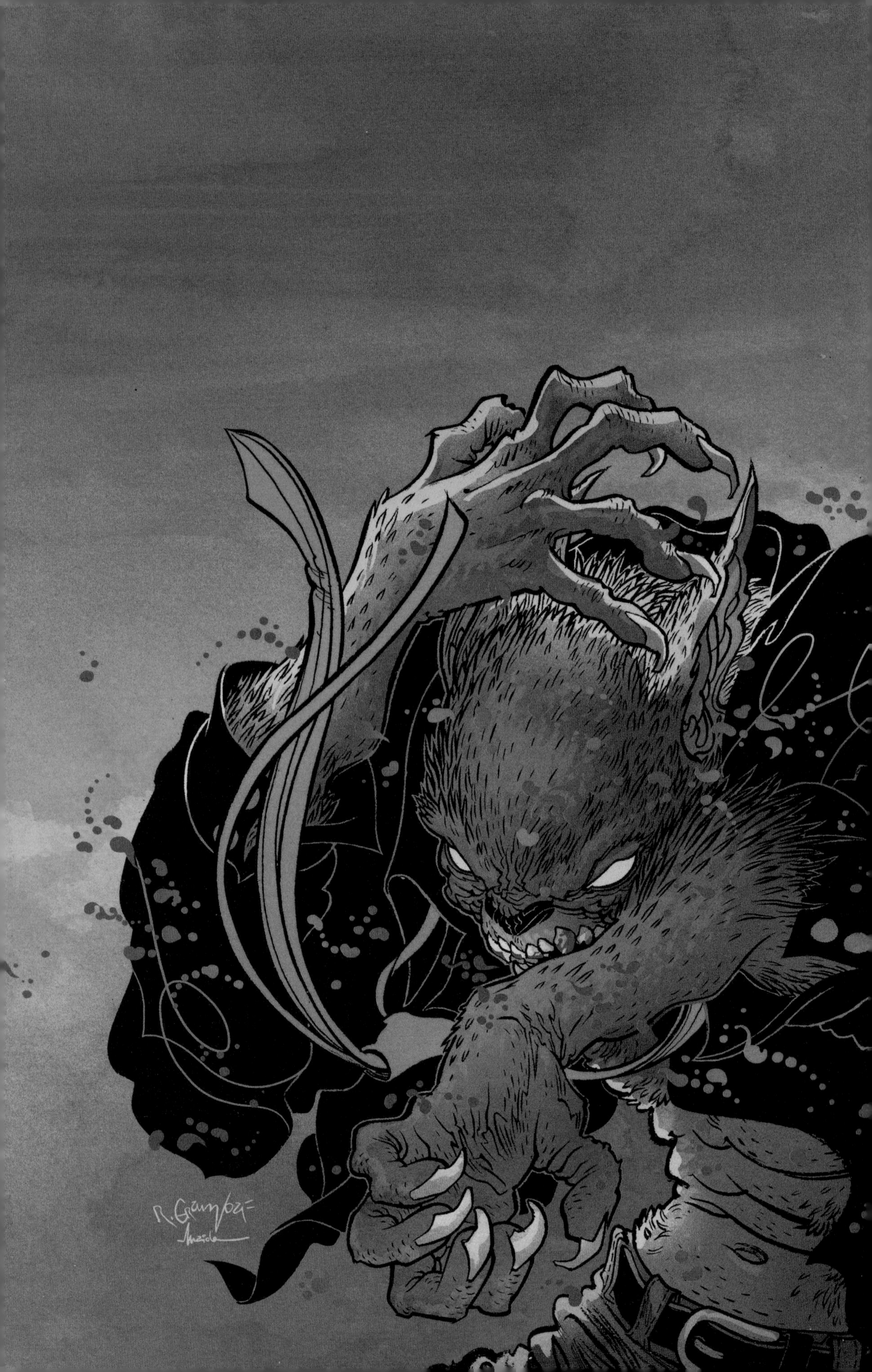

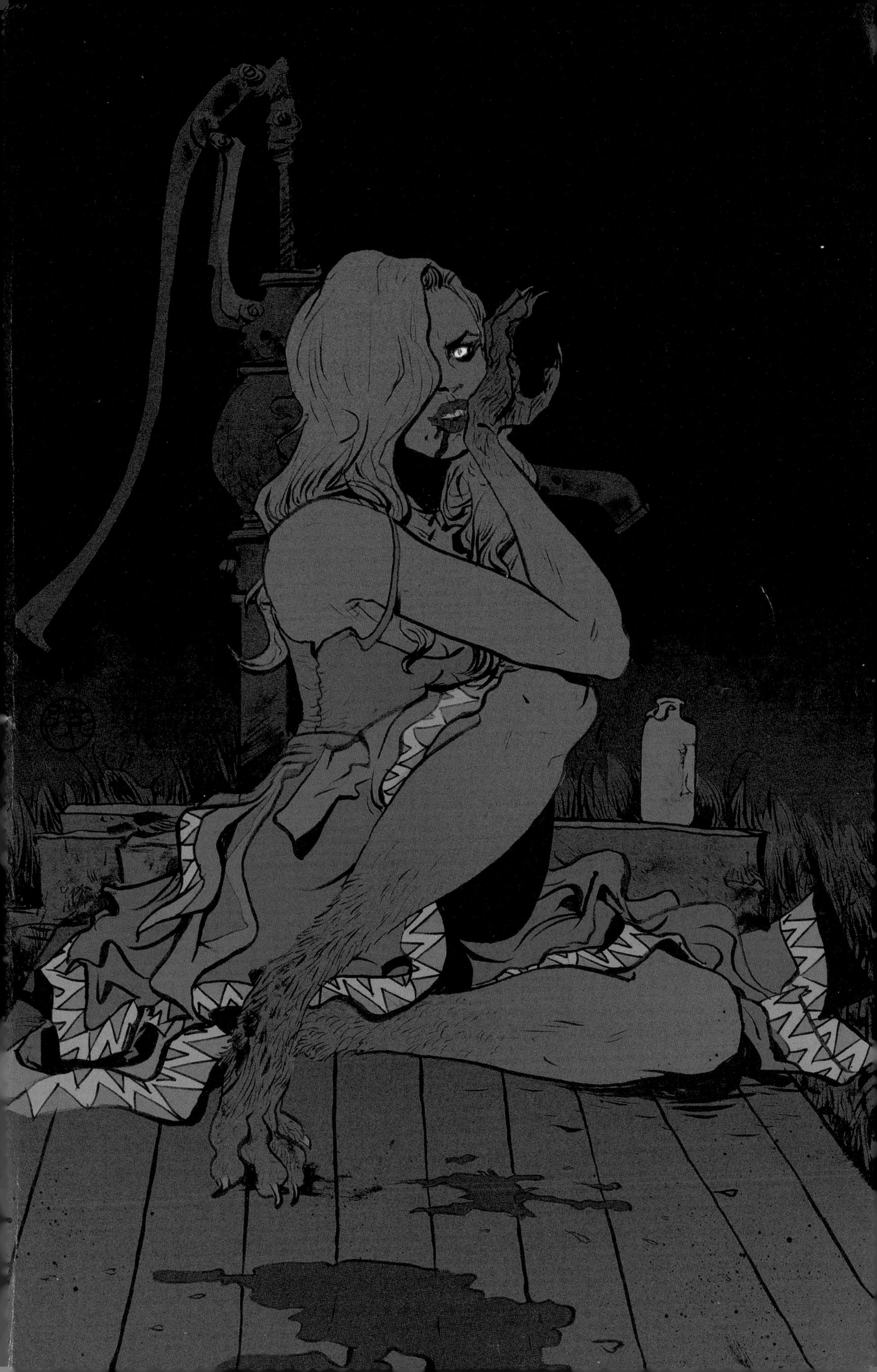